the god-man

SEED OF SATAN

BRUCE BILLER

WestBow
PRESS
A DIVISION OF THOMAS NELSON

WestBow Press books may be ordered through booksellers or by contacting:

WestBow Press
A Division of Thomas Nelson
1663 Liberty Drive
Bloomington, IN 47403
www.westbowpress.com
1-(866) 928-1240

ISBN: 978-1-4497-6631-3 (sc)
ISBN: 978-1-4497-6630-6 (hc)
ISBN: 978-1-4497-6632-0 (e)

Library of Congress Control Number: 2012916259

Printed in the United States of America

WestBow Press rev. date: 10/15/2012

Dedicated to my special gifts from God—
my wife, Kay, our daughter, Carrie Biller,
and our daughter and son-in-law,
Rich and Petria Gonzalez.

And to my parents, Charles and Avelyn Biller

PROLOGUE

In the beginning God created the heavens and the earth.

*   *   *

Lucifer, God's model of perfection, honored above all created beings in heaven and earth, was anointed a guardian cherub who was privileged to walk among the fiery stones. But Lucifer's heart became proud on account of his beauty, and his wisdom was corrupted because of his splendor.

So he rebelled against his Maker and was driven in disgrace from the mount of God.

Later, perhaps millennia later, the insurrectionist arrogantly drew near God's throne, demanding dominion, even if only over some far-flung planet concealed in the remotest corner of the universe. "Send me anywhere in the cosmos, and there, let me rule with power and authority."

God laughed in response, taunting the fallen angel.

"You were the model of perfection, full of wisdom and perfect in beauty," he reminded Lucifer. "You were blameless in your ways from the day you were created till wickedness was found in you. So I expelled you, O guardian cherub!"

"You gave me a choice," Lucifer accused, "and I chose for myself. I had grown weary of merely being the guardian to your throne!"

"You led the rebellion!"

"Yes, and a third of the angels, the seraphim and the cherubim, followed me," the defiant Lucifer retorted. "I was once given dominion over the earth. But you have cast me out and have despoiled the earth by your judgments! It is now formless and empty; its surface is shrouded in darkness."

"Yes, and for your sinful pride, I will yet bring you to the depths of the pit!"

"Have you forgotten," Lucifer sneered, "that of all your created beings, I am the wisest and the most beautiful? I will yet ascend to heaven; I will raise my throne above your angels. I will make myself like you!"

Then Satan, once graced with the titles of Morning Star and Son of the Dawn, was expelled from God's holy presence.

*   *   *

The earth was formless and empty, and darkness was over the surface of the deep.

God said, "Let there be light," and there was light. God said, "Let the water under the sky be gathered to one place, and let dry ground appear." And it was so. God called the dry ground land, and the gathered waters he called seas. And God saw that it was good.

Then God said, "Let the land produce vegetation: seed-bearing plants and trees that bear fruit with seed." And it was so. And God saw that it was good. God said, "Let there be lights in the expanse of the sky to separate the day from the night, and let them serve as signs to mark the seasons and days and years, and let them be lights in the expanse of the sky to give light on the earth." And it was so. God made two great lights—the greater light to govern the day and the lesser light to govern the night. He also made the stars. And God saw that it was good.

God said, "Let the water teem with living creatures, and let birds fly above the earth across the expanse of sky." And God saw that it was good. God said, "Let the land produce living creatures according to their kind: livestock, creatures that move along the ground, and wild animals, each according to its kind." And God saw that it was good.

And God said, "Let us make man in our image, in our likeness, and let them rule over the fish of the sea and birds of the air, over the livestock, over all the earth, and over all the creatures that move along the ground." So God created man in his own image, in the image of God he created him.

And God saw everything that he had made, and behold, it was very good.

And Lucifer, once the model of perfection with authority over the highest rank of the angelic hosts, was delighted with the work of God's hands.

The fallen angel vowed he would rule over this magnificent creation, including the creatures called man, created in the very likeness of God.

CHAPTER ONE

Christmas Day, 1977—Baselga di Piné, Northern Italy

It was a bitterly cold morning in Baselga di Piné, a sleepy *frazioni* cradled on a plateau in the Trentino-Alto Adige region of northern Italy. For more than a week, snowstorms had pummeled the mountainous area and temperatures had fallen as low as –20 degrees Celcius. More than sixty inches of snow had already buried the picturesque hamlet, and ANSA, the Italian news agency, warned that blizzard conditions could continue for another forty-eight hours.

Alone in her sprawling estate, Emiliane Guiseppina pressed closer to the massive stone hearth as if to coax warmth from its dancing flames. She slowly rubbed her abdomen, anticipating the birth of her firstborn. It was fitting that he would be born here, in the land of her own birth. Emiliane fervently wished for a son, a son she vowed to rear in the likeness of Napoleon. A true Bonapartist says, "I am the nation," but her son, she dreamed, would someday proclaim, "I am the world."

In 1797, Napoleon Bonaparte and his French soldiers had conquered the Austrians, who then controlled the region of Trentino-Alto Adige. It was a history Emiliane proudly made her own. It mattered not to her that the French occupiers had pillaged, murdered, and raped the Italian peasants. What mattered was that Napoleon was a *generalissimo* who worshiped the god of war. Napoleon was ambitious. He could be all things to all men but was ruthless to any who opposed him. He ruled by the sword.

After Russia and other European states defeated Napoleon at the Battle of Leipzig, Bonaparte's Italian-allied states abandoned him and aligned with Austria. Trentino-Alto Adige was eventually absorbed by the Austro-Hungarian Empire, remaining thus until it was returned to Italy at the end of World War I. But the inhabitants of the region were deeply divided, and in 1939, Mussolini allowed them to either accept Italian citizenship and remain or assume German citizenship and emigrate north, leaving behind the beautiful mountains they called home.

Emiliane's widowed father, Mario, chose German citizenship. While he experienced immense pleasure in the viridity and breathtaking beauty of the Alps, his love for its saw-toothed ridges and snowcapped peaks did not exceed his insatiable hatred for the God he blamed for his many misfortunes, including the tragic death of his young wife. Martina had been killed when she lost control of her car on a precipitous mountain pass near Baselga di Piné. He also blamed the Jews, the race that claimed to be God's chosen people, for his impoverished financial state.

Emiliane's father believed the best way to strike back at God was to transfer his allegiance to a nation that would soon rid itself of the *untermenschen,* "apelings," as Hitler called the Jews. An art appraiser by profession, Mario had learned that most Jewish companies in Germany had either collapsed financially or been sold as a means for the owners to emigrate to other countries. When on April 26, 1938, the official Nazi newspaper, *Volkischer Beobachter,* declared "The Jew must go—and his cash stays here!", Mario began to formulate his plan to leave beautiful Baselga di Piné, his strategy for becoming a very wealthy man now clearly established in his mind. Mussolini's policies only played into Mario's own desires.

With great satisfaction, Mario remembered Kristallnacht, "the night of broken glass," in which a wave of anti-Jewish hatred, fueled by Nazi Party officials, swept across Germany and its occupied states. Kristallnacht earned its name from the shards of broken glass that lined German streets in the wake of the violence. On November 9-10, 1938, members of the SA and Hitler Youth violently attacked their helpless victims. Jewish homes were ransacked, along with multiplied thousands of Jewish shops, towns, and villages. Many Jews were beaten to death, and thousands more were relocated to concentration camps. Almost two thousand synagogues were plundered and hundreds set ablaze.

Nearly two years after Kristallnacht, Mario read about the special Nazi agency Einsatzstab Reichsleiter Rosenberg (ERR), an organization formed to confiscate cash, artwork and cultural objects from private homes, archives, and libraries. This bit of information brought into focus the tactics he would use to amass his fortune.

Leaving Baselga di Piné behind, Mario Guiseppina and his young daughter, Emiliane, traveled north to Waldkraiburg, a Bavarian town in the district of Muhldorf, Germany. After quickly establishing his reputation in the community as a committed Nazi and devoted disciple of Hitler, Mario began to implement his plan.

Mario attended patriotic rallies in local beer halls as a means of meeting new friends, particularly women who were impressed by his charming personality and handsome appearance. At one of these meetings, he noticed Anna Kappel sitting alone and immediately made his way to her table. Anna was a compulsive shopper with expensive tastes, and she was graced with average looks and a somewhat loud manner. He already knew that Anna's young husband had been killed on September 1, 1939, the day Germany launched its attack on its eastern neighbor and ignited World War II. Anna was fiercely anti-Semitic. Mario also knew she was employed as a low-level, low-paid secretary in the Inland-SD, department five of the Sicherheitsdienst, the agency that secretly monitored the activities of Germany's "high society" citizens.

Anna soon fell under the spell of her charismatic, Italian-born suitor. Unlike other men she had met, Mario seemed to care about every aspect of her life. He listened to her stories. He laughed at her jokes and expressed his concern about the long hours she logged. He asked questions—probing questions—about her job. Anna also learned that Mario passionately believed the Jews were the source of the world's woes. So Anna was happy to share the secrets she learned in the office, such as the names and locations of wealthy high-society Jews who were next on the Sicherheitsdienst's list of planned expulsions.

While Anna had fallen in love for the second time, she was simply a means to an end for Mario. But he wanted her secrets, and she needed his money. So the charade would continue for now. Anna's most recent disclosure seemed especially promising. The following day the Sicherheitsdienst would surprise Frederick Schneller, a wealthy doctor living in the town of Haldenstein, a community not far from Waldkraiburg.

Early that morning, Mario knocked on the front door of Dr. Schneller's spacious mansion. After completing his studies at the University of Berlin, Schneller had founded a highly successful family practice in the town. However, Nazi ideology had poisoned the community, and he and his family now feared for their lives.

"May I help you?" Dr. Schneller asked nervously as he answered the door.

Mario suppressed his disdain for the Jewish doctor, pretending instead to be a trustworthy friend. "I've learned that in less than two hours, you will be visited by the Sicherheitsdienst."

Dr. Schneller stifled a cry of terror as Mario continued.

"We must act quickly. It's common knowledge that you have impressionistic artwork in your home. The Fuhrer has classified such works as degenerate, ideologically unsuitable for the Reich. Security Service thugs are on their way to confiscate them."

"What are you proposing, my friend?"

"Write a brief description of each painting and any other possession you want to protect. Indicate that you have entrusted the property to me for safekeeping, with the understanding that it will be returned to you at war's end. I will sign the document, which you may keep." Mario was no longer surprised by how quickly his victims agreed to his proposals. With the brutal, widespread persecution of the Jews, most placed their trust in anyone they believed would befriend them. They had little choice.

With some hesitation, Dr. Schneller scribbled descriptions of his most prized possessions. Two paintings by Emil Nolde, several Kathe Kollwitz drawings, and a painting by Franz Marc.

"Please protect these for me," the doctor pleaded. "They're my children's inheritance. You'll be generously rewarded for your efforts when I return."

After signing and dating the worthless scrap of paper, Mario returned the document to the doctor. He followed Dr. Schneller as he led him to his library; there the paintings and drawings adorned the mahogany-paneled walls. Mario quickly assessed the works as genuine, thanking the gods for his training as an artist and appraiser.

They hurriedly wrapped the artwork in blankets, placing each piece in the backseat of Mario's 1938 Horch 853 Sport Cabriolet. The automobile never failed to impress his dupes, helping him quickly win their confidence.

Schneller stood on his porch, nervously waving his farewell as Mario exited the circular driveway. He acknowledged the send-off by feigning a sympathetic nod as he gunned the Cabriolet in the direction of Waldkraiburg.

Less than two miles from Dr. Schneller's home, the brutal German Security Police raced past the Sports Cabriolet, followed by members of the ERR. Within minutes, the group had forced their way into Dr. Schneller's residence. Dr. Schneller, along with his wife, daughter, and two young boys, would never be seen again.

One week later, Mario Guiseppina and his beautiful little daughter, Emiliane, moved into the Schnellers' abandoned Heldenstein mansion.

Mario flawlessly executed his looting plan for almost another year before transitioning to the next stage of his life—disposing of his stolen art, investing some of the proceeds in additional properties and depositing the remainder into several Swiss bank accounts. The members of the community presumed that Mario was a wealthy widower, successfully raising his daughter in very difficult times.

Shortly after Mario's makeover as a respectable citizen of the Third Reich, Anna vanished without a trace.

In the years to follow, Mario maintained contact with several of his wartime buddies. He managed his fortune well, and it continued to multiply in the decades following Germany's crushing defeat. Life was good. Emiliane blossomed into a gorgeous, albeit self-absorbed and egotistical, young woman with no particular vocation in mind.

Mario's friends saw him for the last time in the fall of 1976. Without warning, he suffered a stroke, followed days later by what the doctors described as a massive heart attack. Mario's carefully crafted will bequeathed his vast wealth, estimated to be in the millions of Reichsmarks, to his grief-stricken daughter. The estate in Italy was only a small part of her inheritance.

A stab of pain interrupted Emiliane's musings. The contractions were increasing in frequency and intensity, prompting her to place the call.

"Maria, please, it's time."

Her close friend lived in Emiliane's spacious, two-story guesthouse facing an ice-covered alpine meadow. Maria hurriedly skipped down the back flight of stairs from the wood-planked deck adjoining her upstairs sitting room and then ran the short distance to Emiliane's home.

A short time later, Emiliane gave birth to her firstborn, a son.

For the hundredth time that Christmas morning, Emiliane whispered the meaning of her last name, "God will add another son," and pondered the irony of her calling. She would name him Romiti, "Man of Rome." It was not important that he share her last name. Soon enough, the world would know *his* name and worship him as their savior.

CHAPTER TWO

1983—Baselga di Piné, Northern Italy

Most evenings, Maria entertained Romiti by reading from a very early collection of tales that extolled the exploits of the legendary King Arthur. The boy's favorite stories depicted the king as the monster-hunting protector of Britain, victorious over giants, cat monsters, fearful dragons, dog-heads, and witches.

"Read one more!" Romiti demanded.

They were relaxing comfortably on a sofa near the fireplace, Romiti's favorite spot in the house. There was no fire, for the evening was warm, but the setting reminded them of winter, the season most eagerly anticipated by the pair.

"I've already read two stories," Maria reminded her precocious charge. But as usual, she quickly gave in to Romiti's demands, selecting a fable about one of the giants Arthur and his band of superhuman heroes would conquer.

"Was Daddy like King Arthur?"

Maria was startled by the question, although she'd known a question like it would someday be asked. "I've never met your father, nor has your mother ever talked about him. But she told me you were very special, Romiti; in fact, she said your birth was mystical. She never explained what she meant, but I know this means you're a remarkable boy."

After reading the third story, Maria playfully asked, "What do you want to be when you grow up?"

"I want to be the king of the world!"

"King of the world? But the world doesn't have a king, Romiti. What else would you like to be?"

"Nothing!" he pouted. "I want to be the king of the world."

"Why do you want to be the king of the world?"

"Just because! Don't ask me any more questions!" he shouted as he ran to his room.

Romiti was almost six years old, and by anyone's account, an extraordinary child. In this respect, he was much different from Napoleon, the nineteenth-century warrior worshiped by his mother. As a young boy, Napoleon was self-conscious about his middling origins. His family was not wealthy and certainly not aristocratic. His snobby classmates, whom he resented, teased him about his thick Corsican accent. And other than math, at which he excelled, he was a pretty average student.

Romiti, on the other hand, was an exceptional student—brilliant, in fact. He was already proficient in German, Italian, English, and Ladin, an ancient, nearly unintelligible mixture of Latin and Celtic dialects spoken by the nearly one hundred thousand residents of Trentino-Alto Adige. The strange tongue dated back to their ancestors' contacts with the Roman legions in the century before Christ.

Romiti also excelled in the basics: reading, writing, and arithmetic. But what his teachers remarked most was his capacity to exercise his natural leadership and organizational skills to his advantage. He had also developed an uncanny, some would even say mystical or supernatural, ability to solve complex problems. Romiti maintained remarkable composure in situations considered stressful by his peers and older children. None of these talents surprised his mother, who had listened carefully to the astrologers who described the attributes of those born under Capricorn, as he had been. His leadership, his social graces, and his enjoyment of things that excited the senses of sight, taste, and smell were expected.

As Romiti grew older, anyone who closely observed his relationships with other children soon noticed that he intuitively sensed rivals. He usually won over the challenger with an engaging smile or flattering words. If this failed, Romiti had other methods.

*   *   *

The boys usually shot marbles during their lunch break. "I'm first," Romiti would always shout as they ran to the patch of dirt in the corner of the playground.

"You're always first!" countered a Jewish boy named Benjamin. "This time, I'm first, and you're last!" He was a year older and a smidgen bigger than Romiti.

Benjamin was already on his knees, positioning his marbles for the first contest, when he noticed the other boys warily watching Romiti. Benjamin stood up and walked slowly toward his young rival.

"Who's shooting first?" Romiti polled the group.

While none of the boys would confront Benjamin one-on-one, in unison they shouted, "Romiti!" Benjamin longed to win this argument but wanted to remain in the group even more. He reluctantly backed down, agreeing that once again, Romiti would go first. Romiti disarmed Benjamin with a smile and a tap on the shoulder and then dropped to his knees to begin the game. But he never forgot this challenge to his leadership.

Years later his teachers, recounting this event and many others like it, offered them as evidence of an impulsive, iron-willed, uncompromising leader. But others who knew Romiti well also observed that he lacked remorse for any wrongdoing and was without sympathy for those he hurt.

Perhaps Emiliane was partly to blame for the dysfunctional behavior of her son. While she cared deeply about Romiti's health, education, and happiness, she was determined to infuse in him her ideology of race supremacy and consequently, her resolute hatred of Jews. While for a time she dabbled in Roman Catholicism, she eventually rejected the faith of her mother and embraced Hitler and his dream of a master race instead. She joined the discredited Nazi Party, the Nationalsozialistische Deutsche Arbeiterpartei, in her late teens, following in the footsteps of her father.

Emiliane ardently studied the writings of Guido von List and Jorg Lanz von Liebenfels, so-called prophets who based their warped beliefs on loose translations of ancient Scandinavian Scriptures and Nordic paganism. Emiliane was fascinated by their ideas and intrigued by the possibility that she could be among the progenitors of a superrace which had its beginnings among the god-men.

Like her heroes Hitler and Himmler, Emiliane was deeply involved in the occult. Hitler was profoundly influenced by Dietrich Eckart, a wealthy publisher and editor-in-chief of an anti-Semitic rag that Eckart named *In Plain German*. Eckart was a committed occultist and a master of magic who belonged to the Thule Society. Thule was a legendary island, similar to Atlantis, which was supposedly the center of a lost, high-level civilization. Their secrets were guarded by ancient, highly intelligent beings ("Masters") who could be contacted by means of magic, mystical rituals. With the help of these Masters, Thule Society initiates could be endowed with supernatural strength and energy, with the objective of creating a race of supermen who would exterminate all inferior races.

Following in their footsteps, Emiliane mixed Nordic paganism, Roman Catholicism, and practices of the occult, and she raised Romiti to believe in the blend as fervently as she.

Her son would be the god-man who would rule the earth with an iron scepter; his kingdom would devour all the kingdoms of the earth—and of his kingdom, she ardently believed, there would be no end.

*　　*　　*

Another "Benjamin incident" marked Romiti's boyhood—but no one but Romiti himself knew the whole story.

Romiti looked forward to his walk to school each morning. His favorite route took him past Serrain Lake at the foot of Dosso Costalta. The lake was small, lined on one side with apartments and shops and forested on the other. A band of cane skirted the northern shore. Romiti was nearing the cane when he heard cries for help.

He scrambled through the trees to investigate the source of the cries and saw Benjamin thrashing in the icy water. Apparently he had been playing on the rocks when he slipped and fell. It appeared that his foot was tangled in some submerged rocks or debris; Benjamin's head barely broke the surface of the water. He was obviously exhausted, but relieved to see Romiti.

"Help me! Get that stick and let me grab hold of the other end," he cried.

Romiti watched in fascination as Benjamin thrashed wildly and gasped for air. Although Benjamin continued his cries for help, Romiti seemed oblivious to the terrible sounds. He set his knapsack down, and positioning himself on a large rock facing the panicked Benjamin, calmly gazed at the scene unfolding before him. After a minute or two, he pulled a piece of wrapped candy from his knapsack and slowly placed it in his mouth. For another fifteen minutes or so, Benjamin struggled to loosen his foot. Finally, with a pleading glance toward Romiti, he slipped beneath the surface of the water for the last time.

Romiti picked up his knapsack and resumed his walk to school. It was a gorgeous morning. The cool breeze was crisp and clean—it felt good to be alive. He didn't mind arriving a few minutes late for class that day.

At a hastily called school assembly the next morning, local officials announced that Benjamin was missing.

"I saw him the day before last; we walked home from school together," Alrick, Benjamin's best friend, said. "We were supposed to skip rocks on the lake yesterday morning before school, but Benjamin never showed up."

A week later, Benjamin's body was discovered in the Marshes of Sternigo, located on the northern tip of Serrain Lake. A small object reflecting the noonday sun caught the attention of the police officer that identified Benjamin's body. Upon closer inspection, he found it was only a candy wrapper discarded by a thoughtless visitor.

*   *   *

It was December 25, Romiti's favorite day of the year. No one else mattered on *his* birthday. The year was 1989, and today, Romiti attained the magical age of twelve. He was a few inches taller than most of his peers. His long black hair and muscular build were the envy of the other boys and a pleasing distraction to the girls. He had mastered two more languages— Spanish and Mandarin Chinese, aided by the language tutors employed by his mother to accelerate his progress. She spared no expense when it came to enhancing his natural abilities, whatever they might be. After she took him out of the public school at the age of ten, Emiliane, Maria, the tutor, and Romiti would spend several months outside Italy each year, learning the languages and customs of the nations they were visiting.

For Romiti and his mother alike, this day was all about him and him alone. Presents, favorite foods, and other surprises delighted him. This particular day was unusually cold, with snow threatening to fall at any moment. Romiti wanted to try out his new sled, but sans the extra clothing demanded by Maria, who was the boy's caretaker for several hours each day.

"You're not to go outside without your cap, coat, and gloves," Maria ordered with a stern, slightly raised voice.

Romiti stared blankly at Maria and then bolted toward the door.

Maria grabbed him by the arm and blocked his exit. Romiti's angry, piercing gaze frightened her for the first time. With his eyes locked on hers, it seemed as though he was staring through and beyond her, at some apparition only he could see.

"You'll be sorry you touched me," he hissed over his shoulder. "Just wait and see."

With this threat ringing in her ears, Maria watched Romiti ascend the stairs to his room and then heard the loud slamming of his bedroom door.

Emiliane had missed the confrontation, having been upstairs to dress. "I'll be back tomorrow morning," Maria called out.

As she climbed the stairs to the rear entrance of the guesthouse she now called her own, she felt the first snowflakes touch her face.

She clicked her tongue and shook her head. Emiliane adored the boy, but Emiliane was blind to aspects of his character, things Maria could clearly see. Romiti possessed all the traits of a classic psychopath—he was obsessed with fire, cruel to animals, and most embarrassing of all, a bed wetter until the age of nine.

That night, Romiti saw the guesthouse darken. He quietly left his room, and with catlike precision, climbed the stairs that led to Maria's upstairs deck. He carefully removed a piece of heavy string from his pocket, tying each end to the posts supporting the handrail of the stairs. The string was about four inches above the step, impossible to detect in the snow that already covered the landscape. He returned to his bedroom and patiently waited. Then he placed a call from the phone on a stand next to his bed.

"Maria, Mother is choking," Romiti whispered into the telephone.

Maria leaped out of bed, threw on a bathrobe, and slid into her slippers. She ran across her deck toward the stairs, slipping and sliding. Reaching them, she tripped over some unseen object and tumbled headfirst down the steep stairway.

Minutes later, she awoke in excruciating pain. "Emiliane! Help me!" she shouted.

But the snowstorm smothered her voice. She knew her elbow was shattered, and she could see a bone protruding from a leg that was grotesquely twisted beside her. She tried to move her head and found that she could not.

She looked up and noticed the bright lights in Romiti's bedroom; she saw the outline of his frame in the window before it quickly disappeared. "Thank God," Maria said as she performed the sign of the cross over her injured chest. "Romiti will get help."

In moments he appeared in the cold darkness, looking down at her.

"Please," Maria begged, "call for help. It hurts so badly, and I'm so cold!"

He glanced at her briefly as he stepped over her injured form, rapidly climbing the stairs. He removed the broken string, placing both pieces in his pocket, and then returned to Maria's side. He stooped down beside her and watched her with expressionless eyes.

"Please," Maria begged once more. "Call your mama. I'm badly hurt."

Romiti continued to watch Maria, only breaking his gaze when he unwrapped a small piece of candy and discarded the wrapper in the snow. He let it dissolve in his mouth before retrieving from his pocket the broken pieces of string. The young killer dangled the pieces in Maria's face and then left without a word, traces of a smile twisting the corners of his mouth. The falling snow covered his footsteps, burying the evidence of his crime.

Trembling in horror at her plight, Maria realized the truth. "You truly *are* the illegitimate, bed-wetting seed of Satan," she cried out. "I pray you burn in hell!"

Romiti stopped in his tracks at the foul insult but quickly regained his composure. He returned to his warm and comfortable bed and promptly fell asleep.

Maria's frozen body was found the next morning. Although one of the policemen did find a cellophane wrapper buried not far from the corpse, they found no evidence of foul play; their report indicated the cause of death was an accidental fall that occurred while sleepwalking.

At the cemetery a couple days later, Emiliane was heartbroken and beside herself with grief. Romiti was impassive; he didn't shed a tear for the woman who had helped care for him all his life. When Emiliane complimented her young son on his remarkable composure, Romiti acknowledged the praise with a slight nod of his head.

*   *   *

Despite his astonishing abilities and strikingly handsome appearance, fourteen-year-old Romiti was a loner, even among those who considered him a friend. This suddenly changed one afternoon in June, 1991—the day he met Mahmoud Aliaabaadi.

Generations of Aliaabaadis had thrived in Garmsar, situated in the Semnan province of Iran. Known for its large population of educated

Iranians, Garmsar is about eighty kilometers southeast of Tehran, on the edge of Dasht-e Kavir, Iran's largest desert. Boasting a population of forty thousand people from twenty tribal groups, the town rests in a fertile plain not unlike the rural farming communities of Midwestern America. In May, the summer crops of cotton and melons are planted, and in the following month, the winter crops of wheat and barley are harvested.

Mahmoud's father, Massoud, was a successful electrical engineer and a moderate Muslim. He had been content with life in the pre-Iranian Revolution culture, but in the years following the overthrow of the shah, Massoud had become increasingly concerned over the radical beliefs espoused by Ayatollah Ruhollah Khomeini and his followers—especially as they had now infiltrated his own family. His brother-in-law, Tahmaseb Heidari, was a fanatical Muslim cleric who held extremist views. Heidari's young son, Hossein, was three years older than Mahmoud. The cousins attended the same school, and despite their age difference were the best of friends. But Massoud worried that a radicalized Hossein could easily persuade an impressionable Mahmoud to do his bidding, so he began to consider the possibility of fleeing his homeland.

For Massoud, the most painful part of leaving Iran would be the severing of ties to his best friend, Yossi Nazemi. Yossi had earned several degrees at the Ferdowsi University in Mashhad and was considered a brilliant nuclear scientist, working side by side with his Russian counterparts in a joint Russian-Iranian research organization called Persepolis. The two men remained very close friends following their university years, and as a result their families enjoyed most holidays together; celebrations were eagerly anticipated by adults and children alike and were carefully planned months in advance.

Nonetheless, after a year of research and preparation, Massoud successfully spirited his family out of Iran, settling in the almost alien world of Baselga di Piné. The Aliaabaadis moved into their new home less than a mile from Romiti's.

Unlike Romiti's potpourri of pagan and occult beliefs, Mahmoud and his younger sister, Sholeh, whom Mahmoud adored, had been raised devout but moderate Shiite Muslims. Many Shiites pray certain prayers together three times each day, a practice Mahmoud and his family faithfully observed. He had been taught the principal tenets of his faith, the seven pillars of Ismailism, and the traditional religious practices of Shia Islam.

Mahmoud was raised to observe the month of martyrdom, Muharram, and to make pilgrimages to the shrines of the Twelve Imams.

While on a walking tour of his new surroundings one morning, Mahmoud shyly waved to Romiti as he and his father trudged along the path that bordered Emiliane's property. Emiliane was picking flowers from the gardens that grew alongside the wide brick walkway leading to the front entrance of her home. She did not recognize the hikers and thought they might be tourists.

"Good morning. Are you visitors to Baselga?" she asked with a smile.

"No, I'm Massoud Aliaabaadi, and this is my son, Mahmoud," the visitor proudly announced. "We moved to Baselga di Piné last week."

"And I'm Emiliane. This is my son, Romiti."

Emiliane noticed that Massoud was carrying a small book. "I'm an avid reader, and I see that perhaps you are too. What are you reading?"

Massoud seemed embarrassed by the question, but he hesitantly offered the name of the book. "It's the Holy Koran," he replied. "I plan to do some reading when my son and I reach the lake."

"I've never met a Muslim before," Emiliane confessed, "but I've always been fascinated by stories about the Twelfth Imam. Do you believe them?"

"They're not stories," Massoud politely but firmly corrected Emiliane's choice of words. "Our prophets simply foretold what Muslims will experience when history comes to a close. And yes, I absolutely believe these prophecies."

"So who is this Twelfth Imam?" Emiliane asked.

"The Twelfth Imam is a direct descendant of the founder of Islam. He never died, but disappeared from earth in about 939 BC."

"What do you mean he never died?" Emiliane interrupted.

"I mean he never died." The helpful Iranian smiled. "He will remain hidden until Allah commands the Twelfth Imam to manifest himself on earth again as the Mahdi. Meanwhile, he is the Hidden Imam who works through *mujtahids* to interpret Koran."

Emiliane set down her flowers, intrigued. "So what's supposed to happen when he manifests himself again as the Mahdi? Is he supposed to rule the world? And when's all this supposed to happen?"

"Mahdi will return at the end of days, during a time of great upheaval. Mahdi will establish peace and justice for mankind, but not before fighting the Jews and Christians, killing them all."

She was taken aback by his candor but wanted to hear more. "I love it!" Emiliane exclaimed. "And what about Jesus? Where does he fit into the picture?"

"Mahdi will bring Jesus with him. Jesus will serve him, and will force non-Muslims to choose Mahdi or death. At Mahdi's direction, Jesus will engage in jihad, eventually killing Dajjal, the devil. As Mahdi's deputy, Jesus will also slaughter Christians who do not turn to Allah."

"So how will we recognize Mahdi when he reveals himself?" Emiliane asked, growing increasingly excited. Maybe her son would grow up to be the Mahdi. More improbable things had happened, she was sure.

"Personally," Massoud replied, "I'll be convinced Mahdi is who he says he is when he destroys Jerusalem. However, an angel will also appear above his head, shouting, 'This is the Mahdi. Follow him.' He will also be carrying Moses's rod, the one he held when he split the Red Sea."

Emiliane smirked at this last description. Didn't this man realize Moses was just a character from ancient Jewish folklore?

"I'll settle for the destruction of Jerusalem," she said passionately. "That'll be good enough for me!"

"Ah! You're almost a believer!" Massoud observed with a smile of approval.

Growing impatient, Mahmoud decided to interrupt the Shia theology lesson by speaking to Romiti.

"Assalamu alaikum wa rahmatullahi wa barakaktuh," he said, and then laughed, realizing Romiti had no idea of the meaning of his greeting. He translated the phrase into English. "Peace and the mercy and blessings of Allah be upon you."

Romiti smiled in return, but did not offer a greeting. "Wanna see the lake?"

Mahmoud agreed, and the two disappeared for several hours.

Romiti and Mahmoud became fast friends. Both born in 1977, they shared a wide range of interests—with several notable differences as well. Romiti was the charismatic leader; Mahmoud, though possessed of a strong will, was inclined to follow. Both were exceptional organizers and speakers. Both were ambitious. Mahmoud was deeply religious, while Romiti had no religious inclinations other than a deep fascination with the occult. Mahmoud possessed nationalistic ideals; Romiti had none. Romiti held fast to no fixed principles; Mahmoud lived by principles firmly implanted by his father.

Not surprisingly, their first pact was to learn each other's native tongue. Romiti agreed to converse in Italian and Ladin. In return, Mahmoud pledged to speak only Farsi, although he was also fluent in English and Arabic. As teenagers they were inseparable. They excelled in their studies, often completing their homework together. Each accompanied the other on frequent holidays inside and outside of Italy. Both boys were quiet thinkers who loved to roam the nearby woods, often hiking for hours without speaking. Occasionally they would chatter in Ladin, but usually communication occurred through sidelong glances and simple gestures.

Their idyllic way of life in Baselga di Piné was fleeting; almost overnight, it seemed, it was time to select a university.

Because English was their common language, they submitted applications to several American universities and were accepted by each one. They finally decided on the University of California at Berkeley.

By the time they began their college days in America, Romiti was fluent in seven languages, including Farsi. Mahmoud spoke five languages, including Ladin and Italian.

CHAPTER THREE

June 1995—JFK Airport, New York

Romiti and Mahmoud landed at JFK in early summer 1995. As they walked toward the baggage claim area, people took notice of the handsome young men, striking in their appearance. Romiti was the slightly taller of the two, several inches over six feet. Women said he reminded them of a youthful Marcello Mastroianni—dark, strong, and confident, with a slightly arrogant swagger. His granite-chiseled features warned, "Don't mess with me!"

Mahmoud was equally appealing to the women whose paths he crossed. Swarthy, sexy, masculine, and ruggedly handsome, he possessed the determined and unruly looks of the classical Persian male.

They collected their luggage before climbing into a waiting limo for the short fare to a "luxury and exotic car" rental agency. Before beginning their studies, they had agreed that a cross-country road trip would be the best way to immerse themselves in American culture. The agency had already received Romiti's rental payment for the sporty new Porsche Carrera 4 convertible. In about seven weeks, the coupe would be returned to the luxury car rental agency's west coast branch, located near the Oakland International Airport not far from Berkeley.

From JFK they headed to the Ritz Carlton-Battery Park, where the convertible would sit idle for the next several days as the young men explored the city. After checking in, they walked to the World Trade Center.

"Check out the height of the towers!" Mahmoud exclaimed.

Awestruck, they strained to see the top of the cloud-shrouded South Tower, rising 1,362 feet above the ground. The majestic buildings were a tribute to American ingenuity and a symbol of the nation's great financial strength and power. They recalled reading about the terrorist attack on the

World Trade Center two years earlier, remembering the explosions that had killed six people and injured a thousand others.

"Imagine what it must have felt like when the bombs went off! It had to be terrifying, especially if you were trapped in the parking structure below the buildings."

Mahmoud agreed with Romiti's comments, adding, "I'm sure no one worried about the buildings coming down; bet they were nervous about falling glass and debris, though."

Emiliane had arranged a surprise for their first full day in the city. She had become a close friend of Francesco Paolo Fulci, Italy's permanent representative to the United Nations, and he had invited them to visit the UN complex. As they entered the gates to the eighteen-acre facility, a guard explained they had actually left the city and were now in international territory belonging to all the member countries.

An aide to the Italian representative provided a first-class tour for the young men, including a brief visit to the General Assembly Hall, in session during their visit.

Romiti was thoroughly impressed with the experience and confidently predicted to Mahmoud and the aide, "Someday I'll be making the speeches around here—count on it!"

Visits to the Statue of Liberty and the Empire State Building, a baseball game at Yankee Stadium, a hike through Central Park, and a couple of Broadway productions rounded out their whirlwind tour of the Big Apple. Next stop: Washington, DC.

"The size of the city is impressive, don't you think?" Mahmoud's remark was more an observation than a question as they headed south on I-295, leaving New York behind them.

"Yeah. Pretty big," Romiti replied. "But I wasn't all that impressed. See all the potholes in the streets, the graffiti on the walls, the weeds growing in the flowerbeds and in the cracks of the sidewalks? Parts of the city looked pretty run-down to me. And so many sleeping on the sidewalks and begging for handouts. Not at all what I was expecting."

Mahmoud agreed. "How 'bout all the strip joints and magazine racks? Right out in the open! Not what I was expecting either." Mahmoud was quiet a moment. "The United Nations disappointed me too. Eight hundred thousand Rwandans were violently killed in the span of a hundred days last year, and yet I sensed no urgency about this or any other crisis among the ambassadors we met."

"The fighting was primarily between two people groups, the Tutsis and Hutus. The world ignores sectarian violence, even genocide," Romiti responded authoritatively. "As long as the mayhem isn't affecting the numbers on Wall Street, London, or Toyko, I've learned that just about anything goes."

*   *   *

As their journey continued, the travelers visited several popular US tourist destinations, including Jackson Hole, Wyoming, the place that most reminded them of the beautiful mountains of northern Italy. After more than a week in Jackson Hole, they reluctantly left for Salt Lake City. Mahmoud wanted to see the Mormon Tabernacle, wondering if it was as grand as al-Masjid al-Haram (the Holy Mosque) in Mecca, or Jerusalem's Kubbat as-Sakhra, better known in America as the Dome of the Rock or the Mosque of Omar, located on the Temple Mount.

Mahmoud believed all Americans were Christians and did not distinguish between Protestants, Catholics, Mormons, or any other "brands" that he considered branches of Christianity. His main interest was to learn whether Islam's great mosques were as imposing as the Christian places of worship, among which, he mistakenly understood, the tabernacle in Salt Lake was preeminent. While not strongly anti-Semitic, he had no desire to see Jewish synagogues, regardless of their importance or grandeur.

"Who gives a rip about the Mormon Tabernacle?" Romiti complained. "In six hours, we could be in Vegas. I want to see if it's really the sin capital of the world."

After a few hours in Park City, a popular resort community outside Salt Lake, they arrived in Las Vegas about midnight and were stunned by the shimmering lights, the heavy traffic, and the crowds of people lining the sidewalks. As the bellhop was unloading their luggage, Romiti tossed the Porsche keys to the valet and entered Bellagio's. *Where else would two guys from northern Italy want to stay?* he asked himself with a chuckle.

The attractive guest-services attendant stationed at the front desk returned the young men's credit cards and passports and then asked Mahmoud if this was their first visit to Vegas.

"Yes, it's our first time," he replied.

"Are you looking for any particular form of entertainment?" she inquired with a coy smile.

"No," Mahmoud responded naively. "We've heard it's the entertainment capital of America and decided to check it out for ourselves."

Less than an hour later, Mahmoud had seen enough. He was dismayed by the sights and sounds of Sin City. He was offended by the suggestive—pornographic, in his opinion—banners that advertised lewd shows, bachelor and bachelorette packages, strip clubs, and topless lounges.

"I've had enough!" Mahmoud said, disgust dripping from his tone. "I'll take mountains and lakes any day over the immorality and perversion that pervade this town!"

Romiti agreed, and soon they were headed toward California's northern coast.

*   *   *

After driving hard for several hours, Romiti and Mahmoud arrived in San Francisco. Enjoying a bowl of Scoma's New England clam chowder and piping-hot buttered sourdough bread, followed by grilled halibut and a baked potato, the young men discussed their observations of their nearly two-month tour of the States.

They agreed America was a beautiful country, rich in natural resources. Its cities and towns had all the modern conveniences one would expect in a nation such as this. Fertile farms, managed by hardworking men and women, supplied its people with an abundance of crops, and livestock was plentiful on its sprawling ranches. Its forests teemed with wildlife, and the surrounding oceans, lakes, and rivers abounded with fish.

But generally speaking, the people of this great nation, the young men concluded, were weak and divided. As early as 1786, *"E Pluribus Unum"* was engraved on the coins exchanged in America—"Out of many, one." But in the last few decades special interest groups had formed, each believing their individual rights were more important than those of their fellow citizens—even those of friends, neighbors, and coworkers.

"It seems that most everyone belongs to a special interest group, splintering the nation along lines of race, gender, sexual preference, disabilities, and religious attitudes," Romiti commented. His lip curled. "They exchange the power of unity for their petty squabbles."

Mahmoud was appalled by America's preoccupation with sex. "Do you know I heard that in February one of the states, Tennessee, I think, ruled that sodomy laws violate the state constitution? And there's no end to the demands of the gay rights activists. Sex seems to be the only topic on the minds of Americans right now."

"I agree," Romiti replied, and then made a grim prediction. "It's only a matter of time before this fractured country abdicates its place as the greatest nation on earth. I'm convinced it will be overthrown by its enemies within."

Although Mahmoud didn't realize it then, the conclusions they drew from their depressing observations would profoundly impact the lives of untold millions.

CHAPTER FOUR

August 1995—Israeli Embassy, Paris, France

The Israeli government was nervous. Around the world, Jews were being targeted by Iranian terrorists. The prior year's Jewish community-center bombing in Buenos Aires, Argentina, was but one among many examples of the escalating violence. Hezbollah and Iranian government officials were linked to the horrific Argentine attack. The US had placed oil and trade sanctions on Iran after accusing the country of sponsoring terrorism and openly trying to sabotage the Israeli-Arab peace process. Most recently, intelligence cables revealed the Iranians had partnered with Russia to resume work on the partially finished Bushehr Nuclear Plant.

Bushehr provoked an immediate response from the Israeli government. Most governments were fearful that the plant was the first step toward Iran becoming a nuclear-armed terrorist state. An assassination team was assembled by senior Mossad operations officer Orit Liberman. He was connected with Metsada, a highly secret organization within the Mossad. Within Metsada, Liberman had access to the Kidon, a specially trained, elite assassination unit. *Kidon,* meaning "bayonet," was the Mossad's operational arm responsible for kidnappings and executions.

Liberman worked closely with his colleague, Yoel Barak, whose official cover was as the first secretary of the Israeli embassy in Paris. The Mossad had established Paris as their regional base for a covert operation intending to disrupt Iran's plans for a nuclear plant.

Besides a small support team, Liberman had selected three Kidon staff officers as the primary engagement unit for the operation. The support team was to enter Iran first and then perform surveillance on their primary target, an irreplaceable nuclear physicist who was leading the group of Iranian scientists assigned to the Bushehr project. The team would also establish two safe houses in the Iranian capital and acquire the weapons and vehicles required for the Kidon action unit.

*　　*　　*

Romiti and Mahmoud arrived in the college town of Berkeley in mid-August 1995. It was too hot, too crowded—and it would be too long, Romiti realized, before this chapter of his life would end and the next one could begin.

Romiti had enrolled in Berkeley's Haas School of Business. It was never his purpose to enter the competitive world of business and finance, although he was keenly aware of the advantages capitalism and a free-market system enjoyed. Long ago he had decided he would not be satisfied to merely lead a global conglomerate or manage a billionaire's portfolio. Those were the dreams and aspirations of mere mortals—mortals who lived and died with scarcely a whisper of their existence lingering beyond the grave.

Romiti understood that nations rise and fall on the strength of their economies. He was determined to discover and thoroughly understand the financial and economic principles undergirding the world's wealthiest nations and then apply those principles in an as-yet-unidentified transnational vocation.

At the same time, he had discarded his mother's superstitious notions concerning the Nordic gods. He had no regard for any god, especially the gods of his ancestors. Romiti exalted himself above all gods, whether real or imagined. But he readily acknowledged that the energy that so powerfully worked within him originated, somehow, from the magical arts and practices of the occult that were very much a part of her, and now him. Like his mother, he pursued this magic, regularly visiting fortune-tellers, mediums, spiritists, and astrologers.

Even as he studied alongside other college students, he practiced sorcery, witchcraft, and divination. He believed this energy, or force, call it what you will, would supernaturally empower him to accomplish some inimitable objective, one that would uniquely set him apart from all other men in history.

Mahmoud chose Berkeley's School of Physics as the gateway in his quest to become a nuclear physicist.

His studies included the study of special relativity, gravitational and electromagnetic fields, heat and properties of matter, particle and nuclear physics, atomic and molecular physics, and advanced quantum physics.

A fundamental physics department objective was "to promote strong independent learning, analytical, and problem-solving skills, with special emphasis on design, communication, and an ability to work in teams." Another objective of the department was to teach the student to "understand the broad social, ethical, safety, and environmental context within which nuclear physics is practiced." Mahmoud gained this understanding—and just as quickly forgot it.

*   *   *

Three years after the Aliaabaadis left their home in Garmsar, Hossein Heidari joined Iran's Islamic Revolutionary Guard Corps. The very opposite of his cousin, Hossein was unsophisticated, unpleasant, and unattractive. He hated Western culture. Freedom was too dangerous to be placed in the hands of common people; such freedom allowed greedy entrepreneurs to openly peddle their fleshly pleasures to eager buyers around the world. While Hossein secretly enjoyed the forbidden fruit, he nonetheless was committed to the destruction of the purveyors of the carnal merchandise. He believed the IRGC would provide the opportunity for him to someday strike at the West.

However, Hossein quickly became disillusioned with the IRGC, as its mandate to protect the revolution lessened its military focus. He had no interest in improving the nation's telecommunications infrastructure—this, he complained, was work for civilians.

"I didn't join the Revolutionary Guards for this," Hossein groused to another guard while sipping boiling hot tea in an Iranian *chai khaneh* (teahouse). The savory aroma of the strong black liquid filled the room. The men gripped the teacups, actually small glasses, as they vainly tried to warm their hands in the numbing cold. "While the infidels are attacking Muslim lands, we're being told to bring the Internet to small towns."

"Not so loud! Look around, you fool!" his friend whispered. "Do you want to get us killed?"

The teahouse was famous for its Persian baklava, a pastry made of chopped almonds and pistachios. Hossein gulped down another as he quickly scanned the dozen or so men who were sitting around six abused metal tables. Blue patterns on the white-tiled walls brought little life to the drab room. No hanging pictures. No windows. Florescent lights dangled from the ceiling, the only source of light that filtered through the hazy smoke. *Is this my future?* he bitterly mused.

It was not. Their conversation was overheard by Hakim Rivad al-Harbi, an operative from a little-known terrorist group called al-Qaeda, posing as a visiting businessman from Saudi Arabia. Al-Harbi said nothing, but he discreetly followed Hossein as he left the building soon after.

Days later, Hossein was reported AWOL by his Revolutionary Guards commander. Soon Hossein was fighting alongside al-Shabaab in Somalia. He quickly proved himself in battle and was selected for a special assignment that brought him to a jihadist training camp in Yemen. It was from there that he placed a call to Mahmoud.

*   *   *

"La hawia wa la quwwata illa biliah!" the voice on the other line greeted him—"There is no power and no strength save in Allah. Do you know who this is?"

Mahmoud recognized the voice immediately, even though he was hearing it for the first time since coming to America.

"Assalamu alaikum, cousin," Mahmoud replied, "Peace be upon you."

Mahmoud and his cousin recounted the events of their lives since the Aliaabaadis had left Iran.

"The world is changing, Mahmoud," Hossein said. "I've been wanting to hear things from your perspective. What are your impressions of America? What drives the Americans' hatred of Muslims? Have you learned why they support Israel's occupation of the land of our brothers, but slaughter innocent Iraqi and Palestinian children?"

The questions caught Mahmoud off guard. He remembered his parents' fear of Hossein's father but was intrigued by his cousin's perceptions of America—a country he had not learned to love.

"Slow down!" he interrupted. "I'm going to be late to class. Are you available later in the week? I'll call you."

Hossein was quiet a moment and then asked, "What's your e-mail address?"

"M-aliaabaadi@yahoo.com." Mahmoud was an avid fan of electronic communication technology and had jumped on the Yahoo bandwagon soon after the start-up went public.

"Very good. I want to hear your views, Mahmoud. Be watching for my e-mail in the next day or so. *Wassalaam.*"

"Wassalaam," Mahmoud replied.

*   *   *

Hossein discarded his disposable cell phone and smiled.

"He wants to continue our conversation," Hossein said to his Saudi al-Qaeda trainer, Hakim Rivad al-Harbi. "On Yahoo—he's afraid of me e-mailing him at his university. It's a good sign. Mahmoud is just beginning his studies in nuclear physics. Give me some time, and we'll have an operative without equal in the US—*insha'llah.*"

The chief of AQAP, the Yemen-based al-Qaeda in the Arabian Peninsula, Mohammed Abdul al-Wadhi—also called the "Saudi Butcher" because of his participation in several savage beheadings—had overheard the entire conversation and smirked at Mahmoud's apparent naiveté. *Insha'llah* indeed. Allah willing.

The trio painstakingly documented the steps they would follow to transform Mahmoud from a peaceful Muslim into a committed terrorist. High on Mohammed's list was to arrange a "chance" encounter between Mahmoud and his three west coast operatives. Shafeeq al-Fayyoumi and Naa'il Faraj were graduating Cal seniors. Abdul-Majeed al-Dossari was a trained-but-never-practicing, hate-filled, wannabe warmongering cleric. His primary calling was to indoctrinate and inflame young jihadist recruits.

They were perfect.

*   *   *

Mahmoud was beginning his sophomore year at Cal but had not yet connected with the Muslim community, a fact that had been bothering him for weeks. Hossein's phone call was the jump start he needed—soon he began to visit the Muslim Community Association often and regularly attend Friday prayers at several mosques in the area.

One Friday afternoon, Mahmoud attended the obligatory *jum'ah* in a mosque several miles from the Cal campus. Attendance was required of all adult males; females were permitted to attend and perform their Friday prayers with other women in a separate chamber of the mosque. Jum'ah was an essential part of Mahmoud's life, as he had been taught that by attending the prayers, the sins he committed between that Friday and the prior one would be forgiven.

As Mahmoud entered the beautifully landscaped, stone-paved courtyard of the mosque, his attention was immediately drawn to the large central fountain circled by benches. Worshipers used the fountain to perform a cleansing ritual, called *wadu,* before entering the mosque to pray. It was surrounded by a spacious, colorful flower garden, accented by a variety of trees imported from the Middle East, including olive, sycamore, and acacia. Mahmoud performed the ritual, washing his ears, face, hands, arms up to the elbows, and feet before entering the building.

Out of respect, Mahmoud had removed his shoes and was placing them on a rack in the entryway when two college-aged men approached him.

"Assalamu alaikum," they greeted him, "Peace be upon you."

"Al-hamdu lillah," Mahmoud replied, "Praise be to Allah."

He introduced himself to the two men, but their brief conversation was interrupted by the first *adhan,* the muezzin's call to prayer. The adhan was intended to communicate an easily understood summary of Islamic belief, and to Christians, was akin to the description of Christ's humiliation and exaltation found in Paul's New Testament letter to the Philippians. The mournful, wailing recitation, sung a cappella, would sound eerie, even frightening, to a non-Muslim visitor, but it was soothing to the experienced ear of the Muslim worshipers.

The first adhan was everyone's cue that jum'ah would begin in about fifteen minutes.

The young men continued speaking for a few minutes and then agreed to resume their conversation after prayers.

As Mahmoud entered the prayer hall, he stepped inside with his right foot first.

"O Allah, open the door of mercy for me," he prayed softly.

Unlike the churches so familiar to most Americans, the mosque's worship area contained no chairs or benches. In this particular mosque, row upon row of superb handwoven Persian wool carpets covered the floor, each with prominent designs and colors. The walls, pillars, and ceiling were decorated with intricate patterns and quotations from the Koran. There were no pictures or statues, since Moslems believe these can lead to idolatry. Shelves laden with copies of the Koran, as well as a variety of books on Islamic philosophy, theology, and law, lined several walls. Mahmoud wanted to be close to the imam, so he headed toward the *minbar,* the raised steps from which the *khutbah,* the sermon, would be delivered.

Overhead was the *mihrab,* a roofed niche that indicated the direction of Ka'aba, the cube-shaped building in Mecca. Ka'aba is the most sacred site in Islam: all mosques face it. Mahmoud aligned himself with the mihrab to be sure he would face the right direction when he prayed.

The second adhan was made, and then a short sermon was delivered. The imam sat down briefly, then stood to deliver the traditional second, pithy sermon. Finally the muezzin called the *igama,* signaling the start of the two prayers of jum'ah. Throughout Friday prayers, Mahmoud participated in the traditional sequences of standing, kneeling, and prostration.

As Mahmoud left the mosque, he left a gift for *zakat,* charity. His gift would be used to help the poor and to support the mosque.

Outside, he sat down on one of the benches next to the fountain, waiting for his new friends to join him. It was a warm afternoon, and the breeze felt good as he rested in the shade of a sycamore tree. Minutes later, Shafeeq al-Fayyoumi and Naa'il Faraj exited the mosque and made their way toward Mahmoud.

"Well, what did you think of the sermons?" Shafeeq asked. He was the smaller of the two al-Qaeda operatives, homegrown terrorists who were bent on the violent overthrow of the US government. The tough-looking jihadist, whose very wealthy parents had immigrated to America from Saudi Arabia, despised the lavish lifestyles of the Saudi royal family and intended to make the US accountable for its support of the corrupt regime. If he could, he would use this unsuspecting physics student to help him do it.

"I thought they were fine," Mahmoud replied. "The imam provided a straightforward explanation for the verses from Sura 41." The verses, long familiar to him, still stood out clearly in his mind:

"And there shall be no way open against those who, after being wronged, avenge themselves; but there shall be a way open against those who unjustly wrong others, and act insolently on the earth in disregard of justice. These! A grievous punishment doth await them."

"The imam gave too simple an explanation for these verses," Shafeeq said sharply. "In fact, both sermons were too Western for my tastes."

Naa'il agreed, explaining that he and Shafeeq regularly attended another mosque where the imam's worldview was more aligned with Islamic thinking prevalent in Iran, Pakistan, Saudi Arabia, Syria, and other Muslim nations. Mahmoud enjoyed their company and was especially pleased to learn they attended Cal. He readily agreed to join them at the mosque they regularly attended the following Friday.

An hour later, Shafeeq left a succinct voice-mail message for Hossein, who maintained frequent contact with him through an Internet café in the city closest to al-Jaza, home to one of several Yemeni terrorist training camps in the lawless district of Mudiyah.

"Naa'il and I have met Mahmoud. Will introduce him to Abdul-Majeed al-Dossari next week!"

Twenty-four hours later, Hossein passed the message along to Mohammed Abdul al-Wadhi. The Butcher was elated with their initial success.

The following Friday, Mahmoud joined his two new friends, along with Abdul-Majeed al-Dossari, for breakfast prior to attending prayers at the mosque.

Mahmoud was startled by al-Dossari's fierce appearance and caught himself staring at the imposing figure who sat before him. The bearded cleric was much older than his two young associates—and quite a bit heavier. His thick, dark-rimmed glasses did not diminish the piercing gaze emanating from his jet-black eyes. Al-Dossari wore a white turban and robe, but his soft attire belied his stern and angry persona.

Mahmoud was introduced to the frowning cleric and was surprised when al-Dossari did not mince his words. "What is the purpose of your life?" he asked. "Is your purpose to exploit your fellow Muslims by supporting corrupt Western democracies or to liberate your brothers through jihad?"

Mahmoud was intimidated and speechless. He swallowed and then forced a weak reply. "I'm focused on my education right now, and seeking Allah's purpose for my life."

"Our goal is to spread Islam worldwide under a restored caliphate," al-Dossari continued, oblivious to Mahmoud's discomfort. "That's the intent of global jihadism, and when required, it involves international Islamic terrorism and guerrilla warfare."

"We've not introduced this subject to Mahmoud before," Naa'il nervously offered, but he was ignored by the animated cleric.

"Global jihadism will continue until Allah commands the Twelfth Imam to manifest himself on earth. If we're alive when he's revealed, we'll join him in fighting the Jews and Christians, killing them all. There is a place for you in this holy war."

Al-Dossari continued his rhetoric for an hour and then abruptly ended the conversation. "I've been candid because your friends vouched for you. Carefully consider my words, but do not repeat them. If you divulge the subject of our conversation to anyone, there will be fearful consequences, I promise you."

The breakfast meeting concluded with that threat, and al-Dossari quickly left the building. Mahmoud shook his head in disbelief as he watched al-Dossari disappear from view.

"Let's go to the mosque," Shafeeq suggested as the young men paid for their breakfast, leaving a miserly tip for the fatigued waitress.

Mahmoud noticed striking differences between this mosque and the one he had frequented. The mosque he had attended the previous Friday was "family friendly." He remembered seeing men and women, young and old, infants, children, and teenagers. The grounds were immaculate; the buildings were well-maintained. The people were cheerful and welcoming.

Here, the majority of the attendees were men, all of whom were roughly his age. He saw a few women, but no infants, children, or teenagers. All the women (young and pretty, he imagined) were completely covered by their burqas, head coverings, and face veils. Most of the men appeared sullen and angry. The mosque was located in a rougher part of town. There was no greenery anywhere, and it appeared the grounds had not received attention in years. The imam enforced the most conservative form of Sharia law, believing the repressive system should govern all aspects of life.

Yet, despite the rundown appearance of the mosque and his usual antagonism toward Sharia law, Mahmoud was mesmerized by the cleric's radical message and blistering delivery. Al-Dossari's haunting question was also tormenting him. *What is the purpose of my life?* He had observed al-Dossari's convictions and commitment to a cause he considered far nobler than the vain pursuit of wealth and pleasure. Throughout his life, Mahmoud had always left mosques feeling empty and alone—he knew something was missing in his soul. Was radical Islam the answer?

The imam was delivering the teachings of Imam Abdullah Azzam, assassinated in Pakistan in 1989 by jihadists more radical than he.

"Imam Abdullah Azzam taught that 'When the enemy enters the land of the Muslims, jihad becomes individually obligatory—*fard 'ayn.* When jihad becomes fard 'ayn, no permission of parents is required, just as parents' permission is not required to perform the *salah* or to fast Ramadan.

"Because Israel and its protector, the Great Satan, America, have entered the land of the Muslims, jihad is obligatory! We have no choice! What is the definition of jihad, you ask? Imam Abdullah Azzam says, 'The word *jihad,* when mentioned on its own, only means combat with weapons.' If any nation is on Muslim soil, uninvited, then we must combat that nation with our weapons! We must take the war to their land!

"Mohsesn Gharavian, a teacher in Qom, has issued a fatwa that declares, 'For the first time the use of nuclear weapons may not constitute a problem, according to Sharia. When the entire world is armed with nuclear weapons, it is permissible to use these weapons as a countermeasure.'

"Some of our fellow Muslims, perhaps even some of you, believe that by donating money to their jihadist brothers and sisters, they're exempt from jihad. But Imam Abdullah Azzam taught, 'Donating money does not exempt a person from bodily jihad, no matter how great the amount of money given. Jihad is the zenith of Islam, and proceeds in stages. Before jihad becomes *hijrah,* then preparation, then *ribat,* and finally, combat.' Now is the time for combat!"

The inflamed audience could no longer be silent. The passionate rhetoric was more than they could bear, and almost in unison they leapt to their feet in a frenzy, crying, *"Allahhu Akbar,* God is the greatest!" and *"Hayya al Khair al amal,* the time for the best of deeds has come! Now is the time for combat!" Tears of anger splashed on the threadbare carpet as several vowed to give their all to the cause of radical Islam.

The imam was pleased with their response, allowing a boisterous interlude before motioning to continue his sermon.

"You may be afraid of injury or even death. But Azzam taught that 'Jihad is a collective act of worship, and every group must have a leader. Obedience to the leader is a necessity in jihad, and thus a person must condition himself to invariably obey the leader. As has been reported in the *hadith,* 'You must hear and obey, whether it is easy or difficult for you, in things which are pleasant for you as well as those which are inconvenient and difficult for you.'

"Let the following words from the Holy Koran give you strength and courage," the imam continued.

"But those who are slain in the way of Allah—
He will never let their deeds be lost.
Soon will he guide them and improve their condition,
and admit them to The Garden (Paradise) which he has announced for them."
Sura 47:4-6

The hearts and souls of many of the imam's audience gradually accepted his hateful rhetoric, much like a cancer that invades, slowly weakens, and then destroys the body of a once-healthy person. Mahmoud left still enthralled by the passionate preaching, but unlike his friends, his upbringing had prepared him to resist the imam's twisted teachings. He was intrigued and questioning, but far from convinced.

* * *

The Kidon unit assembled in Paris for a final briefing before leaving for Iran. Liberman distributed the official passports for the remainder of the mission and then began to recap their assignment. "Our target is a nuclear physicist whose daily activities are very predictable."

"Is he being given any protection?" one of the team members asked.

"No security measures are being taken. The support team has been recording the target's movements—they're pretty routine. Upon our arrival, their surveillance documents will be given to us. The advance team will provide us with a positive identification of our subject, which will conclude their role in the mission."

Liberman completed his briefing and then asked if there were any questions.

The handpicked assassins shook their heads. Collectively, the team members had nearly two dozen successful terrorist hits to their credit. Other than operating in a hostile country, eliminating a scientist seemed like a relatively routine assignment.

CHAPTER FIVE

Berkeley, California

Day by day, Romiti enjoyed the lifestyle made possible by Emiliane's generosity. Finances were not a problem, of course. His body and spirit were renewed with only three hours' sleep each night. He was in marvelous physical condition. He awakened at four o'clock each morning, enjoying a small breakfast that included a glass of orange juice, two slices of dry wheat toast, and a cup of strawberry or blueberry yogurt. He showered after a brief workout that included some weightlifting and a three-mile run. By five-thirty, he was deep into his studies. He adamantly refused to enroll in classes that began before ten, providing four hours of study time before his first class began.

Romiti would usually return to the condo after classes, again devoting the time before dinner to his studies. He never snacked. Except for his early-morning breakfast, he never prepared his own meals. The evening meal was the highlight of his day. It was vitally important to him that it be perfectly prepared and served with excellence. There was no lack of exceptional restaurants in the towns and cities surrounding Berkeley, so this inimitable fetish was always satisfied. Romiti would normally return to his home in the early evening, allowing him to devote his energies to what he considered his most important mission: to identify the universal and most important problems facing the family of nations and to develop explicit strategies and tactics that would resolve each one.

The Internet was his closest friend. He was a voracious and disciplined reader and would spend three or four hours each evening studying the formidable issues and crises facing the key nations of the world. He called these "challenges" and classified them in four categories.

The first category, labeled "Acts of God" by insurance companies, included the natural disasters suffered by individuals and nations alike. A second group, almost always the consequence of poor planning, included problems that could be resolved with sufficient financial resources or new economic models. The third category of challenges encompassed conflicts caused by racial or religious differences or jealousies. And the final group included challenges that were simply the result of incompetent and/or corrupt government.

Romiti carefully documented the strategies and tactics he would employ to resolve each challenge as if he were the leader of the particular nation he was analyzing. Over time, he charted the policies implemented by heads of state to resolve the challenges, noting the root causes of their successes or failures. He also compared their actions to the ones he would have taken, tallying his own successes—which were many—and failures, which were few.

By the time his Berkeley career was over, Romiti possessed an astonishing understanding of the problems facing the world's leading nations, regardless of their causes. And most importantly, he believed he had acquired the knowledge to solve them.

*   *   *

Mahmoud was awakened by the incessant beeping of his cell; he instinctively knew the call was from Sholeh. The highlight of his life was the weekly conversation with his beloved sister. Quick to laugh, her lust for life and uproarious sense of humor never failed to bring great joy to Mahmoud's lonely existence.

"Hey, Sholeh! What's the latest? Planned your next visit? You know I'll keep my promise to let you hike to the top of Big Dome the next time you're here!"

"I'll be there soon. But I'm calling to let you know that all my paperwork has been approved. I'm leaving for Iran on Friday!"

"Wish you weren't going, Sholeh. What happens if something prevents you from getting out?"

"Don't worry about me! Wish you could come too. I wouldn't miss Souroor's wedding for anything. Besides, Father's arranged for Yossi to pick me up in Tehran. I'll be fine."

The animated conversation continued for a few more minutes before Sholeh ended the call. "Hey, some friends just showed up. We're hanging for a day or two before my trip. Gotta go!"

Mahmoud sighed discontentedly as he said his good-bye. Like a returning fog that shrouds a harbor, the powerful emptiness enveloped him as he began his morning jog.

*   *   *

Headlines in June 1996 announced that Benjamin Netanyahu was the newly elected prime minister of Israel. Hard-liners were pleased with the outcome, believing Netanyahu would confront the burgeoning acts of terror perpetrated by Islamic radicals. Israel's allies were pleased too. Perhaps the tiny democracy would serve as their proxy by keeping the Iranian quest for nuclear power in check.

The Mossad assassination team now embedded in Iran wondered if the new prime minister would scrub their mission. They did not wait long for their answer.

*   *   *

The vehicle parked across the street from the target's home contained three Kidon assassins. Their Baretta .22 caliber pistols were hidden beneath their jackets as they awaited the signal from a female support asset. Her assignment was to make a positive identification of the scientist and then follow him to his home. As she passed the parked vehicle, she was to extend her arm through the open driver's-side window, the signal indicating positive ID had been made and the operation was a go.

*   *   *

"You've grown up!" Yossi exclaimed as he picked up his passenger from the Tehran International Airport.

"Hello, Yossi!" Sholeh greeted the close family friend with an affectionate hug. "We've missed you so much! Father said you'd be here on time. You're still a man of your word, aren't you?"

The two friends did not observe the frowning woman who was carefully watching them crawl into Yossi's brown and aging Pakyan. *Who's the young woman?* She remembered Liberman's warning: "There is to be zero collateral risk." He had also reminded the team of the botched Salemeh assassination: "If an innocent is killed, the mission will be a failure!"

We cannot make a mistake.

*　　*　　*

Yossi and Sholeh were oblivious to their surroundings as the chatty friends made the two-hour drive to their hometown of Garmsar, the site of the wedding now two days away. They reminisced about their former lives in Garmsar and the divergent paths their families had taken. Yossi was especially excited to hear about Mahmoud's life in the United States, and he expressed his wish to someday visit America.

As Yossi neared the vicinity of his home, he swung the Pakyan to the shoulder of the road to allow an impatient woman to pass. Then he pulled back into his lane behind the woman's car, noticing that she slowed slightly as she approached and then passed his home.

The two men in the parked vehicle saw the support-team member extend her arm through the open window, their signal to execute the plan. *Just don't shoot the girl,* she thought.

Yossi slowed down too, as a pedestrian slowly crossed the street in front of him. Sholeh's eyes sparkled as she watched the aging scientist carefully park his prized Pakyan in front of his home.

The men got out of their car and quietly approached the unsuspecting couple from the passenger side of the Pakyan, while Yossi and Sholeh greeted the smiling pedestrian who approached the driver side.

"Yossi Nazemi?" one asked.

"Yes," Yossi answered hesitantly. "I'm Yossi Nazemi."

With positive identification established, the three assassins drew their weapons, killing Yossi as Sholeh screamed in terror. She instinctively raised both arms for protection, but a bullet ricocheted off the car's frame, striking her temple. Sholeh's head snapped to the right, striking the passenger's-side window. Eyes opened wide in shock, the mortally wounded woman gaped briefly at her assailant, and then her body slumped forward in the seat.

"We screwed up! Stray bullet struck the female passenger! Let's go!" The three men dove into the car driven by the fourth member of the Mossad assassination team, who sped to the prearranged drop site. There the men abandoned the vehicle, discreetly climbing into another before making the leisurely drive to the safe house.

*　　*　　*

College life passed more quickly than Romiti or Mahmoud had ever imagined it would.

Romiti had recognized many changes in Mahmoud over their four years at Cal, some of which he himself had carefully orchestrated. Of course, the tragic murder of his sister had terribly affected Mahmoud. He read numerous accounts of her death and was convinced her killing had been carried out by the Mossad. "Collateral damage." He despised the term and reviled the people who had conspired to take her life. Romiti's childhood friend was no longer the friendly, ebullient kid he had met at age fourteen. Mahmoud had become gloomy, forlorn, openly sympathetic to Islamic causes and intensely anti-Semitic and anti-American. To all but his closest friends, he appeared remote, even angry most days. While he and Romiti were no longer inseparable, they remained devoted friends. However, Mahmoud spent most of his free time with others—friends, classmates, or fellow worshipers from the local mosque. Romiti really didn't know for sure, and he never asked.

They were kicking back in the condo one night, cooled by the lazy summer breeze that drifted through the window. Graduation was days away. "What's next, Mahmoud?" Romiti asked.

Mahmoud chewed his lip a little as he pondered his answer. He didn't know if it was wise—it certainly wasn't safe—to disclose just how radically he had changed.

Before he could answer, his thoughts were interrupted by Bennett, a friend of Romiti's and a partying type who lived in the adjoining condo.

"Hey, Mahmoud! We're goin' clubbin'. Grab Romiti and let's go!"

"What's the point?" Mahmoud fired back at the face in the open window. "You know I don't drink, and Romiti doesn't hook up with women. Besides, I'd fit in as much as one of the Louisiana swamp people at a Washington DC cocktail party."

Bennett tried another approach. "We'll get a few bottles of wine. There's a couple yeses in every bottle," he promised, referring to one of the methods they used to conquer the ladies.

"Sorry, man. Gotta pass. Catch ya next time."

Romiti chuckled quietly at the interchange. While he enjoyed a few drinks from time to time, he simply had no desire for women. He viewed them as a distraction. Mahmoud, on the other hand, was afraid of the "honorable scribes," the angels responsible for recording the deeds of men. Mahmoud remained a devout Muslim, believing that apart from martyrdom, one's eternal fate would be determined when the final tally of his good and bad deeds was made. Drinking and bad sex would increase the bad deeds count, so he abstained from both—most evenings, anyway. Romiti had tried the party scene a little in their early years but quickly decided it was beneath him. He wasn't sure why Bennett and others like him kept trying.

Mahmoud was still grappling with Romiti's question and the events that had shaped his life. He recalled the phone call from Hossein during his first few weeks of study, the call that had torn from him his simplistic view of life—now forever left behind in Baselga di Piné.

In the years that followed, Hossein had told stories of the miserable plight of Muslims in Gaza and the West Bank, laying the blame for their misery at Israel's feet. He would describe the interference of America, the Great Satan, in the affairs of Islamic countries such as Iran, Afghanistan, Iraq, and Pakistan. Hossein explained that if America were not supplying Israel with military weapons and training, the Middle East could rid itself of the Jewish nation. Overnight, he claimed, the Arab nations surrounding Israel would flourish. Poverty would be abolished; peace and prosperity would finally come to the region. Of course, Hossein never failed to mention Sholeh—another innocent victim of Israeli aggression.

Massoud Aliaabaadi's worst fears had come to pass. It was *kismet,* or fate, Massoud would later explain, that had brought Hossein into his son's life again. Hossein's influence on Mahmoud was overpowering, reinforcing many of Mahmoud's negative views of America formed during his summer road tour of the country. But it was Sholeh's death that had provided the clear answer to the radical cleric's haunting question: "What is the purpose of your life?"

So what was next? What came after graduation? Mahmoud didn't know for sure. He only knew one thing: he had made his decision. He would soon wage jihad against Israel, the nation he found guilty of the murder of his sister, and America, the Great Satan who aided and abetted Israel's crimes.

*   *   *

Shafeeq had been the first of the trio of terrorist operatives to receive the surprise call from Mahmoud.

"*Assalamu alaikum.* Shafeeq, this is Mahmoud. You've been a good friend, and I've valued our friendship through the years, but we must part company. I no longer accept the notion that the Americans are our enemy. We can't continue our friendship. It's time to go our separate ways."

Shafeeq wasn't quick enough to offer a meaningful response. Before he could reply, Mahmoud had ended the call.

"*Rahimahullah,*" Shafeeq spoke into a line that was already dead—"Allah have mercy upon him."

In the days and weeks to follow, Mahmoud would often think about his three friends, especially Shafeeq and Naa'il, but he was confident they would someday learn the reason for his actions. The trio was widely known in the college community as anti-Israel and anti-American. With Islamic terrorist activities on the rise throughout the world, Mahmoud thought it best to break his ties with the committed jihadists. It could not be long before his outspoken friends would be on a CIA or FBI watch list. For his plans to succeed, he had to form his own cell and locate and connect with other hidden cells inside and outside the United States.

Hossein was dumbfounded and furious when Shafeeq informed him of Mahmoud's decision to suddenly end the friendship, but he wisely instructed Shafeeq to honor Mahmoud's wishes.

"Leave Mahmoud to me. Don't contact him. Give Naa'il and al-Dossari the same instructions. Tell them today!" He pocketed his phone, heart racing. He was terrified of how Mohammed Abdul al-Wadhi might react when he learned of Mahmoud's sudden separation from his terrorist friends. Hossein's mission was to radicalize his cousin, and he had failed. He had witnessed the execution of an operative who had botched his mission and exposed members of al-Wadhi's terrorist cell to the American authorities. While Hossein's failure would not have the same consequences for his own cell, he nonetheless feared a confrontation with the violent Saudi Butcher.

Pushing down his panic, Hossein carefully considered how he should approach his cousin. He could not reveal that Shafeeq and Naa'il had been his operatives. He finally decided to conceal the purpose of the contact by feigning interest in the progress of Mahmoud's education.

"Mahmoud, haven't spoken to you for some time. What's happening?" he asked.

Mahmoud wasn't ready to confide in Hossein—not until his plans were firmly established.

"Not much, Hossein. Just concentrating on my studies. Guess the only new news is that I've decided to pursue a doctorate in nuclear engineering, specializing in neutron transport theory."

"Are you ready to come over to our side?" Hossein asked in a lighthearted, half-kidding tone of voice, although he meant it with all seriousness. He still could not believe that Sholeh's death had not pushed Mahmoud into the arms of radical Islam.

"I'm taking a break from everything other than my studies, Hossein. When I'm finished, I'll decide where my allegiance lies."

Their conversation rambled for a few more minutes, each trying to poke and peek into the secret recesses of the other's mind. By the time their call had ended, Mahmoud had convinced Hossein only that he was sincerely pursuing his education, that he would stay in contact with him but not by phone, and that he desired to remain a devoted servant of Allah.

*   *   *

"What's next?" Mahmoud repeated Romiti's question before he answered the query. "I really don't know. I have a friend who wants to expand a small warehousing and distribution business in Bethesda, just north of DC, by opening a new facility on the west coast. His family's been in this line of business for years, so he's established connections with exporters throughout Europe, Japan, and China. He's invited me to be his equal partner, providing I cough up a million bucks. But there's no chance of that happening. Regardless, I've signed up to earn my doctorate in nuclear engineering, specializing in neutron transport theory, so I'll be at Cal for a while longer. Being involved in a business is a far cry from the work I'd do as a nuclear physicist, but I'm just not sure what I'm gonna do next. Maybe I'll try to do both."

Romiti's gut told him Mahmoud was playing him for the money. He smiled.

"Introduce me to your friend. If I believe the business can be successful, I'll put up the mil for fifty percent of the company. Fifty percent will remain with your friend. Twenty-five percent each for you and me. And whenever the company or your shares are sold, you can repay me—with interest, of course," he added with a smile.

*   *   *

Shortly before Romiti earned his degree in business administration, the university announced it would offer a Master of Financial Engineering degree for the first time. The Haas School of Business advertised the program as one that "would prepare students for jobs as risk managers, investment bankers, asset managers, derivatives traders, and developers of specialized securities at the world's leading commercial and investment banks, insurance companies, and corporate and public treasury departments." Students could also choose to concurrently earn their MBA and MFE degrees in a two-year graduate studies program.

Romiti was one of the first to enroll in the new MFE program; days later, Emiliane sent a cashier's check for $53,000, covering her son's nonresident tuition fees for the two-year term.

For the next two years, Romiti maintained his daily schedule, graduating with honors.

He regularly spoke with Mahmoud, but their conversations were almost exclusively related to the progress of their flourishing distribution business in Long Beach, California. Mahmoud had introduced his friend, Ebrahim Akbari, to Romiti, and soon after, Romiti purchased fifty percent of Akbari Enterprises.

Romiti and Mahmoud sometimes discussed world events too, but the subject of these conversations was almost always centered on the perceived evils perpetrated by Israelis or members of the Jewish-American community.

Along with his interests in Akbari Enterprises, as Romiti later learned, after earning his doctorate Mahmoud became employed as a nuclear physicist in a Southern California-based scientific research and development laboratory. In this capacity, he spent a great deal of his time writing proposals for the grants needed to keep the lab's research projects going. Mahmoud was also a highly regarded member of a project team that constructed complex prototypes of nuclear-based tools that could be used in nonmilitary ventures, such as large-scale earthmoving projects and propulsion mechanisms for space travel.

Interesting set of skills, Romiti concluded as he surveyed his friend's life. *Wonder how I might put these to use in the future?*

CHAPTER SIX

June 2001—Berkeley, California

When Romiti graduated summa cum laude from Berkeley's Haas School of Business, Bank of America, Citibank, Microsoft, the Guardian Life Insurance Company of America, and several other financial institutions were among the first who failed to seduce him with their high-end employment packages and significant sign-up bonuses. Much to their surprise, Romiti spurned their generous offers, explaining that his future plans would return him to Italy. He did not explain that the salaries they offered were mere pocket change to one accustomed to spending multiples of their offers on his toys each year.

His imminent return to the village of Baselga di Piné excited him. He had not seen his mother, Emiliane, for over two years, although they were in frequent contact by phone and the Internet. He planned to stay in his childhood home for several weeks as he looked for a place of his own. While he did not yet have a steady source of earned income, Emiliane deposited the equivalent of twenty thousand US dollars into his bank account each month, a generous allowance that gave him a great deal of freedom to pursue his interests.

After a couple of months of leisurely research, Romiti decided to purchase an estate outside the beautiful cosmopolitan city of Trento, the region's capital. The city was ranked high in terms of its quality of life, standard of living, and business and job opportunities, and it was home to some of the wealthiest and most prosperous citizens of Italy.

There was also an episode in the city's history that strongly appealed to the dark side of Romiti's mind. It was known as the Trent Blood Libel. On the eve of Good Friday, 1475 AD, a three-year-old Christian boy had disappeared. The city's small Jewish community was accused of murdering him and draining his blood for Jewish ritual purposes. Eight Jews were tortured and burned at the stake for the killing of Simon of Trent, as he was called today. Emiliane had often used the story to incite Romiti's hatred of the Jewish people, just as her German schoolteachers had inflamed her anti-Semitic passions when she was a young girl in Waldkraiburg, Germany. It seemed a fitting place for Romiti to live.

Romiti's sprawling, gated, twenty-acre purchase was magnificent. The three-story mansion had 9,611 heated square feet and over 14,000 gross square feet, including outdoor sleeping rooms, decks, and waterfall balconies. The terrace level was designed for entertaining, boasting a wonderfully equipped gourmet kitchen as well as a second summer kitchen. The guest entry gallery emptied into a spacious great room; the adjoining family room easily accommodated the overflow for the frequent occasions on which Romiti planned to entertain large groups of guests. A lavishly appointed formal dining area and sitting room completed the floor.

Bedroom suites for guests and family members, palatial bathrooms, and an exercise/recreation room made up the second floor. The third floor included two luxurious master bedrooms, a sitting room, and Romiti's personal study. A modest maid's cottage was located on the property as well.

The back of the estate ended at the shore of a sparkling lake. With vineyards on either side, Romiti had no privacy concerns. It was the perfect location, he decided, from which to launch his long-studied political career.

Shortly after moving into the beautiful estate, he received a call from an obviously upset Emiliane.

"Are you watching the news?"

"No. I've been outside." He was about to explain what he had been doing, but his mother cut him off.

"They're attacking America! Passenger planes have crashed into the World Trade Center; one tower has already collapsed. Another was flown into the side of the Pentagon!"

Romiti cut her short. "Thanks for letting me know. I'll get back to you later." He sprinted to his study, flipping on his television and laptop.

The date was September 11, 2001. Romiti was mesmerized by the news coming out of the United States, thinking of the summer road trip that had begun at the World Trade Center. His eyes were riveted to the footage of the second plane slamming into the South Tower, followed by the collapse of both buildings. He would never forget the terrified looks on the faces of men, women, and children who fled the imploding towers as clouds of smoke and debris raced through the corridors of the city. Romiti watched people wash away the chalky white powder that choked their lungs and covered their clothes and faces. He witnessed the raw emotions of survivors grieving over those who would never return home. Nonetheless, he remained strangely detached from the calamity, unfazed by the suffering caused by the national tragedy. He marveled at his own emotionless response to the attack and wondered if his heart was made of stone.

But then, he had never been much moved by death.

He placed two calls to Mahmoud in the days immediately following 9/11. Mahmoud was also glued to the television, but his reaction was very subdued, much different from anything Romiti expected.

"I guess what goes around comes around," Romiti said on his first call. "America should have kept its nose out of Saudi business, don't you think, Mahmoud?"

Mahmoud's only reply was, "They're vulnerable. They're really vulnerable." There was no surprise or anger in his voice. The words were spoken softly, almost as if he were speaking to himself.

The two spoke for a short time on each call, vowing to keep in touch. But the promise was soon forgotten as each returned to his busy life.

Hossein also called Mahmoud on the day of the attack.

"Have you been watching CNN?"

Mahmoud was alone, reveling in the pain inflicted on the nation. One moment he was weeping over the memory of his sister, and the next, shouting that the Americans and Jews who ran Wall Street deserved the attack.

"Yes . . . been watching the news and surfing the net all day long. Maybe now Bush will ease the unfair and punitive economic sanctions imposed upon Iraq. Maybe the Americans will have some sympathy for the Palestinians whose fathers and sons have been murdered by the Zionists!"

Hossein hesitated for a moment, momentarily taken aback by his cousin's bitter outburst. His confidence buoyed by Mahmoud's apparent sympathy, he charged ahead. "Mahmoud, listen to me. We've taken the war to the infidels' turf! Today's attack has been in the works for years. Be listening for the name *al-Qaeda*. In a few days, the entire world will know who we are! We'll wage jihad until every drop of infidel blood has been spilled or every infidel has retreated from our blessed soil. We want you to join the side of Allah, Mahmoud. Join al-Qaeda. *Aliahu akbar*—Allah is the greatest!"

Mahmoud's voice was carefully controlled. "America props up the illegitimate Zionist state, so I hate America as much as you do, Hossein. But I will not join this al-Qaeda. I will find my own way to wage jihad against my sister's killers!"

* * *

More than anything else, Romiti craved power—power he knew lay only in the hands of politicians. While he disdained Hitler's many failures, he hungered for the control and authority that had once belonged to his loathsome idol. He knew the only means to achieving such power was through the political process, so his first objective was to enter politics as quickly as possible. His allegiance was to himself; nonetheless, his instincts told him that to realize his ultimate goal, he must align himself with the political party he could best use to his advantage. With his outstanding academic credentials and Emiliane's wealth and influence, his strategy was to offer his services gratis, essentially becoming an unpaid apprentice. From this position, he believed he could quickly navigate his way to the top of the political pile.

On 9/11, Margherita Cogo was president of the Trentino-Alto Adige region. She led the Democrats of the Left (DS), a left-wing party aligned with the Olive Tree electoral coalition. An alliance with the DS, a party that seemed out of step with the issues deemed most important by most of the region's population, would not be in his best interests, so he quickly rejected an association with Cogo.

Lorenzo Dellai was the president of the Province of Trento and was affiliated with the Daisy Civic List, the *Civica Margherita,* the party he and other local politicians had formed. The party's roots were primarily found in Catholic social teachings and Christian Democratic doctrines, along the line of the Italian People's Party. They rejected Marxist ideology, preferring a social market economic model. Best of all, some described Civica as a catchall party that appealed across numerous party lines. Romiti decided he would offer his services to senior Civica operatives.

It was not difficult to set up a lunch appointment with Dellai's chief of staff, Salvatore Rizzo. Prior to the appointment, Romiti supplied Rizzo's administrative assistant with a resume that was short on experience but high on scholastic achievements, capped by an impressive list of influential references. Rizzo would know, too, that Emiliane had made several substantial donations to Lorenzo Dellai's election efforts. Romiti also did his homework on Rizzo. While he found the man's record to be clean, Romiti discovered there were looming financial problems in Rizzo's future.

Rizzo was surprised to learn the lunch appointment would be at Romiti's estate, but he looked forward to the visit with much anticipation. As Rizzo was escorted from the beautifully decorated gallery of Romiti's home, he was intrigued by the little horn he saw resting alone on an elegantly carved console table. Rizzo guessed it had once graced the head of a young bullock. It was reddish-brown, nearly seven inches long, and slightly bowed. He carefully picked it up and touched the pointed end with his finger. *With such a sharp tip, the horn could be used as a weapon!* It was obviously meaningful to Romiti, so Rizzo made a mental note to learn the significance of the piece as they continued to a table that was pleasingly set for two.

Romiti watched his guest carefully and observed that Rizzo was suitably impressed with his surroundings. The two men enjoyed an appetizer of sautéed shrimp with ceci, grilled onions, pancetta, and pomegranate. The truffled mushroom salad with capers, red onions, and parmigiano was delicious, and then they focused their attention on the main course— grilled swordfish with green tomato marmellata, kale, potatoes, and smoked almonds. To complement the meal, the duo enjoyed a bottle of wine recommended by Romiti's personal sommelier—a Pinot Noir, 1985. The red wine had originated in Romanee-Conti, a vineyard of one of Romiti's favorite wineries, the Domaine Bella Romanee-Conti, located in Burgundy, France.

"What's the significance of the little horn that sits on the console table?" Rizzo inquired.

"I really don't know," Romiti answered. "It was a gift given to my mother by a fortune-teller. She promised my mother the symbolism would become clear to me in the days ahead. So for now, I keep it as a reminder and a promise of the future."

"And why does a young man with your wealth and background want to enter politics?" Rizzo abruptly interrupted their casual conversation with a question that was insightful and to the point.

Romiti was deliberate in his carefully crafted response. "Since I was a young boy, I have wanted to be Italy's ambassador to the UN. I want to begin the pursuit of my goal in the region of my birth." Rizzo smiled at the frank response, unaware that Romiti was being modest—his lust for power was far greater than he let on.

"I see that you earned your MBA at Berkeley, as well as an MFE degree. What kind of degree is that?"

"MFE is an acronym for Master of Financial Engineering, a new master's degree offered for the first time at Berkeley. The brochures advertised that the program prepares graduates for careers in corporate and public treasury departments, risk management, and investment banking."

"And did it prepare you for any of these jobs?" Rizzo asked.

"I think so, but the best way for you to find out is to bring me into Civica," Romiti replied.

"And how can Civica benefit from your knowledge?" Rizzo was enjoying the interview almost as much as the delicious meal.

"Frankly, I'm far more interested in how the people of the region will benefit from my knowledge," Romiti countered. "Civica is only a means to help them."

Romiti noticed that Rizzo bristled at his retort, but he quickly defused Rizzo's rising temper with a smile as he continued.

"As in many regions of Italy, Trentino-Alto Adige is facing economic challenges. Unemployment is rising, prices are skyrocketing, and our jobs are being exported to other countries. I believe Civica's economic policies provide better solutions to these challenges than any other party. But having said that, I also believe there are additional policies which if put into practice, will improve Civica's economic platform. I want to help formulate these policies and practices. I don't pretend to have all the answers . . ." His eyes glimmered. "But I've got some of them."

Romiti sat back and sipped his wine, clearly master of the interview. "I've also done my homework. No one comes close to your political knowledge and experience. Civica owes most of its success to you. You're the architect. I want to learn from you. I would like you to mentor me."

Rizzo smiled at the flattery but said nothing. Romiti sensed that Rizzo was waiting for him to seal the deal. He remembered Rizzo's looming financial problems, so he pitched the close without flinching at his own boldness. "Take me on as an unpaid member of your staff, and I'll see that a generous sum is deposited into one of your bank accounts each month."

In the staff meeting the following Monday morning, Rizzo introduced his new economic adviser to the senior members of his team.

Civica performed well in the 2003 election, returning Lorenzo Dellai to office for a second term. A split in the party resulted in the formation of the Union for Trentino in 2008. Under the umbrella of the UpT, Dellai was reelected for a third term. Romiti and his mentor, Rizzo, had worked tirelessly in their respective roles. While they were unknown to the public, party bosses across Italy knew very well the remarkable contributions these men had made to Civica and most recently, to UpT. They also knew that while Rizzo had no illusions about running for public office, it would only be a matter of time before his understudy, the charismatic, brilliant thirty-one-year-old economic strategist, catapulted into the public arena.

Soon after Dellai's reelection, Romiti ran for mayor of Trento and was elected by a small margin. He quickly improved Trento's financial position by eliminating many of the social programs the city was known for and quietly transporting citizens who were financially dependent upon local government programs to other locations throughout Italy. Many such citizens received one-time payments in return for a pledge of silence, a promise that was seldom broken without the promise breaker reaping severe consequences. Inordinately excessive fines replaced jail sentences, bringing added revenues into city coffers.

The amenities so common in the prison system disappeared overnight, and the inmates became "volunteers" who cleaned and maintained the public squares, parks, and roads, saving many more tax dollars. Inmates who rebelled against the new environment were given even tougher assignments. Those who continued to protest their treatment either disappeared or, much to their dismay, learned they had been found guilty of fabricated charges. As a result, they found themselves beyond the jurisdiction of local law enforcement (the *Polizia Municipale,* or municipal police) and instead in the custody of the *Polizia Penitenziaria,* the penitentiary police, well outside the purview of Trento.

With crime down and revenues up, the citizens of a sparkling clean Trento were thrilled with their new status and wondered why other politicians had not implemented similar practices.

After serving a term as mayor, Romiti was determined to become the next president of the Province of Trento. Working closely with Rizzo, Romiti easily won his election under the umbrella of the UpT.

Under the rules of the government of Trentino-Alto Adige, the president of the Province of Trento and the president of the Province of Bolzano alternated at the post of president of the region; the one who was not president served as first vice president. This term, Romiti would become the new president of the region as well.

Once again, Romiti performed remarkably well in his new position. He was a willful and calculating leader. His reputation as a passionate and gifted orator was firmly established. He earned the respect, and fear, of his peers—friend and foe alike. He seemed to have the Midas touch. His next goal was to become Italy's permanent representative to the United Nations, a key stepping-stone to the post he coveted most: UN secretary-general.

CHAPTER SEVEN

Long Beach, California

While Romiti was enjoying his meteoric climb to the top of his world, Mahmoud was slowly, methodically, and meticulously building a terrorist cell he named *'Abd al-Mumit,* Servant of the Bringer of Death.

Mahmoud studiously analyzed the activities of the major terrorist groups, especially those craving the world's attention, but he deliberately avoided any contact with them. His greatest fear was failure. Whatever method he chose, he knew the greatest risk was discovery by the government agencies that were spending billions to locate 'Abd al-Mumit and other similar terrorist cells. There must be no trail leading to Mahmoud Aliaabaadi. *Plausible deniability. Another thing I learned at Cal.*

The fledgling terrorist had studied America's short- and long-term responses to terrorist attacks, particularly the October 2000 attack on the USS *Cole* in the port of Eden, the August 1998 terrorists bombings that destroyed the US embassies in Nairobi and Dar es Salaam, and the Benghazi attack in eastern Libya. These cowardly strikes had killed several hundred people, among them thirty-three Americans, including Christopher Stevens, the US Ambassador to Libya, and injured more than five thousand others. By and large, the government appeared to be passive in its response to such attacks—the exception, of course, being 9/11. No doubt because the violence had occurred on American soil and the casualties were extreme, the US and its allies had retaliated there with a vengeance. But US administrations subsequent to 9/11 began to view the efforts in Iraq and Afghanistan as police actions rather than as wars to be won. Many Americans grew weary of the fight, and the liberal media exacerbated these feelings by the subtle ways it distorted the news. These responses merely emboldened the enemy, spurring them to greater action against America and its allies.

Mahmoud's conclusion was that another major attack on American soil, dwarfing the casualties of prior operations, would cause America and its puppet, Israel, to retreat from Muslim lands. And he was determined that 'Abd al-Mumit would become Allah's chosen instrument for the next major strike.

He meticulously researched the four types of terrorist attacks: biological, chemical, nuclear, and radiological. Mahmoud sketched out various scenarios for each type of attack, identifying the probability of success for each. However, because he was most familiar with nuclear technology thanks to his excellent Berkeley training, and because he had concluded that a nuclear attack would inflict the greatest physical, economic, and psychological harm on the nation, he narrowed his focus to this form of warfare.

Mahmoud would spend the next several years perfecting his plan.

*   *   *

Ebrahim Akbari had done his homework well. Under Akbari's skillful leadership, Akbari Enterprises was building a reputation as one of the leading west coast warehousing and distribution companies of high-volume products manufactured primarily in China. The four-hundred-thousand-square-foot Long Beach facility, the first of several west coast facilities, stored about fifty thousand pallets of approximately six hundred different SKUs. The warehouse boasted forty-two truck dock doors and four rail doors; the company employed seventy full-time workers and between fifteen and twenty seasonal workers.

"Susan, page the building engineer for me," Akbari directed his secretary. The engineer appeared in Akbari's swank office a few minutes later. An expensive oval Persian rug was positioned in the center of the floor. A large, handcrafted walnut desk was the centerpiece of the room. Behind the desk, a comfortable leather chair supported Akbari's large girth. Two leather chairs were positioned in front of the desk. If visitors were to look closely, they would discover the legs of the guest chairs were two inches shorter than normal, allowing Akbari to more easily dominate the business at hand. Strangely, a painting of the ayatollah hung prominently on one wall.

"I want you to take charge of a very special construction project for me," Akbari ordered. "I'm adding a new line of business: storing and transporting precious metals and gems."

Akbari outlined his basic requirements for a facility within a facility. A highly secure, forty-five-hundred-square-foot storage area was to be constructed inside the warehouse itself. It was to be located behind the last truck dock door, which, except for an emergency exit, would be the only visible means of entering the secure area. A fifteen-foot-by-fifteen-foot compartment was to be positioned in the center of the room, initially accessible by no one but Akbari. The area surrounding it would be home to a ten-man team that would provide around-the-clock security. The security area was to be configured with a communication/surveillance room, a kitchen, a common media/reading area, a small fitness center, restrooms, and sleeping quarters.

"I want the new facility operational within twelve to eighteen months; take it slow, but spare no expense in its design and construction," Akbari emphasized. He half-jokingly added, "Build a fortress! Design it to withstand an assault by the marines if need be! Oh yeah, and one more thing. Every square inch must be continuously viewable by selected personnel from within the warehouse—however, no access to the interior via the Internet."

Akbari was a successful businessman and by his many friends was thought to be a moderate Muslim. But he was actually a zealous disciple of the long-deceased Ayatollah Ruhollah Khomeini. He dreamed that America would soon become an Islamic state, subjugated by Sharia law. He longed for Israel's destruction. He fervently prayed to be alive the day Mahdi revealed himself to the world as its much-anticipated Messiah. And he was a fanatical jihadist.

Akbari had been recruited by Mahmoud to become the first member of 'Abd al-Mumit. Recruiting the second member of the cell was far more difficult. Mahmoud had convinced Akbari to hire a new truck driver for Akbari Enterprises. He stressed that the qualified applicant must not have a criminal record, must be proficient in Spanish and English, and must be a current US citizen. One qualification was not advertised, but it was the most important: the applicant must have a deep and abiding hatred of America.

It took Akbari almost a year to locate Natalia Gutierrez, one of the earliest female members of the Revolutionary Armed Forces of Columbia, a designated Foreign Terrorist Organization (FTO). Before joining the RAFC, she was a drug trafficker with the Medellin drug cartel, transporting marijuana and cocaine from Columbia through Mexico and into the United States. Natalia joined the RAFC after her brother, Carlos, was killed in a joint DEA/Colombian National Police operation, fueling her hatred of the governments of Columbia and the United States. Despite her criminal and terrorist past, Natalia had never been arrested for any illegal activities. She was very lucky, as her friends would often acknowledge.

A freak accident had ended Natalia's active involvement in the RAFC, leaving her with no means of support. Once Akbari had found her, she was easy enough to recruit. Soon, she was regularly transporting specialty products from Akbari Enterprises' Long Beach facility to points south of the border, including Mexico, Guatemala, Panama, and Columbia.

* * *

A year after being elected president of the Province of Trento, Romiti was invited to Rome, the Eternal City, for an appointment with Italy's prime minister, Enrico Lanza.

The private meeting was to be held in the Palazzo Chigi, the official residence of the prime minister and meeting place of the council of ministers. As he was escorted to the palace overlooking the Piazza Colonna and the Via del Corso, Romiti recalled that construction of the palazzo had begun in 1562, almost five hundred years earlier. He observed the pinkish hue of the famous five-story landmark as he walked toward its main facade on Via del Corso. He noticed the round and triangular *tympanums,* decorative wall surfaces, that highlighted the row of first-floor windows. A column stood on either side of the main entrance to the palace. Two flags—the green, white, and red flag of Italy and the gold-starred flag of Europe—caught his attention as they were whipped by a strong gust of wind. The flags were hanging from poles attached to the base of a small balcony that acted as a canopy over the entryway. His gaze turned upward as he glanced at the large clock embedded in the front face of the bell tower that loomed over the roof of the palace.

Romiti noted with smug satisfaction that he was precisely on time.

He stood still for a moment, absorbing the impressive sight, before being ushered into the interior courtyard of the palace.

Romiti was enthralled by its ancient beauty. The courtyard, known as the Cortile della Greca, contained a fountain decorated with the coat of arms of the Chigi and Della Rovere families. He was led up the flight of steps leading to the first floor, which housed the *Salone del Consiglio dei Ministri,* the Council of Ministers. In the ceiling of the Salone d'Oro, a neoclassical hall designed by Giovanni Stern, the *Sleeping Endimion* by Baciccia looked down. He quickly glanced at the rare paintings and sculptures that adorned the palace, wishing he could spend an hour studying each one, before he was personally greeted by the smiling prime minister.

The two men had met formally on several occasions, but this was their first informal meeting. Lanza was clearly impressed with his young friend, now in his early forties, and knew that no position, including his own, was beyond his grasp.

"It's good to see you again. You're looking well. Under your leadership, Trentino-Alto Adige is the envy of Italy. You've performed miracles once again, my friend. What's next? Will your next move be to Rome?"

Romiti smiled at the not-so-subtle reference. "Thank you for the compliments, Mr. Prime Minister. No, I have no plans to ever sit in your chair. You have many accomplishments too, Mr. Prime Minister, and our nation will always be grateful for your service."

"Well, what is the purpose of today's visit?" questioned Lanza.

"I have come to request a favor. I want you to remove Carlo De Luca as Italy's permanent representative to the United Nations and nominate me as his replacement. It's a post I've dreamed of since my youth. I'm confident I'll do an excellent job."

The prime minister hesitated for a moment. Italy's current ambassador was his protégé, a close personal and family friend. In fact, the two families had been involved in various business ventures that spanned several generations.

"I'm sorry, Romiti, but I cannot honor your request at this time. I agree that you are eminently qualified for the position, and your service would no doubt bring great honor to the republic." Lanza paused once more before continuing, choosing his words carefully. He did not want Romiti to become his enemy. "But I groomed Carlo for this position, and he's remained a loyal friend and colleague during his tenure as Italy's ambassador to the UN. I'm sorry, but I cannot remove him. I promised him the office, and it will remain his as long as he's able to perform the job. Is there another position in my government that's of interest to you? You're a man of many talents, and your involvement in my administration would be of great value to me and to our nation."

For an instant, Romiti's countenance turned dark as a deep scowl crossed his face. But just as quickly, the angry expression was replaced by his pleasant facade. "No, Mr. Prime Minister. I want no other position. I would like to become Italy's ambassador to the UN. I appreciate your candor and your allegiance to a good friend, but there's a strong possibility that De Luca is involved in a scandalous matter that could compromise his position as ambassador. I'm sorry I'm not at liberty to divulge more information, but I will when specific details are confirmed."

It was Lanza's turn to scowl. "I have no knowledge of any behavior that would bring embarrassment to De Luca or his family, but based on your allegation, a through investigation will follow. Discreetly, of course."

"Of course."

"And should Mr. De Luca step down from his position, or be forced to resign, I will nominate you as his replacement—and further, will do all in my power to see that you're confirmed."

*   *   *

Several months later, Carlo De Luca received an invitation to visit Romiti. Carlo's wife; his two young daughters, ages nine and eleven; and his six-year-old son were also invited to spend the day on the Trento estate. The morning and early afternoon were set aside for the children, with a formal dinner planned for the evening in honor of the ambassador. Romiti arranged for a variety of activities for the three kids, including pony rides, a sail on the lake, and a variety of games.

"You're a kind and generous man, Romiti," the ambassador's wife gushed. "Thank you for providing such an entertaining outing for my children."

"You're welcome, Arianna. Carlo is fortunate to have such a beautiful wife and family. You are always welcome in my home."

Hours later, Romiti greeted the other guests as they arrived for the formal affair. The invitees included the president of the Province of Bolzano, several provincial deputies, and two judges of Italy's constitutional court, along with their spouses.

He had once heard De Luca jokingly complain that he was not invited to the White House dinner held in honor of his excellency Silvio Berlusconi, so Romiti decided to mimic the menu enjoyed by the former prime minister. Delicata squash soup with citron. Maine lobster fondue. Artichoke and reggiano cheese ravioli. Rosemary-crusted Elysian Farm lamb. Crispy eggplant and Swiss chard. Along with the various wines, the dinner was capped by Santa Maria chocolate napoleon, Romiti's favorite dessert.

Before the first course was served, Romiti stood to propose a toast in Carlo De Luca's honor. Arianna De Luca smiled at Romiti, pleased that her husband was being honored for his service. She was also smitten by Romiti's striking appearance. He did not carry an ounce of extra weight. Romiti's features still looked as though they had been chiseled from a block of granite. His once jet-black hair now showed traces of silver, lending a distinguished air to the generous host. Dressed in a black tuxedo and white shirt and tie, Romiti was obviously enjoying the prime of life.

"This evening, I want to honor Carlo De Luca for his service to our great country. The world is a dangerous place, but men and women like Carlo work tirelessly for the peace and prosperity enjoyed by the citizens of Italy and soon, we hope, by the citizens of the world. Thank you for your selfless service, Mr. Ambassador. It is greatly appreciated by me, and certainly by the men and women who are in this room tonight."

Following dinner, the guests mingled on the outdoor terrace. The reflection of the full moon was clearly visible on the glassy surface of the tree-rimmed lake. The view was breathtaking, complemented by the delightful sounds of a small waterfall that fell onto a rocky ledge before splashing into the lake.

Romiti saw that Carlo was enjoying the view alone, so he made his way to the ambassador.

"Beautiful view," Carlo said. "Thank you for such an enchanting evening. The dinner was delightful. And how did you learn of my fantasy of someday dining at the White House? Is nothing hidden from you?" He grinned. "But thank you. You've been very kind to my family and me."

"You're welcome, Carlo. I know the intense pressure today's statesmen are under. I don't know how you perform your duties in today's hostile environment while at the same time balancing family life and a political career. Are you ever able to relax?"

Lulled by the wine and the warm air, the ambassador confided, "It's difficult, that's for sure. I need time alone each day. I don't have a chance to work out often, so every morning I walk alone for an hour or so along the shoreline. No wife, no children, no attendants. I love the quiet solitude, and I use the escape to mull over my more difficult assignments. This habit has made the early morning the most profitable part of my day."

A month later, the headlines of *La Repubblica* blared, "Italy's UN Ambassador Slain!" Carlo De Luca's body had been found on a beach near his home early one morning. His throat had been slashed. The assailant left no evidence, although the municipal police did find a cellophane candy wrapper in the vicinity of the ambassador's body. However, since there was no evidence that the wrapper was linked to his death, it was ignored in the investigation.

Later, the ambassador's widow was surprised and grateful to receive a letter of condolence from Romiti, the president of the Province of Trento. The letter expressed deep sympathy for her and her family, and as a personal expression of his appreciation for her husband's service to the republic, explained that Romiti had established a substantial trust fund that would provide a generous lifetime income for Arianna De Luca and her three children.

A copy of the letter mysteriously landed in the hands of the chief editor of *La Repubblica*. The editor published its contents, lauding Romiti's generosity.

Romiti smiled as he read the *La Repubblica* article. The praise and adoration of a nation were his.

Weeks later, *La Repubblica* reported the lack of progress in identifying the ambassador's assassin. On the same page, a related story announced that the prime minister's nominee to become Italy's permanent representative to the United Nations had been confirmed by the senate of the republic. Many in government were surprised by the nomination, considering the nominee was not a career diplomat and had never served in the foreign ministry, the cabinet, or the Italian senate. Nonetheless, all agreed that Romiti was an excellent choice for the vacant ambassadorship.

* * *

Even before he submitted his resignation as the president of the Province of Trento, Romiti prepared for his new assignment as Italy's ambassador to the United Nations. He would participate in his first UN committee meeting, along with representatives of many other nations, the following week in Berlin. Carlo De Luca, the slain ambassador, had accepted the appointment to become Italy's representative on the committee; Romiti agreed to replace De Luca at the opening session.

After extensive analysis of several active regional conflicts, many caused by religious differences among warring factions, the committee's findings and conclusions were to be released in a document entitled *The Impact of Sectarian Religious Violence on Regional Economies*. This was a subject Romiti had been analyzing since his Berkeley days. He knew how opposing religious beliefs sparked conflicts that decimated regional economies, and he had concrete solutions for the problems the committee would undoubtedly document. It was the ideal forum in which to make his entrance onto the world stage.

Before attending the Berlin conference, Romiti made plans to visit the Westphalian district of Paderborn, Germany. Here was Schloss Wewelsburg, a castle Himmler had rented from the Paderborn government in 1933. If Adolf Hitler was the evil autocrat, Heinrich Himmler was his vile magician, furtively manipulating Germany's laws to achieve his wicked purposes. Providing the muscle needed to enforce the wills of the emperor and his sorcerer were the Black Knights of the SS, the racially pure Aryans whose ancestors were the supposed god-men.

And Himmler was the man Romiti most admired. Himmler was energized by a force unlike any other on earth. Romiti had meticulously studied Himmler's life and was convinced that his involvement with the spirits of the occult was the key to his power. Following in the footsteps of his mother, Romiti would also place his trust in the spirits of the occult. And he would find another Himmler, a man who would be as committed to Romiti's cause as Himmler was to Hitler's.

Himmler had remodeled the cold, dark castle that sat alone atop a hill. The castle contained a 14,500-square-foot dining hall, configured as a gathering place for the Black Knights. Here they celebrated the winter solstice instead of Christmas. Pagan baptisms, human sacrifices, seances, and other rituals were performed in the torchlit hall. The foreboding castle was a fitting place for Himmler, who was described by General Heinrich Hossback as "Hitler's evil spirit, cold, calculating and ambitious . . . undoubtedly the most purposeful and most unscrupulous figure in the Third Reich." Himmler would often resort to the castle alone, communing with the evil spirits that pervaded its rooms.

Before his planned morning visit to the Schloss Wewelsburg, Romiti was abruptly awakened from a deep slumber by an eerie, spine-chilling coldness that pervaded every crevice of the suite in which he was staying. Despite his familiarity with the occult, he was frightened by the powerful, unseen presence he knew was in his lavish sleeping quarters. He had often communicated with spirits from another world. But this was different. His skin tingled. His throat was constricted, as though tightly clenched in the vice grip of a powerful but invisible hand.

"Who are you?" he whispered hoarsely. *"Where* are you?" Romiti was on the verge of panic and could scarcely utter a word.

Then he saw the serpent. It was coiled on the bed, less than a meter from his face. He was petrified with fear, unable to move. The reptile's unblinking eyes gazed at Romiti, who watched its flicking fangs in absolute horror. He was already imagining the pain he would feel when the fangs delivered their deadly venom.

"I am Lucifer, the god of this world," the Serpent breathed.

Then, as if in a trance, Romiti was suddenly transported to the peak of an exceedingly high mountain and shown all the kingdoms of the world, and their glory, in a moment of time. In his vision, he saw presidents, prime ministers, and kings bowing humbly in his presence. He recognized powerful military leaders submitting to his authority. He heard the world's inhabitants acknowledge him as their leader, their god. And he saw his enemies die at his command.

The voice whispered, "All these things I will give you if you fall down and worship me. You have experienced what your abilities can deliver. Now your eyes have seen what I will deliver if you worship me alone. I made this offer once before, and it was rejected. What is your decision?"

Suddenly the Serpent was transformed into a majestic being, unlike anything Romiti had ever imagined. The reptile had become a dazzling angel of light, earning Romiti's worship and adoration.

Romiti staggered out of his bed and fell prostrate in the direction of the majestic being.

"I accept your offer, my lord. I declare my allegiance to you and acknowledge that you alone are worthy of my worship. You must be god, and beside you, there is no other!"

In response, the voice continued, "Ask! What shall I give you?"

Romiti's heart raced. He knew instinctively that the Serpent was asking him to state every desire he had ever harbored, everything he had worked to attain. "I want riches, wealth, honor, and glory. I want the lives of any who would oppose me. But most of all, I want to rule the world."

"All your petitions I will grant. You will rule my people over whom I will make you lord. I will also send you a helper who will guide you into my truth. He will not speak on his own authority, but whatever he hears from me, he will speak to you. He will glorify me, just as I demand that you glorify me. Wait for him. Soon, he will come to you."

With that promise, the voice became silent.

For over an hour, Romiti sat on the edge of his bed, jubilant, empowered, but trembling in fear. Finally he was able to lie down again and sleep. Then he found himself unable to awake from the horrors he witnessed as the future unfolded before him, one terrifying nightmare after another.

Later that morning, Romiti began the short walk to the Schloss Wewelsburg, still reeling from his early-morning visions. It was an unusually warm morning, he noted, but it felt good. Perhaps because it was so warm, his attention was drawn to a man who was sitting on a park bench not far from Himmler's castle. He was warmly dressed. A dark shawl, similar to the *tallit* worn by Jewish men during prayers, wrapped his body like a shroud. *Strange-looking old man. Why the heavy clothing?*

Romiti reached his destination, and as he gazed at the Wewelsburg complex, he was reminded of the so-called Spear of Destiny, also known as the Holy Lance. Romiti knew that the footprint of the castle, when viewed from the air, was triangular, in the shape of a spearhead. Had Hitler's defeat not cut short the ambitious Wewelsburg construction project, Himmler would have built a wide boulevard, the shaft, which would have connected to the spear point, the north tower of the castle. For Himmler, it was convenient that the lance pointed north, toward Thule, the mythological beginnings of the Germanic race.

According to legend, a lance was used by a Roman legionnaire named Longinus to pierce the side of Christ while he hung on the cross. Hitler had supposedly seen the lance and believed the fable that the one who possessed it would rule the world, so Himmler's architects designed the Holy Lance pattern into the plans for the soon-to-be meeting place for Hitler's Black Knights. Romiti smiled. He did not know if the lance had ever existed, but he vowed he would be the one to rule the world—whether he possessed the Holy Lance or not.

Romiti's thoughts of world power were interrupted by the approach of the old man he had earlier observed on the park bench. As he drew near,

Romiti was startled by the man's appearance. He was actually middle-aged, tall, and lanky. But his emaciated frame reminded Romiti of women who debase their bodies by denying them the food and nourishment they desperately need. The man wore a hat, but tufts of sandy hair were visible above his collar. Yellowing teeth were conspicuous beneath his beaked nose. His thin lips naturally curled downward, forming a perpetual frown. His breath was putrid. His pallid skin appeared almost transparent, with tiny blue veins visible on his face, neck, and the backs of his hands. His lifeless eyes were milky blue, without expression.

Romiti shivered, thinking, *This is a vile, malevolent human being, one who has no soul.*

"You are right. I have no soul," the stranger agreed out loud.

But then, in a commanding voice that belied his slight frame, he continued, "You too have sold your soul to Lucifer, the one who has sent me to be your helper. The world will recognize me as the prophet of Lucifer. I will perform great signs on your behalf, even causing fire to come down from heaven in the sight of mankind. The signs will glorify you and cause the earth's inhabitants to worship you. All peoples and nations will obey your commands; none will stand against you. Napoleon longed to rule the world of his time—but failed. Hitler and Himmler had visions of a Third Reich, an empire that would continue a thousand years—but it never came to be. But we will succeed where they so wretchedly failed. Today's democracies and dictatorships will be brought to an end. You will rule the world with an iron fist.

"Most importantly, religion will finally be abolished, every shred of its existence removed from the pages of history—Islam, Taoism, Buddhism, Hinduism, Confucianism—all will disappear forever."

Romiti inwardly smiled at this last statement. *If only it were so now!*

The man's face turned malicious, even menacing. He fearlessly and repeatedly jabbed his bony finger into Romiti's chest, emphasizing his hatred for the People of the Book. "But I revile Christianity and Judaism far more than any of these!" He began to sweat profusely, and beads of perspiration fell from his face. White flecks of spittle clung to his thin lips. Romiti was startled by the transformation of the soulless old man but greatly encouraged by his predictions. The prophet finished, his tone at once accusing and proclaiming.

"Until now, Lucifer has tolerated many of these religions because they have served his purpose. But Christianity and its intolerant system of beliefs have obstructed his progress for millennia. No more! No more! Lucifer, you, and I—we three supplant the Christians' Trinity! I will cause the world to worship you, and yes, through you, they will worship Lucifer, our sovereign lord!"

Chapter Eight

Bogota, Columbia

Mahmoud was uncharacteristically anxious, vomiting for the second time that evening. The nausea had not subsided since he made the decision to involve Hossein in his plans. He believed he was taking a risk by bringing Hossein into his confidence, but he had no other choice. His plans had reached a critical stage, one that required the involvement of resources outside the US. One mistake and his years of preparation would be in vain. He wiped his mouth and dialed Hossein, using the disposable cell phone he had purchased for this purpose. On the other end, someone picked up and waited for Mahmoud to speak first.

"La hawai wa la quwwaata illa biliah!" Mahmoud used the same greeting Hossein had used when the cousins spoke for the first time following Mahmoud's arrival in America.

"Ma sha'llah!" Hossein sounded surprised and pleased to hear his cousin's voice, quickly launching into a series of questions about Mahmoud's life. Mahmoud abruptly ended the customary exchange of greetings.

"I have come to your side," Mahmoud announced, hoping that Hossein would recall the invitation he had once extended, "and plan to celebrate your father's birthday in Bogota, Columbia, this year. I'll be staying at the Hotel Casa Deco. Will you be joining us?"

There was silence on the other end for a long moment. Then Hossein's voice came through, strong and confident:

"I've been looking forward to the celebration as well," he answered. "Yes, of course I'll meet you at the Hotel Casa Deco. It's been on my calendar for months."

*   *   *

It had been some time since Mahmoud had decided to launch a nuclear attack on an unsuspecting American city. His first choice was Washington DC, but he had abandoned the idea when his research showed the city's defenses to be almost impregnable. He had initially considered a "dirty bomb" which dispersed radioactive materials using conventional explosives. However, he had quickly discarded that option too, as it would not inflict enough harm on the government he considered an enemy of Islam.

He wanted the attack to cause multiplied thousands of fatalities, many more injuries, and substantial damage to the target city's infrastructure. Almost as importantly, he wanted the psychological impact of the blast to be devastating. The survivors must lose confidence in their government's ability to protect them. He wanted anxiety and fear to overwhelm the public. It was vital that the nuclear explosion unleash an economic catastrophe that would sweep across the country, much like an enormous tsunami racing across the sea.

Nuclear explosions are measured by the amount of energy they produce. The bomb dropped on Hiroshima was a sixteen-kiloton uranium bomb, and the one dropped on Nagasaki was a twenty-one-kiloton uranium bomb. However, both of those weapons had been detonated in the air at an altitude of about sixteen hundred feet. Mahmoud's weapon would have a yield of about twenty kilotons, or roughly twenty thousand tons of TNT, but would be detonated on the ground. By Mahmoud's estimation, the explosion would cause extensive shock-wave damage that would extend about one mile from ground zero. Severe thermal damage would extend out about two miles, causing major fires in the affected areas. Flying debris, fires, and other damage would extend out three to four miles from the detonation site. Unprotected people within a mile of the bomb site would be exposed to nuclear radiation; if windy conditions existed at the time of the blast, unprotected people would be exposed to radiation as far as eight miles from the initial site of the blast.

With these statistics in mind, Mahmoud had carefully researched potential sites soon after forming 'Abd al-Mumit. The location of Akbari Enterprises' warehouse and distribution center had not been selected at random. It was the ideal facility in which to secretly assemble and detonate the nuclear device. Now he only needed one thing: weapons-grade plutonium or enriched uranium from overseas.

In the month following his conversation with Hossein, Mahmoud began the long trek to Bogota. He preferred to fly but did not want to arouse the suspicions of any counterterrorist agency that might be snooping around. He knew the Department of Homeland Security would be all over him if its monitoring software identified a young single man of Iranian descent, with multiple degrees in nuclear physics, flying to Columbia alone.

Natalia Gutierrez, one of the drivers employed by Akbari Enterprises, regularly made the round-trip run from Southern California to Bogota. Mahmoud became her passenger at a truck stop outside Calexico, a few miles north of the United States-Mexico border.

As they headed toward the border crossing, Mahmoud rehearsed their story.

"You're being considered for another opening in the company, and I'm your potential replacement. I'm learning the route. Tell anyone who asks that we'll be making the Bogota run a few times together."

As expected, the Akbari Enterprises truck was briefly held up at the border. The guard obviously knew Natalia well and greeted her like a long-lost girlfriend.

"Hola, senorita! Who's your new friend?" The border guard was instantly jealous of the bearded Iranian, assuming Mahmoud was a handsome Mexican-American who had cut in on his action.

The guard ignored the two burly men in the backseat. The first time he'd met Natalia and her bodyguards, Natalia had explained the passengers were her muscle for some of the more dangerous areas they had to pass through. Natalia didn't explain that these ex-commandos possessed enough firepower to take on a small army. The border guards would have had to take the truck apart to find the weapons, but the commandos could access them in seconds if they had to.

Natalia's rehearsed explanation for Mahmoud's presence satisfied the guard, and he waved her through.

"See ya again in about two weeks?" he asked.

"Yeah, a little more than two," she replied, "but you're close!"

"We gonna have dinner sometime?" he shouted, but the truck was already in Mexico.

Mahmoud and Natalia made good progress, eventually joining the Pan-American Highway as they traveled through Mexico. They headed south on the highway toward the Darién Gap, the infamous fifty-seven-mile stretch of rainforest near the Panama-Columbia border. The Gap was perilous, known for its bandits and dangerous animals, so rather than continuing by land, they loaded the truck onto a cargo ship headed for Tolu, Colombia, a beautiful town on the Caribbean. From Tolu, they followed Columbia Highway 62 south to Medellin. The violence of the city made Natalia uneasy, so they made no stops in this drug capital. Instead, they took Highway 25, the most direct route possible to Bogota, the capital of Columbia. The one-way, seven-day, thirty-five-hundred-mile trip was uneventful, just as Mahmoud had fervently hoped it would be.

Natalia deposited Mahmoud at the Museo Nacional de Colombia, one of the great museums of Bogota.

"I'll be standing on this spot at noon on Thursday, three days from today," he informed her. "Pick me up at noon. Don't be late!"

Moments later, Mahmoud boarded a taxi and headed for the Hotel Casa Deco, arriving two days before his "uncle's birthday" on March 14. He wanted a day to relax before revealing his plan to Hossein and any associates, seen and unseen, who might have accompanied his cousin.

He was more exhausted than hungry, so shortly after checking into his room, he hung the *"Por favor, no molestar"* sign on the doorknob and was soon dead to the world.

*   *   *

As the implications of the last few days sunk in, Romiti grew euphoric. His extraordinary encounter with Lucifer had changed everything. He had traded his soul, he knew. But if it were possible, he would have given even more for the bargain offered by the fallen angel. If the story be true, only one other mortal in history was ever promised such power, such wealth, and the adulation of the entire world in exchange for his soul. The man called Jesus had declined Lucifer's offer, choosing instead to suffer an ignoble, agonizing death on a barbaric Roman cross. By contrast, *this* Roman's proud, boastful, and calculating spirit was already imagining the glory that would soon be his.

Following his visit to Schloss Wewelsburg, Romiti headed for Berlin, anxious to begin his first UN assignment. He viewed his new position as an important milestone in the quest to realize his destiny, and he was eager to see how together, he and his satanic handler would orchestrate his rise to power.

The first couple days of the conference on sectarian religious violence were unexpectedly boring. From time to time there was some excitement as delegates jealously and openly jostled for the more prominent committee assignments, but for the most part, Romiti concluded that unless something unusual happened, the conference would end like the countless meetings of its kind before it.

After listening to yet another delegate express her opinions about the Israeli-Arab conflict without citing a shred of evidence to back up her claims, Romiti was quick to stand after the delegate yielded the floor. "Madam Chairperson." The chairperson recognized the Italian ambassador, but called for a fifteen-minute recess before allowing Romiti to proceed with his prepared remarks.

Romiti stood alone during the break, relaxed and impassively observing his imposing surroundings. The assembly room was not large—its seating capacity was less than four hundred. The comfortable theater-style seating provided ample desktop space for the delegates' favorite electronic devices. The ambient light provided by several frosted windows and skylights brightened a room otherwise darkened by cherrywood paneled walls and rich navy-blue carpet. A nook toward the back of the hall housed a Starbucks bar that was doing a brisk business, serving up flavored iced teas, lattes, macchiatos, frappuccinos, and other favorites.

Several delegates threaded their way to Romiti's location. He was familiar with this primarily male ritual, where the established kingpins' strutting and cocky language were intended to reveal their privileged status to the uninitiated. The routine was meant to intimidate, to ensure the newbie knew his place. *So here we go. Let's hear how great you are! Take your best shots!* Romiti reveled in the exercise, completely poised, assertive, and self-assured.

They had no idea who was on his side.

He quickly identified the leader of the pack, the hefty British ambassador who tossed out the first challenge. "Romiti—means man of Rome. So, man of Rome, giving De Luca's speech this morning, are we?" The group laughed at the mild insult, waiting to see how Romiti would react.

Romiti smiled at the Brit as he casually flicked an imaginary speck from the sleeve of his very expensive Luigi Borelli suit. "I glanced at De Luca's speech. It reminded me of the others I've heard over the past couple of days—somewhat boring, assuming facts not in evidence, generally irrelevant to the matter at hand." Romiti paused to let his criticism hit its mark. He thought, but did not say, *Though even it would be better than the drivel you dished out this morning!*

"We can do better." He pointed to the mild-mannered South African delegate. "You did your homework yesterday." Rattling off a number of facts, figures, and statements lifted from the South African's speech, Romiti earned a smile of appreciation from the beaming ambassador. "But you didn't close the deal. You didn't call us to action. Let's make our mark. Let's end this conference with a concrete plan to accomplish something!"

Romiti's oracle was interrupted by the chairperson's call to order, and then the floor was yielded to the Italian ambassador.

Romiti spoke passionately concerning the economic impact of regional conflicts, focusing particularly on the human side of the tragedies. He explained the differences between state-based conflicts, non-state conflicts, and one-sided violence, drawing on the data compiled by the Uppsala Conflict Data Program, sponsored by the Uppsala University in Sweden. He described in detail the economic model that was a byproduct of a little-known case study entitled *The Economic Costs of Conflict: A Case Study of the Basque Country.* The study provided compelling and quantifiable evidence of the effects of terrorism on per capita income, investment ratios, industrial production, and the better-educated labor force. Further, Romiti presented a model that predicted the amount of domestic and foreign direct investment a region would lose because of terrorism.

The depth of his knowledge and his grasp of the details were breathtaking. His audience sat spellbound as they listened to his forty-five minute speech. Some delegates were furiously surfing the net to confirm the mind-boggling number of facts and figures offered by Romiti, checking whether any were fabricated or exaggerated. While many of the sources were journals which endorsed and published studies prepared by Romiti, the group of skeptics were amazed to discover that not a single fact or figure was misrepresented.

Romiti saw several number-crunching ambassadors shaking their heads, obviously baffled by his ability to accurately recall so many details. The Austrian delegate, Max Knaus, was especially expressive. Twenty minutes into Romiti's speech, many in the audience would instinctively look to Knaus to confirm or contradict another Romiti detail. An exaggerated thumbs-up signaled his confirmation, a frequent signal during the Italian ambassador's presentation.

What startled them most, however, were Romiti's surprising conclusions.

"For too long the world has coddled the ringleaders of terror. When terrorist leaders and their minions are captured, we try to rehabilitate them like petty criminals. Our heads of state take extraordinary measures to pacify the religious leaders who breed these terrorists, not wanting to be branded as religious bigots. The toll on the victims is staggering, while we stand by, either heartless or helpless, as thugs pirate the wealth of the nations.

"I've proven how quickly regions embroiled in conflict can recover economically when terrorists are eliminated. The UN can no longer sit idle while the world's economies are held hostage to religious zealots. In matters regarding the protection of the citizens of the world, the UN must transition from its traditional peacekeeper role to that of a peace enforcer. We must become the aggressor. Our oppressors must be eradicated by whatever means are necessary, and the sooner we accomplish this task, the better!"

The hall was deathly quiet for several seconds, and then the silence was broken by thunderous applause, accompanied by a standing ovation. While none of the ambassadors had ever expressed their opinions in language that even remotely resembled the words spoken by Romiti, it seemed his words conveyed their thoughts exactly. One of the delegates later described the voice of Romiti as "The voice of a god and not of a man!" It was as if a sorcerer had cast his spell on an unsuspecting audience. The chairperson was calling for order, vainly trying to maintain the proper decorum in the assembly room.

For years to come, the speech would earn Romiti the moniker of "the Fierce Ambassador" because of the intensity with which he had delivered his brutal conclusions.

As the chairperson brought the very successful conference to a close, she publicly acknowledged Romiti's unique contributions to the proceedings, taking care to give him the credit for the majority of the recommendations contained in the conference documents.

Romiti nodded his head slightly from the front row where he was sitting, showing his appreciation for her remarks. Led by the chairperson, the conferees applauded once more while Romiti, breaking protocol, strode purposefully to the podium.

"Thank you for your gracious compliments, Madam Chairperson. It's a great honor for me to be counted among this most prominent group of diplomats. Each of you is far more experienced than I." *And yet you have little to show for it!* He smiled to himself as the prodigious egos of his audience swelled at his words. "But this was a team effort. The problems we're facing are without parallel, but I'm convinced the brilliant men and women in this chamber are up to the task." *And if you're not, I'll make sure this is your last conference!* "I'm looking forward to working with all of you as we collectively impress upon the secretary-general the need to rapidly and fully adopt our recommendations."

As Romiti concluded his impromptu remarks, a dark cloud seemed to fill the chamber, and out of it a voice whispered, "In you I am well pleased."

No one but Romiti heard the softly spoken tribute, and the cloud vanished as quickly as it had come. Most of those present just blinked several times, assuming their tired eyes were playing tricks on them. But an unassuming spectator to the proceedings, the strange man Romiti had met at Germany's Schloss Wewelsburg, took notice of the cloud and excused himself from the gallery, beaming as he discreetly exited the hall.

The secretary-general later received letters from several ambassadors who had attended the conference. The correspondence lavished praise on Romiti, exclaiming that no one had a better grasp of the issues, nor did anyone else possess the courage needed to implement the tough measures that could end the regional conflicts. Later the secretary read the conference manuscripts, and he too was impressed with the Italian ambassador. Brute force was a term rarely used in the United Nations, but Romiti was correct. And the secretary privately agreed: a combination of diplomacy and force could quash the uprisings that were taking place around the globe.

As the head of the UN Secretariat, one of the principal organs of the United Nations, the secretary-general was also the de facto spokesperson and head of the UN. Until now, he had not believed such views could be shared publicly. Romiti had suddenly changed the rules of the game, and the secretary-general was determined to elevate him to a more prominent role as quickly as possible.

*   *   *

The morning following his arrival in Bogota, Mahmoud spent a couple of hours canvassing the area surrounding the Hotel Casa Deco. The weather was perfect. Blue cloudless skies, a light breeze, and temperatures in the mid-seventies. He was searching for a spot from which to observe the hotel entrance without being seen. He noticed the remarkable colonial architecture, straight streets, tall palm trees, and abundant patches of lush green grass that marked the traditional Bogota neighborhoods, some dating back hundreds of years. A street vendor noisily hawked his wares in front of the hotel, attracting much attention from visitors and passersby.

Satisfied that he had found the right location, a busy outdoors café near the central square, he returned to his room and waited for nightfall.

Mahmoud arrived at the café early the next morning, tipping the server handsomely for the prolonged use of the table. About three hours later, Hossein exited a taxi alone and entered the lobby of the Hotel Casa Deco.

He had not seen his cousin in more than twenty years. Hossein was a few inches taller than Mahmoud remembered, but still shy of six feet. He was thin and wiry, probably a solid 170 pounds, and obviously in good shape. Hossein's clothes did not conceal his muscular build. A casual glance revealed the powerful arms and chest of this al-Qaeda terrorist. His hair was cut short, and he sported a two- or three-day-old beard. *Almost exactly as I pictured him,* Mahmoud thought.

Hossein was out of sight for about twenty minutes before returning to the passenger drop-off area. He spoke briefly to the parking attendant and a couple of bellmen but evidently did not obtain the information he was looking for. Mahmoud watched him closely for another hour or so. *Didn't use his phone and hasn't made any contact with hotel guests. Looks like he's alone.* Mahmoud started to push back from the table when Hossein noticed the café and began to amble in its direction.

"*Al-hamdu lillah,*" Mahmoud cried out. Hossein was startled for a second, but then recognized the familiar voice of his cousin.

Hossein returned the greeting as he trotted to the café. They shook hands and briefly embraced. "You're as solid as a rock! Put on a few pounds, no?"

Smiling at the compliment, Hossein whispered, "Al-Qaeda trains well! *Al-hamdu lillah.*"

"So what's this all about?"

Mahmoud flagged a cab while explaining that it was best to play the role of tourists before getting down to business. The cabby dropped them off at an open-air restaurant, where the cousins ordered a Colombian meal of *ajiaco,* a traditional soup made of chicken, corn, potatoes, and avocado.

The generous bowl of soup was served with white rice, salad, and salty tostadas. After lunch they walked to a nearby park, finding a wide-open but isolated section of land where they could speak without fear of being overheard.

Mahmoud quickly explained that he had formed an Islamic terrorist organization. Hossein knew the name meant "Servant of the Bringer of Death," and wondered aloud at its significance. Grimly, Mahmoud explained, "It is Allah's wish to bring death to the Great Satan. I and 'Abd al-Mumit will be his servants in this mission."

As Hossein shook his head, wondering at the unexpected change in his cousin, Mahmoud continued, "You know I've earned degrees in nuclear physics. I plan to detonate a nuclear weapon on US soil, crippling and killing as many Americans as possible."

Hossein caught his breath, and his eyes widened at the revelation and the matter-of-fact manner in which it was revealed. He inhaled deeply, trying to regain his composure. His mind was still racing, already fantasizing about how this news would improve his standing with fellow senior al-Qaeda operatives and more importantly, his dangerous friend Mohammed Abdul Al-Wadhi. The Saudi Butcher was now head of al-Qaeda entire. Osama bin Laden, the celebrated leader of al-Qaeda, had been unceremoniously ushered into Paradise by an elite squad of US Navy Seals in 2011. Five years later, after a string of Bin Laden successors were assassinated by snipers and American drones, Al-Wadhi had maneuvered his way to the top of the terrorist organization.

When his tongue was able to form the words, Hossein clapped his cousin on the shoulder and asked, "What can we do to help? Al-Qaeda can provide whatever materials you need to construct the weapon."

"I already have the weapon," Mahmoud admitted, "but I need a weapons-grade material—ideally, highly enriched uranium fuel—before I can detonate it. It's not possible for me to obtain this material in the States. That's where you and your confederates come into play." Mahmoud suppressed the urge to brag about how he had managed to smuggle the weapon parts into the United States.

"Let's assume we can obtain the fuel," Hossein said. "When do you need it, and how can we get it to you?"

"I'm ready now. And I've decided it must be delivered here. Your source must provide detailed instructions on how to safely store and transport the fuel. I'll play no role in that part of the operation, but will assume responsibility once it has arrived in Bogota."

As his mind began to raise doubts about the possibility of success, Hossein saw three younger men emerge from a wooded area, walking directly toward them. Their dress, loud speech, and confident swagger marked them as Americans. *Think they own the world! Tourists, or CIA posing as tourists?*

Hossein gave a slight nod in the direction of the men. Mahmoud caught the signal and immediately changed the subject. How much had the men heard?

The intruders were less than thirty yards away. If they were CIA, Mahmoud and Hossein could not escape. The weaponless cousins held their breaths, tense and frightened but trying to appear as relaxed as possible to the approaching men.

The Americans briefly glanced in their direction and nodded. One of the three smiled and raised his hand in greeting as the group walked past the conspirators, laughing at a one-liner tossed out by the shortest of the trio.

Mahmoud warily watched the men as they passed by, wondering if they were using eavesdropping equipment. He silently berated himself for being so careless. *If there's another meeting, it must be held in a place where voices can't be picked up by snooping CIA or Mossad agents.*

The conspiring terrorists breathed more easily now and began their return walk to the hotel. The boulevards were bustling with pedestrians absorbed in their private conversations and errands, giving little heed to the cousins who casually walked their streets.

"When you know the arrival date, you must text it to me at least two weeks in advance so my operatives can be here, on site, a day or two before the package arrives. Here's how you'll communicate the pick-up date to me. I want you to choose a recent catastrophic event, one that had worldwide coverage, and then add 250 days to the date it occurred. Text a simple message to me, such as 'Found the article on the major hotel fire in Toronto—will forward it to you soon.' I'll find the date of a major hotel fire in Toronto, add 250 days to the date of the incident, and then arrange to have the materials picked up on the calculated date. Is this perfectly clear? I want no breaches of security."

"Understood," Hossein replied.

"Return to the hotel and then to the airport," Mahmoud ordered. "I'll return to the hotel later. *Barakallahu feek*—may the blessings of Allah be upon you."

"*Fi-Amaan-Allah,*" Hossein offered in return, "May you be in the protection of Allah."

The cousins briefly embraced, and Hossein immediately left for the hotel. Mahmoud ran behind a small hedge and vomited, pleading for assurances from Allah that by confiding in his cousin, he had not made a fatal blunder.

CHAPTER NINE

Bogota, Columbia

Tall and lanky, Larry Phelps, or "Pastor Sticks" as he was affectionately called by the members of his mid-sized Jackson, Mississippi, congregation, was well known and respected in the community as a man who remained unswervingly loyal to his God. His personal and public life were unmarked by scandal, unlike some church leaders who mistook God's favor as a license to harbor selfish ambition or indulge in secret sin. The three Gs—girls, gold, and glory—had been the downfall of several of his high-profile colleagues, so Phelps had diligently built the hedges he needed to help him resist these temptations.

A gifted athlete, the former University of South Carolina standout was a first-round draft pick and an ex-NBA All-Star. He proposed to his high school sweetheart, Cyndi, the night he was drafted, and they were married three months later. But after fulfilling his first five-year NBA contract, he traded a basketball for a Bible. Teammates and coaches were not surprised by Sticks's decision to leave the sport, having experienced firsthand his burning passion to share his faith with all who would listen.

The ex-NBA forward and team captain was accustomed to measuring his success in terms of numbers. He considered his pastoral performance to be average, a grade he was not accustomed to receiving, primarily because he had been unable to grow his church beyond the two-hundred-in-attendance barrier.

Phelps's racially diverse congregation was mostly comprised of middle-aged and senior adults, with a small number of grandchildren thrown in for good measure. The neighboring communities were blessed by his congregation's willingness to share their resources—time, talents, and money—a generosity with which the pastor was well pleased.

But Sticks had not been sleeping well. Something was amiss. He believed God was trying to tell him something, but he wasn't catching on. What was he missing?

In his quest to determine what the Holy Spirit was trying to say to him, Sticks observed that many church members were becoming preoccupied with their imminent "rescue" from the world's woes through the rapture and less focused on sharing their faith with their nonbelieving friends and family members. In response, the pastor had been teaching a series on the role of the church, particularly its role in a world embroiled in wars, economic upheaval, natural disasters, and political intrigue.

This Sunday Sticks was teaching on the rapture of the church, and he had reached his favorite part of the sermon. His eyes quickly scanned his audience of about 150 adults, noting the large number of empty seats. *Down around thirty from last week. The auditorium seats nearly four hundred. Wonder if it will ever be full?* Most of the people were his faithful regulars. He saw no visitors. Even the faithful looked a little sleepy. *Some are listening expectantly, but most are thinking about the Bears-Packers game, I'd bet. God, may your Word ignite a fire in the hearts of your people!*

"Many teach that at any moment the church will be raptured, snatched away to heaven, leaving the world in the hands of a very angry God. I, too, fervently believe in the rapture of the church and yearn for that blessed day. But I also believe Scripture teaches that the church—that's you and me—will have a window of opportunity to practice our faith in a time of unprecedented trouble that will take place just before the church departs this troubled world."

The last statement raised some eyebrows, and several of the old-timers began to stir uncomfortably. The unspoken question on their faces was pretty clear: *He's not going to ask us to knock on doors, is he?*

"God has been calling my attention to world events as never before. I'm coming to believe we're the generation Matthew says 'will not pass away' until all the things described in chapter 24 of his gospel have happened. A general would be making a grave mistake if he promised his marines they would never see combat. Similarly, I feel I would be as guilty if I taught you that God will snatch us away before the time the world needs us most.

"Don't misunderstand me. I don't believe the church is subject to God's wrath—Paul makes this very clear in the opening chapter of his first letter to the church in Thessalonica. But I understand Scripture to teach that God's wrath is not poured out on earth's inhabitants until the sixth seal—I'll talk more about seals, trumpets, and bowls pretty soon—until the sixth seal is opened, exactly as John describes in the Revelation. By the way, I want to make an important point here: when I use the term 'earth's inhabitants,' I'm referring to the majority who has bought into the world's system of values and priorities. You might say the 'world is their home' in contrast to we who are pilgrims, just passin' through.

"True, a lot of bad stuff happens during the first five seals. But while these seals are being opened, the church—remember, that's you and me—will have extraordinary opportunities to share our faith in a culture gripped by fear in a world gone mad."

Several more in the audience were becoming antsy. This wasn't the usual rapture message of deliverance from all trouble before the tribulation began. One of the elders, Jimmy Boyer, a member of the church for more than forty years, was especially ill at ease. Over breakfast one morning, Sticks had shared his thoughts about the rapture—but Jimmy had never expected to hear them from the pulpit. *He's not saying the church will be here during the tribulation, is he? Surely he knows the rapture takes place before God's wrath is poured out on the world!*

Sticks continued, pretending he didn't notice how uncomfortable he was making some of his church members. "The problems we're facing now, exceedingly difficult as they are, will be remembered as childhood puzzles when compared to the trials and tribulations that are coming upon this earth. I expect we'll be at the forefront of a worldwide revival that happens during a seven-year period I'll often refer to as 'the seventieth week of Daniel.' Many Bible teachers have called the entire seven-year period introduced by Daniel 'the tribulation,' but I understand the tribulation to be a short period of time, occurring *within* the seventieth week, that is interrupted by the rapture of the church. The seventieth week of Daniel also encompasses a brief span called 'the day of the Lord,' which follows the rapture and is when I believe the world and its inhabitants experience God's wrath. We'll discuss this topic in much greater detail in future studies.

"Now, I know the pretribbers have a different view, believing the church will be raptured *before* the seventieth week of Daniel begins. And they may very well be right. I certainly won't argue with God if the rapture occurs earlier than I expect! But after studying this subject extensively, I've personally reached the conclusion that the church will be on earth for a portion of Daniel's seventieth week."

Sticks knew many of the people were hearing this view for the first time, so he wanted to put them at ease. He smiled down at Jimmy Boyer. "Now Jimmy and I have discussed this a bit, haven't we, Jimmy?" Many in the congregation looked toward the aisle seat, third row from the front, right side of the auditorium—Jimmy's seat. Jimmy nodded, but his mind was racing. *Hey, don't make me an accomplice! I'm not sure I buy this!*

Returning his attention to the congregation, Sticks continued, "Much of this material may be new to you, so we'll take our time and go through it carefully.

"Some believe that the Great Tribulation cannot precede the rapture because believers would focus on it rather than on our blessed hope, the rapture of the church. Not so. A student who is prepared and equipped for her midterm exams looks beyond the midterms to the exciting Christmas break, while an unprepared and unequipped student nervously focuses his attention on the time of testing. Similarly, it seems to me that a prepared believer looks beyond the Great Tribulation to the coming of the Lord.

"Others believe this notion of a church triumphant in any part of Daniel's seventieth week destroys the doctrine of imminence. You may remember that this doctrine teaches that there are no prophecies that must be fulfilled before the church is raptured—that is, the rapture is *imminent;* it may occur at any moment. Perhaps this is so, but many of those who subscribe to this belief will also tell you that the rapture and the day of the Lord are intimately linked. In fact, most of them would say the rapture is what sets the day of the Lord in motion. And I agree. Writing to the Thessalonians, Paul affirms their understanding when he says, 'You know very well that the day of the Lord will come like a thief in the night. But you, brothers, are not in darkness so that this day should surprise you like a thief.'

"So the rapture and the day of the Lord will come like a thief to those who are in darkness, but we who are in the light will not be surprised. We're encouraged to look forward to our homegoing. We don't know the day or the hour, of course, but we will not be surprised when it comes.

"So the question that must be answered is this: when does the day of the Lord begin? I'll provide a general answer to that question in future studies."

Sticks gripped the pulpit a little tighter. It wasn't comfortable giving a message he knew was controversial, but this message *mattered*—it mattered because his people mattered. There might not be more than two hundred of them, but they were his heart and soul.

"If I'm understanding my Bible correctly, then it's my job to prepare you for the coming storm. I don't want us to be AWOL from the greatest battle ever fought. I want us to not only stand firm, but to be on the offensive. Satan has captured the hearts and minds of this generation, and he would have us believe that the souls of men and women across our nation and throughout the world are safely behind his gates. But the gates of hell cannot prevail as we take the battle to Satan's turf! That's the mission of the church today, and it must be our mission leading up to the rapture and the day of the Lord."

Pastor Phelps finished his sermon and closed the service in prayer. *You got it right, Sticks! That's what you've been missing,* a voice seemed to whisper in his heart.

*   *   *

Pakistan had become one of the most dangerous places on earth. Since 2004, Pakistani Taliban groups had engaged in terrorism against the Pakistani armed forces, killing more than three thousand civilians and armed personnel by suicide bombings and other terrorist activities in one year alone. Pakistan's nuclear arsenal had steadily grown, though not as rapidly as the number of terrorists who called Pakistan home. Years before, it was alleged that Prime Minister Benazir Bhutto, unwittingly perhaps, had helped North Korea in their quest to join the nuclear club of nations. The secrets she divulged helped the North Koreans develop a uranium enrichment program that ultimately led to the construction of a nuclear weapon. A.Q. Kahn, the founder of Pakistan's nuclear program and "the Father of the Islamic Bomb," admitted in a 2004 televised "confession" to providing nuclear know-how to Iran, China, Libya, and North Korea.

Al-Qaeda was next in the growing line of terrorist groups to receive a handout from its all-too-willing Pakistani accomplices.

The best-organized branch of the Pakistani Armed Forces was the army, formerly led by General Muhammad Saleem Rajput. The general longed to conquer India but knew his dream would never be realized so long as the United States was strong. He was a reluctant ally of al-Qaeda, playing a key role in frustrating the numerous attempts of the US Special Forces to locate and kill Osama bin Laden in the mountainous region of eastern Pakistan. Each time the Rangers were close to their target, OBL was tipped off, mysteriously disappearing from the face of the earth. The general was at his best in this cat-and-mouse, life-and-death game, hedging his bets by playing roulette with his two most dangerous partners. This time, he placed all his chips on al-Qaeda and delivered to al-Wadhi and Hossein the materials they were so desperately seeking.

The general learned that a cask containing 5.2 kilograms of highly enriched uranium (HEU) was to be transported to Russia via a Russian Antonov 124-100, a heavy transport plane. In a deal negotiated between Pakistan, Russia, and the United States, the US had agreed to pay Russia one million dollars to remove the HEU from Pakistani soil and safely dispose of it in Russia.

In a brazen daytime operation, al-Qaeda terrorists overpowered the six Pakistani marines guarding the cask on the tarmac adjacent to the nuclear facility, killing them before the giant transport plane arrived. The stolen cask was loaded into an unmarked truck commandeered by an al-Qaeda unit.

The general kept his part of the bargain, ensuring minimal security at the time of the heist. The cask containing the HEU was sealed for transport and storage, greatly simplifying the next phase of the al-Qaeda operation.

In a secret cable sent to Washington, an employee of the State Department warned, "Given the highly transportable nature of the HEU and the shoddy security at the nuclear facility, any mention of this issue in the press could pose serious security concerns." In response, the incident was kept under wraps for several months.

The world had no idea that al-Qaeda terrorists finally possessed the materials they needed to enter the nuclear age.

*   *   *

"Received article re:Tokyo building collapse. Didn't know 38 died. Will be useful in my research."

The text came from Hossein. Mahmoud jumped on the Internet and Googled *hotel collapse, Tokyo,* and *fatalities.* The search engine returned multiple references relating to the hotel catastrophe that had killed thirty-eight people on June 19 the year before. Mahmoud added 250 days to June 19 and sat back, stretching his back against the growing tension.

The materials he so badly wanted would arrive in Bogota on February 24, now just three weeks away.

Just as he finished the calculation, Mahmoud heard car doors slam, followed by a hard rap on his door. Two men flashed their badges, introducing themselves as agents from the Department of Homeland Security. One of the men appeared much more hostile than the other. Mahmoud immediately decided he did not want to cross this man, and he made a mental note of the agent's name—Holcombe.

"Are you Mahmoud Aliaabaadi?"

He prayed silently to Allah. Desperately hoping he would not vomit, Mahmoud answered the agent's question. "Yes, I am. Why do you ask?"

"May we come in?" they asked.

"Yes, please come in," Mahmoud responded, but he was nauseated by the fear rising in his throat. "How can I help you?"

"Just some routine questions," Holcombe snapped.

"The computer selected your profile as a person of interest. We thought so too, and since we're in the neighborhood, we thought we'd get acquainted. The computer says you came to the States from Iran via Italy. Also says you're single and have degrees in nuclear physics. Eye-opening combination in today's world—Iranian, single, and a nuclear physics background, don't you think? Computer says you haven't been outside the country since starting Berkeley. That true?"

Mahmoud fought to keep his composure. "No, I haven't been out of the country," he lied. "Until recently, I was employed as a nuclear physicist at a local research lab . . ."

The belligerent Holcombe interrupted. "Yes, we have that information, but we'd like to know where you're currently employed."

"I'm not employed at the moment. I'm taking a little time to oversee some of my investments, so that'll keep me busy for a few weeks." Mahmoud cursed himself for revealing too much information. "So no, I'm not employed at the moment," he continued, "but I've applied for a position at one of the nuclear regulatory agencies. I left the laboratory on very good standing, and my references are excellent, as I'm sure you already know."

"Yes, we know that too. By the way, any interest in applying for a position at Homeland Security? A person of your nationality, education, and experience could be of great service to our nation?"

The surprise question startled Mahmoud. "No," he stammered. "Well, I mean, I've never thought about it. I'll, uh, give it some thought. May I have a business card?"

"Thank you for your time, Mr. Aliaabaadi," Holcombe offered as he gave Mahmoud a couple cards. "We'll keep in touch. Have a good day."

Mahmoud closed the door and ran to the bathroom.

"Wonder what investments he's overseeing?" Holcombe's partner, Hector Rivera, asked. "And what's with the job offer? Mahmoud nearly choked."

Jack Holcombe chuckled as he remembered the expression on Mahmoud's face. "Let's check out the investments. Who knows? They may lead to something."

*   *   *

Ebrahim Akbari, president of Akbari Enterprises, read Mahmoud's text. "Red. Long Beach Convention Center. One-thirty." Red—Mahmoud's code word for problems.

Akbari quickly left his office, passing by his secretary's desk. "Something's come up that needs my attention. Please cancel my appointments and reschedule my conference calls. I'll call you later."

"Is anything wrong, Mr. Akbari?" his doting and efficient secretary asked.

"Not particularly. Something's come up that I need to take care of right away."

Akbari jumped into his Mercedes-Benz CL-class coup and a minute later was speeding east on Ocean Boulevard toward the convention center. He entered the valet parking area, tossing his keys to the attendant as he quickly scanned the pedestrians, looking for Mahmoud.

Akbari spotted his friend standing on the steps leading up to the front of one of North America's premier convention facilities. Levis, a Raiders jersey, a pair of sandals. And a Giants baseball cap. Akbari smiled. *Can't get any more American than that!* A home improvement trade show was in full swing, so hundreds of attendees were walking around the busy concourse.

Mahmoud had seen Akbari as well and was already moving in his direction. The two joined up on Seaside Way and then walked east toward Victory Park. The cool breeze and salty smell of the ocean were invigorating.

Both men commented on the beautiful weather, neither considering for a moment the disastrous effects their violent plan would have on the beach community.

"Just received a visit from two Homeland Security officers. They asked if I've been out of the country. Wanted to know where I worked. They were bothered that I'm a single Iranian male." Mahmoud grimaced. *Prejudiced jerks!* "Just snooping. I didn't mention anything about Akbari Enterprises, of course, but needed to give you a heads-up."

"That's not good," Akbari noted. "But it is what it is. I'll keep my eyes open."

"Just received confirmation the package will arrive in several weeks. Is the facility ready?" Mahmoud asked.

"Yes, it's ready, although we have not lowered the weapon into its berth."

The disassembled weapon, without the weapons-grade nuclear material, had been spirited out of Russia via a freight train that regularly crossed the Kazakhstan-Russian border. It was eventually delivered, one piece at a time, to a building owned by Akbari Enterprises. Here it was carefully reassembled under Mahmoud's meticulous supervision.

"Shall the security force begin its rotation?" Akbari continued.

"Not yet. I'll let you know," Mahmoud responded. "But for now, keep the weapon in its hangar. We'll lower it in place after the package crosses the Mexican-American border."

*   *   *

"One of Aliaabaadi's investments is Akbari Enterprises, a warehousing and distribution company," Jack Holcombe noted. "Crazy successful, from the look of things. Records say our friend, Mr. Aliaabaadi, owns fifty percent of Akbari. Ebrahim Akbari owns the other fifty percent. Hey, and look at this. Italy's ambassador to the United Nations once owned twenty-five percent but transferred his ownership to Aliaabaadi about four years ago. Wonder what the connection is?"

"Interesting," Hector Rivera replied. "Why don't we sniff around Akbari? I'll work with the fire marshal in Long Beach to arrange a complete inspection of the warehouse. One of our agents can pose as a member of the inspection team. If any hanky-panky is going on in that warehouse, we'll soon know about it."

"Sounds good," Jack agreed, his eyes still on the computer screen. "I see that a couple years ago, a building permit was issued for the construction of a secure facility within the warehouse itself. Be sure to check it out."

*　　*　　*

After receiving detailed instructions from Mahmoud, Ebrahim met with Natalia.

"You're to make the normal stops along the route to Bogota," Ebrahim explained. "It's imperative that you reach Bogota by February 24, so leave a few days earlier than usual. I've made arrangements for you to stay at the Hotel Casa Deco for several days. Bring along some magazines. Once you've arrived at the hotel, I want you to remain inside. Under no circumstances are you to leave the hotel until you receive a message from me. Is this clear?"

Natalia nodded agreement and then asked, "What happens to me after I deliver the package to the warehouse?"

"We've discussed this before, Natalia," Ebrahim replied impatiently. "I will have $750,000 wired to your Colombian account the day you deliver the package. And as you have already confirmed with your bank, $250,000 has been deposited into your account."

Though she didn't show it to her employer, Natalia was elated with her good fortune. In her wildest dreams, she had never imagined she would have so much money. She, along with her two bodyguards, began their last run to Bogota. *Funny,* she thought, *how easily a million bucks can turn a poor member of a terrorist organization into a decadent capitalist mercenary!*

*　　*　　*

Early one morning, two weeks after the surprise DHS visit to Mahmoud's condo, inspectors from the Long Beach Fire Department arrived at Akbari Enterprises unannounced. They began their standard inspection, looking for blocked exits and hazardous materials, evaluating fire-protection systems and searching for minor and major fire-code infractions. Dressed in the uniform of a fire inspector, DHS agent Hector Rivera was looking for anything that might link the company to terrorist activities. Everything appeared normal . . . until they entered the small compartment within the facility. "What's stored in this room?" Rivera asked.

Akbari, who was monitoring the inspection team's every move via the surveillance system, held his breath.

The warehouse supervisor simply stated what he knew.

"We receive, store, and ship precious metals and jewels. They're stored in this secure inner compartment. We made a delivery yesterday, so at the moment, our inventory is minimal. You're free to have a look."

Before entering the compartment, another inspector asked the purpose of the corridor that surrounded it and showed special interest in knowing the reason for the sleeping quarters. Again, the warehouse supervisor was direct and forthright in his answers.

"When we have a substantial inventory, the outer area houses ten to twelve security guards. They work thirty-six- or forty-hour shifts, rotating three days on and four days off, and are not to leave these premises during their workweek. They have access to the kitchen, showers, weight room, sleeping quarters—everything they need is contained within the four walls of this facility. Akbari Enterprises has a perfect security record, and we intend to keep it that way."

"Why does your firm make so many trips to Bogota?" Rivera questioned, feigning a bored expression.

"The emerald trade in Bogota is enormous," the warehouse supervisor explained. "Millions of dollars of rough and cut emeralds are bought and sold daily. Many of these emeralds are sold to brokers in the United States. While most of the emeralds are transported by air, there are special circumstances which require moving them into the US in a more, shall we say, discreet fashion."

The inspectors entered the empty internal compartment and found nothing out of the ordinary. The chief inspector scribbled a terse entry in his notebook, reminding himself to explore the space above the ceiling during the next inspection. Rivera also paid close attention to the ceiling, wondering what might be hidden above his head. He decided not to raise any more questions but made a mental note to discuss the ceiling with Holcombe.

Akbari let out a sigh of relief when the inspection was over. The warehouse would not be on the inspection tour for another year, he speculated, much too late to foil the joint 'Abd al-Mumit/al-Qaeda operation now entering its final stage.

*   *   *

Natalia checked into the Hotel Casa Deco on February 22, two days ahead of the planned delivery. She texted the Akbari transportation traffic manager, letting him know that she had arrived safely in Bogota. She spent the next couple of days watching old reruns, as she was not an avid reader, and running up her room service tab. She planned to enjoy the rare luxury often in the coming months.

On February 24, she received a text message directing her to a warehouse located in Zona 4 Sur, the southern end of the capital. Zona 4 Sur was the industrial zone and included large labor barrios. Natalia arrived at the dilapidated warehouse by noon, noting what appeared to be groups of unemployed workers surrounding the building. However, the bulky weapons beneath their loose clothing betrayed a well-equipped, though relatively untrained, security force. She was waved inside the warehouse. After she and her two companions exited the cab, they were led to a small room guarded by several Colombian men carrying AK-47s. She made a mental note not to tangle with these guys, although she and her two bodyguards were less than happy with the hospitality they received.

Natalia's stint with the Medellin drug cartel paid some dividends, as she also recognized Farsi tattoos on more than a half-dozen men in the warehouse, tattoos she knew could be traced back to Iran and its proxy army, Hezbollah.

"So Hezbollah is connected with this operation," she wondered aloud. "What's Akbari up to?"

The connection between Hezbollah and the drug cartels was well known. Less known was the extent of Hezbollah's activities in Central and South America. The past president-dictators of Iran and Venezuela, Ahmadinejad and Chavez, had supported the connection, united in their common hatred of America. Their common goal was to transport terror to the US through activities Hezbollah operatives practiced throughout the world—car bombings, suicide bombings, and other forms of murder of targeted military and civilian populations.

Natalia and the two bodyguards were kept in the securely guarded room for several hours and then led back to their truck. Nothing appeared to have changed since they were escorted from the cab. However, she noted the lingering odor created by the gas tungsten arc used to fuse a large metal compartment in the truck's covered bed. Even to a trained eye the compartment was hidden, appearing as the forward wall of the truck. So they would be transporting a special cargo, stored in a hidden compartment and delivered by terrorist operatives. *Interesting,* she thought.

They left the warehouse and were soon on their way to the States, planning to arrive at the US-Mexico border sometime during the second week of March.

*   *   *

The Akbari truck containing the illegal cargo was near the end of a long column of commercial vehicles, all in line to cross the US-Mexico border into California. Natalia did not know what she was hauling, but she knew that whatever it was, she did not want to get caught with it. Her stomach was in knots as the truck crawled closer to the customs booth, but she was a pro. Her facial expressions and body language would not betray the fear she could literally taste at that moment.

"Hola, Natalia! Whataya bringing in today?" The voice asking the question belonged to Frank, a US border inspector she knew well from her frequent crossings.

"Not much. We shipped a boatload of faulty Simple-Slide metal filing cabinets to a Colombian distributor. Heard the stupid drawers won't slide open when they're full. Owner threatened to dump them in the street if we didn't pick 'em up soon, so here I am!" Natalia replied.

"Pull into the inspection lane and we'll take a quick look," Frank ordered.

Knowing Frank's bark was much worse than his bite, Natalia flashed her sexiest smile and gave a thumbs-up. The act seldom failed. She was good-looking with a great personality, knew it, and had used these assets to her advantage her entire life.

"Yes, sir! On my way!" she playfully replied.

She pulled into the inspection lane and hopped out of the cab, giving Frank a sly wink. One of the bodyguards also exited the truck and pulled back the rear tarp. An inspector studied the shipping manifest and then jumped into the back of the truck for a quick inspection, confirming the cargo was in sync with the shipping documents. Final clearance was granted by the inspector and then recorded in the automated manifest system.

The inspector knew that Frank had worked with Natalia for several years, so his inspection was not exceptionally thorough. He also knew that Akbari Enterprises was a member of C-TPAT, the Customs-Trade Partnership Against Terrorism. To join C-TPAT, companies provided customs with documentation of the measures they had implemented to strengthen the security of their supply chain and their commitment to meeting the supply-chain best practices required of customs. Akbari had fulfilled these requirements and in return received expedited processing at all US border crossings.

"Everything appears to be in order, Frank. Shall I send her through?"

"Yeah, trucks are lining up. Natalia, free up some space! Outta here, now! We'll see you in a month or two!"

"Got it! See ya later, Frank."

She exited the inspection area, expelling a huge sigh of relief. "Three more hours, guys, and this run will be history!"

Natalia had no idea just how prophetic her statement was.

*   *   *

Natalia and her crew rolled into the Akbari unloading dock late in the afternoon of Friday, March 12. The bodyguards collected their paychecks and checked into the closest bar, a tradition which had begun after their first transnational haul for Akbari. Neither man reported to work the next day or the following. They were never seen again. Natalia was on call for a final, one-way trip to Columbia, so she returned to her condo, awaiting the call and dreaming of luxuries soon to be hers.

After close of business Friday, Mahmoud supervised the removal of the highly enriched uranium hidden in the specially designed compartment of the truck. Mahmoud's associates carefully transported the HEU into the storage area, where Akbari and his companions began to process the radioactive material, taking the first steps that would conclude with the fueling of the nuclear device two weeks hence.

CHAPTER TEN

McLean, Virginia

Baby-faced, thirty-one years old, genius, and bored, the whiz kid with the ponytail sat in a top-secret, high-tech office in McLean, Virginia, home to the Central Intelligence Agency.

The kid was analyzing scores of mostly meaningless electronic intelligence accessed through a network of PCs haphazardly positioned in his small and very cluttered cubicle. The US navy's "White Cloud" space-borne electronic intelligence (ELINT) system, one of three American reconnaissance satellites that worked together to pick up radio transmissions and get a fix on the emitters' signals, sent chatter the kid's way. His job was to use his nearly photographic memory and brilliant mind to extract what was important.

One particular message, comprised of a series of digits, letters, and brackets caught his eye, only because he realized he had seen it several times over the past few weeks:

F8F0[B66[[A6F6I2BK36B2D2H

The signal originated in the mountains of eastern Pakistan. He was aware of the recent heist in Pakistan, and he, like many others, was feverishly searching for any clues that would lead to the stolen uranium. After several hours of analysis, he was positive he had decoded the message. He raced upstairs to report his findings to his supervisor, a senior agent whose team monitored suspicious movements on the Afghan-Pakistani border, a hotbed of terrorism.

"I think I found something!" he shouted to the senior agent. "Whoever created this cipher wasn't very sophisticated. The message originated in the wilds of north Waziristan, situated on Pakistan's border with Afghanistan, and was picked up by White Cloud. It's been linked to an al-Qaeda cell that conducts joint operations with the Taliban."

By mentioning north Waziristan and White Cloud, the whiz kid earned his supervisor's full attention. The senior agent punched a comm line, barking an order to the occupant of the office. "Drop what you're doing! Need you and Rick in my office *now*—on the double!" A minute later, two winded cryptologists, members of a CIA cyber ops team, sprinted into the secure conference room, and the kid began his impromptu presentation.

"My software program first broke the cipher into individual segments, using the nondigit characters as separators." He quickly jotted down the string of characters on a whiteboard.

F8 F0 [B66 [[A6 F6 I2 B K36 B2 D2 H

"Then the program substituted the letters and brackets of the message with their numeric equivalents, using the ancient over-punch methodology used by COBOL programmers in the sixties. The left-bracket plus A through I represents positive digits, zero through nine; the right-bracket plus J through R represents negative digits, negative one through negative nine."

"Hey, dispel with the software lessons," one of the latecomers directed. "We're all familiar with over-punch methodology. But I think you're wasting your time. I really doubt al-Qaeda would depend on coding conventions from the sixties to get out an important message!"

"No, wait! Hear me out! So the second pass of the cipher looks like this." He rapidly scribbled a second line beneath the first, now substituting digits for characters:

68 60 0 266 0 0 16 66 92 2 -236 22 42 8

"These figures still didn't make a lot of sense to me, so I began to manipulate the smaller sets of values. I unlocked the message when I divided the smaller sets of numbers in half," he boasted as he hurriedly jotted a third series of numbers on the whiteboard.

34 30 0 133 0 0 8 33 46 1 -118 11 21 4

"The results resembled two sets of latitudes and longitudes, with trailing values that I easily equated with the month of a year once I determined the locations based on the latitude and longitude I was seeing."

Now the whiz kid commanded everyone's attention. Each analyst leaned forward, waiting for the locations to be revealed.

"The first segment, 34 30 0 133 0 0, contains the latitude/longitude coordinates for Hiroshima: 34′ 30′ 0″ / 133′ 0′ 0″, followed by 8, which corresponds to the month of the year in which the bomb was dropped on Hiroshima."

The kid was so animated, and talking so fast, that he began to stumble over his words. He stopped to catch his breath and then continued his monologue.

"The second segment, 33 46 1 -118 11 21, represents the coordinates of Long Beach, California: 33′ 46′ 1″ / -118′ 11′ 21″. The last digit, 4, represents the month of the year—in this cipher, April. If I'm right, and I pray I'm not, I believe the message is warning terrorist cells in the US that a nuclear weapon will be detonated in Long Beach in April—sometime this month!" He stood triumphant, shoulders thrown back, and then slumped in momentary confusion. "But why Long Beach?"

His question was ignored, but his findings quickly moved up the chain. The consensus of all counterintelligence agencies was that the cryptic message indeed referred to the stolen HEU, revealing that the highly enriched uranium fuel had fallen into the hands of terrorists. Armed with the knowledge that a major terrorist attack on US soil was imminent, various US security and defense agencies scrambled to eliminate the threat.

All the major security organizations were placed on high alert, including the DHS, FBI, CIA, NSC, Secret Service, and several counterintelligence agencies of the US government.

*   *   *

One-fifth of all containers entering the US were processed in the Port of Long Beach—over eight million metric tons of cargo each year. More than twenty thousand twenty-foot containers were handled every day, employing more than thirty thousand people in Long Beach alone and almost two million people nationally. With over five thousand vessels entering the port each year, it was the second busiest port in the US, generating tens of billions of dollars in local, state, and federal taxes. A nuclear explosion in or around the port would be catastrophic in terms of the national psyche, killing tens of thousands of innocent Americans; its devastating impact on the US economy would be felt for decades.

Before the Homeland Security Advisory System was replaced by the two-level National Terrorism Advisory System, only once since 9/11 was the threat level ever raised to red. On that occasion, the warning applied only to flights coming in from the United Kingdom. Under the new system, alerts were issued under either the category of *elevated* or of *imminent*.

Less than two weeks after Natalia's entry into the US via the Mexican border, DHS issued its first NTAS imminent alert. Simultaneously, a bulletin was circulated to the employees of the various agencies charged with the control and protection of US borders at and between the official ports of entry. The bulletin warned of imminent danger to the US—an attempt would be made by al-Qaeda, or a homegrown terrorist organization affiliated with al-Qaeda, to smuggle a weapon of mass destruction into the United States.

Mahmoud and his 'Abd al-Mumit cadre of homegrown terrorists completed their work on the nuke the same day the NTAS alert was issued. A team of radical jihadists, all heavily armed and eager to sacrifice their lives for Allah, took up their defensive positions in the corridors surrounding the secluded compartment in the Akbari warehouse. While they had no idea what it contained, they were unafraid. They knew their last act would please Allah.

*   *   *

Holcombe and Rivera left a briefing related to the DHS bulletin early that afternoon and went straight to Holcombe's office to brainstorm a course of action while they awaited more specific information. The chief of the local DHS branch had announced the anticipated attempt by al-Qaeda to smuggle a weapon of mass destruction into the US. The city of Long Beach was identified as the likely target of the attack, information that did not sit well with the two Southern California-based DHS employees.

"So it appears the attack will occur sometime this month," began Rivera.

"Yeah, and two targets come immediately to mind. The most likely is the Port of Long Beach. Another possibility is the Long Beach Toyota

Grand Prix on Sunday morning, the day after tomorrow. More than two hundred thousand spectators will be lining the streets!"

"I'd go with both," Rivera responded. "I'll bet the port is the primary target, but the terrorists are timing the detonation with the Grand Prix. They'll take out both targets with a single explosion."

"If you're right, we've got less than forty-eight hours to stop the bad guys," Holcombe announced. "Remember Akbari Enterprises? It's as close to the port as you can get. My gut tells me the nuke's hidden somewhere in that warehouse! Either the inspection team missed it or it was assembled after the inspection . . . but I'd bet my life it's there!"

"Let's hope not," Rivera grimly answered.

The two men ran their suspicions past their director, who in turn notified an undersecretary at the DHS headquarters in Washington, DC. The potential terrorist threat was immediately classified as "Pinnacle Nucflash," the highest precedence in the OPREP-3 reporting structure.

The National Nuclear Security Administration, operating under the United States Department of Energy, was quickly brought into the loop. NNSA oversaw the Nuclear Emergency Support Teams, whose mission was to be "prepared to respond immediately to any type of radiological accident or incident anywhere in the world." NEST was not made up of military personnel, but of nuclear physicists and scientists who typically were employed by the nation's nuclear labs. As first responders to a potential nuclear incident, their job was to find the nuclear weapon before it exploded.

It was Friday, midnight, Pacific Standard Time.

NNSA and the FBI had just concluded counterterrorism exercises in Southern California, the latest in the NNSA's Silent Thunder series. The games gave federal, state, and local officials and responders hands-on experience in prioritized alarm assessment and response, crisis management, threat assessment, and emergency response in the event of a terrorist incident involving radiological materials. NNSA performed a quick inventory of its resources and found that more than two dozen NEST team members remained in Southern California, enjoying a little R&R before returning to their normal daily routines. They were immediately dispatched to a parking lot a short block away from Akbari Enterprises, now the designated Incident Command Post for "Nucflash Jihad," the code name assigned to the potential mass casualty incident. A temporary heliport was also established from which helicopter-centered air operations could be conducted.

NEST team members fanned out in the threat zone to locate the weapon. Using unmanned aerial vehicles, the NEST "pilot" would launch a Styrofoam drone by hooking a one-hundred-foot bungee cord to the aircraft before launching it like a slingshot. Each eight-pound drone was equipped with a GPS, two onboard computers, and two cameras, snapping 1,200 images per flight. The drones communicated the georeferenced electronic data to a mobile communications lab, painting a picture of the area for the analysts who were combing the graphics for clues. Early Saturday morning, more investigators began to scour the threat zone on foot, going in and out of buildings, desperately searching for the telltale signs of a WMD. To preserve secrecy, they carried gamma and neutron detectors inside laptop cases, large purses, and backpacks.

Most buildings were unattended; some were guarded by local security services, all of which had been notified of the potential threat. When security resources were present, the flashing of a NEST badge and a one- or two-sentence explanation were usually enough to gain entrance to most buildings. Uncooperative security personnel were threatened with arrest for obstructing the investigation of a threat to national security; all but a couple hardheads quickly backed down. Access to unattended buildings was gained with the full cooperation of local law-enforcement personnel.

Four local SWAT teams, under the command of the first responder and incident commander, Captain Thomas O'Malley, had already secured the perimeter of the commercial warehouse of Akbari Enterprises and were keeping it under surveillance. Other sites that met the profile of a possible nuclear weapon site were also being methodically evaluated, but it was a daunting task. Almost a thousand locations met the initial search criteria. For now, Akbari's warehouse was receiving the lion's share of the attention.

A thrice-decorated veteran of Operation Iraqi Freedom, O'Malley was a former Navy SEAL who had led special ops teams on numerous missions in dangerous Baghdad neighborhoods. An expert in urban warfare, the lieutenant guessed that everything he learned in the streets of Baghdad would soon be put to use.

"Whadda we have here?" O'Malley peered over the shoulder of the SWAT team technician as they studied blueprints of Akbari's warehouse. They were inside a Freightliner MCV-9000/FL Command Center, a high-tech office on wheels. "What's this?" he asked, pointing to the compartment within the warehouse. "And where's Akbari? Has anyone tracked him down?"

One of his lieutenants, named Spencer, answered O'Malley's last two questions. "LBPD has been unable to locate him. He's not at home. An APB has been issued, naming Akbari as a person of interest. His secretary was cooperative but unable to provide any helpful information. She told me Akbari was in the office several times last week. It was a normal workweek, she said. No unusual activity."

The SWAT team's computer forensics expert quickly accessed the Long Beach Development Services database via a secure wireless link, downloading Akbari's construction permits, planning permits, and the latest building inspection reports.

The expert hurriedly scanned the Adobe PDFs displayed on his monitor and then announced, "Looks like construction permits were issued two years ago. According to the docs, this is no ordinary storage closet. It's a bloody concrete bunker!"

The forensics expert added, "The last inspection uncovered no violations, although the fire department was intrigued by our mysterious compartment. The chief inspector scribbled a note to himself—a reminder to check the area above the ceiling on the next inspection. Hmmm. Here's something interesting."

"What's that?" O'Malley demanded.

"Well, the report says the DHS inserted one of their men on the inspection team. DHS must have suspected something was going on some time ago!"

"I'll check it out. Spencer! Look here," O'Malley said to the lieutenant as he again pointed to what he believed could be the location of the nuclear bomb. "This bunker may house the weapon. Appears there's no one home. Get into the warehouse, and be careful!" he barked as he flipped the security key to the SWAT team leader. "The key box is mounted on the west wall of the main entrance."

An LBFD captain had given O'Malley the special security key that allowed access to the box. It contained the keys emergency personnel would need to gain entrance to various areas in the building.

"Palomar! Begin the evacuation of all the businesses in a half-mile radius of the incident site. It's Saturday morning; most businesses are closed. Horton! Follow Palomar. Learn everything you can about Akbari Enterprises. Contact me immediately if you hear anything suspicious."

As O'Malley awaited word from Spencer, his mind began to race through various scenarios. *Is the warehouse booby-trapped? Is this a setup? Have we been lured to this location, but the bomb's somewhere else?* He began to formulate a few quick-and-dirty contingency plans as he awaited the arrival of additional SWAT teams.

His thoughts were interrupted by Spencer's excited voice on the ruggedized mil-spec radio. "No key box. It's been ripped from the wall!"

"Breach the front entrance," O'Malley commanded. "Secure the warehouse. Do not, repeat, do *not,* attempt to breach the compartment."

The SWAT team formed a single-file snake with Spencer as the point man. Once the building's front entrance was breached, an officer tossed several "flash-bangs" into the open area. A brilliant flash lit up the inside of the warehouse. Loud explosions thundered throughout the building. The grenades were meant to temporarily blind and disorient any shooters while the SWAT team members quickly covered their area of responsibility.

"No terrorists sighted!" Spencer snapped into his lapel mic. "Area clear and secured."

After their explosive entry, a Remington Technologies Division Eye Ball was carefully rolled toward the bunker. In the now quiet warehouse, the baseball-sized surveillance device sounded like an errant bowling ball as it rolled toward its destination, transmitting live audio and video to the monitor mounted inside the mobile command vehicle.

"Clear! No encounters," Spencer reported. "Bring in the radar!"

A radar system was hurriedly wheeled into position about sixty feet away from the mysterious compartment. The microwave unit saw through concrete walls, providing a real-time video of what was hidden to the naked eye. The team hunched over the tiny eight-inch display monitor, straining to see what lay behind the walls. The resolution was not great, but Spencer could easily count the shadowy gray figures moving in the compartment in front of them.

"Looks like we have eleven combatants!" Spencer reported as he stared at the monitor. "Permission to engage?"

"Engage," O'Malley responded.

As the SWAT team moved into position, they momentarily froze as they heard a scream coming from inside the bunker. *"Al-Hamdu lil-Allah! Allah be praised!"*

Gunfire suddenly erupted from the assault weapons that protruded from the small slots embedded in the compartment walls. The noise was deafening as the sounds of the firefight echoed through the warehouse.

A SWAT member howled in pain, falling backwards after taking a three-round burst to the chest. "Medic!" another yelled as he pulled his wounded partner out of the line of fire.

The injured officer was the only casualty, as the terrorist's spray-and-pray combat techniques were sloppy and ineffective, making much more noise than damage.

"Pull back!" O'Malley calmly commanded.

Over a secure line, O'Malley gave a brief assessment to his boss, the Long Beach chief of police. "We've entered the target building. Receiving automatic weapons fire from eleven heavily armed, probably Islamic, terrorists. They're housed in a strongly fortified bunker within the warehouse. We've pulled back." He added, "If there's a nuclear device, it's likely in that room. Even if we're able to secure the nuke, we have no way to disarm it."

"Got it covered. Maintain sufficient resources to secure the area, but evacuate nonessential personnel. FBI SWAT teams will arrive in less than an hour," the chief replied.

Just before noon on Saturday, O'Malley gave the order to evacuate civilians and as many nonessential resources from the incident site as possible. His teams maintained visual contact with the bunker in which the terrorists were hiding but initiated no further action. Less than an hour later, the out-of-area NEST and FBI SWAT teams arrived and were hurriedly escorted to the ICP and staging area. Until they arrived on the scene, O'Malley was the single incident commander. Now, with the involvement of multiple agencies and the presence of resources more experienced with nuclear terrorism, command was transferred to NNSA's General Franklin.

O'Malley briefed his successor on the operation.

"What's been discussed on the subject of evacuation?" was Franklin's opening question.

"We've evacuated civilians within a half-mile radius of the warehouse. We've also evacuated civilians and nonessential resources from the incident site. City and state officials have maintained close contact with the feds, but at this time, no general evacuation alerts or evacuation orders have been given. In the absence of any concrete evidence of an actual nuclear device, the fear is that a wholesale evacuation of Long Beach would cause pandemonium, exposing the evacuees to unnecessary risk."

After listening to O'Malley's recap and consulting with nuclear scientists, the general concluded the best course of action was to destroy the bunker they believed contained the armed nuclear weapon. "As soon as the terrorists have been neutralized, NEST personnel will use explosives to trash the bomb's wiring and prevent the triggering of the nuclear detonator."

Hooking a towing package to a specially configured SSI Python ground robot, the FBI SWAT team placed a six-pound package of C-4 plastic explosive bricks on the trailer. The robot was carefully maneuvered so it could not be crippled by terrorist gunfire. It slowly crawled to the wall of the bunker. Using his remote-control joystick, a SWAT officer remotely lifted the package from the trailer and fastened the plastic explosives to the bunker. This procedure was carefully repeated several times.

"Evacuate the warehouse!" the general ordered.

Minutes later, powerful explosions rocked the warehouse as the C-4 blew gaping holes in the concrete walls. Several terrorists were killed by the blast. Injured jihadists screamed threats and obscenities as they wildly fired their weapons, missing their intended victims. The SWAT teams returned fire, and soon, the spirits of the terrorists who survived the blast joined those of their dead comrades.

A NEST team quickly entered the blast site, their gamma and neutron detectors searching for any signs of elevated radiation levels.

To the team's shocked surprise, no radiation source was found.

SWAT teams continued to patrol the secured perimeter as the mop-up operation proceeded into the night. The next morning, NEST teams resumed their citywide search for a nuclear weapon, but without specific intelligence, it was like searching for the proverbial needle in a haystack.

*   *   *

To the casual observer, the building less than a hundred yards from Akbari Enterprises looked empty. The dilapidated sign over the sagging front entrance read, "Shamrock Technologies Corporation." The building's lone occupant, who had ignored the prior day's SWAT warnings to evacuate the area, was studying the security device attached to the nuclear weapon hidden in the basement of the building. Called a Permissive Action

Link, the purpose of the device was to prevent unauthorized arming or detonation of the weapon.

The PAL currently under scrutiny was primitive, little more than a lock that was inserted into the control-and-firing system of the weapon. The nuclear scientist-turned-terrorist was obviously intimately familiar with the technology. He quickly performed his task. Kneeling toward Mecca, he began to chant the last words he would speak before being welcomed to a jihadist's paradise: *"Inna Lillahi wa inna Ilahi raji'un;* we are from Allah to whom we are returning."

Since turning over command of the operation to General Franklin, O'Malley had been monitoring the operation from the former LBPD command center. He was standing outside the trailer, sipping a cup of coffee, happy to be alive.

As the unknown jihadist whispered his ominous prayer, O'Malley heard Rivera loudly calling his name. "O'Malley! Akbari's also the owner of the vacant building a block south of here—Shamrock Technology. We need to get inside!" O'Malley let out a cry of dismay but did not have a chance to respond to Rivera's urgent call.

* * *

The Larsens had spent a cold night in a grassy community park not far from the Yellow Tickets Entry Gate to the Long Beach Grand Prix. The family looked forward to the carnival atmosphere of the three-day event as eagerly as the thousands who flocked to Pasadena's annual New Year's Day Parade. The two Larsen children spent the night on comfortable cots in a warm pup tent while Larry and Megan, their parents, tossed and turned in their undersized sleeping bags. Larry had just finished frying some sausage and eggs, while Megan was trying to balance the meal by enticing the children with generous portions of fresh fruit.

"Come and get it!" he shouted. The kids raced to their father as Megan finished slicing the last of her children's favorite health food. "Want bananas, pineapple, or both?"

* * *

In the nearby city of Anaheim, thousands had descended upon Disneyland, the "happiest place on earth." Chung and Hua, UCLA computer science majors from China, had never experienced the thrills of Disneyland, so they chose the Magic Kingdom for their first date.

"So Hua, you choose! We'll start with your favorite ride."

"Sounds good to me. Since I was a kid, I've seen pictures of the Matterhorn. I know there are scarier rides, but that's the one I want to go on most."

"Let's go!"

* * *

Jack Preston, a seasoned driver for Metro, the Los Angeles County Metropolitan Transportation Authority, was fuming as he left the Del Amo station. *What was I thinking! Why in the world did I answer the phone?* Preston glanced at his watch. *Supposed to be in Big Bear 'bout now!* He and his wife had planned this weekend retreat months ago. He replayed that morning's unexpected telephone conversation.

"Hey, buddy, Mike here. Hamilton called in sick. Gotta cancel your weekend plans. Real sorry, buddy, but I'm down several drivers. Tell you what. Take the Compton to Long Beach route today, and I'll tack an extra day on your next three-day weekend."

The Metro bus was pushing seventy miles per hour as Preston and his passengers rolled south on the Long Beach freeway. Traffic was heavy, but fortunately, no traffic jams. *Everyone's moving about the same speed—a little too fast,* Preston said to himself, *but hey, this is Southern California!*

* * *

Suddenly a groundburst nuclear explosion created a blinding flash of light.

The temperature of the fireball instantly reached tens of millions of degrees. The intense heat vaporized everything inside the fireball and was carried upwards, forming a twenty-thousand-foot-high mushroom cloud. Simultaneously, an electromagnetic pulse drove an electric current through underground wires, causing extensive physical damage and severely interrupting communication networks in Long Beach and the surrounding communities.

Not far away, Megan Larsen screamed in terror as she vainly tried to shield her children from the incredible brightness.

*   *   *

Chung and Hua were standing toward the front of the line, waiting to ride the Matterhorn, Disney's signature roller coaster, when they heard a thunderous explosion.

"What was that?" Hua yelled as she stared into the skies to her east. "It sounded like a bomb went off!" She saw the quizzical expression on her boyfriend's face suddenly turn to fright as he too stared into the heavens behind her. "Look at the mushroom cloud! Someone's dropped a nuclear bomb on Los Angeles!"

Hoping he was making a terrible joke but choking back her fear, Hua whirled around to see the frightening cloud spiraling into the clear blue sky. She grabbed Chun's hand and began to urgently pull him toward the exit. "Come on, Chun! We gotta get outta here!"

Thousands of theme park visitors began to scream hysterically as they, too, raced for the exits. Chun and Hua leaped over several elderly visitors and a few small children who had been knocked to the pavement by the panicked crowd, ashamed for not stopping to help but driven by the instinct to survive.

*   *   *

The explosion generated a shock wave that caused enormous damage to structures within a several-mile radius of Akbari Enterprises. Older buildings collapsed into mountainous heaps of plaster, brick, and twisted rebar. Almost every window of every building in the blast area was blown out, the explosion propelling millions of sharp shards of glass into anything that would hinder their flight—bodies, vehicles, trees.

The Larsen family died quickly as the violent shock wave obliterated the small park in which they were camping. More than one hundred thousand others suffered the same fate as the Larsens, two-thirds of whom were Grand Prix spectators lining the streets of Long Beach. Most were killed by the intense heat, while many others died when their bodies were hurled into immovable objects by the shock wave, crushed by falling buildings, or struck by flying debris. Thousands more suffered severe burns to their skin and eyes.

Still pushing seventy miles per hour, the speeding Metro bus was nearing the point where the 710 becomes Shoreline Drive when the brilliant flash blinded Jack Preston's vision. Just before he lost his sight, Preston thought he saw the brake lights of the car ahead of him, so he instinctively swerved to his left to avoid the crash, striking two cars in the process. He slammed on his brakes as he twisted the wheel sharply, much too sharply, to his right. The bus began to slide and then tumble end over end, crushing a dozen vehicles in its path. Sparks flew as the roof of the tumbling bus scraped the rough pavement, coming to a shrieking and sudden stop as it crashed into the belly of an overturned eighteen-wheeler.

Injured, dazed, and blinded passengers crawled out of their vehicles, clueless and terrified by the smell of gas that drenched the surface of the highway. The sparks ignited the gas-laden air, and in seconds, a mile-long stretch of the 710 was an inferno.

Hundreds of others along the major highways were temporarily blinded by the blast, causing massive accidents and traffic jams within a ten-mile radius of the detonation.

The devastation was beyond belief. Besides the homes and businesses that vanished at the moment of the explosion, thousands of others were destroyed as downed power lines sparked fires throughout the city, fed by ruptured gas lines.

Broken water mains severely hampered firefighting efforts, and damaged roads, bridges, and tunnels prevented first responders from reaching countless numbers who survived the initial explosion but later died from untreated injuries.

The buildings in and around the Port of Long Beach were damaged as well, but not destroyed. The detonation site was simply too far away to cause major damage, although many ships did suffer harm.

Radioactive fallout became the immediate concern of the survivors, of whom 150,000 or more were exposed to hazardous levels of radioactive materials. The panicked patients began to flood the hospitals and medical centers throughout the Los Angeles basin, overcrowding facilities that were already filled to capacity by critically injured and dying victims. Fistfights erupted, and heated arguments and violent threats became commonplace as thousands were refused treatment because of the overcrowded conditions.

There was pandemonium in the suburbs as more than six million people frantically tried to evacuate the area on a severely damaged transportation system, while some of the desperate souls who had no means of escape resorted to looting and robbery. Newly formed gangs of thugs roamed the streets, shattering store windows as they gained entry to the unprotected buildings. The mobs, devoid of conscience, targeted markets and electronics stores first, emptying shelves in minutes. Angry and jealous latecomers to the looting frenzy torched pillaged facilities, now emptied of their merchandise. Fearing for their safety, law enforcement ignored the sound of blaring alarms and breaking glass, focusing on the injured instead. It was even more frightening in the suburbs, as terrorized homeowners indiscriminately fired their weapons at neighbors and intruders alike.

*   *   *

The loss of the port, while not permanent, had a rippling effect across the nation. Some politicians and citizens' groups were calling for the closure of all ports, reducing the possibility of a second attack. Over a million jobs had been lost in an instant, many permanently. Major insurance companies declared bankruptcy because they could not cover the claims; insurance premiums skyrocketed, making it impossible for many transportation companies to operate. Throughout the US, millions of workers were relocating away from the ports for fear of another attack, causing additional port closures that further increased the ranks of the nation's unemployed.

The economic losses were staggering. Immediate costs exceeded one trillion dollars, covering costs that ranged from medical care to reconstruction and dwarfing the one-billion-dollar cost of 9/11. Fearing a collapse of the market, the New York Stock Exchange temporarily halted trading. Many economists began to predict that the US would enter a deep recession. Their predictions launched a global recession. To make matters worse, Iran vowed to launch its nuclear arsenal against America if the US retaliated against any Islamic state. The US government was paralyzed with fear and indecision, and many of its leaders were furious as they recalled the timidity and naivete of past administrations that had allowed Iran to become a nuclear power.

The attack severely damaged the people's confidence in their government. Since 9/11, taxpayers had given the government an open checkbook so it could make sure the country was safe from attack. But vast sums of money had not bought the nation's protection.

The citizens' deep distrust of their government was exacerbated by a deeply divided nation, the fracture that had begun long before 9/11. It centered on the core values upon which many believed the infant nation was founded.

Half the nation had come to believe that freedom was the most honorable national goal, loosely defined as the ability to do whatever one pleased so long as no one of value was harmed in the process. They worshiped a god called *tolerance,* again loosely defined as the acceptance of any behavior, however reprehensible it might seem to the other half, as long as no one they considered of value was offended.

The other half believed that the nation had been founded on principles that had remarkably guided and guarded it for over two centuries. They recalled Alexis de Tocqueville's solemn warning: "When America ceases to be good, she will cease to be great."

Because each group believed its views represented the moral high ground, there was no room for compromise. And so a deeply divided people, frightened and skeptical of their government's ability to lead and protect them, had tragically lost its way.

CHAPTER ELEVEN

Bolshaya Dmitrovka Street, Moscow

"Now is the time to act! America's lost its will to fight! We can plunder the Zionists without fear of reprisal." Viktor Pavlovich, the truculent president of the Russian Federation, made his case.

An extraordinary closed session of the Federation Council of Russia was underway in what was known as the Main Building on Bolshaya Dmitrovka Street in Moscow, the council's customary meeting place. The chairman, Nikita Mihailov, an old crony of the president's, was moderating a debate on Pavlovich's directive that the military invade and occupy Israel. As the supreme commander of the armed forces, the president's demand was within the scope of his authority.

After years of exploration by Israeli companies such as Delek Energy, Givot Olam, Noble Energy, and Zion Oil & Gas, Israel's huge investments of time and money had paid off: following multiple discoveries of vast gas reserves and oil deposits in northern Israel and the Mediterranean, almost overnight the tiny nation had become oil and gas independent. Israel was only one of a handful of the world's democracies that could make this boast. The discovery of a huge offshore natural gas field, dubbed *Leviathan,* would by itself supply all of Israel's energy needs through 2035. And Leviathan was just one field among many. Now Israel was competing with the Russians, piping large quantities of natural gas to energy-hungry western Europe, dramatically curtailing the vast profits desperately needed by the Russian government to fund its military and economic comeback. The Russians and their allies were infuriated by Israel's achievement and alarmed that the little country's success posed a grave danger to national security. To make matters worse for its enemies, Israel was on its way to becoming one of the wealthiest nations on earth.

For decades, the Kremlin's clandestine objective had been to resolve the problems of the Middle East by annihilating the miniscule state of

Israel. Its leaders knew their ambition could not be realized as long as the powerful US was in a position to protect its long-term ally. But of course, that had changed.

"The recent nuclear attack on US soil has paralyzed its government," Pavlovich continued. "The nation's in mourning. Their economy is in a free fall. Their military is standing down throughout the world."

Most members of the council were vigorously nodding their heads in agreement, some shouting occasional words of encouragement.

"Without US protection, Israel is little more than a land of unwalled villages. To maintain, even accelerate, our economic recovery, we must have access to the enormous quantities of magnesium chloride, potassium chloride, and other minerals we could extract from the Dead Sea. But most importantly, we must control Israel's natural gas fields. If the Zionists become the major energy supplier to western Europe, our economy will collapse. Understand: the future of our nation is at stake. While a surprise attack is out of the question, we have an overwhelming advantage in sheer numbers of weapons and personnel. We'll suffer losses, yes, but ultimately, we'll control the Middle East. And the world will thank us for introducing peace to a region that's been at war for generations. Let's not squander this historic opportunity!"

In support of the military action, the president listed a small alliance of nations that was firmly committed to the invasion, including Iran, Ethiopia, Somalia, and surprisingly, Germany and Armenia.

Vladimir Vasiliev, Russia's powerful defense minister, stood and began his own speech. "I agree with our president. Beginning in 2011, we initiated a comprehensive, large-scale rearmament of our armed forces under the direction of then-president Dmitry Medvedev."

Vasiliev was a giant of a man, a head taller than anyone else in the assembly hall, and carried nearly three hundred pounds of solid muscle. He had been a young soldier in the Soviet 40th Army when it invaded Afghanistan on September 24, 1979. While the Soviet military was humiliated by the Afghans, Vasiliev was repeatedly commended for acts of heroism that eventually won him the Medal of Valor, the highest military medal that can be awarded to a Soviet soldier for bravery earned on the battlefield. He rapidly moved up in rank, a genuine hero to the men he led in battle.

Vasiliev knew the Soviets had totally miscalculated the response of the US government to their ill-fated invasion and had grossly underestimated the level of resistance by the Mujahideen, the fierce Afghan guerrilla fighters. The Soviet-Afghan war had been a disastrous mistake for the Soviet Union, but he believed the outcome of this invasion would be different.

"The president's goal was to enhance the combat readiness of all our combat units. In addition, the security council endorsed a national security strategy that takes us through 2030. We have made excellent progress and are equipped and ready for any form of military action."

Eyes turned toward Boris Kozerski, the commander-in-chief of the Russian air force. Like most of the military leaders present, Kozerski feared Vasiliev more than death itself. No one dared to contradict Goliath, the mocking name attached to Vasiliev by the cowardly officers who spoke often behind his back.

Kozerski was customarily assigned the seat next to Vasiliev, and he hated it. Sitting next to Vasiliev, his diminutive stature was even more humiliating, and the marked contrast in size evoked innumerable jokes at his expense. He recalled with embarrassment the stinging rebuke of Makarov, chief of the general staff, who had mockingly said of Kozerski's air force, "They can run bombing missions only in daytime with the sun shining, but they miss their targets anyway." This time, he would prove Makarov wrong.

The red-haired commander was the smallest member of the council, so he stood to make his presence known. "Yes, we're prepared for this mission," the freckled redhead pledged. "Our upgraded air force is better trained and equipped than the Israelis. We'll control the skies over Palestine within hours of the opening attack."

Kozerski's newfound confidence was based on recent weapons deals with the Chinese. As a key component of the rearmament initiative advanced by the former president, the Russian air force had dramatically upgraded its fighter-bomber arsenal by purchasing nearly two hundred of China's new fifth-generation stealth fighters, dubbed the J-20. The Russians chose the Chinese-manufactured fighter after abandoning numerous attempts to build a fighter of their own that could compete with the Americans' nearly invisible F-35 Raptor and the Israelis' F16 and F-35I fighters.

Boris Kozlov, commander of the Russian navy and a closet Christian, vehemently opposed the defense minister. "I believe this strategy will spell suicide for our nation. History demonstrates that God has protected Israel. I realize this isn't a popular position to take, especially among all of you, but I'm a patriot and believe an unprovoked attack may bring about our destruction." His voice held steady, though his heart was anything but. *What a coward I've been! Why have I been so afraid to reveal my belief in a living God?*

Kozlov was a decorated veteran who, like Vasiliev, had moved rapidly through the ranks to admiral. His wife, whom he cherished, was raised an atheist but became a Christian on a holiday in the Czech Republic. A chance conversation with a bold believer in the lobby of Prague's stately Hotel le Palais resulted in her conversion. She matured rapidly in her faith, and by her quiet and steadfast witness, her prominent husband soon followed her lead.

The council members were aghast at Kozlov's suggestion that Israel was protected by God and outraged that he would oppose Pavlovich's scheme. The president, the military leadership, and most of the council stridently ridiculed Kozlov's position, derisively labeling him a religious lunatic, dismissing him as "weak and irrelevant to the debate."

The surly Vasiliev was not accustomed to opposition. He laughed in Kozlov's face. "I heard rumors your wife might be a lover of Jews," he spat. "But I never dreamed she would someday lead you around like one of her favorite pets!"

His career effectively at an end, Kozlov cast the lone dissenting vote to the ill-advised invasion and then excused himself from the council, submitting his letter of resignation the next day.

The military operation, code-named Operation Jericho after the first Canaanite city conquered by the Israelites following their exodus from Egypt, was approved by the council. Following the near-unanimous vote to proceed, the president promised, "Jericho is remembered by Jews as the site of Israel's first military victory in the Promised Land; now it will be forever linked with her destruction."

Operation Jericho would not be a complex operation. The only planned element of surprise was the massive scale of the opening surface-to-surface (SSM) missile attack launched from Russia's ally nations, which would be followed by an assault by the Russian air force. The sole objective of the missile barrage was to cripple Israel's offensive capabilities as quickly as possible. The primary targets would be Israel's air force bases and commercial airports. Once these assets were eliminated, the Russian air force was directed to inflict as much collateral damage as possible on the secondary targets and then maintain air superiority until its mission was accomplished.

After the Russians achieved air superiority with their new J-20s, the coalition, coordinated by the commander of Russian ground forces, would commence the ground assault. Russian, German, and Armenian troops would join the Iranian army at a massing point in northwestern Iran and then follow the winding Turkish-Iranian border west into Syria, eventually assembling in the zone that separates the Golan Heights and Syria. The Ethiopians and Somalis, aided by twenty thousand soldiers of the Quds Force, a special unit of Iran's Revolutionary Guards, would attack Israel from the south, gaining entrance to Israel through the Jordanian port city of al-'Aqabah, just east of the Jordan-Israel frontier. The council anticipated fierce objections—this tactic would be a blatant violation of Jordan's sovereignty—but fences could be mended later. For now, the Russian government would simply warn Jordan not to interfere or the consequences would be severe. Al-'Aqabah would provide easy passage through the mountains, allowing the southern coalition forces to penetrate Israel's southern flank.

* * *

A buffer zone about 8 kilometers long and between 0.5 and 10 kilometers wide separated the Golan Heights and Syria. The Israeli border was called the Alpha Line, not to be crossed by Israeli forces, and the Syrian border the Bravo Line, not to be crossed by Syrian forces. Between these lines was a smaller buffer zone called the Area of Separation, within which the United Nations Disengagement Observer Force operated. The Russians had decided the AOS was the perfect location from which to launch the northern ground attack on Israel, so they commandeered the zone from the UNDOF, which wisely and readily conceded to the demands of the superior force.

Mossad and the Israeli Defense Force were closely monitoring the troop movements on their northern and southern borders. Although they had successfully fought five major wars since Israel's reemergence as a nation in 1948, never had they been in such a perilous situation.

Ariel Shalev, the Israeli prime minister, placed several calls to the president of the United States. His initial calls were not returned, heightening Shalev's dark sense of foreboding concerning the future of the state of Israel.

The US president knew what his response ought to be, but he was struggling over what protection the United States could provide in light of its own calamities. The Senate and the House of Representatives had been brought up to date on the coalition's advance toward Israel. While many of the politicians believed a strong US response was essential, the majority had no stomach for what they knew would be required to protect Israel. In fact, many had already given up hope for their ally, concluding it was only a matter of time before the small democracy was overrun by its enemies. Perhaps now was the best time to let Israel fend for itself; history would be kind concerning the United States's lack of response, they reasoned, given the nature of the recent attack on America and the economic meltdown it had spawned.

When the president finally returned the call of his friend and ally, he sadly informed the prime minister that there would be no help coming from the United States. He assured Ariel that the US, along with its Western allies, had already lodged strong protests with Russia and the United Nations. But apart from that, no other form of aid would be forthcoming.

Shalev was devastated. "Mr. President, Thomas, I implore you! Make every effort to persuade Congress to act on our behalf. The Russians fear your Advanced Hypersonic Weapon . . . I know they fly at five times the speed of sound, giving you the ability to strike targets anywhere in the world in less than an hour. Use them, Thomas! Israel's future rests in your hands."

The president shook his head with deep emotion. Not even the projects coming out of the Pentagon's Prompt Global Strike program would be enough in this situation. "I'm sorry for our response, Ariel, but my hands are tied. I believe the fate of Israel rests in God's hands—not mine. I will do all I can to provide some form of aid, but at the moment, that's all I can promise."

Shalev was not a religious man, but as he hung up the phone and lowered his head into his hands, he instinctively questioned God. "Why is this happening? Why on my watch?"

A decorative prayer book was sitting on a stand in his office. It had never been opened. He picked it up, and it fell open to Isaiah 41:

"All who rage against you
will surely be ashamed and disgraced;
those who oppose you will be as nothing and perish.
Though you search for your enemies, you will not find them.
Those who wage war against you will be as nothing at all.
For I am the Lord, your God,
who takes hold of your right hand."

Shalev was startled by the words. He had been an agnostic all his life—he did not know if there was a God or not, nor had he given the question much thought. But Shalev thought now that if there was a God and the Jews were indeed his chosen people, now would be a good time for him to come on the scene in a big way.

If there is a God and you can hear me, please make yourself known to Israel once more, he pleaded silently.

Unexpectedly, he recalled stories he had read that described a major attack on Israel. The stories were based on future events predicted by an ancient Hebrew prophet named Ezekiel. Shalev called for an aide, directing him to contact a rabbi for the reference to the visions described by Ezekiel. Minutes later, Shalev sat spellbound by the 2,600-year-old story that could have been written yesterday. He was shaken by the striking similarities of Ezekiel's vision to the nation's present circumstances and was somehow encouraged as he left his office to address a hastily convened, emergency session of the Israeli cabinet.

Ariel Shalev was a warrior, toughened by years of combat experience and political maneuvering. But for several minutes, he silently stood before the cabinet, searching for the right words to say. The members waited expectantly, as though Shalev was about to perform a miracle before their eyes. Finally, he bluntly recounted his conversation with the president.

"I've spoken to the president of the United States. While he expressed his outrage at Russia's egregious behavior and great sympathy for our plight, he told me the United States is not in a position to provide any military assistance to the state of Israel." He was silent while all the implications of his statement were fully considered by his audience, and then he continued.

"I have also learned from our ambassador to Russia that the timing of this invasion is no coincidence. The Russian president, Mr. Pavlovich, correctly concluded that the United States will not come to our defense. The ambassador's sources have provided evidence that the Russians' intentions are not to destroy us with their nuclear weaponry but to defeat us in battle, plunder our wealth, and bring to an end the state of Israel."

Shalev left the safety of the podium and marched into the midst of the cabinet members. He raised a clenched fist into the air, punctuating each word of his next sentence with a shake of his fist, shouting hoarsely, "We cannot allow this to happen! Stand up if you're with Israel!"

The entire council stood to its feet, solemn, proud—and very angry.

"We must fight as we've never fought before! The IDF will inflict huge casualties on our enemies; perhaps they will abort their evil mission when it's clear the price of victory is too high. The defense minister has my full support and cooperation for whatever tactics he must employ to defend the state. Consequently, I recommend that this body approve the defense minister's request to use nuclear weapons on the condition they be used only when and if our survival is at stake."

The cabinet members listened intently to the prime minister's every word. Even the opposition voiced their approval of his proposals, and shortly thereafter, the recommendations were passed.

Following the vote, the prime minister returned to the podium to make another brief statement. "You know that I am not a religious man. But in this extraordinary crisis, I've sensed that if there is a God, he is our only hope."

He shared what he had learned from the Ezekiel 38-39 passage and concluded by saying, "May the God of Abraham, Isaac, and Jacob save Israel." Shalev quietly adjourned the session and dismissed the solemn assembly.

* * *

The coalition ground forces north and south of Israel were commanded to hold their positions until the punishing missile and air assault on Israel was completed.

Russia had secretly moved many of their J-20 strike fighters to bases in Armenia, providing for quicker access to their Israeli targets. Each J-20 was carrying air-to-air and air-to-surface missiles in the large J-20 belly weapon bay. The job of the Russian air force was to maintain air superiority after the missiles had destroyed Israel's offensive capabilities and most of its infrastructure.

The Russian navy was the second largest on earth. It was also well equipped, with forty-five percent of its military inventory replaced since 2011. And it knew the Middle East like its own backyard, having established a permanent presence in the region in 2014. Every year since 2008, the Russian navy had completed large-scale deployments in the Mediterranean. The task force currently assigned to the Mediterranean Sea included Kuznetsov-class aircraft carriers, Udaloy-class destroyers, and Slava-class guided missile cruisers.

The order was given to commence the first stage of the Russian attack; at the same time, the coalition forces moved from their positions in the north and south, poised to invade Israel on a moment's notice.

The Mediterranean fleet coordinated the launch of its submarine-launched ballistic missiles with the release of land-based intercontinental and short-range ballistic missiles from various launch sites in Russian, Germany, and Armenia. Cruise missiles were also aimed at Israeli targets from Russian fighter-bombers originating from Russian bases in Libya and Somalia. The decision against the use of nuclear weapons had been made early in the planning stages, so all missiles were carrying conventional warheads. Literally every military base in Israel was targeted, as well as strategically located bridges, ammunition plants, radar command centers, and electric power plants.

Israel's elaborate, overlapping sensor-fused early-warning network was designed to pinpoint the location and speed of incoming aircraft and missiles and was connected to the United States's ballistic missile early-warning system as well. Senior analysts with Israel's National Security Agency were closely monitoring the warning systems when their monitors suddenly lit up like Christmas trees.

"There's a boocoo bunch of destruction comin' our way," one of the calmer analysts muttered to himself.

The eyes of a nearby colleague rolled as he overheard the Jewish-American analyst's slang. "'Boocoo bunch,' huh? Just how many is that?"

"Let's see what David's Sling can do," an analyst cried out, referring to a very sophisticated rocket interceptor system that had been recently deployed.

The dozen or so analysts, along with senior military commanders, were in a secure military situation room outside Tel Aviv. Several left their desktop monitors so they could watch the live satellite feed of the entire Middle East, projected onto a very large viewing window. They were horrified as they watched hundreds of blips, each representing a missile, speed toward their borders. Unless the Defense Ministry's third-generation Arrow interceptor system worked, and worked well, the missiles would strike the tiny nation in minutes. The men and women realized their lives were in jeopardy, knowing the military situation room would be one of their enemies' prime targets. Two or three began to pray for their safety, and the safety of family members whose lives could soon be lost.

"We'll be lucky if we kill one bird out of ten," a controller cried out.

"We're done! There's no way to intercept these missiles," another concluded, and then pleaded, "God, please, no nukes or Israel's gone! Oh God, please help us!"

Then unexpectedly, over the course of a couple minutes, the hundreds of blips disappeared from their monitors and the large screen. "What's happening?" the NSA director shouted in disbelief. "What's going on?" Assuming a catastrophic software failure, software engineers began to shout out the possible causes.

One analyst was pointing to the grid that was projected on the wall-sized monitor. "Can you believe this!" he shouted above the din.

Using the coordinates of the location where each missile had seemingly disappeared, the software program had marked each position by a white dot. The entire monitoring team viewed the screen incredulously, mesmerized by what they saw. Instead of a random series of white marks, the dots created an almost perfect outline of Israel's borders. It appeared that a colossal, invisible wall had surrounded the nation, somehow shielding it from all incoming fire!

Their Russian counterparts were also monitoring the attack from the safety of their ops center in Moscow. They were poised to celebrate their victory when they, too, were dumbfounded when the missiles seemingly exploded at the borders of Israel. They were at a loss for a satisfactory explanation, concluding the computer graphics were simply not credible.

"What happened?" Kozerski was screaming at the intelligence professionals and analysts as they scattered from his presence.

One of the braver military officials stammered an explanation. "There was a server failure; the processor couldn't sift through the masses of data fast enough to accurately project the outcome of the attack." As he spoke, he realized his explanation was wrong, but it was too late to backtrack. "The window froze, giving the appearance that the missiles disintegrated before reaching their targets."

"Get outta here!" Kozerski yelled. "An imbecile could offer a better excuse than that!"

However, Kozerski was also skeptical of the data, unwilling to believe the missile attack had failed. Swearing at the strange complications, he immediately ordered the J-20 strike fighters into Israeli airspace.

Sweeping south from Europe, traveling at twice the speed of sound, the first eight-ship formation of Chinese-made F-20 fighters was quickly in sight of Israel, with successive formations staged several minutes apart. A squadron of F-35I stealth fighters and F-15C Eagles from Israel's elite 133 Squadron, assigned to protect northern Israel, was already at an altitude of ten thousand feet, preparing to engage the invading aircraft now less than eighty miles away. Other Russian formations were also zeroing in on Israel from the Mediterranean Sea to the west, the Red Sea to the south, and even from the east, flying over Jordan.

"Twelve o'clock, dead ahead. Zionist bad boys welcoming us to Palestine," the cocky Russian colonel radioed to the squadron. "Let the games begin!"

"Magniv! It's dogfight time!" The Israelis were itching for a fight. *"Freiers* comin' our way!"

Major Miri Levin, the flight lead, was in the foreship. His wingman, Captain Danny Ben-Ari, was his number two. Ben-Ari spotted the Russian's gray J-20 first, no longer hidden by the patchwork of white and gray clouds that crowded the early morning skies.

"Russian at twelve o'clock!" he cried. Levin got a quick radar lock on the bogey, his five senses now fully aroused by the addictive and all-too-familiar blend of excitement and fear.

"Permission to open fire," the major radioed to ground control. His finger was on the tickle button, waiting for the clear.

"Affirmative; clear to fire," came the immediate reply.

Levin's body tensed as he launched his missile. Out of the corner of his eye, he saw the bright explosive flash as the radar-guided Sparrow blasted out of the F-15 at Mach 3, chasing the elusive enemy aircraft. The J-20 jinked hard to its left and dropped low, breaking the radar lock. *Nice move,* Levin begrudgingly complimented his foe. The violent maneuver caused the Sparrow to miss its target as the missile slammed harmlessly into the desert. Levin copied the hard turn to get on the J-20's tail, its tailpipes now exposed to Levin's heat-seeking missiles. *Gotcha!* Again, Levin locked up the bandit and fired. He heard the muffled blast of the missile as it was launched from beneath the starboard wing of his fighter, but the alert Russian released flares and chaff to decoy the projectile. The Sparrow's navigation system was tricked by the tactic, guiding the missile harmlessly into the chaff. A second miss! Levin's adrenaline was really pumping now. For the third time, the bogey was within weapons parameter, but before Levin could lock up the target, he heard Ben-Ari's excited voice.

"Requesting permission to fire!"

"Affirmative. Clear to fire, Captain," the flight lead responded. Ben-Ari punched the release button, and the missile flew up the hot pipes of the J-20. Ben-Ari's F-35 was rocked by the blast, causing a few creaks, pops, and shudders, but no damage.

"No ejection! First blood," Ben-Ari yelled exultantly.

Within minutes, Levin's squadron had dispatched five J-20s, while the Russians had blown up a couple F-15s and an F-35. The three J-20s that evaded the Israeli missiles streaked toward Israel, their pilots determined to finish their mission.

The Israelis were quickly on their tails, but before their Russian targets reached the kill zone, three brilliant fireballs lit up the darkness as the escaping J-20s appeared to explode in midair. Flaming, twisted aircraft carcasses fell to earth, raining debris on the terrain below. From the ground, it appeared that the fighter jets had collided with a solid but transparent shield. Civilians on the ground saw bright orange fireballs followed by thunderous explosions and wreckage falling directly below the point of impact. It was an amazing sight.

The Israeli pilots were stunned. They quickly performed one-eighties and returned to their cruising positions, waiting for the next wave of fighters to come within range of their missiles.

The NSA director had already witnessed the destruction of the hundreds of incoming missiles, and now he observed the fate of the three Russian J-20 pilots. He radioed the squadrons throughout Israel and quickly outlined his new strategy. "Fly directly toward the enemy, but before you're within their weapons parameter, do a one-eighty and return to the safe zone."

"What happened?" The team leader of the second Russian formation was swearing. "They've disappeared!" One moment the lead squadron was minutes away from their targets deep within Israel, and the next, the J-20s had disappeared from his radar. "Our radar must be malfunctioning. So much for Beijing's advanced radar technology!"

He didn't have time to give the first squadron's disappearance much thought. His radar detected a squadron of Israeli fighters coming straight at him. Suddenly, the formation performed a tight one-eighty and went streaking toward the safe zone within Israel's borders.

"What's *that* all about? Let's smoke 'em!" he encouraged his formation as they approached Israel's border.

Those were the last words spoken by the team leader as he led his fellow fighter pilots into the transparent shield.

As before, the aircraft exploded in midair, unable to penetrate the invisible barrier. Many other squadrons were soon destroyed in the same manner.

Throughout Israel, the IDF fighter pilots were engaging their foes in a dozen or more dogfights, zipping in and out of Israel at will. But invariably, when the Israeli formations baited their foes by feigning retreat, the pursuing Russian fighters would slam into the "wall" while the Israelis passed through unharmed.

"Return to base! Repeat! Return to base!" the commander of one of the Russian squadrons screamed. He was nearly hysterical. "The Israelis have destroyed most of our squadrons! Remaining squads return to base!"

The Russian brass coordinating the strike had lost communication with the several squadrons that were to attack Israel from the western Mediterranean Sea and assumed they also had also been destroyed by unidentified weapons. They were staggered by their losses, with no explanation for the technology that had eliminated their advantage.

The Israeli pilots circling over Israel were screaming with delight, overjoyed by the turn of events. "What's the name of IDF's new weapon? It's incredible! It destroyed almost all the inbound bogeys!" one pilot shouted. Over the radio, another suggested, "Maybe it's the Iron Dome— we've spent over $200 million developing it to shoot down short-range rockets. Maybe it's been secretly deployed."

Israel's defense minister, the Mossad chief, and high-ranking IDF commanders were speechless when they heard the news. "Perhaps the US had a change of heart," the defense minister proposed, but a quick call to the prime minister dispelled that hope. The US had done nothing. For now, they had no natural explanation for the intervention—only euphoria over the miraculous turn of events.

CHAPTER TWELVE

Southern Lebanon

In the late 1980s, a very young Igor Dmitriev had fought valiantly in Afghanistan beside Vladimir Vasiliev, Russia's defense minister. Years later, Dmitriev's promotion to general was strongly endorsed by his long-term friend and comrade in arms. The stubborn curmudgeon was the perfect choice to lead the multinational invasion of Israel, Vasiliev urged. The operation would not be easy, but the obstinate, disagreeable general was the right man for the job. Dmitriev had accepted the difficult command over the strong objections of Mikhail Tretyakov, the commander of the army who expected the top assignment. Tretyakov's objections did not prevail, and he reluctantly agreed to remain in Russia during the invasion.

Dmitriev was speaking to his superiors in Moscow from his temporary command post in southern Lebanon. It was his first briefing following the opening air attack; he was outraged by the disastrous news.

"What do you mean, air superiority has been eliminated? Where's Kozerski?" *Makarov was right. That cretin dwarf couldn't command a group of schoolgirls, let alone the Russian air force!*

"Kozerski's been executed," was Vasiliev's terse reply. "Colonel Gorbachyov now commands the air force."

"When will the second air attack begin?"

"There will not be a second attack," Gorbachyov answered. "The Zionists seem to have perfected a transparent shield that prevents our fighters from penetrating their air space."

Vasiliev changed the subject. "Dmitriev, you're commanding twenty-two divisions; are you prepared to launch the ground invasion?"

"Yes, I have twenty-two divisions, each comprised of fifteen to twenty thousand soldiers. Four hundred thousand troops. But they're from a dozen nations," Dmitriev complained. "The failure of Kozerski's almighty air force may turn what should have been a playground scuffle into another Afghanistan!"

Vasiliev was unmoved. Air coverage or not, he made it clear the invasion was to proceed.

The IDF ranks had ballooned to more than seven hundred thousand troops after Israel mobilized its reserve force. The general was outnumbered, but he was confident the Russian technologists would quickly sabotage the Israeli shield, and soon the air force—under competent leadership this time—would provide the cover he knew he needed.

Overconfident, the general began to review his battle plans.

The northern coalition forces, comprised of twelve divisions, would invade the mountains of Israel via the Golan Heights in the north. Three divisions would move west with the objective of controlling the port city of Haifa and the Mount Carmel area. Six divisions would push south toward the region surrounding the Sea of Galilee. Three more divisions would win control of the Yizrael Valley.

The southern coalition forces, comprised of ten divisions, all of whom were radical Islamics, would follow Highway 90 north through the Paran Desert until the road connected with Highway 40 just north of Ketura. Marching under their black flags, called *al-Raya,* the Muslim warriors would continue north, traversing the winding Highway 40 through the mountains of the southern Negev to the Ramon Air Force Base. The plan was to win control of the base, and then continue until they reached the biblical city of Be'er Sheva, Israel's seventh largest city. After subduing Be'er Sheva, four divisions would follow Highway 60 to the prize, Jerusalem, while the other six divisions pushed west to capture Tel Aviv.

General Dmitriev gave orders to launch the invasion.

*   *   *

Unlike the divisions in the south, the northern army was a force of well-trained, well-disciplined soldiers, most of whom could not care less about Allah, Muhammad, or even Buddha, for that matter. The hilly terrain in which the northern invasion force was operating lay within the Anti-Lebanon mountain range, with Mount Hermon, on the Lebanese border, being the highest point. They descended on the mountainous towns and villages like swarming locusts, quickly defeating small bands of defending soldiers and civilians. After wrestling control of the Golan

Heights, three divisions headed west to engage the defenders of Haifa. After days of fierce fighting, the invaders prepared for a final assault on the city. It would doubtless be bloody, with tens of thousands of Israeli deaths anticipated.

The southern invasion force moved slowly north, delayed by repeated aerial attacks by the Israeli air force. They also encountered strong resistance from Israeli ground forces as the march to the Ramon Air Force Base continued. Located in the sand dunes of the windy Negev, Ramon was one of the nation's most strategic sites for its defense. While the fighter pilots and ground forces assigned to protect the base were still exulting over the destruction of their enemies in the skies of Israel by an as-yet-unidentified form of weapon, they knew the war was not won.

After days of heavy fighting and thousands of casualties, the base was finally overrun by the much larger enemy force. It was captured and destroyed, along with most of its defenders. A short time later, the predominantly Muslim forces overran Midreshet Ben Gurion, a well-known communal settlement. The invaders remained overnight in the settlement, resting in advance of their planned assault on Be'er Sheva the next day.

After taking Be'er Sheva, again with great loss of life, the divisions moved north toward Hebron, planning to capture the ancient town before beginning their ascent to Jerusalem. No one doubted the battle for Jerusalem would be marked by ferocious fighting, with the defenders determined to repel any assault on the holy city. However, while the Iranian Revolutionary Guards were disciplined soldiers, the Ethiopians and Somalis were a ragtag band of undisciplined, uneducated teens, much like the street gangs that terrorized and looted the poverty-stricken neighborhoods of the world's larger cities. The Somalian Islamic Courts Union had sent the young boys into battle, anxious to play some role in the destruction of Israel.

The Iranians knew the angry teens would be no match for the Israelis. Nonetheless, all were confident many Israelis would lose their lives in the next forty-eight hours. And this gave the Islamic soldiers great satisfaction. Soon, some would reap the rewards of martyrdom, while many of their enemies would be slaughtered.

*　　*　　*

Early in the third evening of the land assault, there was a dramatic and unexpected shift in the weather. Satellites revealed a sudden and massive storm front charging east across the Mediterranean, projected to slam into the Israeli coast by early evening. Meteorologists were stunned by the size of the storm but even more astounded by the freakish timing. The first seasonal storms were not expected for another two months.

Given the local weather history, the massive size of the storm took the meteorologists by surprise. As predicted, the rain began to fall a few hours after sundown.

"Let's see what the World Meteorological Organization is saying about this front," the head of the Israel Meteorological Services directed. "We're already seeing record rainfall with no sign of its letting up. Seems like the storm's stalled over Israel, with heavy rain falling in every region of the country . . ." He shook his head, incredulous. "Including the Negev."

*   *   *

After overrunning Hebron, the southern coalition forces had moved on to al-Arroub, a town of nine thousand situated on the edge of the Wadi al-Arroub, midway between Hebron and Bethlehem. The Iranian commanders directed the troops to pitch their tents on higher ground, but the Somalis and Ethiopians ignored their orders, preferring the dry, soft riverbeds to the rocky desert terrain.

It was a fatal mistake. The torrential downpour was flooding the springs that discharged their overflow into the wadis, and a huge amount of water was accumulating on the higher ground north of al-Arroub. The dry desert sand had soaked up as much rainfall as it could; the runoff was pouring into the riverbeds. The storm had already dumped more than eight inches of rain in six hours, with no relief in sight.

Dozens of Somalis were suddenly awakened to what sounded like a roaring waterfall. Their camp was about a mile north of the Ethiopians, so they were the first to hear the terrifying sound. Before they could react, a thunderous wave of water, tangled trees, and barrel-sized boulders crashed through their makeshift camp, sweeping thousands of men to their deaths. The murderous flow of water continued its deadly course, crashing into the Ethiopian camp with the force of a hundred freight trains. Thousands more drowned in minutes, while the less fortunate were mercilessly carried along, crushed by the tumbling rocks and debris that were one with the river.

In the mountainous terrain of northern Israel, the coalition forces were also being pummeled by the driving rain. Trucks, equipment, and weaponry were crushed by a relentless barrage of hailstones the size of softballs. Explosive claps of thunder terrorized the soldiers, and bolts of lightning rained fire on men and supplies alike.

Then, without warning, the ground beneath their feet began to roll, slowly, almost rhythmically at first . . . and then the earth began to violently shake, releasing rivers of mud and debris into the valleys in which the forces were positioned. Unable to bear the weight of thousands of tons of water, the sides of the mountains began to slip, spawning catastrophic landslides that buried entire divisions.

The earthquake ended the coalition's assault on Tel Aviv and Haifa as well. All the major bridges leading into the cities collapsed. The highways buckled for miles, and major city streets were blocked by the rubble of fallen buildings. The troops themselves were under a major assault by the forces of earth and sky.

In the ensuing chaos, communication became impossible. A German special warfare combatant crew, manning several miniguns, misunderstood their orders and turned their six-thousand-rounds-per-minute machine guns on the Russian forces, killing hundreds, perhaps thousands, of fellow soldiers. Fierce fighting broke out among the various coalition forces, abetted by the darkness and the screams of the wounded and dying as they mistook each other for bands of Israeli defenders.

The next morning's assessment was grim. A quick polling of the surviving division commanders revealed that hailstones, flash floods, mudslides, and friendly fire, combined with the toll from the gigantic earthquake, already accounted for the death or injury of more than 250,000 coalition forces.

Dmitriev was stunned by his immense losses.

"Retreat is our only option," an aide offered.

"Retreat?" the general roared. "You sniveling coward!" The aide stumbled backward, terrified by Dmitriev's malevolent glare. The furious general yanked a pistol from the holster of a battalion commander standing nearby, firing twice into the aide's chest. The young man fell to the ground, mortally wounded by the gunshots.

"Any other suggestions?" the general asked the petrified witnesses to his act of cold-blooded murder. There were none. Dmitriev stomped to his tent in a smoldering fury while the intimidated group disposed of the body.

In light of the horrific casualties, coalition forces assumed the next order given by their commanding officers would be for the invaders to withdraw from the occupied territory. As the troops were packing their gear in preparation for the inevitable retreat, an Armenian soldier began to complain of a headache that seemed to come from nowhere.

"Quit your whining. A little headache is the least of your worries right now!", a member of his unit responded.

"But I was fine a few minutes ago. And then this splitting headache . . . and fever too, I think. I'm burning up!"

The perspiring soldier feverishly scratched a rash that was spreading across his itching face, neck, and back as his capillaries burst. He dropped to his knees and then fell to the ground, writhing in sudden intense muscle and joint pain.

He looked up at the small group of soldiers who had gathered around him, his eyes opened wide in fear. "My stomach . . . my throat . . ." Blood began to trickle from the mouth of the dying soldier. "Breathe . . . can't breathe . . ." he choked out.

"Medic! We need a medic here!" a friend of the Armenian screamed.

Another soldier sprinted to the circle of men. "I'm a medic. What's wrong?"

As the friend described the symptoms, the medic, who was familiar with tropical diseases, was reminded of similar symptoms linked with dengue hemorrhagic fever, although he had never seen the disease ravage a person's body so quickly. If it was dengue fever, or something closely related, he was sickened by the knowledge of what would follow. There was no vaccine for this dreadful disease.

"Doc, now his nose is beginning to bleed! You gotta stop the bleeding!" a soldier cried out.

Moments later, the disoriented soldier began to vomit greater amounts of blood as the hemorrhaging ruptured his gastrointestinal track.

"Help . . . please . . . help me!"

His breathing became shallow, and seizures gripped his body. He began to shake violently before going into shock, dying minutes later.

Soon dozens, then hundreds, and then thousands began to show the same symptoms. Panic swept the troops as the mysterious plague attacked the survivors of the prior night's carnage. Some asked for God's mercy and forgiveness as they neared death's door, while others cursed and blasphemed God because of their pain. Soon it was quiet. Pools of blood covered the ground, and the bodies of another hundred thousand would-be conquerors littered the open fields, mountains, and deserts of Israel.

Humiliated by defeat, Dmitriev gave the order to retreat before taking his own life.

*   *   *

In another closed session of the Federation Council of Russia, the president angrily attacked the heads of the various branches of the armed forces. This time, Mihailov, the council chairman, said nothing other than to sarcastically suggest to the president that perhaps Israel wasn't a "land of unwalled villages" after all.

Pavlovich turned on Defense Minister Vasiliev first. "You assured the council the military was equipped and prepared for military action, Vasiliev! What happened?"

Vasiliev was still reeling from the events of the past few weeks. Without a logical explanation for their stunning string of bad luck, he had nothing to say. He simply shook his head before giving a rambling defense of their performance. "The Israelis have some kind of an electronic defense shield that our pilots were unable to penetrate. No ELINT, no HUMINT. Not even the Americans are aware of the new system. We'll figure it out, but it will take time."

"Time you don't have!" the president screamed. "We must defeat Israel now!"

Vasiliev glared at his superior. "Nearly four hundred thousand men have died; almost two hundred of our new J-20s have been destroyed; and vast amounts of weaponry, vehicles, and supplies are scattered throughout Israel. How do you expect to launch another invasion now? It will be years before we recover enough to launch another attack, if ever."

Tretyakov, quietly pleased that Dmitriev, and not he, had been chosen to command the invasion, listened to the heated exchange. Despite his relief at not being in Dmitriev's shoes, he was livid that they were being ridiculed and held accountable for events beyond their control. *Our defeat was not at the hands of mortals.* In an extraordinary act of defiance, he boldly confronted his president. "Perhaps Kozlov was right. Perhaps God protected Israel. There is no natural explanation for our defeat."

Enraged by the very suggestion of God's existence, the president unloaded his wrath on the reckless Tretyakov. "There is no God! Do you hear me? There is no God!"

Tretyakov stood fearlessly, his steel-gray eyes locked on Pavlovich as the president continued to harangue the decorated veteran.

"Hundreds of thousands of lives were lost by your incompetence! I want your resignations today—both of you!" the president shouted as he pointed at Vasiliev. "Your disastrous performance is unforgivable. Operation Jericho has brought embarrassment to our nation, squandered years of military preparation, and wasted billions of rubles."

The president returned his attention to the council. "We will destroy Israel once and for all. The next attack will not be for plunder. We'll turn Palestine into a desolate wasteland, unfit for any form of life. And as for this preposterous talk about a god who watches over Israel—it is foolishness! If such a god exists, then let him confront me if he dares! No god of any nation can deliver Israel from my hand!"

A thundering voice interrupted the president's blasphemous rant, striking fear into the hearts of the council as they jumped up and turned to find its source. The voice seemed to come from nowhere.

"The nations will know that I, the Lord, am the Holy One of Israel. I am against you. I am the one who dragged you into battle for the purpose of judgment. I have given your hordes a burial place in Israel, and now I will rain fire upon you and your allies."

The council members had sunken back into their seats; the president stood at his podium, petrified and unable to speak. They were overcome by a dreadful anticipation of imminent judgment. The leaders instinctively knew they had been judged by God and been found wanting. Trembling, they awaited their fate, fully conscious that their lives were now in the hands of the very God whose existence they and their predecessors had denied for generations.

*   *   *

At the University of Moscow, a Russian School of Astronomy professor was presenting his lecture on meteors at the same time the pompous Russian Federation president was challenging God.

"It's a mistake to believe meteorites slam into the earth. It's more accurate to say the earth passes through their paths, colliding with them in much the same way a speeding train collides with a swarm of insects—often with similar results." The professor chortled at his humorous remark, but the students just yawned, anxious for the lecture to end.

At that very moment, traveling sixty-six thousand miles per hour, the earth began to pass through a spectacular meteor shower.

"Approximately five hundred meteorites that are less than thirty-three feet in circumference strike the earth each year. While some of these minor impact events do cause deaths or damage, most do not," the professor droned.

The lackluster lecture was interrupted by the explosive sounds of objects striking the campus. The building trembled violently with each strike, causing students to run to the windows of their fifth-floor classroom, desperate to find the source of the violence. Others screamed in fright, diving under desks or running into the interior hallways of the aging building.

"That building's going to be hit!" one of the students shouted as she pointed to a complex about two hundred yards away. There was a spectacular explosion as a large flaming ball struck the physical sciences wing. A fiery hail of smaller, golf-ball-sized globs was pulverizing the campus, destroying trees, gardens, and the many statues of luminaries that had graduated from the prestigious school. Thick black smoke billowed from windows as buildings gave way to the flames.

"Oh God, please! Look out! We're going to be hit, too!"

This meteor shower was different from the ones described by the monotonous professor. Besides the multitudes of smaller pieces of fiery rocks, hundreds of larger meteorites, no smaller than a Volkswagen van, were also striking the earth.

Moscow was the first Russian city to be destroyed by the meteorites that were wreaking death and destruction upon the proud land. Bolshaya Dmitrovka Street, the location of the council meeting where the president was making his speech, was turned into a mountain of rubble. No council members survived.

Tobolsk, St. Petersburg, Novosibirsk, Omsk, Uta, and dozens more of Russia's largest cities were destroyed as they passed through the immense brimstone shower. Naval, army, and air force bases across the nation became smoldering ruins. Almost a thousand commercial aircraft were struck by the flaming pieces of brimstone, causing enormous damage as they crashed into towns and villages. Tens of millions of citizens died in the unnatural disaster. Livestock, crops, and timber were destroyed, and the nation's infrastructure soon rivaled those of the world's poorest countries.

Overnight, Russia's world status was reduced to that of a third-world nation. The once-great nation would become an insignificant bystander to the events that would soon impact the lives of every inhabitant of earth.

Meteorites also damaged cities bordering the coasts of Ethiopia and Somalia, as well as the heartlands of Germany, Armenia, and Iran. While the punishment meted out to the coalition of nations that had attacked Israel was not nearly as severe as that experienced by Russia, they were crippled economically and agriculturally, never to fully recover.

The calamitous misfortunes of Russia and its allies received most of the world's attention, although the Islamic world was in a frenzy because of the destruction caused by a spectacular hail of fire and brimstone that attacked a religious shrine which for centuries had stood watch over the Temple Mount. The building obliterated by the wayward fireball was reverently called Kubbat as-Sakhra by Muslims and the Dome of the Rock by Westerners. Amazingly, no other damage was inflicted on the site revered by Jews, Christians, and Muslims alike.

*　　*　　*

Romiti was restive. It was past midnight in Washington DC, and the ambassador was sitting alone in his spacious Embassy of Italy office, located just off Embassy Row in the US capital. He was not in control. Nothing was more maddening to the imperious diplomat. He was fuming over that day's ill-considered United Nations decision to relocate its headquarters to Babylon because of America's diminishing leadership role among the nations of the world. It had always been his dream to lead the international body from its prestigious New York location.

An attack like the one in Southern California had been anticipated by Romiti, but the extraordinary number of casualties and the magnitude of the economic losses had not. And now the disastrous conclusion of the so-called Ezekiel's War would undoubtedly upset the balance of power among the nations of the world even more. Worse, the destruction of Israel's enemies focused new attention on the God of the Jew and the

Christian. Around the globe, Jews and Christians, and even a number of Muslims, were publicly giving God the glory for Israel's deliverance. *How can I use this global upheaval to my advantage?* he wondered. *I will become more powerful than any god and fix the mess. Nations will someday rise and fall at my command.*

*   *   *

In the solitude of his office, the Israeli prime minister pondered the events of the past several weeks. His nation had been miraculously spared certain destruction. There was no natural explanation for the shield that had prevented the missiles and jet fighters from entering Israel. The natural disasters that devastated the invading forces could not have been mere coincidence. Shalev read and reread Ezekiel 38-39, struggling to hold his emotions in check as tears of amazement, joy, and gratitude fell from his eyes. Without a doubt, he knew the ancient prophet's predictions had been fulfilled before his very eyes.

He recalled the words he had spoken aloud just days before the failed operation. *"If there is a God, and you can hear me, please make yourself known to Israel once more."*

Shalev recognized that God had answered his prayer in ways that far exceeded his capacity to comprehend.

He prayed once more. "I now know there is a God of Israel. Forgive me for failing to recognize this truth before today. But I don't know what to do with this knowledge. Please God, reveal yourself to me in a personal way. Show me how to shepherd your people, as you showed David, the second king of Israel."

Outside Shalev's office turned prayer closet, people were celebrating in the streets over their unexpected and astounding rescue. He could hear the pleasing sounds of music and laughter drifting through his window, and he smiled. The prime minister had declared a national day of celebration, officially naming it *Yom Peletah,* Day of Deliverance. Upon learning of the national holiday, many heads of state sent congratulatory letters to Shalev, some even crediting God for Israel's victory. Many of the letters were spread across his desk, further reminders that God had broken into his life. People were literally dancing in the streets of Israel as they celebrated from one house to the next. Many *bet knessets* opened their doors in the evening, inviting passersby to enjoy readings from poignant passages of the Torah.

Virtually every messianic congregation held special services, honoring the God of Israel for his miraculous intervention.

* * *

Disillusioned Muslims, already in despair over the failure of Islamic governments and religious leaders to address the most basic of human needs, were searching outside their religion for truth. Many had abandoned Islam, no longer believing it could give them a sense of purpose or meaning in life. After seeing Israel's miraculous deliverance, millions of Muslims flocked to the Internet, eagerly reading the blogs of Christian teachers that had predicted the conflict and its unlikely outcome, written months and even years before Ezekiel's War took place.

After meeting privately with former Muslims who had converted to Christianity, several radical clerics acknowledged that God had intervened on behalf of the Jews and publicly confessed Jesus as their Savior.

Al-Jezeera was the first network in the Middle East to air interviews with the converted clerics. After allowing two of the imams to present their stories without interruption, the correspondent began to ask probing questions of the converts.

"If you believe that God intervened on behalf of the Jews, why did you convert to Christianity and not to Judaism?"

"That's a good question," one of the men replied. "I have learned firsthand that many rabbis deny the possibility of having a personal relationship with God, and several we have talked to are ambivalent about God's role in their defense."

The al-Jezeera correspondent was disgruntled with the partial answer, so he pressed his point. "These may be valid reasons for not choosing Judaism, but why choose Christianity? Do you believe—"

Another imam, clearly excited about his newfound faith, interrupted the correspondent. "May I answer the question? Christians clearly credit God for supernaturally protecting Israel. Given the evidence, this is a logical and truthful conclusion. It seems to me that rabbis, and even liberal theologians who claim to be Christians, who are ambivalent about God's role in Israel's supernatural deliverance are denying the truth. Secondly, Christians believe that through Jesus, one can be reconciled to God. Even as an imam, I longed to know if I was loved and accepted by Allah. But until my conversion, this knowledge eluded me."

The first imam wanted to make a final point. "After Jesus appeared to me in a vision, I contacted two or three people who I was told were Christians. They evidenced a divine encounter with a living God, provoking me to seek a similar experience."

The interview ended with the al-Jezeera correspondent asking a pointed question. "Your conversion to Christianity is not popular among the peoples of the Middle East. Are you concerned for your safety?"

"We are not," one cleric answered boldly. "To be absent from the body is to be present with our Lord." He laughed softly, confessing, "I just memorized this verse today!"

The next day, al-Jazeera was shooting live on the Temple Mount; the destructive effects of the meteorite shower that had rained on Kubbat as-Sakhra were clearly visible in the background, serving as the backdrop for the news story. The converted clerics who had been interviewed the previous day were boldly proclaiming their newfound faith to a small crowd of Muslims gathered near the impressive al-Aqsa Mosque. The scene was tense as the passionate crowd was divided, with some wanting to hear the imams' story and others threatening violence if the men continued to speak.

"We cannot deny that once again, God has miraculously defended the Jewish state," one of the imams began.

It was not the most sensible way to start a dialogue. The words inflamed many in the audience, several of whom began to shout that the men must leave the Temple Mount.

Still, he continued. "We know that many Muslims are carefully studying the acts of Jesus through a host of websites and blogs created and maintained by committed Christians who are not intimidated by our threats or the threats of radical atheists and religious opponents.

"In the past, we have issued fatwas prohibiting Muslims from visiting these sites. But in his mercy, God has used this technology to reveal himself to Muslims around the world who genuinely want a personal relationship with him. The miracles we witnessed confirm that the People of the Book serve the true and living God, and as a result, great numbers of Muslims are becoming followers of Jesus."

This news was more than a young Saudi visitor could accept. Looking around, he picked up several rocks the size of small eggs. "Shut up, you blasphemer!" he shouted, to the boisterous cheers of some in the audience. Encouraged, he threw one of the stones at the speaker. The rock glanced off the imam's temple as blood gushed from the wound. The injured cleric bravely concluded his story, a rag pressed tightly to his head.

"We've dismissed testimony from fellow Muslims who claimed to have received visions of Jesus, beckoning them to place their faith in him. We've ridiculed and threatened these former followers of Muhammad with violence, but now Jesus has appeared to each of us in a similar manner, giving irrefutable proof that he is the Christ, the Son of God."

* * *

There were other unexpected benefits from "Ezekiel's War," the name quickly attached to the failed Russian invasion. One month after the invasion, Shalev, along with the Knesset, was listening to a glowing report presented by his environmental protection minister.

"For the first time in decades, all the lakes, reservoirs, and spreading basins of Israel are filled to the brim with fresh, sweet water. This national resource is as valuable as gold. Incredibly, new groundwater sources in the southern, semiarid regions have also been discovered, fed by numerous new underground springs. And most mysteriously, brackish and polluted water, a significant percentage of Israel's total freshwater resources, has been found to be sweet. It seems that as the ancient prophets put it, God has turned our desert into pools of water and our parched ground into flowing springs."

"What about Hamanoh? What's happening there?" one of Shalev's cabinet members asked.

The presiding speaker redirected the question to Yariv Harat, the national infrastructure minister.

"We've set aside one of the valleys north of Jerusalem, designating it a burial ground for the slain Russian coalition forces. We believe it will take as long as seven months for the teams to locate and bury the bodies of the invaders. The Orthodox Jews are clamoring for this work to finish, saying the land is defiled by the rotting corpses. Defiled or not, we're worried the bodies will spawn diseases that will kill innocent Israelis, and we're moving as quickly as we can to cleanse the land.

"Thousands have been employed to bury the dead, so many, in fact, that we've been forced to construct a new town not far from the valley. We named the settlement *Hamanoh,* or multitude, because of the vast number of bodies that are being buried there."

Shalev sat back, marveling anew at his nation's reversal of fortune. The president of the Russian Federation had once boasted of the plunder he would extract from Israel, but instead, the victors had plundered vast quantities of weapons, munitions, and vehicles that had been abandoned by their enemies. Perishable assets, such as food, clothing, and medicines, were burned in the giant dumps created for this purpose.

Truly, he thought, God had been good to Israel.

CHAPTER THIRTEEN

Jackson, Mississippi

The temperature was in the low thirties. Jagged spears of lightning lit up the predawn sky, followed by loud claps of thunder that urged the town's inhabitants to remain in their beds. Sticks sprinted from his parked car, unable to escape the torrential downpour. The howling winds whipped across the parking lot, driving stinging pellets of rain into his face. The thirty-yard sprint to the Village Bakery left him breathless and wet. *Need a better set of wheels!* He was soaked to the bone, his teeth chattering.

As he entered the bakery, he saw several pastors chuckling at his predicament. They had commandeered a table next to a blazing fire and were already sipping their coffee and appreciating their escape from the violent storm.

"Laugh now, men, but in about an hour, y'all will be as wet as me!" Sticks predicted. He thought, but didn't say, *Good to see the smiles on some of your faces!* It had been almost two months since the terrorist hit on Long Beach. Since the attack, the breakfast meetings had been somber occasions as the men rehashed the graphic and heart-rending scenes that were repeatedly shown on the various news outlets. The nation's economic meltdown, Wall Street's reaction to the explosion, was also affecting many members of their respective congregations—skyrocketing prices, layoffs, and plant closures were beginning to take their toll.

Among his fellow pastors, Larry Phelps had a reputation for being an excellent teacher and pastor. Among this group, he was the pastor of pastors.

As their weekly breakfast meeting began, one of the men expressed his uneasiness over his congregation's misplaced priorities.

"It just seems like Christians are hunkering down, too timid to stand up for what's right," the pastor lamented aloud, bits of scrambled egg stuck to his chin.

"Give us a break!" another said as he poked fun at his colleague. "You've got egg all over your face!"

"I've noticed the foxhole mentality too," another admitted. "Many are embarrassed by the name-calling—they're intimidated by people who label them 'narrow-minded' or 'homophobic.'"

"Or the worst label of all, 'intolerant,'" another added. "In fact, it's worse than that. Now, not only are we condemned for being intolerant, we're being attacked for not *affirming* lifestyles and behaviors which are contrary to Scripture! It's only gotten worse since Long Beach—seems like most people are determined to defend their 'freedoms' more than ever. Many believers can't take the heat. Of course, on top of all this, now some insensitive Christians are blaming 'sinners' for the Long Beach attacks, causing grief for multitudes of believers who are trying to share their faith in the aftermath of the blast."

Sticks listened to the conversation as he recalled his dash to the restaurant. "None of us wanted to get caught in this morning's storm. I saw how happy you were to escape the hail, lightning, and thunder. In fact, y'all looked pretty cozy right now, sitting by the blazing fire. Likewise, it's natural for the folks in our congregations to want to escape the virulent attacks of people who don't understand what it means to have a meaningful relationship with God."

Ken Stoddard, Sticks's prayer partner, jumped into the conversation. "You've made a good point, Sticks. We're also living in an age when the church is being divided between those who *profess* to be Christians and those who are the true followers of Jesus. The apostle John warned that segments of the church would lose their first love—some would tolerate jealous bickering and gossip, sexual immorality and false teaching; and others would be lukewarm in their faith, even dead."

"As pastors, we must lead by example," Sticks encouraged the small group. "We want our churches to be representative of the faithful churches John writes about, right? So we must warn our parishioners that the world's attitudes toward believers will only get worse. We must teach them to endure the hardships that will come because of their refusal to go along with the crowd. Unlike our present refuge from the storm, there will be no easy escape from a culture whose values are becoming so radically different from ours. Our refuge must be in Christ alone."

Sticks paused, aware that he might be about to step on some toes. "And part of this may be our fault. We've been teaching a rescue mentality in some of our last days sermons—and I don't think we can keep doing it. If Long Beach taught us anything, it should be that we're not just going to escape unscathed. Some of us may be imprisoned for our faith. Some may even die. So it's our job to prepare the church for what may be ahead so that when things begin to heat up, no one will be surprised."

Stoddard added, "John warns us to be faithful, even to the point of death. Through John's pen, we know that Jesus commands us to endure patiently, never denying him. I feel this is the message I must get across to my church."

As their discussion came to a close, Sticks quickly outlined the sermon series he had prepared for the coming weeks. He explained that it would address many of the topics they had just discussed over breakfast. The NBA pro-turned-pastor's series was entitled "The Seventieth Week of Daniel."

One of the pastors closed the meeting with a brief prayer, and then seven men made a dash for their cars.

* * *

Interest in the end times was high, and soon, record crowds were in attendance at Larry Phelps's church. What began as a Sunday morning series soon expanded to Sunday evenings, and then to Tuesday and Wednesday evenings as well. The chapel, which could only seat four hundred guests, was packed to capacity every service. He delivered the same sermon four times every week, each time to an almost entirely different crowd.

The sermon that first caught the attention of his rapidly growing audience centered on the war of Ezekiel 38-39. Sticks explained that the event this passage described was one of the birth pangs leading up to the seventieth week of Daniel—and he hardly had to explain what a stunningly accurate portrait it was of Russia's recent and spectacular demise. Even Russia's allies in the failed invasion could be found in the list of peoples identified in Ezekiel 38. His congregation, all of whom had seen images from the attack on TV, could not keep silent. Every day, they repeated to their friends and neighbors what Sticks taught would happen next.

David Lowry, the founder and president of a biotechnology firm called Innovative Biotech Solutions, already a follower of Jesus, was invited to one of the services. He was quickly impressed by the clarity and relevance of Sticks's message. Lowry knew that hundreds, more likely thousands, of pastors, teachers, and evangelists were delivering similar sermons in the aftermath of the Long Beach attack and the failed invasion of Israel. He was convinced that he needed to lend his strong support to a local voice that was addressing the end-times issues confronting the church and the culture, and he wondered what talents and resources he could offer the pastor.

Lowry caught up with Sticks after one of the services.

"Hey, Pastor Phelps. Informative sermon on the coming one-world government. It's remarkable how clearly world events are mirroring the voice of the prophets, isn't it?"

"Folks 'round here call me Sticks," Phelps said. "Glad you were able to visit this evening. And yes, it's very remarkable."

"Are your messages uploaded to the church website?" Lowry asked.

Sticks laughed. "No church website. We've discussed one several times but never had the budget for it."

"We'll fix that in a hurry," Lowry promised.

Soon, IBS had built and launched a site that featured Sticks's sermons, links to related sites, sermon notes, and information that fully explained how one becomes a follower of Jesus. Within weeks, the site was responding to the requests and questions of several hundred thousand seekers and skeptics around the globe.

*   *   *

Romiti's surroundings had changed, but his objectives had not. *Nations will someday rise and fall at my command.* His embassy office was no longer in DC, but he was still enthusiastically analyzing the mind-boggling challenges confronting the nations of earth, continuing the obsessive pastime he had practiced since his days at Cal. The only difference between then and now was that the world's problems were immeasurably worse.

He glanced at his watch. Already midnight! He moved away from his desk and walked to his leather recliner. Loosening his tie, he fell deeply into the comfortable chair. Feet up and eyes closed, he began to reflect on the changes and challenges that were confronting *his* world.

The world's centers of power were changing faster than a Hollywood celebrity could swap partners. The United States, once the most powerful nation on earth, was on the sidelines, refusing to play—or incapable of playing—its traditional role as the world's peacekeeper. Russia was decimated, no longer relevant to the planet's future. China, now unquestionably the world's single great power, had decided to capitalize on what it viewed as a fortuitous turn of events. Its leaders had made the decision to withdraw from the global community, choosing instead to put their own house in order by investing billions in infrastructure improvements for their citizens.

Following the nuclear attack on the United States, the UN had moved its headquarters, almost overnight, to Babylon, Iraq, a far cry from its former home in the upscale NYC neighborhood called Turtle Bay. The city on the Euphrates was modern and beautiful and located at the crossroads of some of the world's wealthiest nations. Oil-rich Iraq was an island of tranquility in the Middle East, and Babylon, its new capital, had been restored to the position of grandeur and prominence it once enjoyed under its famous King Nebuchadnezzar. All this had come about in the years following the end of the Second Gulf War. After the withdrawal of US forces, a period of violent instability bordering on civil war gave way to an uneasy peace. The government finally stabilized after placating the squabbling Iraqi tribal clans, and soon, the liquid black gold flowed billions of *dinars* into the booming economy.

However, inflation now ravaged the buying power of the world's currencies. Governments were collapsing because of the irresponsible, even criminal, actions of their leaders, who had presided over decades-long spending sprees without a thought of the long-term consequences. The citizens of earth were in a fury over the sinking economies, which drove demonstrations in virtually every major city on earth. In Brussels, masked youths threw rocks and firebombs through bank windows. Germans rallied against their government, furious that their standard of living had collapsed because their leaders had bought the lion's share of the debts of bankrupt eurozone countries. Across the Atlantic, there were massive and violent protests against a sweeping round of austerity measures that were designed to keep the US solvent but dramatically reduced the number of entitlements on which many Americans had come to depend.

Banks and financial markets were screaming for an international agency to manage a single electronic international currency. They believed such a system would stabilize the currency's value, eliminate problems with a foreign currency exchange, and prevent governments from creating massive foreign trade imbalances.

The decline of economic activity in the industrialized nations had dramatically lowered the cost of oil, wreaking additional havoc on the economies of many oil-producing nations of the Middle East.

The Middle East was volatile, threatening to erupt in another bloody war. And now in Jerusalem, the capital of Israel, there were daily, and often deadly, clashes as thousands of Muslims and Jews fought over the future of the Temple Mount. Muslims were adamant that their beloved Kubbat as-Sakhra be rebuilt on its former site. Orthodox Jews were equally determined to begin construction on the Third Jewish Temple, absolutely convinced that God had destroyed the Muslim mosque so that Solomon's temple could be rebuilt. There was no chance of compromise as adherents of two of the world's three great religions battled one another, with dozens of demonstrators being killed or injured every week.

Since the collapse of the Tunisian, Egyptian, and Libyan governments in the Arab Spring of 2011, nationalistic youth movements had been rebelling against autocratic regimes throughout the world, including the Middle Eastern nations of Syria, Jordan, Yemen, Bahrain, Algeria, and Iran. And while millions of moderate Muslims had become followers of Jesus, radical Islam was alive and well, threatening the world's democracies with its intolerant Sharia law.

The African continent was no better off, with armed conflicts in Angola, Chad, Eritrea, Uganda, and other nations.

Even relatively stable countries, such as Turkey, Great Britain, France, and Belgium, were experiencing unusually violent demonstrations, usually spawned by radical Islamic student immigrants who were confronting the beliefs and traditions of the natural-born citizens.

Most of the world was clamoring for a one-world government. It was not a spontaneous, global response to a newfound sense of brotherhood or euphoric feelings of a shared destiny, but a frightened reaction to the ravages of war, famine, disease, and poverty. Long ago, citizens had lost hope that their national leaders could lead them from the abyss. Now they longed for a strong leader who would transcend nationalistic pride and politics and restore what they remembered as their paradise lost.

It was in this dangerous, confusing global environment that Romiti quietly and methodically orchestrated his rise to power. He knew he had been born for a time such as this. And wasn't this the promise? *"All your petitions I will grant. You will rule my people over whom I will make you lord."* Yes, he had sold his soul to Lucifer, but in return, he had received the promise. *"All these things I will give you if you fall down and worship me."*

He was energized by the chaotic conditions, seeing them as dangerous adversaries, rivals to be conquered. He imagined himself on a magnificent white steed, bow held high, a conqueror bent on conquest. He would be the one to restore peace and prosperity to a world in desperate need of a savior.

Romiti's musings were interrupted by an unexpected visitor. "How did you get in?" Romiti demanded to know. He remembered his first encounter with the intruder. *This is a vile, malevolent human being; one who has no soul.*

"I told the security guards that I was your helper," was the only explanation offered by Francois Laroque, the mysterious helper Lucifer had promised Romiti. "We have much to discuss."

Until dawn, the scelestious partners charted their heady plans for the future.

CHAPTER FOURTEEN

Jackson, Mississippi

"Scripture teaches that one of the next events on the horizon is the emergence of a one-world government," Sticks said, delivering a message to another overflow crowd one Sunday morning.

"Even now, the stage is being set for this remarkable event. Now what I'm going to describe is a little complicated, but I'm going to try to coalesce what Daniel and the apostle John have told us about the times we're living in. Stick with me, all right?" Phelps began to laugh at the unintended pun. "Stick with me," he repeated. The crowd picked up his reference to his own nickname and noisily groaned at his clumsy humor. This caused Sticks to laugh even more as he picked up his laser pointer.

"We can't go much further into tonight's topic without some charts. Let's pass them out, okay, fellows?" The volunteers began to distribute the handouts as Sticks continued his teaching.

"The Old Testament prophet Daniel, in chapters 2 and 7 of his book, describes four successive Gentile empires. We know that the first three empires mentioned in King Nebuchadnezzar's famous dream were the Babylonian, the Medo-Persian, and the Grecian, or Hellenistic, empires. But Daniel pays particular attention to the fourth empire, predicting it will go through a series of five phases.

"Daniel chapter 2 describes three phases of this fourth, or last, Gentile empire; chapter 7 describes four phases. By interlacing the descriptions given to us in the two accounts, we see that the fourth Gentile empire, which shall 'devour the whole earth,' is different from the others, not only because of its ferocious nature, but because it evolves through phases.

"The Roman Empire was the first phase of this empire. The second phase began when Emperor Valentinian essentially split the Roman Empire in two. This divided empire has continued for quite a long time, with the eastern power rooted in Russia and the western balance of power unevenly distributed among the Western democracies. I'm convinced the third phase, that of a one-world government, is now at hand. Are you with me so far?" Sticks's laser pointer was focused on the part of the diagram that depicted the coming global government. Several members of the congregation voiced their encouragement.

"The coming one-world government will be comprised of ten regions, or quite possibly will form and then divide into ten separate kingdoms. This ten region configuration represents the fourth phase of the empire. Still with me?"

Heads nodded in agreement. Many in the audience were feverishly writing notes, not wanting to miss a detail when they reviewed the subject with friends and family.

"Now, let me digress for a moment. The apostle John, in Revelation chapter 13, introduces a beast with seven heads. The frightening *sixth* head of the beast to which John refers corresponds to the first four phases of the *fourth* Gentile empire that Daniel describes. Clear?"

A few in the audience again nodded their agreement, while several extroverts shouted, "We're with you!" An old-timer actually bellowed, "Amen!" while some begged, "Slow down! Can't write as fast as you can talk!" All were spellbound as Sticks continued the lecture.

"All this leads to a terribly frightening period of time, a period I believe you and I are about to experience. I know things are very grim right now. Some of you lost friends and loved ones in the Long Beach attack. Many of you are out of work or fearful that you may lose your jobs at any moment. So things aren't looking good. But as bad as things are, I believe they're about to get far worse. And let me say that as your pastor, until we meet the Lord in the sky, I'll have your backs. And you'll have mine. We'll go through this together and victoriously, for we already know the ending! We're going to win!"

More shouts of "amen!" spurred him on. "Let's move on, shall we? We're about to enter the one-world-government phase of Daniel's fourth Gentile empire. As I said, it will eventually give way to the fourth phase—the group of ten. Soon after, a strong ruler will emerge, eventually uprooting three of the ten kingdoms or regions; this powerful ruler will eventually become the head of all ten kingdoms, and by extension, all the nations of the earth. He will reign over the fifth phase of Daniel's fourth empire, which is also represented by the seventh head identified by John in Revelation 13.

"We've all heard of this extraordinary man. He's called by many names in the Bible, such as 'the little horn,' 'the king of fierce countenance,' 'the Beast,' the 'desolator,' and 'the man of lawlessness.' But he's most commonly called the Antichrist."

Sticks paused as a heaviness came over him, and his voice softened. "I believe that very shortly, we'll see this beast of a man emerge on the world's political scene. He will be empowered by Satan himself, and if it were possible, his smooth talk and miraculous deeds would deceive the very elect of God. This fifth and final phase of the fourth Gentile empire will be utterly destroyed by the Messiah, whose coming will inaugurate his messianic kingdom."

He cleared his throat. "I've just given a brief overview of what we'll be studying in the coming weeks as we drill down into the details of Daniel chapters 2 and 7. But before we close this morning, we have a little time for some questions."

A young lady, one of over a hundred college-aged adults who had been regularly attending the series for weeks, stood. "So do you believe the Antichrist is alive today? And if so, do you believe he's in power?"

"Your questions have been asked for centuries," Sticks answered with a warm smile. "But if the events we're witnessing today are the ones spoken of by Daniel, John, Matthew, and other Bible authors, then yes, I believe the Antichrist is alive today and is probably in some politically based leadership role right now."

The young lady quickly raised her hand again. "May I ask a follow-up question?"

"Sure, go ahead."

"What about Romiti? Could he be the Antichrist?" she asked nervously.

"Good question," Sticks replied. "Sure, he could be, but it's really too early to tell. As you know, prognosticators have been guessing names for centuries, but none have been correct. But for the sake of illustration, let's talk of Romiti's accomplishments.

"He used an awfully big stick, but he resolved a deadly conflict in Africa that has taken thousands of innocent lives. The war raged continuously for almost a decade but in a matter of months, he put an end to the violence."

Heads nodded appreciatively, remembering the widely heralded truce that brought peace to the African continent.

"Let's look at another example. The Chinese government recently decided to stop buying US treasury securities. Incidentally, Americans are paying more than $500 billion a year in interest on the debt our government has foolishly rung up. If we didn't have that debt, our personal income taxes could be reduced by forty percent! But I digress, don't I?

"If the Chinese had followed through on their decision, interest rates would have skyrocketed. Home prices would have tumbled lower than they are now. The US, already bordering on bankruptcy, would have been pushed over the edge. Romiti understood the seriousness of the situation and single-handedly brought the parties to the negotiating table. The Chinese government reconsidered its decision and has continued to invest heavily in the US, despite that fact that our fiscal house is in chaos.

"I could provide several more examples of Romiti's extraordinary skills, but here's the point I want to make. While it's much too early to predict who the Antichrist is, it certainly can be argued that Romiti is a prototype of the one who is to come—he's charming, an extraordinary speaker, and a brilliant, ruthless, and cunning leader. But I think I've said enough about Romiti for one night, okay?"

"I thought the purpose of the tribulation was to persuade Israel to accept the Messiah, and that the church would be raptured before the tribulation began," a first-time visitor offered.

"I don't have time to repeat some of the ground we've previously covered, but let me say that I believe the Great Tribulation will occur *inside* the seventieth week of Daniel. It will be cut short by the rapture of the church, setting the stage for a period called 'the day of the Lord.' I believe the church will be a powerful witness to the world *during* the tribulation, but will be raptured *before* the day of the Lord, a brief but terrible time in which God will primarily, but certainly not exclusively, be dealing with Israel.

"Okay, we have time for one more question," Sticks said. It was always difficult to draw a session to a close because of the number of questions on the minds of his audience. Once the meeting was over, he knew he'd be there, talking and answering questions one-on-one, for hours more.

An elderly gentleman asked, "What's going to happen to the United States? And how about China? What's going on with them?"

"It seems that neither America nor China are directly mentioned in Scripture. I believe both nations will be represented during the various stages of the Gentile empire, but the extent of their involvement is unclear.

I will be mentioning China in a later study, so I'll refrain from going down that particular rabbit trail right now, okay?"

Sticks closed the meeting in prayer and prepared himself for a long evening.

*   *   *

The United Nations General Assembly was in an uproar, debating what policies must be implemented to restore order to a world that was teetering toward chaos. The representatives of many nations were forcefully arguing that the sovereign rights of every nation be temporarily subjugated to the UN, at least until order was restored throughout the world. Although considered a pipe dream only decades earlier, this scheme, if adopted by the General Assembly and subsequently by the Security Council, would effectively position the secretary-general as a one-world leader. The very idea of a one-world government, led by a single individual, was breathtaking—almost beyond imagination.

What would the new world look like? Weaker nations likened it to a playground without bullies or a neighborhood without gangs. Poorer nations compared it to being adopted by a rich aunt or uncle. Nations ravaged by disease and driven to bankruptcy by corrupt governments imagined a one-world government as the means to making things right.

Historically, the strong, wealthy, and powerful nations had unanimously and vehemently opposed any notion that smacked of surrendering their national sovereignty, but now they were the exhausted casualties of an unending string of bad luck. Perhaps by temporarily agreeing that the sovereign rights of individual nations be subjugated to a set of principles agreed upon by all, a longed-for era of universal peace would ensue.

The Chinese ambassador, Zhang Chanchun, opposed the notion, nodding at his colleagues as he slowly made his way to the podium.

"Mao Zedong. Jozef Stalin. Adolf Hitler." After each infamous name, the ambassador paused briefly for effect.

"Hideki Toji. Pol Pot. Kim Il-sung. These mad dictators ruled with absolute power. History shows they were responsible for well over one hundred million deaths. Untold millions more were beaten, tortured, and displaced by these evil men. This happens when too much control and authority is placed in the hands of an autocrat.

"My nation suffered greatly at the hands of Mao, whose goal was to cleanse politics, economics, and ideas. His goals gave birth to the Cultural Revolution, the revolution with its mission to abolish the status quo: old customs, culture, habits, and ideas. Thirty million Chinese died as a consequence of his ruthless programs.

"I too am perplexed by the enormous problems facing humanity, and I am fearful for our future. But we cannot abolish the status quo, eliminating our proven systems of checks and balances, by recklessly implementing a dangerous experiment that might give us the likes of another Mao, Stalin, or Hitler."

Many were openly sympathetic to the millions of Chinese who had suffered atrocities at the hands of Mao's evil government. But their sympathy did not alter the immensity of the problems they faced now, problems a one-world government could perhaps fix. There was polite applause for Chanchun's speech, but most ambassadors remained on the fence, anxiously waiting to hear Romiti's address.

The Italian ambassador's speech was scheduled to follow a brief recess in the General Assembly proceedings. The Fierce Ambassador, as he had become known, was the unequaled favorite of the UN: innovative, eloquent, passionate, and persuasive, he had successfully implemented several of the recommendations he had introduced during the Berlin conference on sectarian violence less than two years earlier. In a widely heralded UN experiment, Romiti, along with his carefully handpicked cadre of bellicose followers, had been given a broad range of temporary powers over a small group of African nations. For generations, tribal conflicts had decimated populations in these nations, leaving survivors, usually elderly women and children, in a disease-laden state of abject poverty. Romiti's job was to turn things around—quickly. Using the military power at his disposal, Romiti had quickly eliminated the violent thugs who terrorized the populations they ruled—no more leaders than the East LA hoodlums who brutalized the helpless trapped in their neighborhoods. Criminal activities were quickly and severely punished. Food and medical supplies were no longer diverted to black market channels, ensuring the most needy towns and villages enjoyed a steady supply of goods and services. While some of his tactics were heavy-handed, even violating human rights, some would argue, all acknowledged Romiti's effectiveness. He got things done. The motto engraved on a plaque atop his massive mahogany desk said it all: "Don't confuse effort with results."

The UN experiment, the first of its kind, had proven to be an extraordinary success.

Romiti was credited with successfully enforcing peace in regions that for generations were wracked by religious rivalries. He had brutally crushed individuals who refused to compromise and elevated, and generously rewarded, those who agreed to his plans. Peace, and some measure of prosperity, had followed, giving Romiti a strong following among the almost two hundred General Assembly members. The question now in the minds of many ambassadors was, could the results achieved on a regional scale be successfully replicated on a worldwide stage? Many fervently hoped that they could.

The ambassador was introduced to the General Assembly, the enthusiastic applause of his colleagues cheering him on. Full of pride, a smiling Romiti strutted to the podium. *The world needs me, an exceptional leader, who can lead you out of the morass you've created by your stupid and spineless leadership.* He wanted to shout this accusation, but instead began to deliver his prepared address.

"The world has been driven nearly to anarchy by an act of terror perpetrated by radical elements of one of the world's great religions," Romiti began. "More than one hundred thousand innocent American lives were taken in this cowardly, despicable act of violence. I refer, of course, to the nuclear attack in Long Beach.

"The madness escalated when Russia's insatiable greed and lust for power trumped reason, leading to the catastrophic consequences with which we are all so familiar. Its reckless leaders ignored weather satellites that warned of a massive storm front bearing down on Palestine, and two or three hundred thousand unsuspecting troops died. The military failed to anticipate the medical needs of the troops, and thousands more died from a bacterial virus to which the populations of Palestine are apparently immune. As their just punishment, it would seem, the nation was severely damaged by a meteor shower, one of the most violent and destructive natural disasters in modern history."

Most of the General Assembly members were glued to their seats, mesmerized by the passionate orator. To a very small minority, it seemed that Romiti was rewriting history. Where weeks before God had been credited worldwide with Israel's miraculous deliverance, now Russia's demise was the result of poor planning, a bacterial virus, and an untimely natural disaster.

"I believe the world is at a critical juncture, a momentous crossroads. For too long, segments of the global community have been bullied by stronger nations and divided by superstitious notions of good and evil, gods and devils. For the first time since our earliest ancestors crawled out of their primordial swamp, we have the opportunity to come together as a single people, united in our common desire for tolerance *toward* all and peace and prosperity *for* all. I implore you to place the good of humanity before nationalistic pride. I urge you to support the temporary subordination of your nation's sovereignty to a single worldwide governing body, one that will act on behalf of *all* humanity without prejudice toward the disadvantaged populations of earth. Accept that whatever is in the best interests of humanity is also in the best interests of your nation. My friends and colleagues, I urge you to change your world by casting your vote in favor of this historic resolution."

Romiti ended his speech to thunderous applause.

For the second time in his life, Romiti observed a dark cloud, this time filling the General Assembly Hall. Once again he heard the voice whisper, "In you I am well pleased." Laroque, Lucifer's varlet and Romiti's helpmate, had managed to secure a pass to the proceedings. Sitting in the upper public gallery to Romiti's left, Laroque's thin smile betrayed his satisfaction with the way their plans were proceeding. He caught Romiti's glance and quickly returned a thumbs-up, leaving the hall as the dark cloud vanished before him.

For almost the entire speech, the audience had seemed hypnotized by the Italian representative's powerful voice and commanding message. After observing the assembly's reaction to the speech, the minority in opposition simply lost heart. They did not have the will to fight the eloquent and imposing figure who had so powerfully captured the hearts and imaginations of the assembly.

The General Assembly was euphoric as its members anticipated the historic vote that was about to be taken. When the final votes were tallied, the motion to implement a worldwide governing body to which all nations would surrender their sovereignty and individual freedoms was carried with fifty-eight opposing votes, all but one of which were cast by representatives of the Islamic states. China was the only non-Islamic state to oppose the motion.

In the first vote cast by the Security Council, the measure failed to receive the unanimous vote of its members. China was adamantly opposed to the resolution, even threatening to withdraw from the United Nations. However, after a week of intense negotiations in which China won considerable concessions from the world body, the Security Council unanimously passed the motion as well.

For decades, so-called progressives had dreamed of the time when nations would surrender their sovereignty and individual freedoms to a global, one-world government. Their dream, which others would call a nightmare, had finally materialized, but in an environment that was marked by anarchy, turmoil, and confusion.

In the weeks and months that followed the historic vote, world leaders were united in their commitment to global governance and uncharacteristically optimistic about the future. Their feelings of optimism were reinforced by several quick wins that averted certain conflicts.

While North Korea had pledged its support of the one-world government, its leaders remained jealous of their neighbor to the south. Great numbers of North Koreans were starving, exacerbated by a prolonged drought that had withered their crops. In the first test of the UN's commitment to the poorest nations, the North Korean ambassador requested emergency aid for his starving nation. The UN acted swiftly, removing the Supreme Commander of the Republic and every member of the Supreme People's Assembly. The Security Council flexed its newfound muscle by appointing a governor to oversee the DPRK, one who deftly coordinated the transport of food and supplies to the starving nation.

After the loss of several population centers in the cataclysmic events that had brought Ezekiel's War to a close, the Ethiopians were beginning to mass the remainder of their decimated army on their undemarcated border with Eritrea. Before Ezekiel's War, Ethiopia's had been the largest economy in East Africa and one of the fastest growing in the world. Now the newly impoverished nation was envious of Eritrea's prosperity; its agricultural production had dramatically increased since the end of the last Eritrean-Ethiopian war of 2000, and the country's infrastructure had been greatly improved. A new coastal highway had been built, and for the first time in its history, rail lines connected the Eritrean capital with the nation's major cities. Now the Ethiopian government intended to conquer Eritrea, using the spoils of war to restore what it had lost through its participation in Ezekiel's War.

At the request of the Eritrean ambassador to the United Nations, and strongly endorsed by the popular and persuasive Romiti, a small but effective UN peace-enforcing army swept into Ethiopia, easily defeating the ill-equipped army and replacing the Ethiopian president with another UN-appointed governor. Supported by the UN military, the new administrator was able to keep the peace while obtaining the significant financial and agricultural resources the country so desperately needed.

However, despite its many successes, the UN was impotent when it came to preventing acts of terrorism spawned by religious rivalries. Even Iraq was not immune to religious-sponsored terror.

Sunni-Shia tensions were raised when a clan of radical Shiites bombed a mosque filled with Sunni Arab worshipers from the town of Tikrit, northwest of Baghdad. They were avenging the execution of several leading Shiite insurrectionists who had been involved in deadly skirmishes with forces supporting Iraq's ruling Sunni elite. Hundreds were killed or injured in the mosque bombing, and now the Sunnis were vowing revenge through more acts of terror. If left unchecked, the ancient rivalries could unravel the fragile Iraqi peace.

For good or for ill, Romiti was unlikely to leave it unchecked.

CHAPTER FIFTEEN

Jackson, Mississippi

Sticks and Lowry, meeting an hour before the Tuesday evening session, noticed that the auditorium was already full. "Our site's getting over two million hits a day," Lowry reported. "We've been monitoring the traffic and have found some really interesting patterns too. For example, as midnight approaches in various Muslim nations, the number of hits goes out of sight. It's remarkable to watch!"

"And what about the social networks?" Sticks inquired.

"I don't have the latest numbers, but the message is getting out," Lowry answered. "There's a tremendous amount of traffic, and every day, many post notes saying they've placed their faith in Christ."

"We gotta come up with some creative aids to help the new believers grow in their faith," Sticks said, rubbing his chin. "I'd also love to connect them with mature Christians, although I don't believe we'll be able to do that for long. Soon the lives of Christians will be in danger. The last thing we want is for unfriendlies to gather information that could jeopardize the lives of people who are seeking information about God."

This was new news. "How soon is soon?" Lowry asked.

"It's hard to say. I'll be speaking about this tonight, but I strongly believe the one-world government should concern every citizen of every nation, and certainly every believer on earth. I can't fathom why our government failed to exercise its veto power over this pernicious UN resolution. Life will gradually worsen for Christians and Jews, although the worst of the persecution is probably three or four years away. The church has a sliver of time to get out the message before the window is slammed shut."

Sticks reviewed his calendar and sighed. It was crammed with appointments. Everything about his world might have changed when the US gave its sovereignty over to the UN one-world government, but his pastoral duties sure hadn't altered much. There were still more people with more questions than he could possibly meet with and answer. "You available again on Tuesday? If you are, let's meet again to see what ideas we come up with between now and then."

"You bet. I'll be here," Lowry promised.

Sticks closed their meeting with a prayer, followed by a glance at the clock. "Well, we're outta time, so let's get things rollin'."

Sticks stood before his overflow audience, requesting God's guidance before he began to speak.

"Unless you've been living in a cave for the past few months," Stick quipped, "you know that we're living under the rule of a one-world government, a global community, we're told. As we've already seen, Daniel describes five phases of a fourth Gentile empire that shall 'devour the whole earth.' With the UN's historic vote, the third phase of this empire, that of a one-world government, has begun."

He paused as the significance of those words weighed on his shoulders. "Scripture teaches us that next, this one-world government will give way to ten empires, if we can call them that. This doesn't mean the UN disappears by any stretch of the imagination. It simply means that the UN will learn that as small as the world has become, it's still too large and complex to be governed by a single mortal. Soon, it will be partitioned into ten regions which we could call kingdoms or empires.

"Daniel and John both refer to these empires symbolically, calling them ten 'horns' and 'kings.' But in any event, a man empowered by Satan will come up among the ten horns and begin his rapid rise to power. He'll eventually overthrow three of the ten, perhaps killing their leaders, and then rule over all ten kingdoms, and by extension, the entire world. Once again, we'll be under a one-world government, led by a mortal—but a mortal empowered and totally controlled by Satan. I believe his identity will be established when he signs a seven-year pact with Israel.

"As most of you know, the UN secretary-general is Marius Nielsen. Some of you have asked if this man is the Antichrist, or 'the Beast,' as John calls him in the Revelation. I really don't think so. Scripture is pretty clear about what this man will do, but only time will tell. When we see events unfold as described in Scripture, then we'll be able to positively identify who the Antichrist is."

* * *

The popular but exhausted Danish secretary-general had summoned Romiti to his office, located in the beautiful UN headquarters complex in Babylon. "Nice view," Romiti commented as he peered west toward the Euphrates River. Tall, lush palm trees swayed in the breeze, a refreshing contrast to the sandy desert terrain. Nielsen's office had an unobstructed view of the reconstructed ancient city of Babylon, a "bucket list" site until Ezekiel's War severely restricted travel. Since the UN's move to Babylon, a trickle of travelers were again making the trek to the city that was once home to the Hanging Gardens of Babylon, one of the Seven Wonders of the Ancient World. Nielsen stood beside Romiti, pointing out several historical sites before getting down to business.

"You're the recognized expert on sectarian religious violence," he began. "The armed forces of sovereign states, supported and guided by the UN, seem to be handling border clashes, regional famines, water shortages, tribal jealousies, and drug wars pretty well. But these forces have been powerless to curb religious-based conflicts around the world. In fact, the frequency and enormity of religious-based acts of terrorism are escalating every day. What's the answer? If anyone can tell me, you can."

"Nonreligious conflicts are invariably traced to one of three sources: a desire for power, the need for survival, or an emotional or psychological need," Romiti answered, and then posed a question of his own, deftly evading the secretary's question. "Tell me: how will you respond to nations whose leaders want to expand their power or level of influence at the expense of smaller or weaker neighbors?"

The secretary-general paused to reflect on the question for a moment and then gave his answer. "Historically, we've passed resolutions but little else. More recently, the Security Council has inserted itself into the affairs of once-sovereign states, replacing power-hungry government leaders and incompetent dictators."

"You're evading my question," Romiti charged. "You simply parroted what the UN has done in the past. I want to know how you will respond to the circumstances I just described."

Nielsen sat back, speechless at Romiti's show of disrespect. Not having a ready answer, he repeated his previous answer with a slight twist. "We must exert control over the once-sovereign states, replacing power-hungry government leaders and incompetent dictators."

"Precisely," Romiti agreed. "We must take decisive action when responding to leaders who thirst for more power. We must either endorse the aggressor nation, if this serves our best interests, or crush it. Either way, our response must be swift and decisive, even ruthless at times.

"When the conflict involves the survival of a people group, let's say they're experiencing famine or severe drought, the UN must also respond promptly, moving resources from an area of abundance to the area of need. Now that nationalistic passions have been suppressed and the concept of a global community is accepted worldwide, the UN's ability to move assets to where they're needed most has dramatically improved."

"That's evident," the secretary agreed. "But you're evading *my* question. How do we handle leaders or people groups who are actively engaged in acts of terrorism because of generational hatreds, religious differences, prejudices, fears, or jealousies?"

"Those situations are more difficult to resolve," Romiti admitted. "There's no one-size-fits-all solution. In addressing nonreligious conflict, we must always evaluate the long-term outcome of our actions and not necessarily do what seems right or fair at the moment. Said differently, regardless of the situation, the law of survival of the fittest applies. We must determine which combatant is the strongest and therefore the most likely to survive, and second, which survivor would best serve the short—and long-term interests of the global community. This means that at times, we may even support an unjust cause to ensure the outcome we want. And if that happens, so be it."

Nielsen laid his hands flat on his desk. "Over the past year, we've responded quickly and forcefully to a number of the situations you've described, and as a result, the global community is enjoying a period of relative calm. But now we must turn our attention to the religious conflicts that continue in the hotspots around the world. The truth is, I have no idea of how to proceed."

Romiti smiled. "Why don't you be more specific? The hotspot of the world is the Middle East. It's absolutely absurd for anyone in the twenty-first century to believe land boundaries allegedly promised over five thousand years ago to a wandering Bedouin named Abraham should be considered inviolable today. And yet this ridiculous belief is the source of the time bomb ticking in the Middle East today."

His voice grew more heated as his passion rose. "More than a billion people follow the teachings of Muhammad, a man they believe to be a prophet and whose tribe worshiped the moon god only thirteen hundred years ago. And because this religious figure claimed to be the last true prophet of God, his most strident followers today decree that the entire earth must dress as he dressed, eat what he ate, visit the places he visited, and repress women as he did. And incredibly, the most radical of his adherents believe that anyone who dares object to any of these ridiculous notions deserves beheading!"

Romiti reserved his most venomous attack for last. "And finally, there are the religious fanatics who believe the claims of a man who supposedly lived in Palestine more than two thousand years ago. Even today, mind you, his most devoted followers believe he walked on water, fed more than five thousand people with a few loaves of bread and some fish, and was able to raise the dead. They believe he was actually God in human form. They teach there's no other path to God. 'Either believe what we teach or you'll burn in hell forever,' they proclaim. They believe in absolute truth and claim to have a lock on it! They even teach that we ought to obey God rather than man—no matter what that might lead to, no matter what that god might command. This kind of thinking must stop! It is ungovernable, untenable in our new world."

Nielsen was listening intently. Romiti continued, "Our long-term goal must be to rid the earth of all forms of religion, but especially Christianity. It has been a historical aggressor and source of antigovernment rhetoric and revolution for centuries. However, religion must be eliminated in stages. I've thought long and hard about this inimical challenge to a lasting peace. First, we must offer an acceptable substitute."

"And what do you suggest?" asked the secretary, sitting up straight. He knew he should not have expected less from Romiti, but the daring of his suggestions still made him catch his breath.

"Adherents of virtually every religion can be divided into two groups: fanatics and casual cultural observers. Take Christianity, for example. Most people in America claim to be Christians, but in truth, they only bear the label. This group of cultural Christians does not believe the Bible is literally true, doesn't practice its teachings, and doesn't go out of its way to share the faith. It will be fairly easy to lure these faux Christians into a new, culturally acceptable religion.

"The same is true of Islam, Judaism, Buddhism, and other world religions. They all have a large segment of wishy-washy adherents. I believe we must extract the common principles of decency found in most faiths and wrap them up in a religion that will appeal to the masses, perhaps even commandeering an existing religion and making it our own." Romiti paused for a long minute, waiting for the secretary to urge him on.

"Continue," the secretary commanded. "You've addressed the easy part. What about the fanatics? They're the ultimate merchants of the world's evils, peddling their religious wares wherever they go!"

Romiti held his pause a minute longer, primarily for effect, and then said, "Any religious zealot who refuses to renounce his faith must be executed. Obviously, this means that laws must be passed that make it a crime to perform certain activities or express particular views. It is my studied opinion that there can be no other alternative. The fanatic faithful are incapable of compromise. And their refusal to compromise is the only great threat remaining to our world."

The room was quiet for a long time as they both reflected on Romiti's solution. Then Nielsen abruptly changed the subject as the men returned to the informal meeting area situated at one end of the large office.

"You are no doubt aware that my first term ends in less than a year. What are your plans? When the times comes, will you support me for another five-year term, or do you want the office?"

Romiti was not surprised by the question.

"You've done a remarkable job during some of the most difficult and troubling times ever experienced on earth," Romiti said, his mouth twisting peculiarly at his own exaggeration. "You have an impressive list of accomplishments. However, I believe the problems we've experienced are mere child's play compared to what's coming. I'm prepared for those challenges now."

Romiti stood. Gone were the disarming smile and charming personality. His appearance had transformed into that of a ruthless and callous professional, one who was used to getting his way. His demeanor, once warm, friendly, and engaging, had become dangerously harsh and overbearing.

Nielsen had often been in the presence of the world's most powerful men and women—he respected them, but never feared them. Romiti, he feared.

"Let me be blunt," Romiti finished. "While I have a great deal of respect for the job you've done, I don't believe you possess the energy, nor the skills and experience, required to successfully manage the next five to six years. Do not seek a second term. Endorse me instead."

The secretary-general, humiliated by Romiti's harsh appraisal, quietly considered his visitor's words before giving his reply. "I'm willing to do as you've proposed. If what you've said is true, and I have no doubt that it is, then I cannot seek a second term. I'm unable to endure another five years of conflict and turmoil, so I promise to be your most loyal supporter. Your appointment by the full General Assembly will not be a problem. Your biggest obstacle will be the possible veto of your nomination by one or more of the Security Council's permanent member nations. I know for a fact that the Russian and Chinese ambassadors are jealous of your success and will do all in their power to block your nomination. Let's plan now to make sure that doesn't happen."

*   *   *

The Muslim world was on edge. Israel's extraordinary deliverance from the hands of its enemies had not been anticipated by the clerics. Once again, the troublesome nation had managed to survive certain destruction. Its miraculous deliverance seemed to contradict Islamic eschatology. It certainly challenged the promises of the militant jihadists. Where was the Mahdi, eagerly anticipated by the Islamic masses?

A group of jihadist leaders had gathered in Cairo, now a safe haven for anti-Israeli sentiment since Egypt's transition to an Islamic government.

"Our focus has been too narrow." Al-Wadhi, the passionate al-Qaeda leader, was heatedly criticizing the tactics and strategies of the terrorist organizations. "We spend months, even years, planning spectacular attacks like 9/11 and the one in Southern California. But dozens, even hundreds, of coordinated, smaller attacks would be far more effective. Imagine the economic and psychological impact if every week, a martyr killed a few dozen people in a shopping mall or at a sporting event."

Mubarak al-Diri, head of the Islamic Jihad Movement, fervently agreed. "The Twelfth Imam is to manifest himself on earth again as the Mahdi when the world is filled with injustice and tyranny. Look around! The infidels occupy our lands, they consume our natural resources, and they blaspheme the name of Allah! We're living in the times Allah warned would come!"

"Mahdi will lead an army of Muslim warriors that will conquer Israel, sparking a worldwide revolution that will establish a new Islamic world order," al-Wadhi added. "Until he comes, we must attack the infidels often and mercilessly. A week must not pass without a successful attack."

The gathering of terrorists pledged their support to the less spectacular but deadly operations, and almost overnight, a series of violent attacks were launched in the major Jewish population centers of the world. Radical Islamic fundamentalist mobs took to the streets in support of the renewed violence, making the skirmishes of the Arab Spring seem like a minor schoolyard brawl.

Every day, citizens of the new global community were reading frightening reports of suicide bombings, assassinations, and kidnappings. The escalating hostilities were threatening to derail the much-heralded "peace and prosperity" lifestyles that were promised to come under a one-world government. While Nielsen continued to be a popular figure, many had concluded that he was an ineffective leader—too weak for the job, just as Romiti had predicted in his private conversation with the secretary.

Prior to the nuclear explosion in America, the General Assembly had been casually debating the merits of a new structure recommended by its Committee for Regional Autonomy. The model divided the world into ten zones, called regional zones. Regional autonomy would be maintained, and the individual member nations comprising each RZ, really a confederation of states, would voluntarily associate with the United Nations. The nuclear attack and Ezekiel's War, followed by the UN relocation to Iraq, disrupted the debate, and the idea had been tabled. However, with the UN now in authority over the one-world government and Nielsen's seeming inability to stem the increasing tide of violence, the CRA model had risen to the top of the UN agenda. While most believed the CRA's regional zone model would curb the violence by placing the enforcement of international laws into the hands of regional governments, others argued that the current model would still work if only it were placed under the leadership of a much stronger secretary-general.

Romiti himself was not thrilled with the model recommended by the committee. In fact, he vehemently argued against the notion of ten powerful heads of state, even if he would someday be the de facto leader of them all. Led by Romiti, the opposition vigorously lobbied for the continuance of the present structure: a single authoritarian figure at the head of a one-world government.

The General Assembly hotly debated the CRA recommendations for several weeks, but in the end, over the strong objections of many, including

Nielsen and Romiti, the General Assembly adopted the model by a wide margin. The Security Council also unanimously approved the proposal.

Nielsen's humiliating defeat on the floor of the General Assembly greatly embarrassed him; Romiti vowed to himself that as secretary-general, he would never suffer such a setback.

The General Assembly's next order of business was to address the need to increase the size and composition of the Security Council. Since its creation in 1945, the Security Council of the United Nations had been comprised of five nations, called permanent members: the United States, the United Kingdom, France, Russia, and China. Now, after years of internal squabbling, the General Assembly voted to increase the number of permanent Security Council members to ten, coinciding with the ten regional zones created by the General Assembly. The General Assembly designated a member nation from each of the ten zones to represent the interests of the zone; the president of the designated nation was named the regional world council representative.

By a special legislative act, Russia and France lost their permanent seats on the council and were replaced by Japan and India, representing the Asian and Indian Regional Zones.

The Security Council also changed its name to the World Council.

The United States, China, and the United Kingdom, dubbed the Gang of Three, retained their veto power—but in the future, only seven permanent member votes out of ten, rather than unanimous consent, would be needed to win the World Council's endorsement.

A new United Nations emerged from the US-dominated era that had preceded the tumultuous events of the past fifteen months. The United States and China had removed themselves from the international scene. Russia was destroyed, powerless and without influence on the world stage.

Alone in his office, Romiti stared at the UN handout that listed the ten regional zones and their corresponding World Council member nations:

Ten Regional Zones	Representative World Council Member
Africa	Egypt
Asia	Japan
Australia/Oceania	Australia
China	China (veto power)
India	India
Mesopotamia	Iraq
Middle East	Syria
North America	United States (veto power)
South America/Caribbean	Venezuela
Europe	United Kingdom (veto power)

"Know your enemies!" he cautioned himself. *Egypt. Iraq. Syria.* Their leaders had never forgiven him for his outspoken condemnation of Islam— it did not matter that Romiti aimed his vilest epithets at the heart of Judaism and Christianity. *Conspire against me if you dare. Soon, the three of you will perish, and all peoples, nations, and men of every language will worship and follow me!*

CHAPTER SIXTEEN

Babylon, Iraq

Marius Nielsen's final year as secretary-general was marked by a worldwide recession, a frightening increase in violence, and a disillusioned citizenry. Whether he was inept or psychologically defeated by his colleagues' lack of confidence in his abilities to govern, the embattled secretary-general was now the titular head of a failing global government. In the absence of a strong leader, the regional zone presidents were beginning to jostle for power, strengthen their militaries, and hoard vital resources.

Unlike Nielsen, Romiti was carefully maneuvering behind the scenes. He had convinced most World Council members that without his leadership, the ten-region model would soon fall apart. He claimed that secret alliances had already formed and that war was imminent. The presidents of the African, Mesopotamian, and Middle Eastern Regional Zones were unconvinced by Romiti's exaggerations—but of even greater concern to them was what they perceived to be his anti-Islamic rhetoric.

After a great deal of backroom negotiation, the World Council nominated Romiti to become the next secretary-general despite the three votes cast against him. Surprising to many, Romiti won the support of the British ambassador, although none were aware of the unexplained fortune recently inherited by the ambassador, nor the prominent position that would be his in the Romiti administration. As expected, the dissenting votes were cast by the presidents of the predominantly Muslim regions.

Despite their strong dissenting voices, the assembly elected Romiti to become the next secretary-general by the greatest margin ever registered for the office.

As was his custom, Romiti retreated from his victory to the privacy of his suite. There he offered praise to Lucifer, praying and burning incense to the fallen angel. In return, Lucifer's presence descended upon Romiti like a mantle. Romiti closed his eyes, savoring the pleasure he experienced as Lucifer filled his heart with pride. The feeling was powerful, akin to the rush an addict feels after mainlining a potent drug. Romiti was grateful that Lucifer so tangibly acknowledged his praise.

*   *   *

Several weeks later, in an informal meeting of a small, handpicked group of senior UN officials, Romiti, the newly elected secretary-general, informed his colleagues of his future plans in a surprisingly open and candid manner.

"I've chosen you because I know you will not fail me. I've worked closely with each one of you over the past several years and have learned by experience that you represent the very best in your professions. Your allegiance to me is proven, and once again, I'm depending on—in fact, demanding—your undivided loyalty and absolute confidentiality."

Several squirmed uneasily in their comfortable chairs, wondering what kinds of clandestine, and probably unlawful, activities they would be told to perform on behalf of their demanding leader. From past experience, each one knew the price of membership in Romiti's elite inner circle. They were also well acquainted with the rewards. A quick study of their financial holdings told the story of Romiti's generosity.

"Despite the fact that most of you are serving in an official UN capacity, ours is not a UN-sponsored meeting. As you have been told, this informal get-together is off the record, an opportunity to candidly and freely discuss what's on our minds. As members of my cabinet, you shall soon become the key players in a new global government that will supersede the present authority of the United Nations. While the UN is functioning in its present role, it's critical that its goals parallel our own. When our goals begin to diverge, we must bring the UN objectives in line with our own. Is this perfectly clear?"

Everyone nodded in agreement, wondering where this conversation would lead.

"Over the past several months, I've had numerous conversations with each of you. Several are already working on initiatives that support my personal goals as secretary-general. Today, I'll discuss some of these goals, but this meeting is also a forum in which you will bring us up to date on the initiatives that are already underway. Are there any questions?"

No questions were raised, so Romiti continued. "Our first challenge is to resolve the status of Jerusalem and the Temple Mount. You may ask why this should be our first. I've devoted my life to understanding why governments fail. Obviously, they fail for many reasons: incompetent leadership, lack of natural resources, famine and disease, and of course, defeat at the hands of an enemy. But in a global community, ruled by a competent, ironfisted, and ruthless—yes, ruthless—leader, most potential causes of failure can be easily addressed. I believe the most significant, perhaps the only, barrier to worldwide peace and prosperity is religious rivalry. Overcome this challenge, and a millennium of peace and prosperity will follow."

"You may as well solve all the problems of the Middle East! The Jews and Muslims are the most stubborn, uncompromising people on the face of the earth!" Dixon, a retired US navy admiral and former chairman of the Joint Chiefs of Staff, bluntly blurted what was on his mind, unmindful of the proper protocol.

The outspoken military man would soon serve as the commander of the Global Security Force. In a plan proposed by Romiti and soon to be adopted by the General Assembly, the armed forces of every nation would retain their national identity and structure, but be subordinate to the UN's mission. In joint operations, they would operate as the Global Security Force, the umbrella name for the agency's international military arm.

Before Romiti could respond to Dixon, Taylor Pattersen, the secretary of the Department of Global Communications, posed a question of her own. "You raised the idea of a global community, ruled by a ruthless leader. Will you be that ironfisted and ruthless leader?"

Romiti frowned, somewhat annoyed with the interruptions.

"Frankly, yes, I will. I will solve problems that have confounded the world for millennia! Now please, let me continue.

"Jerusalem is center stage for the deadliest, longest running, and most resource-draining conflict in the world today. Almost every leader says peace between the Jews, Christians, and Muslims is unachievable." He didn't state his thoughts: *Peace is achievable, even if it means we must kill every one of them!* "Resolve the impasse, ladies and gentlemen, and it will give us the time we need to eliminate the problem that has plagued the Middle East for millenniums. Any disagreement?"

Romiti had chosen his words carefully; he did plan to "eliminate the problem," but he was not yet prepared to reveal what "problem" he intended to eliminate.

Dixon cleared his throat to catch Romiti's attention. "Just to be clear, Mr. Secretary, can you describe the impasse you intend to resolve? It seems to me there are several impasses that must be considered."

"Yes, there are specific issues that must be addressed, but for now, I'm referring to only one—the control of Jerusalem. All of it must be under either Jewish control or Muslim control. A divided Jerusalem is like a scab that is never allowed to heal. Until the status of Jerusalem has been settled, there will be constant feuding in the region and by extension, the nations of the world."

Francois Laroque, Romiti's newly appointed deputy for Religious Affairs, smirked as he offered his comments. "I agree the status of Jerusalem must be resolved, Mr. Secretary, but I also strongly believe this problem is symptomatic of a broader, much more serious illness, if you will. The world will be in continuous conflict until all religions are abolished."

"Strange observations coming from a deputy for religious affairs," Richard Dixon wryly observed.

"Let me finish," Laroque snapped. Dixon made a face at the deputy's putrid breath. Romiti seemed to rely on the odious man, but it was anyone's guess why.

Laroque went on. "So yes, let's fix Jerusalem first, while we begin the process of consolidating all religions into a unified religious order; and then, when the time comes, the new order too will be destroyed. That, my friends, will be the final step to world peace and prosperity."

"The idea of a unified religion was gathering steam in the US in the years before the attack on Long Beach," Dixon began. "To be sure, the proponents of a one-world religion were the liberal theologians who denied most of the essential tenets of Christianity . . . but the idea had plenty of support. Even so, to pull this off, you'll need a strong military force. Seems to me the radical elements in almost every religion would resort to terrorist activities to preserve their influence. Perhaps more importantly, you'll need to infiltrate religious organizations worldwide."

"I'm already on it," interrupted Max Zagmi, the former head of Albania's Directorate of State Security and now chief of the UN's Center of Intelligence and Security. Zagmi was the protégé of a particularly brutal director of the infamous Sirigumi, Albania's feared secret police.

He had learned his trade well, and Romiti had been impressed. "I had the opportunity to discuss this subject with Romiti and Laroque over a year ago. We've been carefully planning, and anticipating, I might add, for this day to come. I already have a large and well-equipped network in place. We're beefing up our counterterrorism units, and within a few months, we'll release cyber-based computer worms that will infiltrate most PCs attached to the Internet. The malware is patterned after Israel's Stuxnet, the famous worm that paralyzed Iran's Bushehr Nuclear Power Plant. I'm in the process of acquiring sophisticated surveillance technologies that will help us monitor, intercept, catalog, and yes, even subvert, all forms of electronic communications. Soon, we'll be tracking every web-based communication that has a hint of religious content. We can also tag web users based on their profiles and then block them from accessing certain websites and social media. The project is being managed out of a new $2 billion cybersecurity center in India."

Max smiled, eager as a child sharing his newest toys. "We anticipate there will be vigorous opposition to the secretary-general's efforts to prosecute the war on religious systems, so we need a tool that will help us monitor the activities of our adversaries. As some of you know, one of the UN initiatives has been to implement a revolutionary airborne surveillance system modeled after America's Gorgon Stare." The group was aware that Gorgon was a mythical Greek creature who turned into stone anyone who gazed into its unblinking eyes.

"The system transmits live video images of any physical movement across an entire town or small city. Under Nielsen, the purpose of the system was to locate local warlords who were slaughtering indigenous people groups in remote Sudanese villages. Now we'll use it to track the movements of the religious opposition."

"Don't forget our drones, Max," Romiti reminded his chief. "You've been bragging about your fleet of model-airplane-sized unmanned drones that can be launched from a slingshot. In less than a year, we'll have deployed the most powerful, far-reaching surveillance system the world has ever seen!"

Max was pleased by Romiti's enthusiasm, chuckling as he continued his report. "We've already hired charlatans who soon will begin to infiltrate every religious organization on earth. All of them are accomplished actors, and each is earning an outrageous salary along with extraordinary perks and benefits. Their allegiance will be to the Center of Intelligence and Security, without a doubt."

"Their allegiance, and ours, must first be to Romiti," Laroque immediately countered.

"Yes, of course," Max stammered. "I didn't mean to offend the secretary-general."

"I'm not offended, Max. You're doing an outstanding job. Superior intelligence gathering is the key to our success, and the center's off to a terrific start!" Romiti placed his hand on Max's shoulder and whispered in his ear, "Don't let me down."

He straightened up again, and Sebastian Ospel, recognized as one of the most brilliant economists of his time, took up the reporting. "We also must control the economies of every nation. This objective will be accomplished as soon as we implement a single electronic international currency." The Swiss economist was the chairman of the newly formed Global Economic Council and a long-time Romiti confidant. "We'll launch a three-nation pilot project within twelve months," he boasted, "and it will be deployed worldwide within two years."

"Thank you, Sebastian, but that's not good enough. Have the pilot online in six months, with full implementation within eighteen months," Romiti directed. "You have an open checkbook for any resources you need; see me for anything you lack. Anything."

Pattersen had been quiet during most of the cabinet meeting, but after listening carefully to her colleagues, she offered her thoughts. "Much of what we've discussed this morning will outrage populations raised in Western democracies. My department will coordinate several media campaigns timed with the release of information from your agencies. The media campaigns will anticipate and aggressively counter the resistance that is sure to come from pockets of the global community."

"Then, my friends, it is underway." Romiti smiled and dropped his bombshell. "I've arranged for a very secret meeting of Islamic revolutionary leaders to take place outside Tehran in two weeks. Leaders of virtually every radical Islamic organization on earth will be in attendance. I will convince them to recognize Israel's right to exist, agree to the rebuilding of the Jewish temple on the Temple Mount, and refrain from further attacks on Israel."

The cabinet looked at one another, incredulous. Was he serious?

"With all due respect, Mr. Secretary. I'm sorry, but that will never happen," Ospel objected. "The Jews and Muslims have been at each other's throats for fifteen hundred years. There's no way the Muslims, especially those enamored by radical Islam, will ever agree to these concessions!"

"I'm being deadly serious, Sebastian. It will happen, mark my words! Soon, you will learn how I will pull this rabbit out of my hat. And Max, I have a job for one of your intelligence officers. I want to be able to track the movements of several terrorists after they leave the conference. Before I depart for the conference myself, give me the tools that will get it done!"

"Consider it done," Max promised.

Romiti surveyed his handpicked cabinet with approval. Not a bureaucrat among them. No sluggards. All focused on the goal.

Soon, I will reign over all the kingdoms of the world.

After dismissing his cabinet, he and Laroque boarded Romiti's private jet for the short flight to Tel Aviv. "Look, Laroque. You're on the world stage now, and first impressions matter. You embarrassed me today. It's obvious that the other members of my cabinet revile you. Your unkempt appearance, putrid breath, the slipshod shave—the cabinet was appalled. Fix it—today!"

The reprimand angered Laroque, but he knew better than to cross Romiti. The charges were not new. He had ignored similar remarks by well-meaning or tactless, even spiteful, people throughout his lifetime, but he would begin his transformation that day.

After the stinging rebuke, Romiti began to reflect on the meeting. He was most concerned about Pattersen's predictions about the reactions of the Western democracies, especially America. She was right, of course, and he could not afford to awaken the moribund giant. He must remember to give her warnings careful attention.

From the Ben Gurion International Airport, they were taken to the regal King David Hotel, within walking distance of the Temple Mount. The VIPs received a warm welcome from the staff selected to escort them to their luxurious suites.

After dismissing his attendants, Romiti enjoyed the quiet solitude, reflecting on the history of the famous hotel. Prior to the creation of an independent Jewish state, the King David Hotel was the temporary home to the British administrative headquarters for Palestine. In July 1948, a bomb was planted in the basement beneath the wing that housed the Mandate Secretariat and offices of the British military. The attack was planned as a response to Operation Agatha, in which British soldiers had confiscated large quantities of documents that linked the Irgun, a right-wing Zionist underground organization, to other violent groups in the region. Telephone warnings placed by the Irgun, the perpetrators of the brazen attack, were ignored by hotel staff. Half an hour later, the explosion caused the collapse of the western half of the southern wing of the hotel. Ninety-one lives were lost. More than half a century later, Israel was no less dangerous. Romiti shook his head in wonder.

Awakened just before midnight, Romiti and Laroque met their chauffeur and guide in the beautiful hotel lobby. Romiti quickly observed the assortment of chairs and tables that were carefully arranged throughout the spacious entrance hall, noting that on each table sat a bouquet of freshly cut flowers. Colorful Persian rugs covered sections of the large squares of gray and gold marble flooring, and impressive paintings hung from walls that were marked by a patchwork of light-colored cubes and rectangles. A group of wealthy tourists circled the grand piano, located in the far corner of the vestibule, as one of their number played a fretful tune. Observations behind him, Romiti purposefully strode across another Persian rug, this one a kaleidoscope of color, as he approached the revolving exit door, noting the Israeli flag that stood next to the long reservations counter. *Soon, that flag will be a relic of history.*

The efficient attaché responsible for the secretary-general's personal concierge services had arranged for an experienced guide to lead them from the King David to the Dung Gate of the Old City. As they walked down King David Street, Romiti turned back to catch a spectacular view of the legendary hotel, bathed golden by the bright lights that cast their beams on the quartz exterior. It was beautiful.

From the Dung Gate, they would follow the Derech Ha'ofel road to Absalom's Pillar in the Kidron Valley. This was a fitting site for Romiti's plans, as the monument honored the man who led a rebellion against Israel's second king, one whom God, the religious believed, had placed on the throne. As they walked along the cobblestone sidewalk, the trio passed the ruins of Ir David, the ancient City of David, the landmark that signaled them to cross over to the other side of the street. Romiti and Laroque followed their guide to an opening that led down a steep cobbled stairway to the valley floor. They were surprised to see two young Jewish Orthodox men sitting on the low stone wall that lined the stepped pathway, rocking silently as they offered their prayers. The young men smiled a greeting, but the visitors rudely ignored the friendly gesture. Soon the Tomb of Zechariah, carved out of solid rock, came into view.

Moments later, the imposing Absalom's Pillar was also visible. The guide quickly climbed to the top of the pedestal on which the four-columned monolith appeared to rest, sitting comfortably while observing his charge.

Romiti and Laroque walked another twenty yards to a large Jerusalem-stone garden that was protected by five small olive trees. Romiti rested on the U-shaped, cement-capped rock bench while Laroque erected an altar on the large patch of earth that filled the planter. It was in this very valley that Manasseh and the early kings of Judah had built the high places, erected altars to the Baals, and used Asherah poles in their worship of the fertility goddess. It was here that Manasseh had practiced sorcery, divination, and witchcraft, and consulted mediums and spiritists.

And it was here, on this starlit Jerusalem night, that Romiti and Laroque committed blasphemy in the manner of the Judean kings who lived before them. They began to burn incense to Lucifer, bowing down to the fallen angel and all the starry hosts.

The guide was faintly amused by the scene. He snickered quietly but honored their request for privacy by remaining a stone's throw from the worshipers.

"Lucifer, generations of Judean kings have come to this valley to worship you. Now we have come to worship you as well," Laroque intoned.

At the mention of Lucifer's name, the guide, an ex-Israeli special forces officer, became edgy. He watched the orange and yellow flames dance on the altar—as the light cast by the full moon and bright stars inexplicably dimmed. The guide was unable to see his own hands and feet through the heavy darkness. A strong blast of wind pushed small pebbles off the ancient grave markers that filled the valley, the stones' noisy clatter echoing through the deserted burial ground.

Romiti closed his eyes, reveling as his spirit communed with the fallen angel.

By contrast to Romiti's blissful trance, the guide was frightened by the unholy ritual. He shuddered as a sudden coldness gripped his body. Goosebumps covered his arms and neck. He jumped when Romiti unexpectedly snapped out of the trance. The secretary-general's body trembled briefly, and then he began to speak.

"We have come to this valley to honor you, my lord," he began, "and to request your guidance. Tomorrow I meet with Shalev, the modern-day king of Judah. May I find favor in your sight, O Lucifer. Lead and guide me, and may our plans succeed."

"You have brought glory to me by renewing this place of worship," Lucifer replied audibly. "Asa, Jehoshaphat, and Hezekiah, ancient Judean kings, destroyed the high places built to honor me, but by your actions tonight, some have been restored. Go in my favor. I will grant you strength and power to accomplish my will in this city."

*   *   *

Romiti and Ariel Shalev were enjoying the panoramic view of the Old City from Romiti's sixth-floor royal suite in the King David Hotel. Built in the 1920s, the locally quarried pink quartz exterior and unusual interiors of the hotel never failed to impress its guests. The view of the city was equally impressive.

"Many of the world's leaders have savored this view," Shalev said with a great deal of pride. "The dowager empress of Persia, the queen mother Nazli of Egypt, King Abdullah of Jordan, the US presidents Nixon, Ford, Carter, Clinton, George W. Bush, and then-Democractic presidential candidate Barack Obama. Even Winston Churchill was impressed with the spectacular views of Jerusalem."

The hotel's King's Garden restaurant catered a delightful breakfast of eggs, hard and soft cheeses, freshly baked bread, an Israeli salad, and Moroccan pastelles. The two leaders spent several minutes discussing world events, particularly those of concern to Israel, as they helped themselves to the delicious meal. Then Romiti outlined the purpose for his visit.

"The Middle East is about to unravel, and no one knows this better than you," Romiti began. "You and I have a historic opportunity to bring peace to the region. I want to broker an armistice between Israel, the League of Arab States, and the terrorist organizations that target your nation to this day."

Shalev raised an eyebrow. "That's a pretty tall order. And what piece of Israel is to be given up this time?"

"Israel must agree that Gaza and the West Bank, with the exception of the Jerusalem District, which will be annexed by Israel, will be an independent, sovereign Palestinian state. Israel will not control Gaza ports and will agree to construct a corridor, at its expense, that will allow unrestricted passage between the two regions. That's it."

Romiti paused while the prime minister considered his words, and then resumed his proposal. "In return, the member states will recognize Israel's right to exist as a sovereign nation. Secondly, they will agree that you can rebuild the temple on the Temple Mount, and third, they will refrain from further attacks on your nation. Finally, to protect Israel from threats from its neighbors to the east, Israel will have unrestricted access to a buffer zone that will encompass the West Bank territory east of Highway 90 to the Jordan River."

Shalev could hardly believe what he was hearing: for the first time in his lifetime, a plan was being offered that seemed far more favorable to Israel than to its surrounding neighbors. But he was also skeptical.

"If you truly brokered such an armistice, I would certainly bring it before the Knesset for their approval," Shalev replied, "but I believe this is a fantasy. The Arab world, especially the more radical Islamic states, would never concede to such a pact."

"Let's not go down that path right now. I want to know that *if* the League is willing to move forward with the armistice as outlined, you will endorse it to the Knesset."

"Yes, I would throw my full support behind such a pact," the prime minister promised, "although quite frankly, most secular Jews have no aspiration to build another temple. We remember the words of Sheikh Said e-Din el'Alami, who said that any attempt to build a synagogue would be done on 'the corpses of a million Muslims.' We prefer peace to bloodshed. Why do you believe a new temple is so important to Jews, other than the Orthodox minority?"

"Do you not know your own history? Israel's reunification of Jerusalem and the capture of the Temple Mount in 1967 was the perfect time to remove the Dome of the Rock. This was Rabbi Shlomo Goren's plan. On the second day of the 1967 war, he pleaded with Central Region Commander General Uzi Narkiss to place one hundred kilograms of dynamite in the shrine, but the general declined."

"And I'm glad that Narkiss was levelheaded! It would have been foolish, even suicidal, for him to follow Rabbi Goren's advice!"

"Perhaps, but since Israel's failure to assert control over the Mount, Orthodox Jews and Muslims have constantly bickered over this piece of real estate. Even radical Christian fundamentalists have joined in the fray.

Now that Kubbat as-Sakhra has been destroyed by natural means, we can diminish the chances of warfare between the radical elements of all three religions by rebuilding the temple. The Muslims still have their mosque. Jews, Muslims, and Christians will be able to worship together in a place that's equally revered by all."

"And do you believe this will bring about a lasting peace?"

"I would hope so, but I recommend we begin in small, achievable steps. To make the idea palatable to all parties, I'm proposing that the armistice initially remain in force for seven years and then be enacted permanently when the world sees that peace is achievable."

The two men shook hands, promising to meet again soon. The prime minister returned to Beit Rosh Hamemshala, his official residence in Jerusalem, while the secretary-general returned to the UN headquarters in Babylon.

Shalev was restless that night, tossing and turning as he struggled to fall asleep. After finally dozing off, an apparition, an angel of the Lord he later realized, appeared to him in a vision. Shalev was gripped by fear at the sight of the mighty angel, the tallest being he had ever seen—a man truly majestic, awesome, and terrible—and in his dream, fell facedown at the angel's feet as though dead. Trembling and raising his head, Shalev shielded his eyes from the brilliant light, a light as bright as the sun.

"What is it? What do you want?" He choked out the words, wishing desperately to escape but unable to move.

The angel placed his right hand on Shalev's shoulder and warned in a loud voice, "Have nothing to do with that man of lawlessness. Soon he will oppose and will exalt himself over everything that is of God."

The room in which Shalev slept seemed to shake as the angel's voice thundered its message. Once again, Shalev fell prostrate before the angel, alone and afraid.

CHAPTER SEVENTEEN

Tehran, Iran

"Please make sure your seat belts are securely fastened. We'll be landing in Tehran in less than ten minutes," the pilot informed his small crew and several passengers.

It was two a.m., and except for this very secret flight, the airport was closed to all traffic. As the jet taxied down the runway, several armored vehicles carrying a counterassault team raced to the designated termination point. Two passengers, along with several aides, exited one plane and boarded another while the counterassault team carefully guarded both planes. Minutes later, they departed from Tehran's Imam Khomeini International Airport, modeled after America's Dallas Love Field, and Romiti and Laroque began the final leg of their journey to the Iranian city of Sabzevar.

On the short flight, Romiti brought Laroque up to date on his conversations with Shalev. Laroque was stunned by the terms of Romiti's proposal, understanding why Israel would readily agree to such a pact but finding it difficult to imagine how the jihadists would possibly concede to Romiti's plan.

"Convincing the ayatollah to become an evangelical preacher would be an easier sale than persuading the jihadists to accede to your demands! How do you plan to pull this off?"

"I will assure them that I am sympathetic to Islam, that I believe the Jews are the source of the world's woes, and that therefore, it is Allah's will that Israel be destroyed. I will promise to work in concert with them to see that Allah's will is done on earth."

Laroque's face showed no emotion as he listened. Finally the silence was broken when he jibed, "And when did you convert to Islam?"

It was Romiti's turn to smile. "Of course there is no Allah. But if by invoking his name I can win a temporary peace, then by Allah, I'll say what I need to say!"

"Why did you choose Sabzevar as the location of the Revolutionary Islamic Conference?" Laroque quizzed.

"Sabzevar was destroyed in the fourteenth century by invading Mongols. After the town was lost to Timur, the lame Muslim Turk who saw himself as Genghis Khan's heir, he killed the ninety thousand soldiers defending the town. There's a square in Sabzevar that is named *Sarberiz*, or 'the place of heads.' After the defenders were brutally killed, their heads were cut off and placed into three pyramids, one of which was located in Sarberiz Square." Romiti smiled again, a smile that would have frightened anyone but Laroque. "I don't want this fact of history lost on the jihadists who are attending the conference. Those who don't go along with my program will also lose their heads."

Laroque was silent, and Romiti went back to reviewing the long list of more than ninety terrorist organizations whose leaders would be present. Abu Nidal Organization. Al-Aqsa Martyrs Brigade. Hamas. Hezbollah. Islamic Jihad Movement. Al-Qaeda. Palestine Liberation Organization. The Muslim Brotherhood. The names on his list represented the organizations responsible for more than seventy percent of terrorist attacks worldwide.

Romiti laced his fingers and smiled in anticipation of the closing session.

*   *   *

"Assalamu Alaikom warahmatu Allahi wa barakatuhu." Romiti opened the third and final day of the conference by invoking the blessings of Allah upon the attendees. The gathering murmured in surprise, appreciation, and skepticism—and then grew silent as Romiti surprised them yet more by greeting the more than ninety jihadist leaders in flawless Arabic, Farsi, French, German, Italian, and English. They were already impressed that the UN secretary-general had arranged the conference for their benefit, each having been personally summoned by the radical president of the Islamic Republic of Iran on Romiti's behalf. Romiti had promised the Iranian president the blood of the Israelis; in return, the president agreed to persuade the radical terrorists to join him in Sabzevar. Now Romiti was working his magic in a more personal way.

After greeting several attendees, he was stunned by the sight of Mahmoud, his boyhood chum. Romiti, the Italian orator widely acclaimed for his powerful discourses, was speechless. *What in blazes is Mahmoud doing in Sabzevar?* He slowly made his way to the 'Abd al-Mumit delegate and affectionately but hesitantly embraced him before greeting him in Arabic: "Mahmoud, my long-lost brother. Is it really you? It's been too long!"

The two men had not spoken since before the 'Abd al-Mumit operation in Long Beach. Mahmoud had carefully followed Romiti's career, often wondering how he might one day capitalize on their friendship. Romiti, on the other hand, had no idea that Mahmoud was the founder of the notorious terrorist cell. Mahmoud knew the dangers of disclosing his connection to 'Abd al-Mumit, but in a strange way, he yearned to impress his former best friend. He wanted Romiti to know that he was the one responsible for bringing the Great Satan to its knees. He wanted Romiti's approval, even his blessing. *La hawla wala quwata illa billah,* he silently prayed, asking Allah for courage as he began to reveal what he had done.

For more than two minutes, the two men spoke rapidly in Ladin, the odd language never forgotten since their childhood days in Baselga di Piné. No one present had ever heard the language spoken, including the translators who had been invited to the conference. But all observed and were impressed that Romiti was accepted as a brother by Mahmoud, the world's most wanted terrorist and the one credited with the successful attack on America.

The conference was being held at the Islamic Azad University of Sabzevar, home to more than sixty-five hundred students during the academic year. The conferees were sitting in a small but comfortable auditorium that was configured in six rows of desks, creating a half-circle that faced the podium. There were no electronic devices in the auditorium—no recorders, no mobile phones, no laptops. Romiti was adamant that his voice not be recorded. In fact, there would be no record whatsoever of his presence in Sabzevar.

When introductions were over, he grasped the podium and looked out at the audience. "I trust this conference has been a profitable exercise for every one of you. Not unexpectedly, the groups you represent are often in conflict with one another. As a result, the general world opinion is that jihadists are a loose confederacy of revolutionaries who randomly murder large numbers of innocent civilians. The world credits you with the occasional overthrow of governments too, but finds it ironic that the governments you topple are often the ones most sympathetic to your cause. The world's perception of you must change!"

Romiti stopped to let the charges sink in before he continued. "Many of you really share a common goal, don't you? It's to Islamize the entire world. To introduce the strictest interpretation of Sharia law into every society and culture on earth. Am I correct?"

Most in the audience nodded their heads in agreement, some clapping and others boisterously voicing their approval. A few were operating under the banner of Islam but were really hardcore revolutionaries and anarchists, committed to the destruction of Western democracies—they could care less about taking Islam to the four corners of the globe.

Romiti smiled and went on. "But this cannot be accomplished until the two Satans have been wiped off the face of the earth. Now, my good friend Mahmoud has bruised America, and for this he is to be commended. But the US has only suffered a bruise." At the mention of Mahmoud's exploit, thunderous applause and shrill cries of praise filled the conference room. Romiti paused briefly, allowing Mahmoud to savor the moment. He winked and flashed a smile at his friend, and then continued his speech.

"If America finds its will, it will engage in the battle once more. However, when Israel ceases to exist, I'm certain America and its crusaders will retreat from the Middle East. Then we'll take the war to America's soil, fighting until the Great Satan goes to its final destruction."

A few of the rowdier jihadists shouted responses in Farsi and Arabic, which Romiti quieted by holding up his hand.

"My goal, like yours, is to rid the earth forever of America, this occupier of Muslim soil. But first, Israel must be defeated and destroyed!"

Upon hearing this declaration, the audience leapt to their feet, raising their fists and shouting their approval. "Israel must be defeated!" they repeated in unison. "Destroy the Little Satan!"

After quieting his audience, Romiti resumed his speech. "We cannot win this victory for Allah by working independently. We must be united. I share your goals, so you must believe what I'm about to tell you, and you must trust me. If you trust me and follow my lead, we will achieve victory, I promise!"

But Romiti's next words seemed to contradict his earlier rhetoric, leaving his audience incredulous, confused, and angry.

"You must rein in your soldiers. I want a three-and-a-half-year moratorium on violence against Israel—no rocket strikes, bombings of any kind, grenade attacks, assassinations—in other words, all violence must immediately cease. You must give up global jihad!"

The audience was stunned into a temporary silence. Then all rose up in fury, shaking their fists and screaming their disapproval. Mahmoud shook his head slowly, wondering whether his old friend was painting himself into a corner from which he would never escape. Many begin to exit the hall, muttering threats as they abandoned the conference.

But then, for no obvious reason, the most vocal leaders began to meekly return to their seats. They seemed to have fallen under a hypnotic spell, angry but no longer threatening. Hidden from view, Laroque had been observing the proceedings from a small nook at the rear of the hall. He smiled and nodded knowingly as the satanic spell worked its magic.

"Why should we trust you?" Hossein shouted.

"Shut up!" Mahmoud hissed to his cousin. "Let him finish!"

The Saudi Butcher, al-Wadhi, heard Mahmoud's muted order to Hossein but would not be silenced." You're no more than a mouthpiece for Israel!" the Butcher loudly accused. "We will not rest until the last drop of Jewish blood has left Muslim soil!"

"Even if we were to trust you, we all saw what happened to Russia when they attacked the Zionists. They were utterly destroyed. How can you possibly succeed where one of the world's strongest nations failed?" The Hezbollah leader and a repeated assassin was trying to give Romiti a chance to explain himself, but he too was seething.

The head of the Islamic Jihad Movement, Mubarak al-Diri, stood and motioned for silence. "I agree with my Hezbollah friend. The secretary-general is a mouthpiece for Israel, and unless he can describe how he plans to defeat them here and now, we should behead him!" The IJM leader turned to face Romiti. "Prove how we'll defeat Israel, or we'll drag you to the square at Sarberiz, where I'll personally sever your head!"

Romiti was not at all surprised by the crowd's reaction, and in fact was patiently waiting for the right moment to demonstrate the extent of the supernatural powers at his disposal.

"Dare you oppose me?" Romiti questioned al-Diri. "Are you willing to forfeit your life by your insolence?"

"You don't intimidate me," al-Diri sneered. "The Islamic Jihad Movement will not comply with your request." He stood with arms folded, a menacing smirk on his face.

Seconds after the words left al-Diri's mouth, the sound of a rushing wind filled the place where they were sitting.

Al-Diri leapt to his feet, his eyes open wide in surprise. He stared intently at the backs of his hands and then slowly raised them to his face, gingerly touching his bearded cheeks and jaw.

"I have no feeling!" he wailed in Arabic.

His fellow terrorists watched in disbelief as al-Diri's dark skin began to lose its moisture, like desert grass dried by the sirocco winds of the Sahara. Suddenly the skin began to shrivel as his cries of pain and terror filled the auditorium. Within seconds, his emaciated and withered flesh gave way to bone and cartilage. His clenched teeth formed a hideous grin on the skull, now sheathed by his white turban. Al-Diri's regal tunic hung loosely on the skeleton, a dreadful reminder of the once-proud leader.

"Does anyone else want to question my authority or power?" Romiti quietly asked.

Silence met his question.

"Let me repeat my promise. I will deliver Israel into your hands. No power in heaven or on earth can prevail against us! Before Allah our witness, you must swear your allegiance to me today. Today's proceedings are not to be revealed to the world. You must temporarily set aside violence; soon, Allah will release you like destroying locusts upon the mountains of Israel. I promise."

With little further debate, the leaders of the various terrorist organizations conceded to the demands of the secretary-general for a temporary cessation of violence.

"Imam Abu Ghait has issued a fatwa that declares it is lawful to take the lives of brothers who violate the oath to which they are now bound. The fatwa is the only tool you need to enforce the peace, and I expect you to use it, if only as a threat. I solemnly give this warning. Anyone who dares to break his oath to me will suffer the fate of al-Diri."

The shaken leaders left Sabzevar with al-Diri's skeletal remains firmly engrained in their memories. Mahmoud remained with Romiti for several more hours, offering many more details of the 'Abd al-Mumit operation—a breach he would later regret.

*   *   *

Two days later, Romiti attended a remake of the Arab League's infamous 2009 Doha Summit in the tiny country of Qatar. When the Arab League had last met in Doha, it was dubbed "The Reconciliation Summit."

Instead, it had highlighted Arab differences, many exacerbated by George W. Bush, the former US president. Bush had cunningly mobilized Sunni Arab governments against Iran, creating unexpected rivalries between various governments. It was hoped that this year, true reconciliation would occur.

Several outspoken leaders preceded Romiti to the podium, including Iran's president. The leader of Hamas, who had attended the Sabzevar conference, and the Palestinian chairman and de facto leader of the Fatah movement, were also present in Doha. Each addressed his perceptions of the Palestinian issue and concern over the rise of the political right wing in Israel, especially following Israel's spectacular victory over Russia. As expected, the Arab states were taking a hard line against Israel, the one issue on which all member states found common ground.

Once again, Romiti took center stage as he eloquently and passionately pressed his deceitful plan for peace in the Middle East.

He repeated what he had told the Israeli prime minister. "Israel must agree that Gaza and the West Bank, with the exception of the Jerusalem District, which will be annexed by Israel, will be an independent, sovereign Palestinian state. Israel will agree to abandon control of Gaza ports and will construct a corridor, at its own expense, between the two regions. The League of Arab States must recognize Israel's right to exist. Further, it must allow the Jews to construct their temple on the Temple Mount . . ."

At the mention of the Temple Mount, a chorus of angry, shouting voices drowned out Romiti.

"We will never allow a Jewish temple to desecrate the former shrine of Kubbat as-Sakhra! We will spill the blood of any Jew who dares to defile this holy site!"

The enraged audience continued their shouting, pumping their fists into the air and striking their chests.

Once again, Romiti stood motionless, waiting for the angry shouts to subside. As the audience watched, they noticed a radiance about him that was far brighter than the lights that lit up the stage. Someone quickly dimmed the stage lights, and the effect was startling. As some would later report, Romiti became in appearance like a god.

The eyes of his audience were riveted to the platform as they witnessed Romiti's seeming transfiguration from mortal to near deity. They stood in wonder at the sight, and then reverently bowed their heads as subjects in the presence of their king.

After observing their stunned reaction, he resumed his speech, speaking persuasively for his peace plan. "Look, Kubbat as-Sakhra was a shrine—not a mosque. Although many in the West are not aware of this fact, you are. Worshipers will recite their prayers at al-Aqsa, the mosque you consider the third most holy place in the Muslim world. It's within walking distance of the Kubbat as-Sakhra site, only two hundred meters to its south. Let the Jews rebuild their temple!"

Romiti began his concluding remarks as Laroque, seated alone in the balcony, stood with his eyes closed and his arms outstretched toward the evil source of his power.

To some in the audience, the secretary-general's closing seemed rather benign.

"It is time for the Muslim, the Jew, and the Christian to live together in harmony throughout the Middle East. Collectively, we long for a period of peace and prosperity in this region. The eyes of the world are upon us. Let us choose peace and renounce our violent pasts! There must be no unprovoked attacks on Israel. None."

But the minds of the radical Muslims in the audience took away an entirely different message. "Allow the temple to be rebuilt, and in less than four years, it and the state of Israel shall be destroyed! I promise that within this time frame, not a Jew or a Christian will remain alive in the Middle East. We will purge the infidels from your sacred soil. Agree to my request, and all I have promised shall surely come to pass!"

Once again, the delegates leapt to their feet—but this time, in harmony with their new leader. Israel's enemies in the conference hall pondered the powerful Romiti, grappling with a mystery. For days, they debated the paradox: their ears had clearly heard the words spoken by Romiti, but inexplicably, their minds had translated the words into an opposing message they knew was intended for them alone

The media was amazed by the sudden transformation of the delegates, puzzled by their startling acceptance of the speech. They left the hall bewildered but nonetheless exhilarated with the outcome.

That evening, in the historic closing session of the summit, the League of Arab States recognized Israel's right to exist, agreeing not to oppose the rebuilding of the temple and to forego violence against Israel.

Many in Israel wept when they heard the news coming out of the Doha Summit II. At last, a lasting peace, one they had never dreamed possible in their lifetimes, was taking shape before their very eyes.

Before leaving Doha, Romiti had a brief, very private meeting with Yehya Saadat, the chairman of the Palestinian National Authority.

"One condition of the armistice is that Gaza and the West Bank must combine to become a sovereign nation. As the current PNA chairman, you're the obvious choice to become its first president, and I'll lend my full support to your bid for the post. But let me be very clear. Within the next four years, if so much as a firecracker is tossed into Israel without my permission, you'll be out of a job and your nation will be reduced to ashes. Make no mistake. I'm deadly serious, and I mean exactly what I say."

"I understand you perfectly. If I'm chosen to be the president of the new nation, I'll implement whatever measures are necessary to prevent attacks on Israel from Gaza and the West Bank," the intimidated chairman agreed.

A few weeks later, the terms of the armistice were simultaneously presented in special sessions of the Israeli cabinet, the League of Arab States, and the United Nations. Although some in Israel and the Arab states opposed the armistice, all parties to the seven-year pact approved its terms. The armistice, called the Treaty of Babylon, was officially adopted at a formal signing ceremony held at the UN headquarters in Iraq.

*   *   *

Sticks's leadership team was gathered in his living room, watching a live CNN special report. The broadcast, announcing the signing of the treaty, was originating in Babylon. "I never thought I'd live to see this day," a solemn Sticks was saying to his friends.

"Today's signing represents a milestone in human history," the senior correspondent enthused. "There has never been a more important armistice. A year from today, thousands of people will be enjoying life who, in the absence of this treaty, would certainly have died violent deaths."

Sticks was unable to move, spellbound by the extraordinary news. *This is it. The seven-year covenant predicted in Daniel 9 has been signed before our very eyes!*

The journalist continued his report. "Not surprisingly, the territories of Gaza and the West Bank form the new nation of Palestine, led by the former chairman of the Palestinian National Authority, Yehya Saadat. For the first time in more than one thousand years, the peoples of the Middle East have agreed to end hostilities for a period of not less than seven years.

It is a remarkable achievement for a secretary-general who has held his post for less than a year!"

The cameras broke away from the journalist to cover the live proceedings now underway in the General Assembly. A motion to erect a tower on the grounds of the new UN headquarters in recognition of Romiti's tireless efforts to negotiate the historic peace accord was presented and adopted unanimously by acclamation. In expressing his appreciation for the honor, Sticks and his team heard Romiti say, "If we as one people have thus begun, then nothing we plan to do will be impossible."

The CNN journalist quickly scanned his notes and then commented on the honor bestowed upon the secretary-general. "Called the Tower of Babylon, it will be the tallest structure in the Babylon. An impressive granite slab will jut out of the tower just above its copper base and will serve as a platform for artists who will entertain the large crowds of visitors anticipated to gather in the beautifully landscaped plaza."

As promised, Romiti was changing his world.

CHAPTER EIGHTEEN

Temple Mount, Jerusalem

"Several hundred thousand Israelis are celebrating the signing of the Doha Peace Initiative negotiated by Romiti." David Cunningham, CNN's Pulitzer Prize-winning Middle East correspondent, was interviewing Ziva Rivlin, a spokesperson for the Temple Institute, an organization whose long-term goal was to "bring about the building of the holy temple in our time."

"He's their champion, an international hero, universally admired by the earth's inhabitants. Three times a day, for nearly two thousand years since the Romans destroyed Jerusalem and demolished the Second Temple in 70 AD, the Orthodox Jews have recited this prayer: 'May it be your will that the temple be speedily built in our own time.' Finally, their prayers have been answered; the temple can be rebuilt."

The interview was being conducted in a seldom-visited corner of the Temple Mount in which piles of archeological finds were sitting. Rivlin was resting on an ancient stone bench, perhaps once used by weary travelers who had made the dangerous pilgrimage to Jerusalem to worship in the Second Temple.

"Many believe Kubbat as-Sakhra, known in the West as the Dome of the Rock, occupied the same spot as Solomon's original temple. They say the unexpected destruction of Kubbat as-Sakhra opened the door for what is being celebrated today. Do you agree?"

Rivlin nodded her agreement, and then explained why. "We at the Temple Institute believe that God has intervened on behalf of his people. The temple could not have been rebuilt while Kubbat as-Sakhra was standing—certainly not without widespread violence and a significant loss of life. We're grateful for the recent decision by the League of Arab States to allow the project to move forward unopposed, and we hope the

Third Temple and al-Aqsa will become centers of reconciliation for peace-loving peoples of the world."

Cunningham was a skeptic, unconvinced that any being, god or otherwise, had intervened on behalf of the Jewish people. Life was so much simpler when people sought natural explanations, cause and effect. But he had to tell this story as it played out, no matter what people believed about it.

Observing the camera crew, a couple dozen Temple Mount visitors began to congregate a few yards away from Cunningham and Rivlin, hoping they would get on television too.

"I understand that architectural plans for the temple now exist and that many of the priestly robes and vessels to be used have already been made."

"You're correct," Rivlin replied. "If you drop by the Temple Institute office, located in the Jewish Quarter, you'll see glass cabinets filled with dozens of objects patterned after the descriptions found in the Tanakh, or Old Testament, including a pure gold menorah, silver trumpets, and an incense altar. Visitors can even take a virtual tour of the new temple, including the Sanhedrin assembly hall known as the Chamber of Hewn Stone."

Cunningham turned to the small crowd of gawkers that had gathered near the cameras. "Did you hear that? How many of you have visited the Temple Institute?"

No one responded, so Cunningham assumed the answer was no one. He was turning back to the cameras when a lady loudly promised to visit, so he quickly asked what she hoped to see.

"I'd like to see the virtual tour—will be interesting to see what the new temple might look like someday. I also want to see the gold menorah."

Cunningham smiled at the tourist, making her day. "Here, let me give you the URL for the virtual tour." The woman jotted down the information, thrilled by the attention she was receiving. Cunningham returned his attention to Rivlin as he asked the next question. "So what's next?"

The answer to this question obviously excited Rivlin, and she stood. "The next few months will be very exciting! The architectural plans have already been submitted to Jerusalem's deputy city planner for approval. We're hoping they'll be fast-tracked so that construction can begin within the next ninety days. We believe the new sanctuary will be occupied within a year of our ground-breaking ceremony!"

Turning to face the cameras, Cunningham began to wrap up the interview for his viewing audience. "Well, we've come a long way since the days of Mahmoud Abbas, the former Palestinian Authority president. Just hours before his famous 2011 speech before the UN, Abbas promised two hundred senior representatives of the Palestinian community, 'We shall not recognize a Jewish state.' Today we hear that construction of the Third Temple may soon begin. Exciting news, indeed!"

The news crew turned their focus away from the archeological finds as they took sweeping shots of the Temple Mount. However, Cunningham turned to his interviewee.

"Ziva, before you go, and off the record, I wanted to ask you another question. What can you tell me about the two strange-looking men who've been seen in various parts of Jerusalem over the last couple of days?"

She frowned. "To tell you the truth, I don't know what you're talking about. I've been preparing for this interview and haven't left my apartment for a week—haven't watched any news. Fill me in!"

"I'll give you the highlights. The pair has been seen in the Jewish Quarter, at the Western Wall and, believe it or not, the Knesset Building. This morning they were seen talking to a group of people in the courtyard of the Temple Mount."

"You described them as 'strange-looking' men. What makes them look so strange?"

Cunningham was chuckling as he described the two characters. "Their clothes. Rumor has it that it looks like they're wearing old gunnysacks—garments made of a coarse cloth, maybe woven from the hair of animals . . . or possibly sackcloth, as the ancient Hebrew prophets did. Reports say they look like wild men, with their strange clothing, long hair, and scraggly beards."

Upon hearing their description, Rivlin turned pale.

"Any—any idea why they're in Jerusalem?" she finally stuttered.

Cunningham cocked his head. *She's hiding something.* "No idea. It has something to do with their religion, apparently. The local police have questioned them a couple times but so far, nothing exciting has come of it. Sure you don't have any idea what they're up to?"

Rivlin was quiet for a moment. "I need to do some research—but do you own a Bible, a New Testament?"

Shouldn't have asked, Cunningham thought wryly. *Is she a religious nut?* "No, but I'm sure I can find one. What's up?"

She hesitated for a moment, then plowed ahead. "Over the years, I've met Christians, invariably evangelicals, who were visiting the Temple Institute. They've told me about two men who are described in Revelation, the last book in their New Testament. 'Read chapter 11,' they always say, so I'm telling you the same thing—read chapter 11. It describes two men—sometimes called the 'two witnesses'—who will suddenly appear in Jerusalem. I wonder if these are the ones. The visitors said to be watching for these men to appear around the time of the new temple!"

Cunningham could hardly suppress the excitement rising up in his chest. He had a sixth sense about prize-winning stories and immediately sensed this one could be the Pulitzer!

Even if he didn't believe in all this religious stuff.

*   *   *

David Lowry was in his company's executive conference room, concluding the weekly status meeting with his operations staff, when his secretary interrupted his recap of the week's key deliverables. "Larry Phelps on two—says it's important."

Lowry had given his secretary permission to interrupt him when Sticks said that. Lowry quickly punched line two on the speakerphone.

"Hey, Sticks. What's up?"

"Lowry? I need to see you right away. Any chance of swinging by the church? It's very important. That's all I can say at the moment."

"On my way, Sticks. Keep cool! Will be there in twenty minutes."

A short time later, Lowry grabbed a chair as he entered Sticks's office and waited for an explanation. One look at the preacher and Lowry knew something was troubling him.

"You're familiar with the famous passage in Revelation 13 that says something like, 'If anyone has insight, let him calculate the number of the beast, for it is man's number. His number is 666.'" Sticks charged on. "Well, about a week ago I discovered something I've only shared with a couple of people. I ran my findings by an acquaintance at the Baltimore Hebrew University first. He confirmed my suspicions, but I wanted a second opinion, so I contacted a friend who is a professor of Hebrew Studies at the Hebrew University of Jerusalem. After I presented my findings, he told me he made the same observation several weeks ago but has been keeping it to himself."

"So go on," Lowry urged, sensing Sticks's excitement. "What have you discovered?"

"Each of the twenty-two letters of the Hebrew alphabet has a numerical value. The values progress as follows: one, two, three, four, five, six, seven, eight, nine, ten, twenty, thirty, forty, fifty, sixty, seventy, eighty, ninety, one hundred, two hundred, three hundred, and four hundred. Well, when you link the letters that spell 'Romiti' with their Hebrew equivalents and then sum up the values, you find the result is 666. The Hebrew letters that comprise 'Romiti' are *resh,* two hundred; *vav,* six; *mem,* forty; *yod,* ten; *taw,* four hundred; and *yod,* ten."

Sticks stood, agitated, and paced behind his desk. "Using this methodology, the names of many public figures throughout history have had the Hebrew numerical equivalent of 666. So by itself, this isn't earth-shattering news by any stretch of the imagination. But based on everything else he's done—his virulent anti-Semitic rhetoric, his rapid rise to a position of prominence on the world stage, the recently signed Treaty of Babylon—it's clear, Lowry. No room for argument or wondering anymore. Romiti is the Antichrist."

He sat down, throwing himself into his chair like his legs couldn't hold him up anymore. Lowry just let his words sink in as Sticks continued. "The most powerful man in our world right now is a man fully empowered by Satan himself. Over the last several days, several other prominent Bible teachers have posted blogs that also identify the secretary-general as the prophesied Antichrist." Sticks jumped up again and continued his pacing, but there was a determined look on his face. He was energized, ready to take the battle to Satan's turf.

Lowry whistled and then asked the obvious question. "What do we know about him? Personally, I mean?"

"Not much, really. He was raised in a village in northern Italy named Baselga di Piné. Romiti's mother, Emiliane, was also an only child, the daughter of a fanatical follower of Hitler named Mario Guiseppina. Mario's wife, Emiliane's mother, was killed in an automobile accident shortly after the birth of their daughter. Although Catholic by birth, Emiliane rejected Catholicism and became deeply involved in the occult."

"Hmmm. What about his father? And what's Romiti's last name?" Lowry questioned.

"That's where it really gets interesting. There's no record of a father. His name is never mentioned—anywhere. When Romiti's birth was recorded, his mother insisted the name *Romiti* stand alone. She refused to give him her last name. Romiti means *man of Rome,* and it's the only name he's ever known."

Lowry whistled again and then asked, "So what happens next?"

"Well, for now, we should just keep our eyes and ears open. We should also watch Laroque, Romiti's deputy for religious affairs. If my hunch is correct, Laroque may well be the 'false prophet' of Revelation 13. In the not-too-distant future, we may discover other information that will confirm my conclusions. For example, based on Matthew 24 and Revelation 6, we should expect to see the Antichrist begin his conquest of nations that oppose his leadership. We can expect widespread famine—the price of food will soar as staples become increasingly scarce. Things aren't going to be easy, my friend.

"Tonight, I'll begin an accelerated, multipart study on the seven seals of Revelation 6. I'm going to out Romiti as I discuss the first seal. Christians need to know. But I don't want to lose our focus—we need to talk about what our response to the coming events should be."

"What do you mean?" Lowry asked, still trying to come to grips with all that Sticks was telling him.

"The church must engage and confront our world in much the same way Jesus and his disciples engaged and confronted the culture of their day. Believe me, after today, it'll no longer be church as usual. It'll be like the early church—persecution, sharing everything we have, being one in heart and mind, and, I fervently pray, with great power we'll testify to the power and grace of Jesus."

Larry whistled for the third time since the meeting began. "Wouldn't miss tonight for the world!"

*   *   *

That evening, regular attendees noticed that for the first time in their memory, Sticks's wife, son, and two daughters had joined him on the platform. Before he began to teach, Sticks called attention to his family. "I'm going to present some disturbing information tonight. It will frighten some, perhaps many, of you. Might even frighten my family. So I want

187

us to be together on the stage. I will also make a vow to my family this evening, and you'll be the witnesses, okay?"

Sticks saw heads nodding. *They know tonight's topic is a serious one. I can see it on their faces.*

Sticks began his teaching by repeating the information he had given Lowry an hour or two earlier. "Based on Daniel 9, beginning with verse 27, most evangelical teachers believe the Antichrist's dominance over the world's political scene begins when he signs or enforces a seven-year covenant with Israel. Toward the end of Revelation 13, the apostle John reveals that 'the number of the beast' is 666."

Sticks noticed an immediate reaction to the notorious term. He watched some lean forward in their seats, anxious to hear his every word. He saw wives glance uneasily at their husbands—some responded to their wives' anxiety with a quick wink or by sitting impassively, masking the dreadful fear that had abruptly gripped their hearts.

"These two pieces of information give us clues as to the identity of the Antichrist. Bottom line, we're being told that someday Israel will sign a seven-year peace covenant with a powerful leader. The newly signed Treaty of Babylon is exactly that. Israel and its enemies have agreed to end hostilities for seven years—the newly elected secretary-general authored the treaty and is one of the most prominent signers of the manifest. And we're being told the 'number of the beast' is 666. For centuries, many have speculated that 666 is somehow connected with the actual name of the Antichrist—a fair conjecture, considering John's testimony."

Sticks stood up straighter and took a deep breath, aware that what he was about to say would put him at direct odds with the ruling power of the world. "Based on this reasoning and other information, I'm convinced that Romiti, the secretary-general of the United Nations, is the ruthless, Satan-energized dictator predicted in the extensive prophecies of Daniel, the apostle John, and other Bible authors."

There were gasps from the crowd as the force of his words hit home. A few started to weep, but most stared stoically at the pastor, waiting for him to continue.

"If I'm correct, we've entered into the brief span of time that Jesus's disciples called 'the end of the age.' You've heard me call this period the seventieth week of Daniel. The events of this period will be our focus for the next several evenings.

"I've already mentioned that I asked my family to be on the stage. I'm not being theatrical. My reason for inviting them to join me is very simple. Until Christ comes for his church, an event called the rapture, the coming days will be difficult, even terrifying, for many believers.

"My natural family and my church family are my most important relationships on earth. They're more important than my job, my material possessions, and my position in the community. Some may say this should have always been true, and I agree. But while we may have believed this with our minds, I'm not sure we've practiced it with our hearts. But from this night forward, our priority must first be to our Lord and Savior Jesus Christ. And our second priority must be to our families, which includes fellow believers."

Sticks asked his family to stand beside him before he made a public vow to the Lord, to his family, and to his church.

His family stood together, hand in hand. Tears spilled from Cyndi's eyes as she looked at her husband, knowing that life would never be the same. For the first time in their marriage, she was frightened for herself and her children. And she was terribly frightened for Sticks. She recalled that morning's conversation, when she had pleaded with him to be careful. "Do you have to publicly announce that Romiti is the Antichrist? What if you're wrong? Or worse, what if you're right?"

He had smiled at her concern, held her close, and then softly paraphrased Mordecai's famous line to Esther: "Who knows, Cyndi, but that I have come to this position for such a time as this?"

"Heavenly Father, I love you and desire to put you first in every area of my life," Sticks prayed before his congregation. "Thank you for calling me from a life lived in rebellion against you, for forgiving me of my many sins, for turning aside your wrath which I so richly deserved, and then, as if all this were not enough, for adopting me as one of your children. Truly, you are an amazing God! I pray that in the short time we have left, I may serve you selflessly and with excellence, making the most of every opportunity you send my way."

Sticks turned to his wife. "Cyndi, honey, I love you. You've been an amazingly supportive wife, lover, and best friend. The coming storm will be very tough on both of us, but we'll make it, won't we? I don't know what kind of choices we'll be forced to make, but understand that apart from my obedience to the Lord, you and the children are my highest earthly priority, even more important than my own life."

He smiled down at his children, who were trying their best to be brave in front of everyone watching. "And Tommy, Samantha, and Laurie. You're the joys of my life. I want each of you to know how much I love you. This is hard for you to understand—you're only five, seven, and ten years old—but many of our friends are going to need a lot more of Daddy and Mommy's time. Some people don't like what I'm saying, and they may even put me in jail. Some of your school friends may not want to be your friends anymore. Remember? We've talked about this, haven't we? I've got the best kids in the world, and I want you to know how very proud I am of you. Each of you are God's gift to your mom and me!"

With hardly a dry eye in the auditorium, Sticks kissed each member of his family before they returned to their seats, and then he turned his attention to the message.

"As Jesus left the temple in Jerusalem, his disciples called his attention to the beautiful buildings and the massive rock walls that protected the ancient city. But Jesus wasn't as impressed as they were. He's not as easily impressed as you and me, is he? His reply shocked the disciples, as he predicted that soon 'not one stone here will be left on another; every one will be thrown down.' Imagine if someone told us that someday, not a building, not even a wall, would be left standing in Washington, DC. We would assume that another power would conquer America or that the world must be coming to an end, wouldn't we?"

"Yes, we would!" a Gulf War vet agreed loudly.

"That's exactly what the disciples concluded. They asked Jesus when these events would happen and what sign would be given to indicate his return and the end of the age. This story, told in Matthew 24, is known as the Olivet Discourse because the setting is on the Mount of Olives overlooking Jerusalem. I've been there—it's a beautiful place! In response to their questions, Jesus taught his disciples what the believers who are living during these 'end times' can expect. You and I are the believers Jesus was talking about! Isn't that incredible? He was talking about you and me!

"There's another New Testament passage that closely parallels the Olivet Discourse. In Revelation 6, John introduces the seven seals. And no, this isn't an ancient Jewish rock group! In his vision, John sees a scroll, or in today's language, a book, held in the right hand of God. The seven-sealed scroll is closed and can only be opened by Jesus, the one in heaven who is worthy to open the scroll. John watches Jesus open the scroll by breaking one seal at a time. As each seal is broken, John writes a brief description of its significance. So for the next few weeks, I'm going to describe the events that are associated with the first five seals. However, to a great extent, the time for teaching is past. I, along with my leadership team, will be charting our course for the tumultuous days ahead."

"Slow down!" a young voice ordered. The unexpected command relieved a little tension, and several laughed nervously at the teenager's interruption. "Yes, sir!" Sticks responded to the blushing adolescent. He waited patiently until the young man looked up, his signal that Sticks could resume talking.

"Some teach that the seals represent the opening salvo of God's wrath on mankind. However, I do not share this opinion. I believe that during this terrible time, God is actually demonstrating his sovereign control over the affairs of earth. During man's wrath against man, the seals represent the fact that God's in charge. Even during the first part of Daniel's seventieth week, before we see Jesus face-to-face, nothing can happen to you or me without God's consent. One of my favorite authors, named John Walvoord, has written, 'The judgments of war, famine, and death, and the martyrdom of the saints, have largely originated in human decisions and in the evil heart of men.'

"When the first seal is opened, John sees a rider on a white horse. Most of you have heard of the Four Horsemen of the Apocalypse—it's a concept that's been used in pop culture and literature plenty of times. The passage we're studying tonight provides the background for this familiar term. The first rider and his horse symbolize the rise of false Christs and religions, epitomized by the Antichrist himself. This figure plays a very important role during the seventieth week of Daniel.

"The true Trinity is comprised of the Father, Son, and Holy Spirit. The counterfeit trinity is also comprised of three figures. Satan will play the role of the counterfeit father and will give his authority to the Antichrist, who plays the role of the counterfeit son. The False Prophet will be the counterfeit holy spirit. So by this first seal, John introduces us to the second person of the counterfeit trinity, the Antichrist. John writes that this person is given a crown and rides out 'as a conqueror bent on conquest.' The Antichrist will assume greater and greater power as he conquers, first by deception and then in battle, all who oppose him.

"While there will be a false sense of security as the Antichrist consolidates his power base, over time we must expect violence to increase as the Antichrist wages war against his enemies, defeating them one by one. This increase in violence is demonstrated by the next seal.

"When Jesus opens it, a rider on a fiery red horse is seen. This rider is given a sword and 'power to take peace from the earth and to make men slay each other.' As the Antichrist gains power, violence throughout the earth will increase. Peace will disappear. The second seal initiates significant wars that will take place during the opening days of the seventieth week of Daniel.

"A natural consequence of war is famine, as farms, ranches, and infrastructure are destroyed in major battles. John next sees a black horse whose rider is holding a pair of scales in his hand. The scales represent famine. John writes that a couple of loaves of bread will cost a day's wage! Today, large populations go to bed hungry each night. Accurate numbers are hard to come by, but there's little disagreement that today, at least ten million children starve to death every year. But when the third seal is opened, severe food shortages will dramatically increase throughout the world—multiplied millions more will die of hunger.

"North Americans, particularly Americans, have been well fed. It's rare that anyone dies of starvation in this country. But as you're all well aware, the attack in Long Beach damaged our country's supply chains. Seventy-five million unemployed parents have been unable to feed their families. I've seen statistics that show there are far more hungry Americans today than ever before. But when the third seal is broken, it's very likely that we in the US will also experience terrible famine—not just supply chain challenges.

"We have assembled packets of information that describe steps we can all take to prepare for this eventuality. As you leave this evening, I urge you to take as many packets as you need and distribute them to friends and family, explaining the importance of planning for the days ahead."

Sticks surveyed his congregation, who were taking notes and listening more closely than ever. And no wonder—his teachings were a blueprint for their lives in the coming days, not just dry doctrine they couldn't understand. His heart moved with compassion for them. "The fourth horse and rider are perhaps the most frightening symbols of all. John describes a pale horse whose rider is named Death. John also notes that 'Hades,' or hell, followed close behind. In the closing months of 2011, the earth's population broke seven billion people. Today, that figure is over eight billion. Eight *billion!* Keep that figure in mind as our study continues.

"The fourth horse and rider were given power over a fourth of the earth—imagine, given power over nearly two billion people—to kill by weapons, famine, plague, and wild beasts. This period, I believe, will be the worst ever experienced on earth. It seems that John is saying that nearly two billion people will perish during this time. It's unimaginable, isn't it? As famine continues unabated, wild animals become fearless and begin to prey upon humans to satisfy their hunger. Yet, even during this most terrible of times, the church must be a beacon of hope to a world that's in utter chaos, one held captive by unspeakable terror, despair, and hopelessness."

Many of the listeners were already familiar with the apostle's grim description of the seven seals, but this time, their imaginations lived the experience as Sticks painted vivid pictures of their future. Some had begun to assess their lives, silently taking inventory. *What should I do—should I sell my home and move out of the city? Maybe I should call off the wedding. If I quit my job, are there things I can do to help Sticks reach our community? Barb wants to start a family—that ain't gonna happen!*

"The fifth seal depicts believers who have refused to worship the Antichrist and as a result have been martyred for their stand for Christ. This is sobering, isn't it? Many Western believers have asked how this is possible. Why would God allow his followers to lose their lives? The truthful answer is simply, 'Why not?' Today, more than 400 Christians are killed each day for their faith. That's almost 150,000 believers a year! In most parts of the world, especially in Islamic countries as well as India, China, North Korea, and others, millions of Christians have been martyred for their faith. In his sovereignty, God has not allowed Satan to attack the Western church through martyrdom. Instead, Western believers have been seduced by the idols of wealth, sex, and convenience. But this is changing and will continue to change as Antichrist reveals himself as the one opposed to God and begins to intensely persecute the church and Israel, committed to their mutual destruction.

"Before we end this evening, let me leave you with some challenges. I've not painted a pretty picture of the next few years, so let me leave you with hope. Earlier this evening, I used China as an example of a nation where Christians have been mercilessly persecuted. But in this nation, more than 30,000 people also turn to Jesus every day. By some estimates, there are more than 150 million believers in China today.

"When the world experiences the pain and turmoil I've described tonight, we in the church must become the first responders. We've already seen this happen on a smaller scale as the church has generously responded with time, talents, and gifts to the victims of the many natural disasters that have plagued the world in recent years. Let's imagine this was practice for the bigger calamities that will surely come.

"I'll offer more details in the coming weeks, but here are some things to consider. Set aside a substantial block of time each day to pray for your family, the leaders of this church, your neighbors, our nation. I'm confident a global revival is on its way—pray it comes soon and that you and I will be a part of it. Launch small groups in your neighborhoods, inviting your unbelieving friends and relatives, rather than other church members, to participate. Take an inventory of your possessions with the idea of *giving away* as much as possible when a need arises. Soon, we'll be announcing some unique new ministries that you can be part of—begin now to evaluate your schedules and personal resources so when the ministries are launched, you'll be ready to participate.

"In closing, set aside some time to study Revelation 6, comparing it verse-by-verse to Matthew 24. Note the similarities. I'll provide some additional details in coming talks, but in the meantime, I encourage you to learn these chapters well. Any questions?"

"I want to know when the church will be raptured," one young mother asked. "I've always been taught that the Christians will be gone when all this happens."

"Here's my quick answer," Sticks replied. "I believe the rapture occurs at the sixth seal. Obviously no one knows the date of the rapture, but Paul reminds the church in Thessalonica that 'this day should not surprise you like a thief.' We should study Scripture diligently, watching expectantly for his return, and as Paul exhorted his friend, Philemon, 'be active in sharing your faith so that we may have a full understanding of every good thing we have in Christ.' I deliberately ended tonight's session at the fifth seal. We'll spend most of the next session on what the fifth and sixth seals represent for the church. For now, suffice it to say that I don't believe we're going to escape the events I described tonight."

Lowry stood and asked, "Matthew writes about the abomination that the prophet Daniel predicted. I understand this sacrilege occurs in the new temple. When do you think this will happen?"

Sticks nodded, glad his friend had brought that up. "We've all been reading about the Jewish temple that's being built on the Temple Mount. As you know, it won't be long before construction is completed. At some point, the Antichrist is going to commit a terrible act in the temple. It will be so blasphemous that it will cause the temple to be desolate: that is, it will no longer be used, emptied of its worshipers. According to Daniel, the Antichrist commits this abomination about three-and-a-half years after the peace initiative is signed—midway through the seventieth week of Daniel. When he commits this blasphemous act, it will cause many Jews to recognize the Antichrist for who he really is. At that point, the Antichrist will unleash his full fury on Jews and Christians alike. This ties into the fifth and sixth seals again, so I'm going to stop for now. Get some sleep, and we'll see you next time!"

Lowry caught up to Sticks after the meeting ended. "I meant to tell you this earlier this evening, but I forgot to bring it up. The church's website has been up and down like a yo-yo today. We've been hit by some kind of a computer virus. I've got the best technicians in the company trying to track down the source; after we've eliminated the virus, we'll construct a better firewall to prevent this from happening again."

Sticks remained deep in thought for a minute and then asked, "Have you heard of any other sites crashing?"

"Yes, as a matter of fact I have. Over the last week or so, several have told me that they suddenly lost connectivity to the Internet. We've figured the service providers were having problems with their web servers."

Sticks smiled sadly and shook his head. "It's more than that, Lowry. I'll bet if you look into it, you'll find they were visiting religious sites when service was disrupted. I doubt our problems were caused by any ordinary virus. I'm guessing the Antichrist's technologists are blocking access to Christian sites. Do you remember the Arab Spring uprising? Syria, under Bashar al-Assad, used technology to identify and murder hundreds, perhaps thousands, of dissenters. Egyptian officials used similar technology to eavesdrop on dissidents over Skype, and Moammar Gadhafi's henchmen snooped on e-mail and chats of Libyan protestors. Your technicians are probably up against some of the best computer wizards money can buy. My guess is the problem is here to stay; we'll have to make do."

*   *   *

Romiti was in his office at the UN headquarters in Babylon, perusing a bulletin from Max Zagmi, chief of the UN's Center of Intelligence and Security. He smiled as he read that Zagmi's cyber-based worms were beginning to corrupt certain religious websites and stealthily infiltrate others, the latter to mine information that would be used to locate, bully, or embarrass particularly valuable evangelical targets. However, Romiti's glee turned into anger as the bulletin also revealed disturbing statistics showing the number of sites that had already identified him as the evil Antichrist predicted in the Bible. This was not a surprise. Romiti knew the Bible, certainly many of the most significant prophecies, better than most preachers, so he also knew he would be identified as the Antichrist as soon as the Treaty of Babylon was signed. But he was incensed by the confident manner in which his detractors predicted his downfall.

What infuriated him most, though, was various sites' effective presentation of the gospel—the "good news," it was called. The last thing Romiti wanted was a resurgence of radical Christianity. It was his greatest fear. He made a mental note to meet with his cabinet soon; they must plot a continuing strategy to counter the religious busybodies who could obstruct his plans for the world.

CHAPTER NINETEEN

Jerusalem, Israel

The Chief Rabbinate of Israel, also known as the *Rishon leZion,* consisted of two chief rabbis: an Ashkenazi rabbi and a Sephardi rabbi. Elected for ten-year terms, they alternated in its presidency, were assisted by the Chief Rabbinate Council, and were recognized by law as the spiritual head of Orthodox Jewry. As such, the Rishon leZion had jurisdiction over the rebuilding of the temple.

Every aspect of the temple reconstruction was subject to the rabbinate's scrutiny and approval. Despite their painstaking attention to the minutest details, ensuring that not a hint of biblical, talmudic, or rabbinic laws were violated, construction of the temple was making rapid progress. While the leaders of the various Muslim extremist groups were honoring their promise to refrain from violence against the Jews, the vitriolic debate on the rebuilding of the temple incited radical individuals to make numerous threats on the lives of the construction workers and religious overseers. At the request of the council, a heavily armed Israeli military protected the construction site, ensuring progress would not be slowed. There were also the occasional rallies of the most militant Islamic devotees who remained opposed to the project. These rallies did not go unnoticed by Romiti, and on more than one occasion, their leaders mysteriously disappeared. But despite their inordinate attention to details, the threats, and the demonstrations, most Orthodox Jews remembered that they had waited two thousand years for this project to begin—a few obstacles would not dampen their enthusiasm. Perhaps with the glorious temple in place, their long-awaited Messiah would come. Perhaps, some fervently prayed, Romiti was the *Mashiach,* the one who would rebuild the temple and renew sacrifices on the Temple Mount

*   *   *

Laroque was excitedly preparing for the UN's first gathering of leaders of the world's great religions, dubbed the International Interfaith Council. The publicly stated, twofold purpose of the IIC was to lay the foundation for greater mutual respect, tolerance, and cooperation among the world's great religions, and to begin an interfaith dialogue intended to reconcile the religions into a single movement. Cloaked in religious symbols and rituals, its disguised purpose was to infiltrate and destroy all religious systems that would oppose Romiti and Laroque.

"What are you going to do about the number of men who proclaim they're the Christ?" one of Laroque's senior religious advisers asked.

"They're popping up over all the world, but especially in the Middle East," a Hindu priest added.

"I plan to ignore them," was Laroque's answer. "They'll come to nothing. Most of these false Christs are deceiving small groups of followers, mostly for financial gain. These religious misfits will cause some to follow them rather than Christianity. They're leveraging the convergence of ancient prophecies and current events with their charismatic personalities, creating small cults of avid disciples who have bought into their hodgepodge of fact and fiction. But the number of converts is small—they'll have no impact on our plans for a unified religion."

"But how about the Christians?" the Hindu priest pressed. "The number of evangelical Christians is growing faster than any religion— even Islam. Islam is growing through the high birthrate of its adherents, but Christianity is growing through new conversions. In Karnataka, we disrupted their meetings. We drove the Christian leaders from our villages. We beat the new converts, we burned their vehicles and their homes. Karnataka was called the most dangerous state for Christians in India."

"Don't worry, Bima. You'll do this again, I promise you. But you must be patient," Laroque replied.

Like the Antichrist, Laroque was acquainted with Scripture, and he understood human nature. "The earth is about to enter a period of severe crisis," Laroque offered. "This means that people will search for spiritual relief in great numbers. They always do. Now is the time to launch a worldwide religious movement that transcends the teachings of Jesus, the Jewish prophets, and Muhammad. Buddhists, Hindus, and Muslims will unite under my global religion."

Laroque continued, "I do not want the various religions to coexist. Our goal is to meld them into one, united in a single religion that will serve my purpose. As for the so-called Christians that align with us—" he smiled. "I want them to have a form of godliness, but to deny its power."

*   *   *

As expected, the chief rabbis of Israel did not attend the International Interfaith Council, nor did leaders of any evangelical or fundamentalist Protestant denomination. There was a fierce debate among the Catholic cardinals, but in the end, a decision against the Pope's participation was announced, hugely disappointing Laroque. However, in attendance were heads of several mainline Protestant denominations, moderate Muslim clerics, rabbis associated with liberal Judaism, and monks representing various Buddhist and Hindu traditions. Not surprisingly, and to everyone's delight, the Dalai Lama, representing Tibetan Buddhism, also attended.

Since Laroque's first encounter with Romiti at the Schloss Wewelsburg, Himmler's Paderborn castle, the prophet seemed to have been reborn. His once sickly and emaciated frame looked strong and healthy. His eyes were bright and penetrating, exuding confidence. Tanned and energetic, the deputy minister was anxious to launch his new movement.

In his opening address, Laroque denounced the notion that any religion had the absolute truth.

"For too long, narrow-minded religious bigots have divided humanity by their dogged insistence that they and they alone have the corner on truth. Some of these dogmatists claim their path is the only path to God and all other paths lead to a fiery hell."

The audience listened intently, transfixed by the power of his voice and vision. "True religion should not divide humanity; it should unify us. The purpose of this gathering is to bring us together as one, to create an inclusive religious system that embraces all people of all faiths. Tolerance will be the first and greatest commandment in this new religious order."

By the end of the conference, Laroque had won the day. The attendees came to the conference representing a myriad of religions, but all were predisposed to accept the founding principles adopted in the closing session of the first International Interfaith Council. Called the Six Pillars of Faith, they were:

1. I believe one knows truth through self-revelation.
2. I believe it is good to pray to deities and their prophets, the most notable of whom are Mohammed, Buddha and Jesus.
3. I believe a succession of prophets were empowered to model diverse paths, all of which lead to ultimate enlightenment and oneness with him.
4. I believe the attributes of deity are revealed through various written forms, including the Koran, the Vedas, the Lotus Sutra, and the Bible.
5. I believe the words of the prophets reveal our personal truth.
6. I believe deity has appeared in human form throughout the ages, culminating in a single manifestation that will bring about a lasting peace on earth.

Believing that the Dalai Lama embodied the newly adopted Six Pillars of Faith, the delegates formally recognized him as the only living prophet to the present generation. The Dalai Lama modestly accepted the accolades of his religious friends, promising the allegiance of his followers to the new one-world religious system that would be headquartered in Babylon.

Laroque smiled as he listened to the Dalai Lama accept his role as prophet. *This was easier than I imagined—five hundred million Buddhists will follow the Dalai Lama's lead.*

The first council also elected Arundhati Gupta, the Hindu delegate from Karnataka, as its Supreme Priestess. Laroque was ecstatic. *And now we've added a billion Hindus! Not a bad start!* Laroque's first choice to head the movement, Gupta would soon rule over earth's religious affairs. She kept secret her deep hatred of Christianity and Judaism. She possessed a quick wit and a brilliant mind—and she was the consummate appeaser.

Gupta was a powerful communicator, an excellent organizer, and most importantly, she had fallen under the spell of Laroque. Her ambition was to meld a diverse set of religions into a hodgepodge replacement that would appeal to the masses, and she was committed to the notion of a universal religion that could accommodate all of India's 330 million gods. Her mission was to build and lead a global religious movement that had no vestiges of Judaism or Christianity. Laroque alone could see how great she would become. She and her followers would soon grow drunk with the blood of the saints.

Coinciding with the ending of the conference, the UN's Department of Global Communications released a worldwide series of moving minidocumentaries that chronicled the accomplishments of the recent International Interfaith Council. The infomercials featured the Dalai Lama and a host of talented entertainers, including actors and actresses, musicians, singers, comedians, and others, all giving credit to the Six Pillars of Faith for their success.

Most heads of state embraced the Six Pillars, encouraging the populations they ruled to join the new movement. Most churches, synagogues, and mosques throughout the world quickly aligned themselves with the IIC, while their members flocked to Omega-ism, the name coined by the IIC and proclaimed as the world's greatest and last religious movement.

The Vatican quickly published a manifesto decrying the false religious system, and in Boston, more than three hundred Catholic bishops gathered to publicly denounce the Six Pillars. Heads of evangelical denominations, conservative Jewish congregations, and devout Muslims also condemned Omega-ism, calling it an abomination and urging its rejection.

*   *   *

Romiti wanted to make certain he could always count on the support of America's ambassador to the United Nations, and therefore, he needed the newly elected president of the United States, James Gladden, to be firmly ensconced in his proverbial pocket.

The president was sitting in the Oval Office, located in the west wing of the White House. He was still basking in his recent victory but was somewhat intimidated by the memories and accomplishments of the men who sat in this office before him. The east door of the office led to the rose garden; the door was open, allowing a cool breeze to freshen the room. He was gazing out the south-facing windows when he accepted Romiti's scheduled call.

"Mr. President, thank you for taking my call."

"You're welcome, Mr. Secretary-General. How can I be of service?"

"I have information that is of vital interest to you and your government. It's a matter of national security and must be discussed with you discreetly and in private."

"Come to Washington. I will be delighted to receive you," the president declared.

Several days later, Romiti was en route to the Washington Dulles National Airport. Following his arrival at Dulles, Romiti was escorted to the White House by motorcade with the usual pomp and circumstance reserved for royal visits. The procession included six armored SUVs, accompanied by police motorcycles that led and followed the motorcade.

He was greeted by the president himself. Then, following a personal tour of the White House, Romiti was ushered into the Oval Office for a private meeting.

Romiti, an avid historian, was inspired by his surroundings. But the power represented by this office would pale in comparison to the power that would soon be his. He stood in front of the massive partners desk, called the Resolute Desk. Romiti knew its history. The desk was made from the timbers of the British frigate HMS *Resolute*. The frigate had been frozen in Arctic ice and abandoned. After being found by American seamen, it was presented as a gift from the United States to Queen Victoria. After its decommissioning, Queen Victoria ordered that two desks be made from its timbers. The queen kept one, and in 1880 presented the second desk as a gift to President Rutherford Hayes.

Romiti noticed the striking maroon drapes that partially covered the three large windows behind the president's workspace, and the striped wall coverings, perfectly accenting the vivid color of the draperies. He slowly turned around, observing the memorabilia, statuettes, and famous paintings mounted on the pearl-white walls.

"Thank you for allowing our meeting to take place in the Oval Office. Since childhood, it has been one of my goals to meet with the sitting president of the United States in this historic seat of power," Romiti declared with a great deal of satisfaction.

"I'm glad you're pleased," Gladden replied, smiling. "Now, tell me the purpose of your visit."

"The perpetrators of the horrific nuclear attack in Long Beach have never been brought to justice," Romiti began. "I have made it my goal to learn the identity of each of the terrorists. I now have their names and whereabouts, and I want to personally present this information to you."

Gladden was stunned by the revelation, but thrilled. The capture of the terrorists, on his watch, would almost guarantee his reelection four years hence. He remembered the huge bounce, though short-lived, that Barack Obama had enjoyed in the days immediately following the death of Osama bin Laden. The nation was still enraged over the Long Beach attack, bent on revenge but without a clue as to the identity or location of the jihadists. With justice served, the president would enjoy unprecedented popularity with his constituents—Republicans, Democrats, and independents alike.

"How did you come by this information?" Gladden asked.

"I cannot identify my sources, nor can it ever be known that I was your source of information. You can take credit or give the credit to whomever you desire, but you must not associate me with this affair."

"And what may I do for you in return?" the president inquired.

Romiti gave the impression that he was carefully considering the question. "As a young man I traveled extensively throughout your country, from New York to San Francisco. My experiences instilled in me a deep admiration for America and its people. In return for my information, I simply want to be considered a friend of the United States. There may be a time when I need your support. Perhaps my act of kindness will be remembered by you should I ever find myself in need of your help."

The president was touched by Romiti's apparent sincerity and pledged his support to the modest secretary-general.

Less than two weeks later, the world was astonished to learn that the terrorists responsible for the nuclear attack on Southern California had been captured in coordinated raids conducted in various parts of the world. General Muhammad Saleem Rajput, the head of the Pakistani Armed Forces, was easily captured in Islamabad, the capital of Pakistan, while attending a military parade. Natalia Gutierrez, the Akbari truck driver, was arrested in her beautiful home in Bogota, Columbia. Hossein Heidari was captured in the city of Garmsar, Iran.

During a routine medical exam performed just hours before Heidari's capture, the examining physician discovered a radio frequency identification tag, smaller than a grain of rice, implanted in the back of Mahmoud's neck. Mahmoud correctly assumed that he had been somehow tagged while attending the Sabzevar conference. The RFID tag did not require a power source; it simply echoed back preloaded identification information to an airborne surveillance system that had been diligently searching for him. Mahmoud concluded Romiti was somehow responsible, and he fled Garmsar hours before his hiding place was discovered by the GSF. In hiding, Mahmoud bitterly vowed revenge for Hossein's imminent execution.

The al-Qaeda chief and Saudi Butcher, Mohammed Abdul al-Wadhi, was among those killed by the Global Security Force during the surprise raid on his training camp in Yemen.

In a joint CNN interview, Richard Dixon, commander of the GSF, and Max Zagmi, chief of the UN's Center of Intelligence and Security, gave full credit to the president of the United States for the operation's spectacular success. Neither man revealed that the RFID tag implanted in Mahmoud Aliaabaadi's neck had led the GSF directly to the terrorists.

Zagmi was first to speak. "The president of the United States has long harbored a secret ambition to bring the perpetrators of this heinous crime to justice. President Gladden's independent investigation of these evil acts uncovered substantial information that resulted in the capture of these radical terrorist leaders and their operatives."

Dixon added a brief footnote to Zagmi's prepared remarks. "The president's information was invaluable to our operation, and without it, 'Abd al-Mumit would never have been crushed. We have learned that an Iranian named Mahmoud Aliaabaadi is the founder of 'Abd al-Mumit. He was able to evade capture, but we will continue the hunt for Mr. Aliaabaadi. We promise this mass murderer will be brought to justice."

Mahmoud was watching the interview from a small but heavily fortified compound in a remote Pakistani village. He was startled to hear his name, choking and spitting his *sabz chai,* black tea. Romiti, that cursed, traitorous snake. He had even given the president his name.

Despite general worldwide opposition to the death penalty, most of the non-Arab world accepted the judgments of the swift military trials. In contrast, Muslim governments implored Romiti to pardon the terrorists, but the secretary-general ignored their pleas. Heidari and Rajput were found guilty of crimes against humanity and were executed by firing squad. Gutierrez was found guilty as an accomplice, although the tribunal determined she had been unaware of her role in the attack. She was sentenced to twenty years in a military prison.

The president of the United States was universally praised for his resolute determination in tracking down the individuals behind the unprecedented attack on his nation, and he enjoyed enormous popularity with the voters.

Romiti was immensely satisfied with the outcome, knowing he had a significant world leader in his pocket. Though America had been financially crippled and militarily subdued, it was still an important ideological card in the world deck. Strangely, he showed no signs of remorse for the betrayal of Mahmoud, his boyhood chum from Baselga di Piné.

CHAPTER TWENTY

Jackson, Mississippi

Bob and Lisa Campbell were the leaders of a small band of people who met in their home several nights each week. The Campbells' group was one of more than a hundred life groups connected with Sticks's church, almost all of them springing up practically overnight. The groups set aside a portion of one evening each week to study Pastor Sticks's weekly "Life Group Notes" in order to sharpen their understanding of current and biblical events. The primary purpose of this exercise was to prepare everyone for the questions that were relentlessly being asked by those with whom they came in contact each day.

The rest of the evening was devoted to training, tailored for members who had become believers over the past week or two. The life groups were following James Kennedy's *Evangelism Explosion* model, quickly learning how to share their newfound faith with friends and family members. The other weeknights they came together were spent in their neighborhoods, demonstrating God's care and concern by providing help to people who were struggling with their circumstances and preparing them for the more difficult times that were coming.

During the day, women volunteered to care for children of working moms, a service that was accomplished on the church campus. Others began to collect shoes, clothing, and other essentials that were given to struggling families. On weekends and evenings, talented men and women who were gifted with carpentry, electrical, plumbing, auto repair, and other skills responded to families who could not afford to pay for the services. Medical professionals volunteered their time as well, and their patients were charged little or nothing for the medicines and supplies that were purchased by the church.

Like in the first-century church, a generous farmer had donated a small piece of property—four acres with a flowing stream—to the church. The fertile farmland was divided into small plots that were assigned on a first-come, first-served basis. Hurting families inside and outside of the church were taught how to grow cucumbers, corn, eggplant, fava beans, broccoli, cantaloupes, carrots, melons, and squash. Food prices were taking bigger chunks of everyone's paychecks, so the community was grateful for the church's generosity, and many began to listen to its message because their new friends demonstrated their faith in practical ways.

Bob and Lisa's small group was meeting in their large living room. Lisa noticed the carpet was beginning to show signs of wear and tear, and the sofa was sagging a bit. The walls had a few dents and bruises too. *Funny. If things had looked like this a year or so ago, I would have been embarrassed to invite anyone into my home. Would have insisted that we replace the carpet, paint the walls, and purchase new furniture.* A single tear rolled down her cheek. *How was I so selfish? How did I believe possessions were more important than people?* She noticed the smiling faces of her friends, despite the trials she knew they were experiencing. *Our priorities have changed, haven't they, Lord? You finally have our full attention.*

"Bob and I have been imagining how terrible it will be for Christians and nonbelieving Jews after the Antichrist commits his blasphemous act in the temple," Lisa shared. "Pastor Sticks says that after the temple is desecrated, the Antichrist will go on a murderous rampage against everyone who opposes him, especially those in Israel."

Lisa looked to her husband, who took up the topic. "Lisa's right. Very soon, life's going to be unimaginably painful for our friends in Israel, believing and nonbelieving Jews alike. So we've been knocking around the idea of teaming up with a small group of believers there. Sort of a sister city idea, but with life groups instead. In anticipation of life after the desecration, the life groups could collect and send money to the sister groups in Israel now. We know that believers will be barred from buying or selling shortly after the desecration, so if they begin now to purchase and store the essentials they anticipate they'll need, they'll have some level of relief then. Even more importantly, our gifts would provide opportunities for them to share their faith in their communities in very practical ways. What do you think?"

The group agreed it was a great idea, and soon, Bob connected with Uri Katz, the leader of a growing messianic congregation in Jerusalem. Uri and his wife, Rachel, were in their early thirties with twin six-year-old sons, Daniel and David. Uri was an archeology professor at a local university and one of the favorite instructors on campus. Thoroughly modern, his ruddy appearance and pleasant charm earned the favor of his students. He had met his wife, Rachel, in one of their archeology classes, where she immediately captured his heart. Pretty and vivacious, with an infectious smile, the outgoing Rachel was the life of every party. The two were the best of friends and rarely apart. The twins kept them busy, but on the rare occasions when they were alone together, their favorite activity was to explore the ancient tels that dotted the Judaean countryside.

Uri was encouraged by the Campbells' idea, and within days had provided them with contact information for fifteen more messianic congregations. Soon forty life groups in Israel were linked with more than eighty groups in America.

Lowry made sure Sticks's life group notes were translated into Hebrew each week, posting them on the website for easy access. Sticks was pleased and honored, never having dreamed that someday, thousands of Israelis would be following his weekly presentations. Lowry knew that shortly, this means of communication would either be too dangerous, or more likely, entirely blocked by the followers of Antichrist. He needed to discuss this with Sticks. What were their alternatives?

Soon, gifts were regularly being sent to Uri, who distributed the money to the forty small-group leaders in Israel. The funds were used to purchase nonperishable supplies that were discreetly delivered and stored in locations carefully selected by Uri and his group leaders. By the time of the desecration, Uri would report that the Campbells' idea had resulted in the purchase and safekeeping of more than one million dollars' worth of nonperishable essentials.

*　　*　　*

Uri had just visited an injured friend in the Shaare Zedek Medical Center, located in southwest Jerusalem not far from Mount Herzl. As he was leaving the hospital, he observed a man wearing a black suit entering the facility. The suit, together with his black hat and beard, told the world he was an ultra-Orthodox Jew. As a young boy, Uri always wondered how anyone dressed as this man was could be comfortable in the stifling Israeli sun. *Things haven't changed much—how can he stand to dress so warmly, especially in summer?* Uri nodded at the man as they passed one another, noting the sad expression on his face.

Two days later, Uri was driving away from his apartment when he noticed the same man he had seen at the hospital. This time, he was walking alone on the tree-lined sidewalk. Uri swung his car to the side of the street, stopping a few yards ahead of the pedestrian.

"Shalom! I'm Uri. I think our paths may have crossed at the Shaare Zedek Medical Center a couple days ago. Do you live in Bayit VeGan?"

Bayit VeGan was a mostly Haredi Jewish neighborhood that was not far from the medical center. Uri had moved to the orthodox community shortly after he was chosen to lead a small messianic congregation nearby.

Uri was addressing a large, barrel-chested man with a heartbreaking countenance. "Yes, I was visiting my young son who has cancer," he replied. "His name is Ehud, and mine is Jacob. Jacob Cohen." He grasped Uri's hand and shook it hard.

Uri was stricken by the man's painful circumstances. "I'm very sorry. I can't imagine how difficult it would be to have a child with a life-threatening illness. Can I give you a ride to the hospital?"

Jacob hesitated a moment before replying, "No, thanks. I don't mind the walk."

Uri noticed the hesitation, so he offered once more. "I'm on the way to the hospital myself. A friend was seriously injured in an automobile accident, so I've been visiting him a few times a week."

"Well, if it's not out of your way, then sure, I'd appreciate the lift."

On the way to the medical center, Uri learned a little more about Jacob. He was an Orthodox Jew, married, with one son. About a year earlier, Ehud had been diagnosed with an especially serious form of leukemia. Jacob visited his son every day, making the four-mile round-trip trek each morning.

"My younger brother, Ezra, also lives with my wife and me. I'm very proud of Ezra. He's a brilliant young man who's studying to be a rabbi. This may sound strange to you, but I believe my brother will someday be known as a great man of God, blessed be His Name. He has devoted himself to the study and observance of the law of the Lord, and his insights into the truths of the Torah are astounding. Almost every day, it seems, he shares a new discovery with me. Nothing gives him greater satisfaction than sharing his insights with anyone who is willing to listen. No rabbi I know speaks of the things of God, blessed be His Name, with such passion and authority. I believe all of Israel will someday speak of my brother the teacher, even if he is derisively called a Haredim!"

Uri was familiar with the Haredim. Translated from Hebrew as "those who tremble" before God, these ultra-Orthodox Jews had been at odds with other Israelis for years. Uri knew that about one-half of the adult Haredim shunned regular work and instead were full-time Torah students receiving a government stipend, a source of great frustration to the secular majority. As full-time students, they were exempt from the military draft as well, further alienating the Haredim from their fellow citizens. They raised large families, often having half a dozen children or more.

Uri introduced himself to Jacob as an archeology professor, choosing to temporarily withhold the fact that he was also the leader of a local messianic congregation. "So you have but one son—that's a rare exception for the Haredim, isn't it?"

"Yes, it is. My wife and I decided to forego a large family so our attention can be focused on Ehud."

As they drove into the hospital parking lot, Uri learned that Jacob began his walk to the hospital at eight each morning. Since Uri left for the university around eight-thirty, Jacob agreed to Uri's offer to drop him off at the hospital each morning on his way to work. Uri was surprised and genuinely pleased, silently asking God for wisdom as he began this new friendship.

*   *   *

World events continued to serve as Sticks's object lessons for his Seventieth Week of Daniel series. One evening, Sticks interrupted his scheduled talk on the seven seals to give a brief presentation on the character of the Antichrist.

"Tonight I'm going to disrupt my series on the seventieth week of Daniel so we can learn what the Bible says about the character of the Antichrist. But even before I go there, let me offer some encouragement in these perilous times. When the apostle John wrote about the second seal, he was foretelling a time when peace would be removed from the earth. But interestingly enough, in the sixteenth chapter of his gospel, John provides the antidote we need in times such as these.

"In this chapter, we see Jesus comforting his disciples who had finally gotten it! They now understood that Jesus was leaving this world and returning to his Father in heaven. As he was preparing to leave his disciples, Jesus reassured them by promising that in him, they would have peace. He reminded his disciples, his friends, that in the world they could expect trouble, but in him they would have peace. I want to encourage you with the words Jesus spoke to his disciples over two thousand years ago—and yet are as relevant today as then. Even during these perilous times, we can stand on his promise: 'Peace I leave with you; my peace I give you. I do not give to you as the world gives. Do not let your hearts be troubled and do not be afraid.'

"Do we have peace this evening?" Sticks came close to shouting the question. His audience shouted back, "We do!" And with that, Sticks began the evening's study on the Antichrist.

"Scripture teaches that the Antichrist will share Daniel's ability to solve complex problems, a gift that is sorely needed today.

"Where did Daniel's gift come from?" Sticks asked.

"God!" the crowd answered.

"And who's the source of the Antichrist's supernatural ability?"

"Satan!" was the immediate answer.

"You're right! The Antichrist is a Satan-inspired, Satan-controlled individual who will avail himself of every bit of help that Satan can offer.

"The Antichrist will worship 'the god of fortresses.' Obviously the Antichrist worships Satan, but he also venerates war, as this passage indicates. This man will seem invincible to all the people on earth. His goal will be to destroy Israel, the nation that gave birth to Jesus. Romiti is crafty and deceitful, a liar par excellence."

The frowns and scowls on the faces of his audience expressed their disdain for Romiti. Some shook their heads while others kept their heads down, not wanting to see the man's picture on the screen.

"Interestingly enough, he will not desire the love of women; instead, as the saying goes, it will be all about him! At some point, perhaps when he desecrates the temple, he will declare himself to be deity. He will exalt himself above God! He will be the god-man.

"Although it's almost impossible for us to comprehend, for a time God will allow Romiti to be wildly successful. Incredible as it seems, it is true. We are already seeing this happen. You can see it with your own eyes. What are some examples of Romiti's successes that you've already observed?"

"He negotiated the Treaty of Babylon," one man noted. "And it seems to be working. I haven't heard of any major terrorist attacks in Israel lately."

A woman shyly raised her hand.

"Yes," Sticks responded as he pointed to her.

"It seems like his idea of a one-world religion is gaining steam. Every time I turn on the television or look at a magazine, I see that more and more people are following the Supreme Chieftess Gumba or Guppa . . . whatever her name is."

Several laughed as Sticks made the correction. "I think you're referring to the Supreme Priestess Gupta! But yes, you're right. She seems to be gaining a following, doesn't she? But this shouldn't surprise us. The apostle John says a false religious system—he calls her the great prostitute—will commit adultery with the inhabitants of the earth. 'What does John mean?' you might ask. 'How does the great prostitute commit adultery with the inhabitants of the earth?' The great prostitute—Babylon is another name for this religious system—uses religion to meet a need that God meant to be satisfied through a relationship with Him alone.

"James, the brother of Jesus, wrote, 'Religion that God our Father accepts as pure and faultless is this: to look after orphans and widows in their distress and to keep oneself from being polluted by the world.' But this false religious system, led and controlled by the powerful Gupta, does not exist to serve but rather to rule, to grow rich, and to destroy Jews and the followers of Jesus." He shook his head. "Sorry! Got a little carried away on my answer, didn't I! Any more questions?"

"I haven't seen any military victories yet," a man in his midthirties observed. "Didn't you say the Antichrist would worship the god of fortresses? He seems to be a man of peace, for the most part."

"That's a good observation, Bill," Sticks acknowledged. "That's an area we should watch closely. It seems that this is an area in which the Antichrist will be making some moves. Now, let's finish up our time on the infamous member of the counterfeit trinity.

"Antichrist will be allowed to speak against God, blaspheming his very name! And not only will he speak against God, but he will oppress and persecute those who follow Christ. In fact, Daniel writes, 'The saints will be handed over to him for a time, times, and half a time,' language that a majority of Bible scholars believe specifies a period of three-and-a-half years.

"The leaders of many nations will follow him, and in return, will be granted positions of authority and status in his one-world government. The Antichrist will greatly reward those who do his bidding and acknowledge him as god. The territories he has conquered will be divided, with parcels of land given to his obedient minions.

"In the book of Daniel, the author also seems to imply that the Antichrist will try to change the 'set times and the laws,' perhaps to mimic the authority Daniel earlier attributed to God. I'm not positive what this verse means, but let's follow the actions of Romiti, and we'll soon find out. Maybe we'll see the Antichrist eliminate religious holidays, perhaps even attempt to remove the significance of the Sabbath, the traditional day of rest.

"Not a nice guy, is he? Follow this man closely! He is not a man of peace. As the name 'Antichrist' implies, he intends to stand in place of, or against, our Lord and Savior Jesus Christ."

Sticks scanned the last of his notes as he concluded. "Next week, our focus will return to the seals, specifically the fifth seal, which represents the martyrdom of the saints. It will be a difficult session, but one no one should miss. In the meantime, you're doing an incredible job in the field! Every day, I'm hearing amazing stories from people who have come to faith because, unlike the Antichrist, your character and good deeds are shouting 'Jesus!' to all who are watching. Keep up the good work, folks! We'll be home soon!"

CHAPTER TWENTY-ONE

Jerusalem, Israel

In the days following his first encounter with Jacob, Uri thought often of his new friend and his ailing son, Ehud. There was a twinge of sadness, perhaps even misplaced guilt for his own good fortune, as he contemplated the events slated for this warm autumn day. It was a special occasion for the Katz family, who planned to celebrate the birthday of the twins, Daniel and David. Uri had arranged for another professor to handle his classroom duties so he could spend most of the day with his family. After he visited Ehud, Uri, Rachel, and the boys would drive to the city of Tiberias, the hometown of Rachel's sister. From there, the group would hike down to the nearby lake, often called the Sea of Galilee, for the celebration. He had not mentioned this to Jacob, whom he picked up at the usual time and place.

"Morning, Jacob. I have more time than usual today. How 'bout introducing me to Ehud?"

Jacob seemed delighted by the suggestion. "I've told Ehud all about you. He's been looking forward to meeting you."

A short time later, Uri was having an animated conversation with a young boy about the same age as his twins. Although the illness had taken its toll, Ehud had a hilarious sense of humor and was obviously the apple of his father's eye. Upon learning that Uri was a professor of archeology, a bit of information that clearly impressed him, Ehud's main interest was learning how many treasures Uri had discovered.

"Well, not many. As a matter of fact, Ehud, I've not discovered any. But my wife, Rachel, has. A couple years ago, we were digging near Megiddo when she unearthed a small clay jar that was filled with coins dating to the time of King Solomon."

"Can I see them?" Ehud asked excitedly.

"I'm sorry, but not today. They're part of an exhibit that's in Belgium right now. But I'll tell you what. Next time I'm here, I'll show you some pictures that were taken right after Rachel discovered her treasure."

Despite Ehud's illness, his antics caused a momentary sparkle to return to his father's eyes. Jacob roared with laughter as his son repeated the various jokes he had picked up from the nurses. There was a serious moment too, as Jacob read and reread the account of David and Goliath, one of Ehud's favorite stories from the Tanakh, the Jewish Bible.

Too soon, the visit was over. Jacob kissed the little guy good-bye, promising to visit him again the next morning. As usual, he wiped away the tears as he left his son alone.

As they walked out of the hospital, Jacob confessed that he was losing hope that his son would ever recover. "What right have I to hope, when our generation has lost its hope?" he asked. "Before you disagree, let me say, yes, it is good that God, blessed be His Name, rescued Israel from certain destruction. I'm pleased our beloved temple is being rebuilt, although I'm fearful at what price—the authoritarian UN secretary-general and his Treaty of Babylon may prove to be our undoing. But there's no question that anti-Semitism is on the rise. When you look at the big picture, you can easily lose hope. My glass is half-empty, you say? Perhaps. In Orthodox Judaism, some rabbis teach that the *Mashiach* will come in a generation that has lost hope. Perhaps he will come soon, eh?"

Uri swallowed hard and silently prayed for wisdom as they climbed into the car. "Yes, I do believe the Mashiach is coming soon. But I must confess something to you, Jacob, something I've wanted to tell you for weeks but haven't felt the time was right. Please don't be upset with me for not being forthright, but I'm a follower of Yeshua."

Jacob looked intently at Uri for a moment and then turned his face to the window, not speaking for several minutes. Jacob broke the awkward silence by quietly saying, "I'm not surprised. The possibility crossed my mind the day I met you, but I deliberately repressed the thought. I've carefully avoided any possibility of meeting a disciple of this man, shunning those like you my entire life. Millions of Jews have been murdered by Christian Gentiles, Uri. My own great-grandparents were slaughtered by these people. But you are a Jew and not a Gentile! How can you possibly be a follower of this Jewish pretender whom the Gentiles call Jesus?"

"Would you like to discuss this, Jacob? Is now a good time? We can pull over and give it our full attention."

"Yes, I'd like to have this conversation. But you told me you were celebrating birthdays today, so let's do this. Let me list the reasons I don't believe your Yeshua is the Mashiach. Then let's set a time to have another conversation," Jacob responded.

Uri made a quick call to his wife. "Rachel, I'll be home in about an hour. Having a conversation with Jacob. Won't be gone long."

Jacob narrowed his eyes as Uri got off the phone and parked his car. They climbed out together, enjoying the fresh air. "So I imagine your wife thinks you're going to convert me, right?"

Uri chuckled. "I doubt that, but I do imagine you're in her thoughts at this very moment. So, take it away. List your reasons. I'll not interrupt you, but I might jot down some notes. And then can we meet again tomorrow?"

Jacob shrugged. "Yes, tomorrow works for me. Until then, here's my opinion on the coming Messiah." Jacob clasped his hands tightly behind his back, and then slowly ambled back and forth as he offered his views.

"Let's assume for a moment that the man Yeshua actually walked the earth and that the Christians' Bible provides an accurate description of everything attributed to him. And by the way, both of these assumptions are disputable."

Uri squirmed as he fought the urge to argue Jacob's last statement. *Only the misinformed, uninformed, or most hardened skeptics question Yeshua's existence today, thanks to the vast amount of textual evidence that has been documented.*

Jacob noticed Uri's grimace, hesitating slightly as he waited for Uri to speak. When Jacob realized he would not be interrupted, he smiled and then continued his discourse. "I see that you disagree with my last statement, but regardless, let's continue, shall we? After years of personal and formal study, I find that Yeshua did none of the things the Scriptures said the Mashiach would do. Throughout Jewish history, many men have claimed to be the Mashiach. But all of them died. None of them completed the mission of the Mashiach.

"I believe the Mashiach will be a great warrior, brilliant and ruthless in battle. He will be a human being, certainly not God, blessed be His Name. He will rebuild the temple and will renew sacrifices on the Temple Mount. He will gather Jewish exiles from around the world and bring them home to Israel. The Mashiach will restore the religious courts of justice. He will restore the line of King David and establish a new government in

Israel. In fact, Jerusalem will once again become the center of all world government."

Uri whistled his admiration for Jacob. "I'm impressed! You've obviously studied a great deal, haven't you?"

Jacob smiled briefly at the compliment and then continued. "For millennia, this is what the Jewish people have always looked for in a messiah. The Christian's idea that an innocent, divine being will sacrifice his life to save us from our sins cannot be found in Jewish theology. This is why I do not use the Gentile term *Christ*. I use the term *Mashiach,* which means 'Anointed One,' instead."

Jacob shook his head. "History just does not point to Yeshua as the Anointed One. A man named Shimeon ben Kosiba, known as Bar Kokhba—Son of a Star—came far closer than Yeshua did to fulfilling the requirements of the Mashiach, a century after Jesus. But the Roman Empire crushed his revolt and killed him, ending speculation that he was the coming Mashiach."

Jacob stopped his pacing and was now looking quizzically at Uri. "As a matter of fact, even Romiti comes much closer to being the Mashiach than Yeshua. He has brokered a peace in the Middle East. The reconstruction of the temple is underway because of his efforts alone. I'll bet he'll be a brilliant military commander. I predict that no nation will be able to defeat him in battle. If I learned there was a drop of Jewish blood in him, I would immediately accept the proposition that he is the one our people have been waiting for." Jacob took a couple of deep breaths, wanting to hear Uri's response to his comments, but appreciating his willingness to listen without interruption.

Uri still did not respond, so Jacob continued. "I also believe the time is ripe for the coming of the Mashiach. Rabbis teach that he will come when he is needed most, that mankind's conduct will determine when he is to come. Some say he would come if Israel repented for a single day, or if Israel properly observed two consecutive Shabbats before he comes. The most ardent rabbis teach the Mashiach will come in a generation that is completely innocent or totally guilty, or in a generation where our offspring do not respect their parents and grandparents.

"My own rabbi teaches the Mashiach will come in a generation that loses hope. And this is what I too have come to believe. Perhaps because of my son's illness, I too have lost all hope, Uri. Life no longer is meaningful to me, and I have lost my joy. Like Job, I say to God, blessed be His Name,

'If only my anguish could be weighed and all my misery be placed on the scales! It would surely outweigh the sand of the seas. The arrows of the Almighty are in me, my spirit drinks in their poison; his terrors are marshaled against me.'

"I do not mean to offend you, Uri. You are a good friend, even closer than many members of my own family." Jacob's conclusion was pained. "Tomorrow I will listen to your reasons for believing Yeshua is your Messiah, but then you must never speak of him again in my presence. I cannot accept your Messiah, nor can I expose my family to your views."

"You have not offended me, Jacob," Uri quickly assured him. "I look forward to our discussion tomorrow. Let's meet at the park bench, my friend."

*   *   *

Uri's boys were playing in a bright red tube slide in one of the many Bayit VeGan neighborhood parks. Jacob slowly made his way to the green metal bench where Uri and Rachel were sitting, reminiscing about the many hours he had spent with Ehud in the very same park. Rachel's presence made him uncomfortable, first because, since his youth, attractive women had intimidated him, and then especially because he believed she was there to help Uri convert him. Her dark, shoulder-length hair was tied in a ponytail, giving the impression of a playful young lady. Rachel was deeply tanned by her many hours in the Israeli sun, time spent digging through the tels for ancient artifacts. Sparkling green eyes, high cheekbones, and a mischievous smile complemented her beautiful features. *Perhaps my brother will someday find such a wife!*

Uri introduced Rachel to Jacob, who shyly nodded, grasping Rachel's hand and exclaiming, "Uri is my closest friend, Rachel. You made a good choice when you agreed to become his wife!"

Rachel laughed in agreement and then asked permission to take a picture of the two men. Both agreed, and the two friends stood in front of a nearby pomegranate tree, both sporting enormous grins on their faces as their picture was snapped.

"I can't believe it! A great photo, the first time! Uri never takes a good picture, Jacob. You must bring out the best in him!" Rachel exclaimed.

Jacob beamed with the compliment as Rachel called the boys for the short walk home. "See you for dinner, Uri."

The two men returned to the bench where Uri and Rachel had been sitting. Jacob spoke first. "You have a beautiful wife, Uri. Take good care of her!"

"I will," Uri promised. His expression showed he knew himself to be a lucky man.

"Another beautiful day in Jerusalem!" Jacob noted as his upraised face absorbed the welcomed warmth of the sun. "Israel seems to have escaped the erratic climate changes that are wreaking havoc on other nations. Things seem pretty normal around here, don't they?"

"Yes, I've noticed that too. God is showing favor to his land." Uri cleared his throat as he began to wrestle with a pomegranate. The wild pomegranate trees were everywhere, and their abundant fruit was a favorite source of nourishment to the community. "I've been thinking about what to cover in our conversation, Jacob. There's much I want to say. But yesterday, you limited your remarks to why you believe that Yeshua is not the Messiah, so I'll limit my comments too.

"I'm not going to explain why I reached a different conclusion about the Mashiach than you did—at least not today. Instead, I'm going to address the results and consequences of our nation's rejection of Yeshua as the Messiah. I hope what I say will provoke you to the point of wanting to meet again on this subject. Is this okay with you?"

"Yes, proceed. I've promised to listen this one day only, and listen I will to whatever you choose to say—but please do not expect another day," Jacob replied.

Uri smiled as he began the conversation. "Are you familiar with a character named John the Baptist?"

"*Yohanan ha-mmatbil,* eh? Yes, I'm familiar with the name. I believe he's called the forerunner of Yeshua," Jacob answered with a smug look on his face. "Am I right?"

"Very good—yes, you're absolutely correct. When Yohanan and Yeshua proclaimed 'the kingdom of heaven is at hand,' their Jewish audience understood what they were saying. The listeners were well-versed in the Tanakh and the nature of the messianic kingdom. Jews were clearly expecting an earthly kingdom, just as you inferred yesterday morning.

"However, as you know, the common belief was that if you were Jewish, you would automatically be included in the kingdom. This thinking was incorrect, so Yeshua and Yohanan both emphasized the need for repentance, not one's Jewish birth, as the means of entry. While this teaching was accepted by some, it was wholeheartedly rejected by Israel's religious leaders, men who should have known better, and by most of their followers. So while the nation certainly wanted the oppressive Roman occupation to end and the kingdom to be established, the nation did not accept Yeshua's offer of himself as their Messiah. The book of Matthew—"

"A thieving tax collector and as such, a traitor to Israel, let me remind you," Jacob interrupted.

"Yes, you're right—a hated tax collector. Do you know more about the *Br'it Chadashah*, the Gentiles' New Testament, than you're letting on?" Uri asked good-naturedly.

A young boy interrupted the conversation by showing them a tempting collection of pastries. "Fresh, from the Mahane Yehuda Market," he announced. The two men looked hungrily at the crumbly halva with pistachios, their mouths watering. "Hmmm. Looks good—how much? Oh, and include a couple bottles of water too." After some playful negotiations, Uri agreed to the kid's exorbitant price, less a couple shekels. "I'll take half a dozen," Uri said as he shelled out his payment to the aspiring entrepreneur.

Jacob had been holding his breath, praying the kid wouldn't blow the deal by sticking to his price. His eyes lit up as he eagerly bit into the delicious dessert. "Now, where were we? Please continue, Uri."

"Let me see. Oh yeah . . . you were attacking Matthew's character, as I recall!" Uri said with a wink. "Yes, formerly a thieving tax collector but now a repentant and forgiven disciple, Matthew records how Yeshua traveled the land, proclaiming that he was the Messiah. The first miracles he performed were signs to the nation. He wanted the people to make a judgment—was he the Messiah or not? If he was accepted, Yeshua would establish the messianic kingdom predicted by the ancient Jewish prophets, the kingdom the people of his day so desperately wanted.

"Let me describe a miracle that Matthew records in his account of Yeshua's life, Jacob. Some people brought to Yeshua a man who was demon-possessed, blind, and mute. The healing of such a person is one of the miracles the Pharisees taught only the coming Messiah could perform. Do you agree?"

Jacob nodded, agreeing that such a miracle was demanded by the religious leaders as proof of one's claim to be the Messiah.

"Yeshua healed the demon-possessed man, so based on what they had been taught, the witnesses to this miracle naturally asked, 'Can this be the Son of David?' They didn't believe they were qualified to answer this question, so they posed it to their religious leaders. But Yeshua didn't walk or talk like the Messiah they were expecting. They were looking for another law-abiding, rule-mongering Pharisee who acted like them. So the Pharisees and experts in the law rejected Yeshua and instead, declared that he was possessed by the prince of demons, Beelzebub. Yeshua countered their declaration by reminding them of a simple observation—the man had been demon-possessed. If Yeshua was possessed by the prince of demons, as they alleged, then by casting demons out of the afflicted man, Satan would be divided against himself and his kingdom could not stand."

Nice tale! If only it could be proven, Jacob thought. *Matthew would have known such a divine act would be a sure sign of the Messiah and could have fabricated the story to win over his Jewish audience.*

"In response to their rejection of him, Yeshua told them he would no longer perform miracles as proof that he was the Messiah. Nor would he give the nation signs, except the sign of the prophet Jonah: 'For as Jonah was three days and three nights in the belly of a huge fish, so the Son of Man will be three days and three nights in the heart of the earth.' The signs and miracles he would now perform would be for the benefit of his twelve disciples, among them Matthew, preparing and equipping them for the work he would call them to do.

"The sign for the nation, the sign of Jonah, would be the resurrection. Israel would see it three times. First, by the resurrection of Lazarus, a close friend of Yeshua who had died. John, another of Yeshua's disciples, wrote that when the Jews who had come to comfort Lazarus's sisters saw what Yeshua did, 'they put their faith in him.' They responded correctly to this sign, concluding he was indeed the Messiah. Others chose to meet with the Pharisees, asking them to render judgment. Was Yeshua the Messiah or not? Sadly, the religious leaders rejected the first sign of Jonah and instead, jealously conspired to put Yeshua and Lazarus to death.

"The second time this sign was given was at Yeshua's own resurrection."

Jacob was obviously uncomfortable with the reference to Yeshua's resurrection, but he managed to remain silent, chewing his lip instead.

"As before, this sign was also rejected by Israel, particularly by the proud and hardened religious leaders." Uri's expression grew more serious.

"The sign of the resurrection will happen a third time, Jacob, and it's likely that you'll be a witness to this event.

"So that's my spiel. If you have questions or want to discuss this again, just let me know.

"Before I forget, I want to mention one more thing. Since the signing of the peace treaty, I'm sure you've seen the two strange-looking men who hang out at various places in Jerusalem—the fellows in sackcloth. I believe they're the two witnesses that the guy I mentioned a minute ago, the apostle named John, predicted would come before Yeshua returns."

An exasperated Jacob held up his hand, signaling for a quick break. "I figured you'd mention those bizarre homeless creatures. Yes, I've seen them. Everyone's calling them what you did—the two witnesses. These panhandlers should not be allowed on the temple grounds, Uri. They're unclean. They haven't taken baths in months, it appears, and they're stirring up the people with their condemning messages."

"Let me finish, Jacob. You're familiar with the miracles performed by Elijah and Moses. They raised the dead, stopped rain from falling on Israel, caused fire to fall from heaven, turned freshwater into pools of blood, and commanded darkness to cover our land. We will see these witnesses perform many of the same miracles that Elijah and Moses performed. The signs they perform should serve to authenticate their claims to be messengers from God and their words, proclamations from God himself."

Jacob interrupted once again. "These men are an embarrassment to Israel, Uri! Visitors from around the world come and mock them, making fun of their strange speech and dress. How can you believe they're from God, blessed be His Name?"

"Look Jacob, not every day, but most days these men can be seen at the Temple Mount or in the Jewish Quarter. Talk to 'em. They'll confirm everything I've told you but eventually, they'll be killed in Jerusalem. Like Lazarus and Yeshua, they too will be resurrected. They will be raised to life after their bodies lay in the city for three-and-a-half days. Israel rejected the first two resurrections, but Scripture teaches that many in Israel will accept the sign of the third resurrection. I'm telling this to you before it happens, Jacob, so you will someday accept what I've spoken as truth."

Uri paused as Jacob stood. Uri knew if Jacob was seriously considering his words, his friend would soon begin to pace. Sure enough, Jacob clasped his hands behind his back and began his familiar ritual. He said nothing as he paced back and forth, but he motioned for Uri to continue.

"In the meantime, Israel's rejection of Yeshua as their Messiah opened the door to the Gentiles."

Jacob's eyes flashed in anger when he heard Uri mention the Gentiles, the *goys* responsible for the deaths of his great-grandparents. *How can Uri possibly follow the God of the Gentiles?*

"I believe the world has been blessed through the first coming of Yeshua. The Gentiles who have repented of their sins and accepted Yeshua as Savior now have a stake in *Olam Ha-Ba,* the messianic age. Jews who have repented of their sins and accepted Yeshua as their Messiah will enjoy all the blessings of the messianic kingdom as well."

Jacob vigorously shook his head. "If I followed your reasoning to its logical conclusion, I would have to believe that through the ages God, blessed be His Name, has intentionally allowed Jews to suffer in order to make room for the Gentiles. The idea is preposterous, Uri. You are mad! I do not see this message in the prophets."

Uri winced at the last charge, but continued. "One last point, Jacob. Yesterday you made a comment about the Christians who murdered your great-grandparents, along with millions of other Jews. Many in Israel are mistaken in the belief that because they're born to Jewish parents, they'll automatically be included in the kingdom of God. Likewise, Gentiles too are mistaken when they believe they're going to heaven simply because they're born to Christian parents or because they live in a country that professes to be a 'Christian nation.' The true followers of Yeshua are ones who have acknowledged that they are sinners, have repented of their sins, and have asked Yeshua to be the Lord of their lives. I do not believe those who participated in the 'final solution' were Christians, nor could their nation be characterized as a 'Christian nation.'

"I know this is not what you expected to hear, Jacob. But I'm asking that you reflect on what I've told you. Continue your research. Ask God to give you a clear understanding of what you're studying. And I believe with all my heart that you'll someday come to believe and accept what I've explained today."

CHAPTER TWENTY-TWO

Babylon, Iraq

The regional zone presidents of Africa, Mesopotamia, and the Middle East were summoned to Romiti's office in Babylon. They were among the leaders who had voted against Romiti's bid to succeed Nielsen as the UN secretary-general. Romiti had prevailed in that battle, but the trio continued to quietly paint him as an enemy of Islam. While the men were not publicly critical of Romiti's leadership, they never missed an opportunity to sow dissension behind his back. They worked collaboratively to sabotage his agenda unless it happened to advance their own. Word of their discordant activities had reached Romiti from multiple sources, and he intended to use this private meeting to put an end to their divisive behavior.

The three leaders were escorted into the secretary-general's plush office. Romiti did not welcome them at once. Instead, hands on his hips, he stood with his back to his visitors, staring at the Euphrates from one of his large office windows. The men stood quietly, waiting for Romiti to begin the meeting.

Romiti finally turned to face them. "Sit," he coldly ordered as he pointed to the large chairs surrounding a marble table on which various beverages had been placed. Trim, fit, and impeccably dressed, the stern-faced Romiti cast an imposing figure. He remained standing, exaggerating his dominant position among the men.

"You're undermining my plans for the Middle East," he said, the rebuke sharp. "And you've spoken disparagingly of my character. This behavior is traitorous, and it must stop!" Romiti, arms folded across his chest, stared menacingly at the men, closely observing their reaction.

The African Zone president sneered at the secretary-general. "And just what are your plans for the Middle East? We've often wondered. You're an enemy of Islam, no matter what you told the Arab League. You're subverting the will of Allah by enticing Muslims to join a one-world religious system that includes the despicable infidels—Jews and Christians."

"Is that what this is about? You're opposing me because of petty religious differences?" the secretary roared. "You're making my point!"

The Iraqi president, representing the Mesopotamian Zone, added, "You win allegiance by appointing your fawning yes-men as heads over territories, distributing land for a price. But you cannot buy our cooperation. We will not cower before you."

Romiti looked derisively at the smaller man who dared confront him and then changed tactics, becoming a bit more conciliatory. He sighed. "I'm not enticing Muslims to join another religion. I've proven that religious rivalries cause the majority of the world's violence against civilian populations. You know these conflicts trigger famines and disease, killing even more people. Omega-ism is my attempt to bring humanity under a single tent.

"As for my plans for the Middle East: It's the birthplace of the world's three great religions. And not by coincidence, it's also the birthplace of Omega-ism, of which the three of you speak so negatively. Unlike Judaism, Christianity, and Islam, Omega-ism will bring reconciliation and harmony among the peoples of the world. And I intend for Jerusalem to once again become the center of an all-world government."

While Romiti's reference to Jerusalem pleased the men, their expressions did not show it, and their heated exchange continued for another hour with no significant concessions made by anyone.

Finally Romiti burst out, "No wonder the Middle East has been embroiled in conflict for thousands of years! Your stubborn allegiance to archaic and irrelevant religious beliefs is beyond my understanding. But let me be perfectly clear. If you continue to oppose me, I will destroy you. Your governments will be uprooted, overthrown, and you will disappear from the face of the earth."

The fuming secretary-general dismissed the men from his office with a wave of his arm, his words ringing in their ears.

Within weeks, observers noted the heightened presence of heavily armed Global Security Forces in and around the capitals of Iraq, Egypt, and Syria. When questioned, Dixon, the GSF commander, sarcastically responded, "Let's just say that the secretary likes to keep his dogs on a leash."

*   *   *

In typical fashion, news agencies worldwide were announcing that the widely heralded era of worldwide peace and tranquility, inaugurated by the coming of Romiti, was coming to an end. Their grim predictions, set in headlines, were calculated to attract readers and were sourced by tidbits of information leaked from Romiti's contentious summit with the three regional zone presidents. The GSF buildup around the three capitals fueled the rumors of widespread resistance to Romiti's policies by Muslim nations. The Organization of Islamic Cooperation, a 57-member pan-Muslim body, was stridently voicing its opposition, furious over Romiti's decision to deploy GSF troops in the capital cities.

Journalists were also nonplussed by the erratic weather. Was it global warming or global cooling? One group of experts claimed a mini-Ice Age was on its way, while others predicted the earth's once-fertile farmlands would soon become desert wastelands.

Romiti was irritated with the reports filed by his fair-weather media friends and had determined to express his annoyance in a scheduled assembly of his cabinet at the UN headquarters in Babylon. But Islamic resistance to his policies and the flaky weather reports were the least of his concerns. He was perturbed by persistent rumors of Omega-ism's stagnant growth. If the rumors were true, it threatened his goal of a single worldwide religious system.

"So tell me how the Omega-ism movement is progressing." Romiti directed his statement to Laroque.

"It's going very well," answered Laroque, contradicting what Romiti had heard. "Almost two billion people have switched their religious affiliation to Omega-ism, just as I hoped. As expected, nominal Christians have joined the movement in droves. We're seeing huge numbers of Hindu and Buddhist conversions. What is especially pleasing is that the Omega-ism adherents, especially in nations where Hinduism and Buddhism were once the dominant religions, have fiercely confronted followers of Christianity, Judaism, and Islam. They have burned down their places of worship, killed their local leaders, and expelled them from their communities. Tens of thousands have been killed. We would be better off if the news would stop reporting it—" he shot a pointed look at Taylor Pattersen—"but all of this is still in our favor.

"Secular and nominal Muslims have joined our ranks too, but at a much slower pace than we expected. It is concerning that a growing number of Muslims are reporting visions in which a man in white, purportedly Jesus himself, invites them to follow him. We're investigating these stories now, but it's not easy. The reports are not limited to a particular geography or branch of Islam. Perhaps the dreams are drug induced, or the number of incidents is wildly exaggerated—we just don't know, but we'll soon find out."

"How about evangelicals and Jews? Are we seeing any movement there?" Romiti queried.

Laroque's lip curled. "Unfortunately, but not unexpectedly, the answer is no. While there have been some Jewish converts, most of whom had no prior religious affiliation, we have made no progress in the Orthodox Jewish community, nor have we made perceptible progress with evangelicals, Catholics, or Orthodox Christians."

Max Zagmi jumped into the conversation. "Our Internet intercepts and polling data are showing some disturbing statistics, even trends, that must be countered. Evangelical Christians suddenly seem far bolder in their efforts to proselytize members of other religions. Thousands of Christian websites are posting seditious messages, undermining our efforts to unite the world's populations under a single religion. Most of these sites are making serious accusations against you, Mr. Secretary, causing an alarming number of people to oppose our programs."

"And what are they posting about me?" Romiti asked Zagmi, keeping his tone deliberately dry and derisive.

"Most sites are now claiming we're living in the end times, and that soon, God will remove his followers from the earth."

Romiti interrupted Zagmi's discourse. "The sooner the better! But I didn't ask you about their future—I asked you what the fanatics are posting about me!"

"The sites claim you're the biblical Antichrist, the one who will oppose Jesus Christ. They say you're possessed and controlled by Satan and that the earth's inhabitants must defy and disobey you every chance they get. The sites also predict you will eventually break the peace treaty with Israel and then launch murderous attacks on Christians and Jews."

Romiti and Laroque exchanged knowing glances at Zagmi's last remark, but Romiti was clearly angered by the feedback, impatiently tapping his pen on the table.

Suddenly Romiti hurled the pen across the room as he stood to his feet. "So be it! Zagmi, begin documenting the names and locations of the religious fanatics who oppose me. I don't care if they're pastors, rabbis, or imams. I want you to accelerate the covert disruption of their activities, whatever they may be. Give special attention to the most prominent religious leaders. Hire prostitutes to seduce them; link them to dubious financial schemes. Publish stories that accuse them of the activities they condemn from their pulpits—pornography, infidelity, embezzlement. You may use any tool at your disposal to discredit them and their message."

He turned on his media representative next. "Pattersen. I'm annoyed by the media's penchant to call attention to every bit of negative news. If you can't manage the media, I'll find someone who can. Take control! Create a campaign that illustrates the Christians' use of libelous speech—take their words out of context, I don't care! I want the world to see them as I see them. Demonstrate a pattern of seditious activities too. I want people afraid to read their materials or visit their websites, let alone have a conversation with them. Especially target the stubborn evangelicals, Christian fundamentalists, Islamic radicals, and Orthodox Jews!"

"I'm on it!" said an embarrassed Taylor Pattersen.

"And I'll sponsor new legislation making it a punishable activity to proselytize and toughen the penalties of existing laws against what I consider to be seditious activities," the secretary-general continued. He clasped his hands behind his back. "And what's this I hear about two madmen at the Temple Mount? Sounds like they're pretty entertaining, although I understand they're preaching that Jesus is coming soon and that everyone should refuse to go along with me. And please don't tell me they're claiming to be the 'two witnesses' mentioned in apocalyptic literature!"

"I don't know about that, but I've asked the local police force to keep their eyes on them. We've pretty much ignored them up until now," Dixon answered. "But as they crank up their rhetoric and their speech becomes more divisive, we'll take action, you can count on that."

"You'd better be right!" Romiti said with some annoyance. The very thought of sitting idle while two religious nutcases were slandering him was maddening. "There'll be a day of reckoning for those two, and you can count on that too!"

One last question. "What progress is being made on the Temple Mount?"

"Before we go there, can I bring up a topic that's not on the agenda?" Pattersen asked.

"What is it?" Romiti asked impatiently.

"My staff is following hundreds of blogs that are describing serious food shortages, even in the wealthiest nations. They're reporting that in some cities, if you're lucky enough to have a job, the first half of the workday earns enough money to buy a loaf of bread. Food riots are everywhere; people are dying. If these shortages aren't addressed soon, today's riots will look like a picnic compared to what's coming."

"Yes, I'm up to date on the situation," Romiti acknowledged. "In fact, at the next meeting of the UN General Assembly, Abdul Odinga, the chief economist for the Food and Agricultural Organization, is giving an address that will deal with the problem. Now, let's continue with the last item on the agenda. What progress is being made on the Temple Mount?"

The members of the cabinet looked at one another as though they were being asked to explain the origins of the universe. Dixon, Zagmi, Ospel, and Pattersen had no idea of how much progress had been made on the temple project. It was apparent that only Laroque had been monitoring the construction effort.

"Excellent progress is being made," Laroque began. "Almost weekly, factions are protesting the construction—but by and large, the project remains on schedule. The finishing work is in progress on the inside of the temple. Outside, a lot of masonry work is underway in the gardens, walkways, and fountains. In fact, the restoration of the massive courtyard is almost complete. The temple furnishings should arrive in about six weeks, with the official dedication ceremonies scheduled for October, just three months away."

Laroque smiled his disquieting smile, an expression that dripped disdain. "I tried to persuade one of the chief rabbis to invite you to give the dedicatory speech, but judging by his stunned reaction, you would have thought I'd asked him to commit blasphemy!"

Romiti chuckled as he imagined being asked to give the opening prayer at the dedication.

"Let's see what happens when the International Interfaith Council mandates the use of the temple for a planned Omega-ism event!" Laroque announced.

There was a look of bewilderment on the faces of the remaining cabinet members, but Romiti quelled further conversation by abruptly ending the meeting.

*　　*　　*

Around the globe, serious discussions like the ones between Uri and Jacob were taking place every day. Especially in Israel, people were fiercely debating whether the Messiah was coming for the first time, returning for the second time, or not coming—or existing—at all. They argued whether there was an afterlife, and if so, whether there was one path or multiple paths to heaven.

For many, the two witnesses in Jerusalem were at the center of this raucous debate.

The older-looking of the two men was soon nicknamed "Moshe" by the hecklers who circled them each day.

The other witness was the taller of the two and was nicknamed "Eli'ahu" by his rude audience. He was the apparent leader and more outspoken of the two, earning his moniker by reminding his predominantly Jewish audience of the ancient Jewish prophet whom King Ahab had called "the troubler of Israel."

Each day, the two witnesses reminded the gathering crowds that judgment was crouching at their door, urging them to repent of their sins and follow Yeshua, their soon-returning Messiah. At first, the reactions of the crowds were mixed. Some snapped their pictures, assuming them to be eccentric but entertaining comedians. Others ignored them, concluding they were just another pair of religious nuts. The religious among the crowds, Muslims, Jews, and Omega-ism converts alike, were often the most spiteful, heckling them at every opportunity and pelting them with stones. The mood of the crowds became increasingly hateful with the passing of time.

*　　*　　*

Sticks's congregation no longer assembled on the church campus on Sundays. The auditorium could not accommodate the large crowds that gathered, so instead, the people met throughout the week in a number of smaller venues—parks, ball fields, and the parking lots of abandoned strip malls. They came together to worship, for encouragement, and to learn ways in which they could be salt and light to a community that was in desperate need of both. Sundays were set aside for providing assistance to families in the surrounding neighborhoods, not unlike other days of the week.

On this particular Sunday morning, Sticks was among more than eight hundred volunteers who were being divided into many smaller groups of five to eight people. Each crew included a couple of handymen and was outfitted with bags of groceries, medical supplies, and an assortment of freshly laundered, previously used clothing, shoes, and sandals. The teams would canvass the neighborhoods, assessing needs and distributing their resources. They deliberately refrained from preaching on these occasions, focusing instead on the physical needs of the many that opened their doors.

As the team walked toward their first stop, a middle-aged woman named Francis was expressing her excitement over the number of people who had volunteered that morning. "The evangelical Christian community has become an activist community unlike anything I've ever seen. The closest comparison I can make is to the Jesus Movement in the sixties," she was saying. "While I wasn't around back then, I've heard enough firsthand accounts to conclude that God is working in similar ways today."

"What's your opinion? Do you think God's working in a unique way right now?" Sticks asked a favorite young couple whom he wanted to draw into the conversation. Greg Reynolds's parents and grandparents had been lifelong missionaries to Zimbabwe; his fiancée, Jeni Williams, was an only child, the daughter of a couple who pastored a large evangelical church in town. Greg was a big, rugged-looking individual and a gifted teacher. He often taught in the young adult Bible fellowship classes, receiving high marks from those in attendance. Jeni was shy, pretty, and very compassionate. Sticks loved the friendly couple, faithful volunteers who never missed a church activity. But he worried about them. They seemed restless, awkwardly out of place at times, perhaps a little sad—they said the right words, and they certainly did more than their share of good deeds. But sometimes Sticks got the impression the two were performing their acts of service as the way to earn a right relationship with God rather than as their response to God's grace.

"Francis is right," Greg quickly answered. "My grandparents lived in Southern California during the Jesus Movement. They've told me a million stories about Chuck Smith, the coffeehouses, the music—Barry McGuire, Mustard Seed Faith, Keith Green, Love Song, Andraé Crouch and the Disciples—I could go on. My grandparents met at one of the Jesus Festivals, and I'm told life was never the same after that."

Jeni nodded in agreement, saying, "My grandparents told similar stories." She wistfully added, "Makes me wish I lived in that generation. I've never experienced God the way my parents and grandparents have."

The conversation was suspended as they knocked on the front door of a home that was in obvious need of repair. A small child peered curiously through tattered draperies before disappearing. "Daddy," the little girl hollered, "there's some people outside."

The girl's sullen-looking father, a young man in his late twenties, opened the door. His disheveled appearance and lifeless eyes revealed a discouraged heart. A youthful woman, perhaps his wife or girlfriend, stood meekly behind him. "Whaddya want?" he growled.

The team leader smiled her brightest smile, hoping to disarm him. "I'm Susan Gates," she said as she held out her hand.

He ignored the friendly introduction and repeated his question. "Whaddya want?"

"The economy is pretty tough right now—lotsa people out of work. We're canvassing the local neighborhoods, finding people who can use a little help. Jim here's an electrician; Bob's a carpenter. Need anything fixed around the house? We also have some groceries and some freshly laundered clothes—might have a dress that will fit your little girl."

He almost snarled in reply. "Buncha religious do-gooders! Heard 'bout you guys. From some crazy church that believes the world's comin' to an end. Well, ain't interested. Take your preachin' somewhere else!" he ordered as he slammed the door. Windows rattled, and the little girl began to cry. "But Daddy, I'm hungry."

The volunteers were always taken aback by the ill-mannered treatment they sometimes encountered, but they never let it discourage them. The next stop would be better, they always agreed. Susan quickly found some shoes and clothing that would fit the child. She and her friends left these gifts, plus a couple bags of groceries, on the front porch before marching to the house next door.

The conversation picked up again. "I agree there are many more activist believers now, but in some ways, our newfound sense of urgency may be having a polarizing effect," Lowry countered. "Statistics prove that millions of people have come to faith in the past couple of years. Leaders of indigenous ministries in Iran, Pakistan, Kazakhstan, and Indonesia, among many others, report that Muslims are coming to faith by the tens of thousands, many through visions in which they report that Jesus himself appears to them, inviting them to place their faith in him. The stories are astounding and are coming in from towns and villages throughout the world. But at the same time, billions of antibelievers have become resolutely, even fiercely, opposed to Christianity. Take the man we just met, for example. At first, I thought he was discouraged—and he probably was—but he was very resentful too. Wasn't interested in talking to us—in fact, he was obviously opposed to anything connected to religion. It's as if a line has been drawn in the sand. People are making their decisions for or against Christ every day."

"You're right, but we must continue to boldly confess our faith," Sticks encouraged the volunteers. "Very soon the freedoms we now enjoy will be curtailed, perhaps removed altogether. The time is short, so we must increase our efforts to engage our community as never before."

CHAPTER TWENTY-THREE

Babylon, Iraq

The Portuguese ambassador picked at his grilled salmon and avocado salad as he lamented the plight of his people to his colleagues. "Eighty percent of Portugal does not have enough to eat—and I'll bet that today, far less than twenty percent enjoyed a meal that was comparable to this one."

"Unfortunately, you're not alone. The same is true in my country," the ambassador from Finland offered. "There are so many pollutants in the air that hardly anything grows well anymore. It's like living beneath a permanent cloud cover." He swirled the ice in his drink as he continued the dire report. "Barley, wheat, and hay figures are down by sixty percent. Potatoes are the size of walnuts. These were once Finland's most significant agricultural commodities—now we're not growing enough to feed our livestock, let alone our citizens."

"We need to go," the Swedish delegate warned as he glanced at his watch. "The General Assembly's already convened. We're late." The ambassadors tossed their tips on the table as they hurriedly packed their leather attaché cases. Walking rapidly to the United Nations General Assembly Hall, they breathlessly entered as Abdul Odinga, the chief economist for the UN's Food and Agriculture Organization, began his speech.

"We have entered a period of global famine," he began. "This is a very perilous time, threatening the very survival of the planet. The global food chain is being stretched to its limit. While populations have decreased in some parts of the world, they're growing in other parts, increasing demand for food. And bizarre weather patterns and horrific disasters, both natural and man-made, are damaging the world's food sources. Prices are soaring, sparking food riots across the globe."

Odinga continued, "The decimation of the Russian harvest, followed by poor harvests in Canada, the United States, and the Ukraine, have drastically reduced global supplies. The meteorites that pummeled Russia released so much dust into the atmosphere that a portion of the sun's energy has been prevented from reaching earth, causing much cooler temperatures. This has really stunted the growing season.

"Dry, hot weather in South America has wiped out much of Argentina's soybean exports, and flooding in Australia has ruined its wheat crop. As food reserves shrink, prices soar. The FAO has reported that its food price index has jumped seventy-seven percent during the year, barreling past the previous record of thirty-two percent set in 2010.

"The Chinese are buying every available crop, dangerously impacting soybean and grain reserves, already at their lowest levels in almost four decades. If even one more natural disaster or conflict occurs in one of the breadbasket countries, we'll see widespread, unimaginable starvation, far beyond our ability to manage."

At the mention of the Chinese, many ambassadors struggled to maintain their composure. Most were envious of China's good fortune, while some from the Western nations were angry. The dour faces scattered throughout the assembly hall betrayed their jealous and angry spirits. For decades, the West had been the People's Republic of China's generous benefactor, granting billions in aid to the once impoverished third-world nation. The Chinese had astutely managed the gifts of capital, and implausible as it seemed, brazenly loaned the capital to their patrons. Adding insult to injury, the Chinese demanded low tariffs on their exports but levied huge tariffs on their imports. Absurdly, the Western governments had agreed to the unsound monetary policies, and soon, the creditor nation was wielding a giant club over the hapless Western democracies. *And now they're the land of plenty, and we're begging for bread,* the US ambassador bitterly reflected.

"Finally, we must prepare ourselves for more regional conflicts as food shortages worsen. Food prices, while going through the roof, are not increasing in the industrialized nations as fast as they are in the developing countries. There are several reasons for this, but one important one is that in the developing countries, more than half the average family income is already spent on food. As prices soar, there is far less money available for other basic necessities, inflaming the passions of citizens against their own government and the people of neighboring countries whom they perceive as more fortunate than themselves."

The UN General Assembly quietly listened to the gloom-and-doom report, wondering what else could possibly go wrong

* * *

Sticks had just read a pirated summary of the *UN Report on the Global Food Chain,* comparing its dire warnings to his understanding of Matthew 24 and Revelation 6. While food supplies in the US were adequate for the time being, the poor, and even the middle class, were beginning to panic over the sky-high prices. At first, higher prices forced them to choose between eating at home or dining out. A short time later, they were choosing between meat and pasta. And now, many were forced to choose either food or medicine.

While anxious, even fearful, over the developing worldwide famine, Sticks was thankful that for more than two years, many churches throughout the world—including his own—had been preparing diligently for the looming crisis. While their efforts would not save everyone, he knew that some people would eat because of their sacrifices, and that supplied a measure of comfort to the troubled pastor.

His cell phone played a familiar tune, alerting him that his wife was on the line. "What's up?" he answered.

"If you're in your office, jump on the Internet. There's rioting in the major cities of India because of the government's decision to eliminate food subsidies."

"I've been watching the news too," Sticks admitted, sheepish since he knew he should be studying. "There's pandemonium in the streets. Food prices have spiraled out of control; the average Indian can't afford to feed his family." *We're days away from food riots too,* Sticks thought.

As Sticks was speaking with his wife, a live interview of Romiti appeared on the monitor of his PC. "Hold on a sec, Cyndi," he told her, and he focused his attention on the familiar face of the UN secretary-general. He was being interviewed outside the UN headquarters in Babylon.

"How is the UN responding to shrinking food supplies and their inflated prices?" the correspondent asked.

"The scope of the worldwide famine is unprecedented, caused by the convergence of many unusual and unrelated events. Of course, mankind bears some responsibility. Famine and disease usually follow conflict, and to this day, we see religious and tribal warfare inflicting great damage on the environment. However, we see natural causes too. Many countries in the West are experiencing severe drought because of abnormally hot weather, while nations in Eastern Europe are coping with unseasonably cold weather. Both weather patterns are wreaking havoc on the growing seasons."

Romiti turned to a UN spokesperson standing at his side. "Do you have anything to add?"

"Yes—in the West there have been a hundred consecutive days of triple-digit temperatures, causing reservoirs to dry up, crops to wither, and fish and animals to perish by the millions," the spokesperson offered. "Pipes are busting due to the dry, shifting ground, cutting off valuable water supplies to small towns. The water tables in scores of regions are also falling precipitously, due to widespread overpumping of their aquifers. This has particularly impacted the wheat harvest in these regions."

The secretary-general was nodding his head in agreement, although his facial expression was screaming, *This is not my problem. What control do I have over the weather?*

"And if that's not enough, in Africa, an epidemic of stem rust has nearly destroyed the wheat harvest. Now the epidemic has jumped to Asia. Ecologists are saying famine conditions will persist, causing spiraling food prices and massive starvation on a level never experienced before."

A dour-looking writer interrupted the spokesperson's ominous forecast. "Yeah, we've all heard the stats." Turning his attention to the secretary-general, he challenged the UN executive. "Now we want to hear what Romiti's going to do about it!"

Romiti glared at the writer before responding. "In my first week as secretary-general, I directed various UN agencies to prepare contingency plans for a potential global famine. Acting on my directive this morning, the UN began the large-scale distribution of vitamins and minerals through fortified sachet powders to the regions most severely impacted."

The correspondent had a surprised look on his face. He had not heard of any UN-sponsored famine relief operations, and he was obviously embarrassed by his lack of knowledge.

The spokesperson interrupted Romiti, winning a scowl from his superior. But he charged ahead, providing additional details of the UN mission. "We're also shipping peanut-butter sachets and Spirulina. These do not require refrigeration or any mixing with water. Additional supplements, such as vitamin A capsules and zinc tablets, are also being transported to the hardest-hit areas." With this last remark, the UN spokesperson stumbled away from the reporter so that Romiti could complete the interview without interruption.

"We're distributing billions of dollars of cash vouchers to hungry families in the nations where food is available but too expensive for most of its citizens. This approach will enable families to purchase food while stimulating the local economies.

"The UN is also shipping tons of hybrid strains of high-yielding crops. While this will not prevent starvation today, it does provide hope for the future. In the past, hybrid strains have improved grain production by 250 percent. Yes, we all know this practice was criticized by greens because the crops required more fertilizer and pesticides than regular seed. However, I believe we must implement measures that will take us through the famine with as few lives lost as possible."

The writer interrupted Romiti once again. "And how many people will die of starvation before the next harvest?" he asked sarcastically. "Do you realize that in some parts of the world, the cost of a quart of wheat or three quarts of barley now equals a day's wage?"

"I'm explaining what steps I've initiated, my friend. And what steps have *you* taken to save the lives of starving children around the world?" Romiti's question quieted the humiliated writer, but much to everyone's surprise, the secretary-general answered his question anyway.

"The UN report projects that eighty-five million people will starve to death before the year is out. There is absolutely nothing we can implement today that will prevent these deaths from occurring."

The anticipated death count stunned the reporters into silence.

"However, it could be much worse. The measures we're taking today will save sixty million lives this year—and many more next year. We have a long way to go, but my intention is to eliminate famine from our vocabulary. The new UN famine-eradication programs I've sponsored will ensure this goal is reached within the next two years. This loss of human life is a calamity that must never been repeated. I will not rest until every citizen on earth has access to an affordable, tasty, and nutritious diet."

The reporters and camera crews, impressed with Romiti's apparent sincerity and the steps he had already taken to avert an even larger tragedy, clapped for several minutes and then began to heap praise on the man who had not only anticipated the global famine, but would triumph over it.

Sticks logged off the site, unable any longer to stomach the press corps' adoration of the man who would someday demand their worship.

*   *   *

Romiti shook hands and exchanged formalities as he left the UN headquarters. While he appeared to have humanity's best interests at heart, Romiti had not publicly shared a fear of far greater concern to him than eighty-five million deaths: the geopolitical implications of a massive worldwide famine. History had demonstrated that famines radicalized entire populations, leading to uprisings that toppled national governments. Romiti realized he did not yet have an absolute grip on the masses, and therefore, he was not immune from a worldwide revolt against him and his policies.

He accepted accolades from a flattering reporter but brushed off more questions as he stepped into his waiting limo. He sat back against the cool leather and closed his eyes. He had also suppressed the confidential and frightening conclusions of the *UN Report on the Global Food Chain* from the eyes of his adoring public. In the conclusion of the report, the UN expert had written, "To avert disaster, the world population must be reduced by two-thirds. Oil production is also peaking and will probably decline, possibly precipitating this agricultural crisis much sooner than expected."

The only bright note on the world scene, it seemed, was taking place in the Middle East. Following Ezekiel's War, weather patterns had dramatically changed in Israel's favor. The Negev was blossoming. For the third consecutive year, the nation's granaries and storehouses were overflowing with grains, nuts, and produce, fed by enormous harvests. In each of the past two years, Israel had exported over four hundred thousand tons of wheat, sorghum, and corn to Jordan, Egypt, and the new Palestinian state formed by the former Gaza and West Bank territories. Israel had also committed to delivering another five hundred thousand tons of food this year—at prices far below market. The king of Jordan and Prime Minister Shalev had become close friends as a result of Israel's generosity, celebrating the fact that no starvation deaths were recorded in the nations fed by Israel.

Romiti was exasperated, even angered, by Israel's success and kindness, somehow believing that Israel's good deeds diminished the glory that should be his alone. Confident that his driver could not hear, he whispered, "Lucifer, allow me to tear down this nation, I pray!"

Much to Romiti's surprise, Lucifer responded audibly to his petition. The voice was like a whisper in his ear. "Be patient. The time is near. Before long, I will give you dominion over the entire earth. My faithful and mighty servant, Abaddon, along with his legions, will soon be released from the Abyss in which they've been unjustly imprisoned for millennia. These comprise a supernatural army under my authority. I will command them to help you. Those they choose to torment will seek death but will not find it. Their victims will long to die, but death will elude them."

Several hours later, Romiti, still burning from Israel's success but swollen with pride over his encounter with Lucifer, was in a private conference with Laroque.

"The timing of the famines is dreadful. I'm pretty confident today's press conference bought me some time, but we must quickly develop a communication strategy to blunt the effects of what will be a rising death toll. In today's skirmish with the press, I stated that the UN is projecting eighty-five million starvation deaths, but the actual number I've been given is more than double that figure."

Laroque agreed with Romiti's positive assessment of the press conference. "Pattersen should fast-track the production of some minidocumentaries outlining the various famine-relief programs being implemented by the UN. She should highlight our successes, obviously, and link them directly to you."

While they were talking, they were startled by Lucifer's sudden visible appearance and imposing voice. "Our lord," they breathed as they slipped to their knees. The imposing figure towered over the two men, who continued to kneel in obeisance to the fallen angel. In appearance, Lucifer was magnificent. Close to seven feet tall, his perfectly proportioned body resembled that of a powerful, larger-than-life, world-class athlete. He was adorned with precious stones. He was handsome. Desirable. And sin in bodily form, corrupted by his beauty and pride.

"Worship me," he commanded his two followers. They did.

"Concerning me, God said, 'You are the model of perfection, full of wisdom and perfect in beauty. You were in Eden, the garden of God; every precious stone adorned you: ruby, topaz and emerald, chrysolite, onyx and jasper, sapphire, turquoise and beryl.' He announced that I am blameless in all my ways. But when I exceeded him in wisdom and beauty, he cursed me and banished me from his presence. Now I have usurped his authority and have become the god of the earth!

"Yes, I am the model of perfection, full of wisdom and perfect in beauty. I am god, and before me, there will be no other! I demand your praise and the worship of those you rule through me! There are many among you who refuse to serve me. For this reason, *I* have struck the earth with a famine.

"Do not believe those who credit God with these disasters. I alone am the god of this world! But famines pale in comparison to what the world will soon experience. A fourth of the earth's population will die by the sword, famine, plague, and the wild beasts of the earth. Do not forget that *I* have dominion over all the earth's inhabitants! I tell you, let the starving starve. Prepare the famine survivors for the punishment I'm about to unleash upon them. For too long they've tolerated people who follow the God of Israel and the feeble-minded who obey Jesus, his powerless Son!"

Romiti and Laroque were still lying facedown, too frightened to raise their heads. When it had been quiet for several minutes, Laroque sensed that Lucifer had left, so he slowly tilted his head sideways just to confirm they were alone. At that moment, a receptionist entered the office unannounced. She quickly viewed the sight of her superiors on the floor before fleeing the scene embarrassed and chuckling, wondering what the two men were up to.

"Lucifer's gone," Laroque was barely able to whisper, ignoring the receptionist's untimely and awkward interruption.

Romiti looked up, relieved to be alone but bursting with a level of energy he could hardly contain. "Oh, what a profound, what a spiritual encounter!" he said excitedly. "It was glorious! Nothing can stop us, Laroque! Nothing! And Lucifer has revealed to us what our next moves shall be."

CHAPTER TWENTY-FOUR

Jerusalem, Israel

Other than the blistering desert heat, it was a beautiful day in Jerusalem as its exuberant citizens prepared for the dedication of the temple. Despite the depressing reports of conflicts, wars, famines, and earthquakes that had the planet reeling, Jewish pilgrims from around the world had converged on the holy city for this festive, historic occasion.

Most of Jerusalem's inhabitants on this day were well acquainted with the temple's sad and turbulent history. Funded by his wealthy father, King David, the First Temple took Solomon seven years to construct. He confessed that the heavens could not contain God, much less the temple he had built. In his dedicatory prayer, Solomon acknowledged that he had built the temple for God's Name so that from his dwelling place in heaven, God would hear the prayers of his people, uphold their cause, and forgive their offenses. Solomon also reminded the people that their hearts must be fully committed to God, that they were to live by his decrees and obey his commands. But as a consequence of the nation's disobedience, the Babylonians, led by Nebuchadnezzar, destroyed Jerusalem in 586 BC. The temple was rebuilt, though not to its former grandeur, and dedicated by Zerubbabel in 515 BC. Hundreds of years later, during the Roman occupation of Judea, King Herod completed his renovation of the Second Temple around 20 BC, but it was also destroyed, this time by the Roman general Titus, in the siege of Jerusalem in 70 AD.

Since that time, generations of Jews had longed for the day a rebuilt Third Temple would become the center of their religious activities. That day had finally come, and the celebrants were trembling with excitement, delighted the dream had come to pass in their generation—confident theirs was a unique and special generation in the sight of God.

To proceed with the temple dedication, the Chief Rabbinate Council announced its decision to resume animal sacrifices, though not on the scale of Solomon's day. And it was especially important that on this historical occasion, the priests were rendered ceremonially clean through strict observation of the purification rites.

While the world was appalled at the thought of animal sacrifices, proper observance of the purification rites required the Levites to slaughter a red heifer on the Mount of Olives. After several rabbis arranged the cedar, pine, fig, and cypress wood on the altar constructed for this purpose, the high priest performed the sacrifice. Descending from the altar, the priest lit the fire before the slaughtered heifer was placed on the burning wood.

The priest wrapped hyssop and a piece of cedar inside a section of wool dyed with scarlet and then threw the symbols into the belly of the heifer before it was consumed by the flames. After everything had burned, the ashes were collected for the next ritual.

The ashes were mixed with "living" water, water drawn from a flowing spring. A bundle of three stalks of hyssop, each with one bud, was dipped into the solution and then sprinkled on the priests who were pronounced ceremonially clean and fit to participate in the temple service.

Ezra Cohen observed with fascination all the steps connected with the animal sacrifice and the purification rites. From years of study, he was acquainted with the rituals, and he was equally familiar with the Jewish meaning attached to the various symbols. But as he reflected on the hyssop, the piece of cedar, and the wool dyed with scarlet, he wondered what the two strangers on the Temple Mount would say these particular symbols represented.

It was odd, but he was strangely drawn to the mysterious creatures, perhaps because they so reminded him of the prophets of old. His older brother, Jacob, despised them—for what reason, he really did not know. But his gut told him mankind was living in the twilight of the age, and somehow, these men were connected to the cataclysmic events he sensed were coming.

*　　*　　*

The temple was magnificent, but the shrill and strident cries of hundreds of Omega-ism devotees were a maddening distraction to the temple celebrants.

"Destroy this temple!" the Omega-ism followers shouted. "It prolongs the life of Judaism!"

"Long live Omega-ism!"

"Judaism opposes Romiti and is an enemy of the global community!"

Laroque was standing apart from the crowd, quietly observing the celebration. He was pleased by the demonstration, ardently wishing for a violent confrontation when he was startled by the loud cries of a woman.

"Worship Supreme Priestess Gupta! She alone is deity, manifested in human form!" Soon others took up the cry, shouting, "Gupta is deity! Give glory to Priestess Gupta!"

In a rage, Laroque left the Mount, the seeds of jealousy planted deep in his soul. *She is not deity! Gupta must not receive the worship due Romiti! Omega-ism has served its purpose!*

*　　*　　*

Visitors were caught by surprise at the thoroughly modern design and appearance of the new temple. It was immediately apparent that the two-story complex was divided into three sections. The width of the midsection was obvious, marked by five striking marble pillars spaced an equal distance apart. The west wing of the temple contained offices, meeting rooms, technology centers, and other required facilities. The east wing housed the Sanhedrin assembly hall.

While not creating a replica of Solomon's temple or the temple that was destroyed in 70 AD, the architects had included some of the more striking characteristics of the temples of old. As worshipers approached the steps that led to the porch entrance, they were stunned by the sight of an immense basin, a laver, that was supported on the backs of twelve bronze bulls. The bronze bulls circled the basin with their faces pointing outward, away from the laver that contained ten thousand gallons of water.

The altar of sacrifice was opposite the laver and served as an incinerator for the sacrifices. The altar, constructed from stones taken from the Dead Sea, was unremarkable in its appearance. It was placed in the center of a thirty-by-thirty-square-foot platform, also constructed of stone, which was ringed by seven steps that led to the surface of the stage. It was shaped like an open, rectangular box, having the same dimensions as two picnic tables set end to end, from which the smoke from the sacrifices could ascend unobstructed into the sky.

The porch was entered by passing through two free-standing pillars that retained their original names, Jachin and Boaz. After passing the pillars, worshipers entered the Holy Place. At the front of the Holy Place, they observed a seven-branched golden lampstand, the altar of incense, and the table of shewbread. The altar of incense, standing about two cubits high, resembled a small rectangular pedestal and was made of acacia wood covered with a thin sheet of gold. The table of shewbread was also made of acacia wood—two cubits long, a cubit wide, and a cubit-and-a-half high. It too was overlaid with a sheet of gold, and on each Sabbath day, twelve loaves of freshly baked bread would be placed on the table.

Behind the Holy Place, completely hidden from view, was the Holy of Holies, only to be accessible by the high priest on special occasions.

At precisely noon, a shofar was blown to proclaim the opening of the temple. The loud blast startled a wealthy American tourist standing next to Ezra. "What on earth was that? I've never heard such an instrument—it sounded beautiful!"

"The shofar is a five-thousand-year-old instrument that looks the same today as it did when some ancient shepherd discovered an animal's horn could be used to make music," Ezra quietly explained. "Shofars are made from the horns of rams, goats, or sheep. But the shofar blown moments ago is made of a ram's horn, an appropriate reminder of Abraham's willingness to sacrifice his only son, Isaac. Scripture teaches that God, blessed be His Name, was testing Abraham's obedience. Would he really obey the bizarre command to sacrifice his son, an act that would violate the most sacred teachings of Scripture? At the last moment, God, blessed be His Name, commanded Abraham to exchange Isaac for a ram caught by his horns in a nearby thicket."

On today's joyous but solemn occasion, the blowing of the shofar paralleled the sounds of Rosh Hashanah. The crowds on the Temple Mount first heard the *tekiah,* an unbroken blast of the shofar lasting three seconds. The *shvarim* was heard next. It too was a three-second blast of the ram's horn, except it was broken into three segments. The next blast, called the *teruah,* was broken into nine rapid-fire notes. And the last sound was the *tekiah gedolah,* three unbroken blasts of the shofar, each lasting three seconds.

Musicians celebrated joyfully with songs of thanksgiving and the music of cymbals, harps, and lyres. Singers from around the world had been invited to participate in the historic dedication. After the priests and

Levites had purified themselves ceremonially, they purified the people as well. And then the Jewish worshipers solemnly and reverently filed into the beautiful temple for the first time.

Everyone stood as an ancient copy of the Torah was carried around the assembly hall. Psalms were sung and Scriptures were read. Everyone stood again as the Ashkenazi rabbi, Jonas Heifetz, opened the ceremony in prayer, quoting excerpts from the dedicatory prayer offered by Solomon thousands of years earlier.

"O Lord, God of Israel, there is no God like you in heaven above or on earth below—you who keep your covenant of love with your servants. You have kept your promise to your servant David. But will God really dwell on earth? The heavens, even the highest heaven, cannot contain you. How much less this temple? May your eyes be open toward this temple night and day, this place of which you said, 'My Name shall be there,' so that you will hear the prayers your people Israel pray toward this place. May your eyes be open to your servant's plea and to the plea of your people Israel, and may you listen to them whenever they cry out to you. For you singled them out from all the nations of the world to be your own inheritance, just as you declared through your servant Moses when you, O Sovereign Lord, brought our fathers out of Egypt."

Following a brief message by the Sephardi rabbi, Isaac Disraeli, the observers stood reverently as the *Aleinu* was recited. The prayer anticipates a time when God is acknowledged by all humanity, and foresees the messianic age. The memorable ceremony ended, and the jubilant visitors were dismissed.

As the crowd began to leave the temple, there was a loud commotion in the outer courtyard. Two men were speaking to the people in powerful voices that could be heard a hundred yards away.

The one nicknamed Eli'ahu was praying earnestly, eyes and arms lifted up toward heaven. "O my God, I am too ashamed and disgraced to lift up my face to you, my God, because this people's sins are higher than our heads, and our guilt has reached to the heavens. From the days of our forefathers until now, our guilt has been great."

The mostly Jewish crowd who heard his confession began to jeer, demanding that he stop his prayer. "This is not an occasion for sackcloth and ashes, nor disparaging speeches about the citizens of Israel," one of the Jewish visitors shouted. "This is cause for celebration! Our temple has been rebuilt. Stop spouting this nonsense about our sins!"

Eli'ahu fixed his burning eyes on the man. "Yes, for a brief moment, our God has been gracious to you and has shown you kindness. He has punished you less than your sins deserve. But you must repent of your sins and accept Yeshua, the Son of God. He is the Messiah whom so many of you seek."

Hearing the name of Yeshua, the spectators grew angrier, threatening violence upon the men who would dare to desecrate the hallowed temple grounds by the mere mention of his name. "Mashiach will come soon. Yeshua is not the Messiah!"

Several security officers unsuccessfully tried to break up the gathering of the several hundred people who by now were incensed by Eli'ahu's words. Finally, they approached the two men, demanding they leave the Temple Mount.

"We will not leave this place. We must obey God rather than men!" the one called Moshe replied.

"Who are you? What are your names? And how did you get past security?" an officer asked.

"Our names and who we are are not important," Eli'ahu answered. "But let it be known today that in the writings of the apostle John, we are called the 'two olive trees and the two lampstands.' We are the two witnesses who stand before the Lord of the earth!"

The officer in charge barked orders to six other officers. "Arrest the two lampstands!" he mocked with a laugh. "Handcuff them and take them to jail."

The crowd laughed with the officer and eagerly awaited the arrests.

As the six men drew closer to the witnesses, Moshe raised his hand, signaling for them to stop. "Come no closer. We are obeying God, speaking only what he has commanded us to speak. We want no harm to come to you or anyone else."

The officers began to laugh and continued walking toward the two witnesses. Moshe raised both hands this time, and his would-be captors tumbled backwards, ten or fifteen feet from where they had last stood.

The six men leapt to their feet, mouths opened wide in amazement. The commanding officer and five of his six men remained motionless, trying to comprehend what had just happened. The sixth officer jumped to his feet in a rage, cursing as he pulled his baton from his belt.

"That's the last time you'll pull that trick! You'll wish you'd never set foot on the Temple Mount!" With baton raised, he charged toward the two witnesses.

This time, Eli'ahu raised his hand and simply said, "Stop!" Once again, the officer was thrown backwards. But this time, as he bounced off the stone pavement, his arm was broken and his head bleeding from his rough tumble on the uneven courtyard floor.

"As the Lord God of Israel lives, there will be neither dew nor rain for the next year except at my word," Eli'ahu pronounced to the shocked onlookers.

The officers led their injured coworker to their car as the crowd silently left the Temple Mount, pondering what they had just heard and seen. Before reaching their car, one of the officers stopped and then ran back to the witnesses.

"Please forgive me for the words I spoke. I was afraid. Can we discuss what you've been saying to the people of Israel?" he asked.

Both men smiled briefly at the police officer, saying, "Of course. Come back when you're able, and we'll discuss what's on your mind."

* * *

Very early one morning during the week following the dedication of the temple, Jacob and his wife, Rivka, were studying a passage from 2 Samuel. King David had been told that his infant son, the one he had fathered by Bathsheba, had died. In response, the king acknowledged that his son could not return to him but that someday, he would go to be with his son. As they discussed the passage together, they were startled by the ringing of their phone.

"Jacob, this is Doctor Livni. Please come to the hospital as quickly as you can. I'm sorry to report that Ehud is not doing well; he cannot live much longer."

Jacob and Rivka hurried to the medical center, already crying and deeply afraid. "Oh God, blessed by Your Name, please don't let Ehud die!" Jacob cried out. "He's our only son. He has never done anything wrong. Oh God, blessed be Your Name, please take me if you must, but please don't take our son."

As they entered Ehud's room, they were relieved to see that he was awake, although very weak. He smiled faintly at the sight of his parents and then said, "The doctors don't think I'm doing so well. But that's okay, Papa. While I was sleeping, an angel told me everything would be all right, that I would be with . . ."

Ehud seemed to fall asleep, but seconds later, his eyes fluttered open. "The angel said I would see you and Mama again soon, so it's going to be okay."

Each parent held one of Ehud's hands until the boy fell into a deep sleep. He died a short time later.

Jacob and Rivka cried as they tenderly touched their son one last time, and then they gathered his favorite belongings. After thanking the nurses and doctors for their loving care, they left the hospital, heading for the park bench that had become their favorite hiding place. They sat quietly together, grieving over the sudden death of their son. They had received word before that his condition had worsened, but little Ehud always recovered. They had hoped, even expected, that he would bounce back again this time, just as he had done so many times before.

Jacob was weeping as he rocked back and forth, quoting verses from Job. "Sighing comes to me instead of food; my groans pour out like water. What I feared has come upon me; what I dreaded has happened to me. I have no peace, no quietness; I have no rest, but only turmoil. On the day of my birth, why was I not hidden in the ground like a stillborn child, like an infant who never saw the light of day? Oh, better that, than to bear this pain! God, blessed be Your Name, why did you allow this to happen? Are you a cruel God, blessed be Your Name, who hurts those who love you most? Have I disappointed you? I cannot bear to live without my son."

Rivka's heart broke even more as she listened to her husband's self-disparaging confessions. *Surely our Ehud did not die because we've disappointed you.* Rivka's cries turned to sobs as she fell to the floor, her face buried in the sleeve of her dress. Her eyes were swollen and her chest heaved; she was tormented by the loss of her child and the sorrow expressed by her husband.

"While the child was alive, we fasted and wept, hoping you would be gracious to us by allowing Ehud to live. We have always honored you and kept your commandments. For what trespass are we now being punished? Can I bring Ehud back again? We will go to him, but he will not return to us."

After a while, there were no more words to utter. Jacob became silent, groaning and weeping beside his wife and before his Creator.

* * *

Although Uri had never met Ezra Cohen, Jacob's younger brother left voice mail, letting Uri know that Ehud had passed away. In his message, Ezra explained that his brother and sister-in-law had left for the park to mourn alone.

Uri and Rachel hurriedly arranged for a neighbor to watch the twins and then went to join the grieving couple. They quickly located Jacob and his wife, and without a word, sat down beside them. Jacob nodded a greeting but for a long while was unable to speak.

When he finally regained his composure, Jacob thanked Uri and Rachel for sharing in their sorrow. His voice quavered. "This morning, my hopes were soaring as I anticipated today's dedication of the temple. Jews have waited so long for this glorious day, praying it would prepare the way for the coming of the Mashiach. And then we received the call from the doctor, saying there was nothing more he could do. My hope died with Ehud, Uri. Our hearts are crushed. We cannot go on without our son."

Uri's eyes filled with tears as he promised the couple, "Listen, Jacob, Rachel and I will walk with you and Rivka on your painful journey. I don't pretend to understand all the reasons why God allows bad things to happen, but I do know he loves you and Rivka deeply. You're not alone. We'll get through this dark time together, I promise you."

CHAPTER TWENTY-FIVE

Jerusalem, Israel

The rude buzzing of an alarm clock awakened Ezra at two o'clock in the morning. He immediately thought of playful Ehud, and his heart began to ache. It had been a month since the little guy died, and Ezra missed him sorely. He longed to hear Ehud's laughter echo through the halls, to see his mischievous grin, and wondered if that could ever be.

For several weeks now, Ezra had been rising much earlier than the other members of the close-knit household. He left his brother's home and hurriedly walked the short block to a vacant apartment. Looking furtively about, he silently entered the dwelling, locking the door behind him. He strode to a small, windowless vestibule. He removed a small battery-driven lamp from his pocket, and as before, began to study the claims of the one called the Son of David. He was reading from a book the Gentiles called the Gospel of Matthew. The two brothers had discussed Jacob's earlier conversation with Uri about the coming Messiah, and Jacob had mentioned Uri's repeated references to Matthew, the tax collector. Ezra was intrigued by Uri's comment that Matthew's primary audience was Jewish and that the intent of his writings was to provide irrefutable proof that the long-awaited Messiah had come. Ezra made the decision to read Matthew's account in secret. He had to learn for himself what the ancient heretical Jewish sect that had become Christianity believed about the one who claimed to be Israel's Messiah.

After two hours of study, Ezra closed his eyes and once again prayed, "Oh God, blessed be Your Name, if this Yeshua is truly the Son of David, please show me. I only desire to please and obey you. You revealed yourself to our fathers, Abraham, Isaac, and Jacob. Please reveal yourself and your truth to me as well. Let me hear your voice."

Ezra quietly exited the apartment, leaving the door unlocked for his return early the next morning.

*　*　*

The two witnesses had returned to the northeast corner of the temple courtyard, near Bab al-Asbat, the Gate of the Tribes, and were speaking to a rowdy crowd of several hundred worshipers and visitors. Angered by their repeated references to Yeshua, the chief rabbis had ordered the witnesses to stay off the Temple Mount. But they ignored the orders, appearing on the Mount every day. The chief rabbis had heard astonishing excuses for how the vagrants had eluded security and why no arrests had been made, but for the time being, they decided not to interfere in police business.

"Yeshua was faithful to the One who appointed him, just as Moses was faithful in all God's house. Yeshua has been found worthy of greater honor than Moses, just as the builder of a house has greater honor than the house itself."

As before, upon hearing the name of Yeshua, the Jewish crowd became belligerent, especially when Moshe gave greater honor to Yeshua than to their revered prophet Moses. A dozen or so stomped off, looking for authorities that could cart away the strange-looking men. Others heckled and jeered the preachers, a cruel game to which the men had become accustomed.

"Every house is built by someone, even this house, this temple, that you are visiting today. But God is the builder of everything. Moses was faithful as a servant in all God's house, testifying to what would be in the future. But Yeshua the Messiah is faithful as a son over God's house. Today, if you hear his voice, do not turn a deaf ear as our ancestors did in the time of testing in the desert, where our fathers tested and tried God and for forty years saw what he did."

Standing in front of the Gate of the Tribes, Moshe continued his brief message by saying, "See to it that none of you has a sinful, unbelieving heart that turns away from the living God. Who were they who heard and rebelled? Were they not all those Moses led out of Egypt? And with whom was he angry for forty years? Was it not with those who sinned, whose bodies fell in the desert? And to whom did God swear that they would never enter his rest if not to those who disobeyed? So we see that they were not able to enter because of their unbelief!"

From across the courtyard, the sound of gunfire interrupted Moshe's closing, causing pandemonium among the tour group that had gathered around the Fountain el-Kas, a site used for Muslim purification rituals.

Panicked visitors ran toward Moshe, trying to escape the outraged assailant. Temple guards quickly captured and subdued the young shooter, an impassioned Palestinian who was furious over the presence of the temple. The Palestinian had shot a young rabbi who was guiding a dozen tourists around the temple grounds.

A policeman who had witnessed the shooting also sprinted toward the two witnesses, quickly elbowing his way through the spectators before stopping in front of the preachers. It was the same officer who, weeks earlier, had tried to arrest and handcuff the preachers, only to return a few minutes later to ask their forgiveness for the words he had spoken.

"One of our rabbis has been murdered by a young Palestinian. Come quickly!" the policeman shouted. "I know God listens when you speak to him. You must pray for the rabbi! Please, come quickly!"

The shocked crowd listened intently to the officer's pleas for help, and then returned their full attention to the two witnesses, unsure of what their response would be.

What kind of men can raise the dead? they wondered. No one in the crowd moved. No one spoke.

The preachers stepped toward the officer, who turned and ran in the direction of the fallen rabbi. "Follow me!" The two witnesses slowly followed the officer to the site of the shooting. A large crowd had gathered around the body of the murdered man.

The police officer and the two witnesses made their way through the crowd, reaching the fallen rabbi who was lying on the hot stone pavement. A doctor, present in the crowd for morning prayers, was leaning over the mortally wounded teacher. Shortly, he looked at the officer and shook his head. "I'm sorry, but I'm afraid he's dead. There is nothing I can do."

The officer looked at Eli'ahu. "Please, sir, I know your God listens to your prayers. Is there anything you can do?"

Eli'ahu closed his eyes for a moment and then, looking up toward heaven, prayed aloud in a strong voice, "O Lord my God, may you alone be glorified. In the name of your Son Yeshua, let this man's life return to him!"

Eli'ahu prayed with great authority, and the simplicity and boldness of his supplication stunned the crowd into silence. The eerie and absolute silence continued as every eye stared at the body of the rabbi. The faces of the other rabbis betrayed their resentment at the mention of Yeshua, but they too remained motionless, staring at their lifeless companion.

Suddenly the eyes of the slain rabbi began to flutter, and he coughed twice. Slowly he stood to his feet, first touching his temple and then his heart, the targets of the assassin's bullets. The searing pain was gone. The wounds had healed. He looked at the two witnesses in wonder as Moshe whispered something softly into his ear, and then the healers began to walk toward the temple, leaving the speechless crowd behind.

The rabbis looked at one another in astonishment and disbelief, none fully comprehending the meaning or implications of the miracle they had just witnessed. One of them said, "We must request a meeting of the Chief Rabbinate Council and report what we have seen and heard today. We must also find out by what power these men are doing these miracles!"

The people were amazed, and the Jews in the crowd asked one another, "Could Yeshua really be the Son of David, the coming Mashiach?" All but one hurriedly left to tell their friends about the miracle they had witnessed that day.

Suddenly left behind and alone with the two witnesses, who had slowed their pace toward the temple, Ezra Cohen could not move. His legs and feet were paralyzed, it seemed. He had witnessed the entire sequence of events and was staggered by the miracle that raised the rabbi to life. His theology did not allow for a resurrection, but he had witnessed a marvelous miracle, of that he was certain. He could not find the courage to ask the questions that were tormenting his soul. He was fearful, afraid of where his questions might lead. Finally, movement returned to his feet. As he began to walk, his questioning gaze returned to the miracle workers.

"Behold, a true Israeli, in whom there is nothing false," the one called Moshe cried out.

"How do you know me?" Ezra questioned.

Eli'ahu replied, "The Son of David knows you, Ezra. He sees you every morning, even while you're hiding. You search in secret for undeniable proof that the one called Yeshua is really who he claimed to be, the Messiah, Israel's coming king. You have it now."

Tears welled up in Ezra's eyes as he covered his ears and fled the truth.

*   *   *

Sticks grabbed his cell phone when he heard the sound of the shofar, the ringtone Sticks had assigned to Uri's calls. "You won't believe it, Sticks.

A rabbi was just murdered on the Temple Mount, but minutes later was raised to life by the two witnesses. There's several YouTube videos—check 'em out!"

The two men spoke for another minute or two about the effects of the recent international launch of the single electronic currency system before ending the brief call.

For the next hour, Sticks was glued to the Internet, fascinated by the events taking place in Israel.

"Honey, quick. Watch this!" he shouted. Cyndi came running. Together, they listened to the eyewitness reports of those who had seen the dead rabbi come to life.

Sticks spoke breathlessly. "It's amazing, isn't it? For thousands of years, theologians have ridiculed the apostle John's account of the resurrection of the witnesses, particularly where John says, 'For three-and-a-half days men from every people, tribe, language, and nation will gaze on their bodies and refuse them burial.' They've taught that John was using symbolic language and therefore, no one should take his words literally. They could not imagine the Internet, could they?"

"Slow down, turbo! You're getting carried away again. But yes, it's amazing, isn't it?" Cyndi replied.

"Someday soon, I believe we'll see the murder, and according to Scripture, the literal resurrection of the two witnesses. Oh, wait! This oughta be interesting. They're about to interview one of the rabbis who's still standing in the temple courtyard. And I can see two men sitting in the background. Wonder if they're the two witnesses? This is live."

The two witnesses were enjoying the shade of several olive trees, growing inside a circular planter made of stone pavers. The planter, sitting in the middle of a wide walkway, contained several water spigots that children were using to splash water on one another. Several dozen people were standing near the two men, while others sat on a raised stone platform that lined the walkway.

"We understand that you were standing next to the rabbi who was killed and later raised to life. Is this true?" a reporter asked.

"Yes, I was actually walking beside Rabbi Aaron Judeh as we were returning to the temple. We were near the Fountain el-Kas when I thought I heard gunfire. For a minute, many of us believed Rabbi Judeh had been shot. However, we now believe that he simply collapsed from shock. There is no evidence of any wounds, nor is there any blood on his clothing."

"Are you saying the entire thing was staged? I've seen pictures of bloody chest and head wounds! Are you denying this happened?" the reporter asked incredulously.

"Absolutely not. This incident was not staged. I'm only saying that we've carefully studied the footage and have concluded that the bright sunlight distorted the pictures, giving the illusion of blood instead of what it really was—the shadow cast by the bronze bulls outside the temple."

"Is Rabbi Judeh willing to be interviewed?"

"No, that will not be possible. He is still shaken from the incident and unable to speak."

"Unwilling or unable?"

"The Chief Rabbinate Council has chosen me to give its official statements. The rabbinate has concluded this was not a miraculous resurrection. Rather, faulty conclusions were drawn in response to the bedlam created by the gunfire. Fortunately no one was hurt, and the perpetrator was apprehended."

"Can you believe that?" Sticks shouted into his monitor. "Can you believe the hardness of their hearts! God, open their eyes! May all Israel turn to you soon!"

Sticks's eyes returned to the monitor in time to see Moshe raise his hands, as if to summon someone or something from the heavens. Suddenly the sky turned dark, as if a thick cloud was passing between sun and earth. A massive swarm of biting flies descended on the Temple Mount, blanketing every object in sight. The spokesperson for the Chief Rabbinate Council looked fearfully toward heaven and then ran for shelter, wondering if his statements were connected with the sudden onslaught of the filthy insects. Revolted by the winged creatures and annoyed by the pinch of their bites, the Temple Mount visitors fled for the safety of their cars, homes, and hotels as Sticks watched from half a world away.

In Bayit VeGan, Jacob, Rivka, and Ezra were outdoors when the dark cloud obstructed the noonday sun. Seconds later, they realized the cloud was actually a mass of flies that had swooped down on Israel. They ran toward their home, slapping the flies from their arms and faces. "Where did they come from?" Ezra shouted in disgust. They entered the apartment, hurriedly slamming the door behind them, and then began to swat the insects that had managed to enter their dwelling through the open windows and door.

An hour later, their home free of the pests, Jacob and Ezra turned to CNN for the latest news. Rivka continued to fearfully stand watch as she peered out her bedroom window, nervously watching hordes of flies collide with the pane of glass that separated her from the awful insects.

As the Cohen brothers observed the scene torn from the pages of Exodus, the reporter announced that the plague of flies was not confined to the Temple Mount; gigantic swarms were now being reported in every city and village of Israel. Airports throughout Israel were shut down, as were the major thoroughfares of the tiny nation. Commerce quickly came to a halt.

Sticks, glued to his monitor, was in awe, wondering if believers were faring better than unbelievers in this latest demonstration of God's power.

As if to read his thoughts, Moshe, still on camera, raised his voice and said, "Give glory to God! You do not believe God is able to breathe life into a slain body. Perhaps you will now believe that even flies do his bidding! Do not harden your hearts. This sign is given to all of Israel. Repent of your sins and turn to Yeshua, the Son of David! God has made a distinction this day between you and his people, those who have placed their trust in Yeshua and those who have not. This winged nuisance will not trouble the followers of Yeshua. As a further confirmation that this plague is a sign from God, know that the flies will be gone from Israel by this time tomorrow. A strong wind from the east will sweep them into the Mediterranean."

"Wonder what that distinction looks like?" Sticks mulled. "Better give Uri a call."

The correspondent concluded the news segment by saying, "These flies remind me of the fifth plague Moses called to strike the ancient Egyptians, but this time, we Israelis are the victims."

You mean the fourth plague, Sticks mentally corrected him. Unbeknownst to the reporter, the bites were already infecting thousands with debilitating diseases that would become news in the weeks to come.

* * *

Some of the angriest people remained on the temple grounds a while longer, tormented by the flies but cursing the witnesses and threatening them with bodily harm. Finally, the angry men and women fled the Mount in a rage.

In the days that followed the plague, Israeli citizens, observant Jews and secular alike, began to contact their government leaders, angrily demanding the two witnesses be jailed, or better yet, deported. They were incensed that on the very day the Jewish temple had been dedicated, the day Jews throughout the world had assembled in honor of their beloved temple, the two men would deliberately profane the sacred assembly.

Believers, meanwhile, grew stronger in their faith, strengthened by the providential acts and miracles they were witnessing, boldly proclaiming their trust in the Messiah to all who would listen. And the church grew, as the Lord added greatly to their number.

* * *

Romiti sat in a cushy leather chair in the private conference room adjoining his comfortable, lavishly appointed office, discussing with his cabinet the recent famines that had stolen the lives of nearly two hundred million people around the world—numbers that had not yet been reported.

The cabinet was enjoying drinks and hors d'oeuvres, especially tasty canapés, as they progressed through the agenda.

"We dodged a bullet," Romiti boasted smugly as the waitstaff served the world's most powerful man a second helping of hors d'oeuvres. "Pattersen, your documentaries highlighted our most successful feeding programs and deflected attention away from our shortcomings. You're to be commended for another excellent job!"

"Thank you, sir. And your idea was brilliant, I must say," Pattersen responded, clearly flattered. "The staged interviews with senior government officials of various nations, all hinting of the vast profits hoarded by the greedy Jews during the global famine, really turned public opinion in our favor."

Sebastian Ospel, the chairman of the Global Economic Council, also chimed in. "Those two crazies on the Temple Mount helped us as well. By claiming credit for the drought and the astonishing infestation of flies, they're making the people angrier about religious intolerance every day! How stupid! Both could have been dismissed as freakish acts of nature."

"Yes, you're right, Ospel, but by claiming that God has empowered them, the 'crazies' are bringing attention to their message. I understand the 'miracle of the flies' actually persuaded a large number of weak-minded people to become Christians. I can't allow this to continue much longer. By the way, how's the single electronic international currency coming along? Deployment's behind schedule. What steps are being taken to get back on track?"

Ospel had been waiting for this moment—showtime. He beamed with pleasure as he gave his report in the hearing of his peers. "Over two thousand beta sites reported zero system errors and zero downtime for three consecutive months. Upon reaching this milestone, the software launched worldwide a month ago, only two months behind the planned go-live date. All things considered, the implementation has gone very smoothly. Our biggest challenges, as we expected, are in the developing countries where many population groups, mostly tribal peoples, don't comprehend electronic currency—besides the fact that these tribal areas have no means to access it. So for now, the vast majority of the transactions originate in developed countries, with minor numbers coming from the least industrialized nations."

That out of the way, Ospel got to the point he knew Romiti cared most about. "By this time next month, we can launch the Global Identity and Allegiance System whenever you give the word. Identity stations have been configured in almost every government office on earth. Pattersen has developed several marketing pieces—which are excellent, I might add—that explain the purpose of the new system. Her clever electronic media demonstrates how GIAS will eliminate identity theft, the crime whose victims now number in the hundreds of millions. It also shows how the system will significantly improve the on-site quality of care provided to crime and accident victims. By swiping a patch, the victim's medical records will be immediately available to attending emergency personnel. Pattersen has also done a brilliant job of connecting GIAS to the warmth and camaraderie of a global family, a sense of community. Those who do not participate in GIAS are estranged from the family—these outsiders are dangerous, treacherous, even evil."

Romiti was pleased with the news, although he had already heard preliminary reports of the project's successful launch. For the first time in days, he was smiling. The normal fare of glum news had begun to take its toll on him, so good news quickly energized the secretary-general.

"Exceptional report, Ospel! Let me know when the system is ready. I want to launch GIAS the day it's available, although I'm not prepared to link it with the electronic currency system yet. I want most of the world registered on GIAS before we integrate the two systems."

The meeting was interrupted by one of his secretaries, who handed Romiti two urgent memos she had received while the meeting was in progress.

Romiti quickly scanned the contents of both memos and then, in utter frustration, crumpled them into balls and threw them at his secretary. "Do not interrupt this meeting again!" he bellowed. The secretary ran from the office, humiliated by the sudden outburst.

Romiti remained quiet for several minutes as his mind grappled with the information he had just received.

"Are there any large-scale military operations underway in Asia or North America?" Romiti directed his question to Dixon, the GSF commander.

"No. As a matter of fact, the most recent GSF operations ended two months ago, and they were minor. We were overseeing the final distribution of famine-relief supplies to the hardest hit regions of Africa and Indonesia."

Romiti kept his tone tightly controlled. "These communiqués are from the presidents of the North American and Indian Regional Zones. It seems massive protests have simultaneously erupted in most of the major cities in these zones. The demonstrations suddenly turned ugly when government forces attempted to disperse the crowds." Romiti's eyes bored into Dixon, and his hands trembled slightly with anger. "The memos state that hundreds of protesters have already been killed."

Dixon and Zagmi were both stunned by the news. "I've seen nothing that would indicate this level of unrest," Dixon stammered.

"I agree," Zagmi added. He had jumped half to his feet at the news, and now he tried to seat himself again without looking too awkward. "We're monitoring virtually every form of electronic communication, and there's been no hint of any kind of coordinated protests in these zones. Does it say what the protests are about?"

"The usual stuff. Food shortages. Big Brother government. Staggering unemployment figures. But obviously your surveillance and eavesdropping systems have big holes. Demonstrations like these are always coordinated through social media. Something's up, and you need to get on it!"

Romiti stood. "There are more items on our agenda, but they deal with future plans. Let's bring this meeting to a close so Dixon and Zagmi can find out what's going on. Watch your e-mail. My secretary will distribute next month's agenda shortly."

As the group left the conference room, the humiliated secretary handed Romiti three more memos, reporting major riots and bloodshed in Western Europe, Africa, and China. "What is going on!" Romiti roared to anyone who was listening.

*   *   *

The violent uprisings continued around the world. Surprisingly, the Middle Eastern Regional Zone was the only one unaffected by the riots. Romiti received daily updates from Dixon and Zagmi, and the reports were alarming. It had been six weeks since the first report of violence, and thousands of deaths had been confirmed.

The conflicts were having other unintended consequences. As the violence spread, valuable crops were destroyed as small skirmishes and major battles were fought in once-fertile farmlands.

While the UN tried to restore the shattered peace, the effects of the worldwide drought, for which the two witnesses were taking credit, worsened. Romiti recalled Lucifer's prediction as well, although he had been hoping it would not come to pass this soon: "A fourth of the earth's population will soon die by the sword, famine, plague, and the wild beasts of the earth."

*   *   *

Odinga, the chief economist for the UN's Food and Agricultural Organization, was summoned to an emergency session of the General Assembly. Before he began his presentation, the motion to enter executive session was carried. There was to be no public disclosure of the General Assembly proceedings.

To no one's surprise, the economist reported that another global famine was imminent.

"There is nothing that can be done. The world's food reserves are depleted, and the greater portion of the current year's crops have been doomed by the record heat wave. Our statisticians have created models that demonstrate a billion people may die of starvation. The figures are staggering, beyond imagination."

The General Assembly was astonished by the magnitude of the looming catastrophe. A few questions were asked, but most members remained silent, trying to comprehend the impact of a billion deaths.

The president of the General Assembly nodded his assent to Romiti's request to take the floor. Romiti stood as he addressed the bewildered leaders.

"I have never acknowledged the existence of any deity, let alone the God of the Jew or the Christian. However, I do believe there is a God."

Most of the delegates were stunned by Romiti's admission. Until this very moment, all of them had believed him to be a committed atheist. They instinctively leaned forward, not wanting to miss a single word.

"Yes, there is a God. I freely admit that he was the 'cause' behind the universe. But he is not omnipotent. He does not possess all power. If he did, there would be no pain and suffering. He certainly is not just and loving, or we would not experience famines and disease. And he certainly is not faithful, or he would have already delivered on his promises. No, the God of the Bible, if he is alive, is a distracted cause, no longer concerned about the plight of his creation. Was not Friedrich Neitzsche correct? The God of the Bible is dead."

The majority of the assembly stood in unison, thunderously applauding Romiti for putting into words what the majority had believed for so long. Two or three were angered by the blasphemous talk and terrified of the eventual consequences.

"The world took a giant step forward when I negotiated a peace in the Middle East, a dream that's been beyond our reach for thousands of years. We have fought valiantly to blunt the effects of a global famine, preventing the deaths of a hundred million people. And yet the two 'witnesses,' as they're often called, in league with their intolerable sponsor, the supposed God of the universe, have called for another worldwide drought. What have the innocent inhabitants of earth done to deserve this awful punishment?

"You've visited the websites of the religious zealots who oppose me. They call me the Antichrist, the beast, the root of all evil! But what have I done? Tell me! What evil acts have I committed against humanity? Name one!"

Even while protesting his innocence, Romiti saw images of his boyhood schoolmate, Benjamin; Maria, his nurse and tutor; and De Luca, the Italian diplomat, all murdered by the cold-blooded killer. He trembled as he saw his victims pointing their accusing fingers toward him and then to a fiery pit he imagined to be hell. What was bringing these images to mind?

"Today I'm taking my stand against the God of the Jew and the Christian. I will not be subordinate to him! I am in league with another god—the god who has authority over the affairs of this world. I have been chosen by him to restore order and prosperity on earth!"

Romiti mockingly turned his face toward heaven. "If there is a God of the Jew and the Christian—the so-called God of Abraham, Isaac, and Jacob—then summon me. Let me defend my ways to your face," he challenged. "Summon me, and I will answer you; let me speak, and I will argue my case before you. Why do you hide your face from me and consider me your enemy?"

Turning back to his audience, he continued his rant. "See, there is no living God of Abraham, Isaac, and Jacob! What kind of deity would overlook my challenge? The God who is revered in these intolerant religions is either dead, alive but powerless, or is a cruel invention of their corrupt leaders, an invisible instrument created to deceive, control, and enslave their pitiful converts!"

The General Assembly listened spellbound, some shouting their agreement. They were also growing angrier with the religious zealots who opposed their leader, one they believed had done everything in his power to restore peace and order to a world in disarray.

"At my direction, Laroque, the deputy of Religious Affairs, founded the International Interfaith Council under the wonderful leadership of Supreme Priestess Gupta. Already, the IIC has more than three billion adherents. Am I opposed to a religion that benefits all of humanity and not just the intolerant few? Of course not! I desire world peace above all else."

Romiti glanced at Laroque, who was smiling his approval.

"Christians and the Jews—these are root of evil! Not long ago, a bus carrying twenty schoolchildren in the nation of Palestine was attacked by a group of soldiers. There were no survivors. You all know the story. Witnesses gave conflicting reports of the carnage; one claimed the leader snapped orders in Hebrew." The terrible massacre had received worldwide coverage, and Israel, while proclaiming its innocence, was swiftly and universally condemned for the attacks. Romiti breathed deeply, seeming to calm but remaining resolute. "We will survive this latest assault on our innocent children and live on to a glorious future. But we must no longer coddle our enemies. With your support, I, along with members of my cabinet, will develop a strategy that will for the first time in history rid the world of the religious fanatics who disrupt our peace and kill our children. Will you join me?"

The speech struck an anti-Semitic, anti-Christian nerve among the General Assembly members. Following prolonged applause for the profane speech and nearly unanimous agreement for the secretary-general to develop a plan to eliminate his opposition, several members launched attacks of their own.

"The Jews are occupiers of Muslim land, oppressing the Palestinians and fanning the flames of violence and discord throughout the region," the Iranian ambassador declared.

The ambassador from Indonesia added, "Christians and Jews stubbornly refuse to adopt the IIC's Six Pillars of Faith, are intolerant of practices which they alone find immoral, and steadfastly reject UN-recommended practices that promote peace and harmony among all peoples. They will not participate in population reduction programs, oppose gender diversity training, and will not enroll their children in Omega-ism coaching classes. The list is endless. And despite all this, we're seeing a record number of people flocking to Christianity. If tracking polls are remotely accurate, their ranks have swollen by tens of millions in the last year alone. They must be stopped!"

Other ambassadors pressed the virulent verbal attack on their enemies until the Egyptian ambassador finally made a motion to adjourn the meeting.

"Mr. Chairman."

The president of the UN General Assembly again acknowledged Romiti's request to take the floor.

"Before this session adjourns, I would like to address my colleagues one more time. And let me remind you that we are still in an executive session of the General Assembly.

"We have heard Odinga's frightening report of the looming famine. He has reported that hundreds of millions of lives will be lost—perhaps as many as a billion.

"I believe we should consider other alternatives that might spare the lives of innocent men, women, and children. I'm going to list measures that may seem barbaric in our modern society, but let me assure you, present world conditions are unparalleled in the history of humankind. They call for radical action.

"Our prisons contain millions of people who have broken our laws—murderers, rapists, muggers, Christians, Jews. Why should criminals be fed while innocent people starve? In many parts of the world, the famines are caused by religious rivalries. Perhaps we should consider mass executions of religious fanatics of all faiths, thus preventing future conflicts. Many people groups have refused mandatory sterilization, the UN's program to reduce population growth. Shall we consider infanticide? How 'bout senicide, the killing of the elderly? I know these are extreme measures, but none can be taken off the table. A billion innocent lives are at stake.

"It is true that such actions would not win us favor with the masses, who would not see clearly enough to condone them. Minutes ago, many of you derided the radical Christians, Jews, and Muslims that violently oppose our programs. Consider implementing some of the ideas I've outlined, and others that are yet to be mentioned, making it clear that our enemies—not the United Nations—are the cause of these measures. I want the global community to loathe Christians and Jews—the world must perceive them as the cause of these 'draconian measures.'"

Romiti thanked the members for their support and yielded the floor following his final comments. "I will present my plan in the next session of the General Assembly. In the meantime, be patient. The next twelve months will be extraordinarily painful for mankind. But let me assure you: we will emerge from this extraordinary trial victorious over our enemies. We will prevail!"

*　　*　　*

Sticks almost choked when he read the leaked contents of Romiti's speech to the General Assembly. *He's in league with another god? One who has authority over the affairs of this world? He's talking about Satan—some god!*

While meeting with his small group leaders that morning, Sticks shared excerpts from Romiti's speech. "This should lay to rest any doubts you may have about this man's true identity. He is the Antichrist. The apostle John tells us this man will 'open his mouth to blaspheme God, and to slander his name and his dwelling place.' Daniel predicted the Antichrist 'will say unheard-of things against the God of gods.' Daniel went on to say, 'He will be successful until the time of wrath is completed, for what has been determined must take place.'

"The fourth seal is about to be opened. After the events of the fourth seal have run their course, the fifth seal will be broken. Then the Antichrist, completely empowered by Satan, the god Romiti claims he's in league with, will vent his fury on Israel and the church. But this morning, I want us to be encouraged by a phrase from Luke's gospel, written by the physician who also authored the New Testament book of Acts. Luke writes, 'Stand up and lift up your heads, because your redemption is drawing near.' Our redemption is drawing nigh, men! We must be consumed by this thought. It must be the first thing we think about when we wake up each morning, and the last thing we think about when we close our eyes each night!"

Sticks's eyes seemed to burn with the passion of his words. "The fourth seal will be marked by warfare, famine, and disease. We must accelerate our efforts to reach everyone in our community with the good news."

The small group leaders leaned forward in their chairs, enthusiastic and laying hold of Sticks's every word.

"You and I must live our lives with a profound sense of urgency. None of us know when the freedoms we take for granted will be taken from us; we don't know how many more days we have before we're imprisoned or killed. Let's use whatever time is remaining to be Jesus's hands and feet to every man and woman, boy and girl we meet."

Chapter Twenty-Six

Babylon, Iraq

As usual, Romiti was the first person other than janitors and security personnel to arrive at the UN's Babylonian headquarters. The janitorial staff was preparing to leave the building as the secretary-general stormed down the hallway toward his massive office. Janitors scrambled to move supplies and equipment from Romiti's path, terrified it would be their misplaced box or piece of equipment that would be the cause of a stumble. Usually, Romiti silently enjoyed their cowering reaction to his presence, but today he was in a foul mood. Nothing could soothe his rage. Conflicts and famine were decimating entire people groups, and their effect on the world's economy was devastating. The prior evening, another passenger plane had crashed, killing nearly three hundred people. The accident would be pinned on the maintenance crews, no doubt. Too many mechanics had died. Even if there were enough mechanics, the spare parts weren't available—there weren't enough factory workers to man the production lines. This bleak outlook wasn't limited to the airline industry. Hospitals were grossly understaffed. Insurance companies were history. Retailers were bankrupt. Only the mortuary business was booming.

Three hours later, at precisely seven o'clock a.m., his first cabinet meeting of the day got underway. Vague talk of another plague had been circulating, and Romiti wanted answers.

"Reports of a new, rapidly spreading HIV-like disease have recently surfaced in major cities around the world," the head of the Global Health Organization explained to Romiti's cabinet members. "It presents many of the same symptoms as the Human Immunodeficiency Virus, but experts have confirmed it is not HIV. This means that at present, the medications that have been developed to combat HIV are of little or no value to the victim."

"Does it have a name?"

"We've named it HIV-Extended, or HIVE—at least temporarily."

"Who's at greatest risk?" Ospel asked nervously.

"From what we've discovered so far, no population group seems to be at higher risk than another. As we all know, the people most vulnerable to HIV are those who have not remained in monogamous relationships. Not so with this disease. And while it may take up to ten years for HIV to progress to full-blown AIDS, HIVE progresses from infection to death within fourteen days."

Several whistled. Romiti just sighed. *When will the bad news stop?*

"For decades, scientists have been warning us of the growth of superbugs that are resistant to all antibiotics. HIVE may be caused by one of these superbugs—so far, it seems that HIVE infections are impossible to treat, even resistant to the most powerful class of antibiotics. This outbreak will be a nightmare scenario if it's not stopped in its tracks."

"And what are the symptoms?" Ospel posed the follow-up question.

"You getting nervous?" Dixon poked at Ospel, who by now was sweating profusely and trembling slightly.

"Like HIV, the initial symptoms are headache, a sore throat, and often, a rash. A few days later, the patient develops a very high fever and a hacking cough and will experience soaking night sweats and swollen lymph nodes. The most noticeable difference between this disease and HIV/AIDS is the tremors which make it impossible for HIVE patients to stand, confining them to beds until their death."

Within six weeks of the first official announcement of HIVE, nations were in a panic as they counted millions of HIVE deaths. Worldwide, over thirty million AIDS-related deaths had been reported from the first reported incident through to 2010, but at the present rate, HIVE-related deaths would triple the total AIDS count within six months of its discovery. Even Romiti's council was not exempt. Ospel was the first council member to contract HIVE, dying days after learning of the disease in the secretary-general's office. To escape the deadly disease, people were choosing to remain in their homes as much as possible, further damaging local economies. There was no proof of an airborne contagion, but if an outdoor trip was necessary, millions of germophobic citizens were wearing facemasks as protection. The source of HIVE was still a mystery.

Owners of restaurants, theaters, and shopping malls were dismayed as their customers dwindled away. Most public events were canceled. People ran from strangers, frightened by the possibility that every unfamiliar person might be spreading HIVE.

Surprisingly, attendance was up in the churches most reviled by the UN, while attendance had dropped significantly in the Omega-ism halls. The most common explanation for the increased attendance in the US was given by the new attendees themselves, citing fond childhood memories of Sunday school and VBS volunteers from whom they had learned the stories of the Bible. When life turned sour, they explained, they found solace and support among believers in Bible-teaching churches.

*   *   *

No community was immune from the effects of HIVE, and Jackson, Mississippi, was no exception. Over a thousand deaths had been confirmed in the city, and many thousands more had been stricken by the mysterious disease.

Sticks was speaking passionately from a makeshift platform in one of the neighborhood parks. "I commend you for sharing so freely of your time and possessions. Every day, for months, I have received notes and heard stories from families you have helped and lives you have saved. But now I'm asking you to do even more.

"The HIVE outbreak is worsening. We don't know its cause. We don't even know how the disease is transmitted from one victim to the next. But we do know that many have died and many more are infected with the virus. The apostle John writes, 'This is how we know we are in him: whoever claims to live in him must walk as Jesus did.' As we've read the remarkable stories of Jesus, all of us have been struck by the company he kept. He was not afraid to associate with tax collectors and prostitutes, those most despised by his culture. He healed the sick and returned dead children alive and well to their grieving parents. And Jesus literally touched lepers, the contagious outcasts whose disease terrified the healthy.

"Today, I'm challenging the church—remember, that's you and me— to walk as Jesus walked. Let's walk into the lives of those stricken with HIVE. Let's share the love of Jesus by doing whatever we can to assist those before whom most of society flees."

The church responded to Sticks's challenge and to similar challenges made by pastors around the world. Believers were trained in how to care for an HIVE patient, and soon, the church became the first responder to the dreaded disease. Some in the media reluctantly gave credit to believers for their courage and compassion, acknowledging that many willingly forfeited their lives while caring for the sick.

*   *   *

Sticks placed a call to Uri. "Haven't spoken to you in weeks. I've been wanting to ask you about the plague of flies. What was it like? How did it affect you?"

"It was pretty incredible, actually," Uri reported. "I've never seen so many flies! For several minutes, the sun was actually hidden from view by the massive swarm. But believe it or not, not a fly came within ten feet of any believer I've spoken to. The pesky insects wouldn't enter our cars, our homes, or our churches. Some Israelis were upset because believers weren't affected by the plague, but most just seemed curious. Gave us a lot of opportunities to witness, too, and some people actually came to faith! It was an amazing experience. Now I know how the Hebrew slaves felt in Egypt! And on another subject. How's the electronic currency system working in the States?"

"Doesn't seem to be any hiccups so far," Sticks replied. "It's a pain sometimes," he admitted, "but it seems to be going pretty smoothly. However, things are going to get ugly soon, I'm sure. Every day, we warn all who will listen that soon, the Antichrist is going to introduce the infamous 'Mark of the Beast.' When that happens, those without the mark will somehow be barred from the electronic system, I'm sure."

"I agree," Uri said. "Any day now, we're expecting the fulfillment of Revelation 13."

"From what I understand, you've been able to purchase and stockpile nonperishable supplies with the gifts we sent you, right?"

"Yeah. Glad we did this before the new system came online. We're not touching the supplies, though, until we have no choice."

"One last question. How's the health of the church in Israel? Is it growing? Are the believers afraid or encouraged?"

Uri thought about the questions for a second before responding. "All the pastors I know are reporting conversions almost daily, but the church in Israel is tiny. So I'd say it's growing at an unprecedented pace, but the overall number of believers is small. As in the States, the endless string of catastrophes have had a polarizing effect on the people. Some are becoming much more antagonistic toward Christianity, and others are becoming more curious and open. Tragically, a small number who once called themselves believers have become so fearful they no longer fellowship with us. We're doing all we can to encourage their return to the faith," Uri reported. "But overall, I'd definitely say the church is growing more healthy every day."

"Well, that's good to hear. Omega-ism has drawn away most of the people who used to attend for show, leaving churches full of committed believers who are on fire for Jesus, plus a growing number of seekers who are seriously considering the claims of Christ. So I agree—the church is growing more healthy every day."

Unaware that he was launching into preacher-teacher mode, Sticks leaned back and launched into another topic that was weighing heavily on his mind. "Have you heard that tomorrow, Omega-ism devotees will be celebrating Mother Earth Day around the world? Supreme Priestess Gupta has prerecorded a message for her followers, requesting that each family bring a piece of fresh fruit or vegetable to what they call their 'halls of peace.' They plan to offer the food as a bloodless sacrifice to the goddess Mother Earth, asking for forgiveness and demonstrating their sorrow for the present state of the global environment.

"They should pay attention to Jeremiah, who asked, 'How long will the land lie parched and the grass in every field be withered?' He answered his own question when he said, 'Because those who live in it are wicked, the animals and birds have perished.'

"Despite the massive problems facing humanity, the Supreme Priestess is continuing to press for legislation that gives 'Mother Nature' the same rights status as humans! Following the UN-sponsored global summit on sustainable development in Rio de Janeiro, radical green groups have been advocating that Mother Nature has the right to be completely restored. In fact, these groups are pushing for mandates that require governments to ban the 'introduction of organisms and organic and inorganic material that can alter in a definite way the national genetic heritage.' Priestess Gupta is now one of their strongest allies! And this, when hundreds of millions of earth's inhabitants are dying of starvation and HIVE! Hard to believe, isn't it?"

Sticks wrapped up the call with an encouraging prediction. "Things will get worse before they get glorious!" And then he rushed to his Sunday evening service where he was to teach on the events associated with the fifth seal.

*   *   *

Before jumping into his message for the evening, Sticks spent an hour checking on the spiritual and physical health of his large audience. "Has anyone gone the day without a meal?" About forty hands were raised. They were directed to a team that had arranged a simple but nutritious meal. The number of meals prepared each day varied, depending on supply. Sticks never ceased to marvel how closely the number of meals matched the number of people who raised their hands.

"Does anyone need a jacket, a pair of shoes, or a pair of glasses?" Again, the responders were directed to a team that would outfit them with the particular items they needed. This dialogue continued until Sticks was satisfied that the basic needs of his audience were satisfied as best they could be.

It was obvious that most were suffering financially as a result of the nation's deep economic depression. However, it was also clear his audience was following in the footsteps of the early church. Many were selling or trading their possessions, giving to anyone who had need. Remarkably, the church was radiating joy. Sticks had never seen such unity among believers, and the expressions of hope and love on the faces of his audience were contagious. The feelings of anticipation were overwhelming, like those experienced by a small child eagerly awaiting Christmas morning. Despite their deplorable conditions, none would trade their circumstances for any amount of money or possessions because they knew how the story ends.

In the pulpit, Sticks found that tears came to his eyes as he looked out over the people he had come to love and respect so deeply. Theirs was a real faith, and it challenged him nearly as much as his sermons challenged and encouraged them. He cleared his throat and blinked back the tears.

"We've experienced what the first three seals have wrought—the rise of the Antichrist and war and famine on a scale that was unimaginable a decade ago. The world is reeling from the effects of the fourth seal—more war and famine, and of course, the plague called HIVE. All creation is crying out for deliverance. If we could hear the cries of nature, we would hear the rocks and trees pleading for the curse to be reversed. That day is coming, and coming soon, I believe."

Sticks's words stirred up memories in almost every person within the sound of his voice. Some fought the urge to cry as they fondly remembered loved ones who had died, or were dying, of HIVE. Others smiled slightly, remembering their prosperous lifestyles of a mere decade ago. Now their livelihoods were lost, their savings were exhausted, and their bellies were often empty. They knew Sticks was going to tell them things were about to get worse, if that were possible. And yet each one was certain his future was secure—what a paradox! They were reminded of two of Sticks's favorite equations: "Everything – God = Nothing" and "Nothing + God = Everything."

"But before deliverance comes, John warns of unprecedented persecution in chapter 6 of the Revelation. Remember, the book opens with the claim that it's the 'revelation of Jesus Christ, which God gave him.' Jesus offers us the assurance of ultimate victory through him. He promises us access to him in these trying times and lauds us for our patient endurance. In the coming weeks and months, let's be diligent to carry out the tasks God has called us to do, the foremost of which is evangelism. And remember, our future is held firmly in his loving hands!

"Very soon, the Antichrist will commit sacrilege in the temple. His despicable act will reveal to the Jews, particularly the Orthodox Jews, that he is an imposter. Overnight, they'll become bitter enemies of this counterfeit Messiah, resisting his every move.

"The Antichrist will savagely retaliate, unleashing his pent-up fury against Jews and Christian believers alike. For the Jewish people, it will be the worst expression of anti-Semitic behavior they've ever experienced, surpassing the Holocaust in terms of its brutality and great loss of life. Believers will also be objects of Romiti's wrath, resulting in martyrdom for great multitudes who are followers of Christ. Jesus called this a time of great tribulation or distress, and so theologians have embraced this term, naming this horrific period 'the Great Tribulation.'"

Heads nodded at the familiar term, one that most understood intellectually, but never expected to experience first-hand.

"For many years, many of you have believed that you would escape the Great Tribulation. There was a time I believed that myself. But as you know, my beliefs on this period of history have changed. Let me again encourage you with the words of Jesus himself, who said, 'But he who stands firm to the end will be saved.' Jesus is not speaking here of our salvation, for that's already been eternally secured. He's encouraging us to stand fast in the faith during times of intense persecution, just as millions have done in the generations before us, and we will be saved, delivered— not from tribulation, but out of it.

"If God did not interfere in the Antichrist's murderous rampage, no Christian would remain alive. But at some point, God will say, 'Enough!' In the Olivet Discourse, Jesus says that 'If those days had not been cut short, no one would survive.' Obviously the seven years will not be shortened, so he must be referring to a period within Daniel's seventieth week. God will 'cut short,' or amputate, these days, speaking of the Great Tribulation, I believe, by removing the church by means of the rapture, which in turn will initiate the day of the Lord, a time of God's wrath.

"I don't know what day or hour the rapture will occur. Scripture teaches that no one knows, not even Jesus himself. Concerning the rapture, I believe Matthew was saying that just as judgment fell the day Noah escaped, so God's wrath will suddenly fall upon the earth the day the church is raptured. Speaking of the rapture, Luke, the physician who wrote the gospel named after him, likewise gave the example of Noah and then added that God's judgment of fire rained down on Sodom the very day Lot left the wicked city.

"Concerning times and dates, Paul reminded the church in Thessalonica that there was no need for him to write on this topic. They knew very well that the day of the Lord would come as a 'thief in the night' to those who were in darkness. Then Paul reminded his readers that they did not belong to the darkness but were 'sons of the light and sons of the day.' Paul was saying that while no one knows the date or time of the rapture, the sons of the light and sons of the day will not be surprised by the sudden day of judgment. We know it's coming, and it's coming very soon. However, like Noah and Lot, we'll be rescued, this time by rapture, and then judgment will suddenly fall, as a thief in the night, on an unsuspecting world.

"During the short period of time that follows the rapture, Antichrist will continue his vicious persecution of the Jewish people. But God will supernaturally protect a remnant that will survive the Antichrist's murderous campaign, and at some point before Christ's second coming, the Jewish remnant will accept Jesus as their Messiah."

The solemn crowd listened intently to the sermon, quiet, but thankful their pastor had thoroughly prepared them for what was still ahead.

Sticks asked young Greg Reynolds to close the meeting in prayer. Greg's prayer was short and to the point. "God, we're grateful that we do not belong to the darkness, but we're sons and daughters of the light. Please give us the strength and courage to serve you during these terrible times, and help us be examples to a world that's lost without you."

Once again, Sticks sensed the lack of passion in Greg's prayer. The words were appropriate, but his delivery was distant, detached.

He made his way to Greg and Jeni. "What's up?" he asked good-naturedly. Both flashed smiles, but their eyes told a very different story. "You both seem preoccupied—a little sad this evening."

"We've been talking about getting married, but we're wondering if it makes any sense, given the times. Yeah, I guess you're right. We're a little distracted right now."

Sticks felt a little better, knowing how he'd feel if he was in Greg's shoes—*A beautiful fiancée, but in a world that's teetering on the brink of destruction. Maybe that's all I've been sensing all along.*

*   *   *

Outside the temple, next to the altar of sacrifice, the two witnesses were engaged in a lively and sometimes heated discussion on the priesthood with a couple dozen rabbis. A few were sitting on the steps leading to the altar, but most were too agitated to sit.

"Yeshua has become the guarantor of a better covenant because he lives forever. And because he lives forever, his priesthood is permanent. You're Israel's priests and rabbis, but someday you will die, bringing to an end your priesthood. But Yeshua's priesthood is permanent, so he is able to save completely those who come to God through him because he always lives to intercede on their behalf. As our high priest, Yeshua meets our needs—he's holy, blameless, pure, set apart from sinners and exalted above the heavens. He was the sinless sacrifice whose death atoned for our sins."

Pointing to the altar of sacrifice, the one nicknamed Eli'ahu continued. "Time and again, you offer sacrifices for your own sins and then the sins of the people. But from the days of Moses, the sacrifice was meant to be a shadow, a symbol, pointing to the real thing. Yeshua sacrificed for our sins once for all when he offered himself."

Several in their audience were listening intently, including Aaron Judeh, the young rabbi who had been raised to life by the witnesses after his death on the Temple Mount. As usual, most were upset and angry at what they were hearing and were trying to convince the witnesses that Yeshua was an imposter whose followers were misguided heretics.

For the dozenth time since their initial appearance in Jerusalem, the witnesses were interrupted by a small GSF military unit whose leader recited the standing order to stop preaching about Yeshua.

Moshe gazed intently at the young leader, saddened by the man's arrogance and hardness of heart. "Young man, we must obey God. We're simply following orders, as you're following yours. Please listen to what we're saying, and you too may be saved from the judgment to come."

Members of the GSF unit laughed, mocking the two men by falling to their knees and asking "What must we do to be saved?"

The unit leader commanded the priests and rabbis to walk away, to stand alongside another GSF unit that was keeping curious bystanders about thirty yards away from the confrontation. Then he ordered his men to ready their weapons.

He returned his attention to the two witnesses. "Upon the authority of the commander of the Global Security Force and the secretary-general of the United Nations, I have been commanded to arrest you and remove you from this site. If you resist, I've been given orders to execute you where you stand. Your vile speeches against the secretary-general and continual provocation of the Jews on the Temple Mount will come to an end today. You have five minutes to make your decision. Consider carefully how you will answer me."

"Sir," Moshe politely but firmly replied, "there is no need for more time to consider your request. Should we obey you rather than God? We'll not stop speaking about our God. But as for you, consider your own life and the lives of your men. Place your trust in Yeshua. Ask him to forgive you of your sins and accept him as your Savior."

The leader and his men ignored the pleas, waiting for the five minutes allotted the stubborn fools to expire, and then asked, "What's your decision?"

"We've given our answer," the witnesses responded in unison. "We must obey God rather than man."

The leader turned to his unit and barked a simple order: "Proceed!"

As the members of the team prepared to carry out their orders, Eli'ahu looked toward heaven and said, "Father, these men have hardened their hearts toward you. They've chosen to follow the Evil One, the prince of this world, rather than you. Demonstrate your power before these many witnesses by sending fire upon the men who call you their enemy even while benefiting from your mercy and grace."

For a brief second or two, bystanders watched in amazement as a fireball descended from the sky. At first it resembled a fiery missile streaking in their direction, a trail of dark smoke spiraling in its wake. Some tried to run for shelter but most stood still, paralyzed by fear. The ball of fire struck the would-be executioners, consuming the men and their weapons. People standing thirty yards from the impact felt the searing, rushing wind that was generated by the fireball's deadly collision with its target, and heard the crackling sounds of matter as it was incinerated. People ran from the courtyard, shouting for others to run for safety. The men and women of the second GSF unit stood in place, unsure of their response. The priests and rabbis were terrified and confused, not yet comprehending that they too had rejected the words of the two witnesses but had been spared the same swift judgment.

Then Eli'ahu spoke to the large crowd of people who had gathered around them. In a voice full of emotion, he cried out, "How long will you reject Yeshua, God's only Son? Salvation is found in no one else, for there is no other name under heaven given to men by which we must be saved!"

Moshe shook his gray head in righteous anger and shouted in a voice that carried across the courtyard, "Beginning at dawn tomorrow, for three days the earth's inhabitants will suffer a painful plague of boils. As you seek relief from the pain, be reminded that neither would the ancient Egyptian Pharaoh obey Moses and Aaron, the ones God chose to speak on his behalf. Their rejection of God's message invited the plague which you will likewise suffer!"

*   *   *

"Oww! What is this?" Jacob roared only seconds after awakening from a restless sleep. He was tenderly scratching his chest and legs while howling in pain. "Boils!"

"I don't know the cause, but I've got 'em, too," Rivka responded. "Oh, they hurt!"

"Ezra! Ezra!"

Startled by the shouts, Ezra leapt out of bed and then began to shriek. The bottoms of his feet were covered in sores, now ruptured and oozing fluid. Ezra fell back to his bed, shaking his head in disbelief as he recalled hearing that one of the witnesses had called for a plague of boils to inflict the earth's inhabitants.

"What manner of men are they?" he asked himself.

Jacob placed a call to the hospital, but the lines were busy. He yelled at his Smart TV, commanding, "On-CNN-boils!" The television obeyed his shouts, bringing up the most current CNN footage on the sudden outbreak. Populations in every nation on earth seemed to be complaining of the painful sores.

A spokeswoman for the Global Health Organization was being interviewed by an obviously distressed reporter.

"Have you determined the source of the boils?" the reporter questioned as she shuffled from one foot to the next, trying to ease the pain.

"Yes, we've concluded the painful outbreak has been caused by contaminants in the world's food supply," the GHO spokesperson answered.

"I've never heard of a disease that has simultaneously affected the entire planet, causing entire populations to wake up with the same symptoms. How do you explain it?" The correspondent who was asking the questions was lying on her side, the only position she could find that didn't aggravate her boils.

"That's a good question," the GHO spokesperson stammered. "We do not have an answer right now. The world is experiencing unprecedented troubles, many of which are affecting our environment. Some biological scientists suggest that a mutation of some form has occurred as a result of the environmental catastrophes, affecting the food chain in some way."

"We've heard that 'born again' Christians and the very young are not affected. Any truth to these reports, and if so, any theories?" the interviewer asked.

"Yes!" the spokesperson snapped, fully aware that she was being baited by the reporter. "I've offered a theory that has been widely reported by the media. But the truth of the matter is, we believe there is a conspiracy among evangelical Christians and Jews—which includes the two witnesses, as you are so fond of calling them—to commit religious acts of terror. Terrorists—not food contaminants—are the cause of this painful outbreak. The boils were predicted yesterday, mind you, by the religious zealots in Jerusalem. How could anyone possibly know this was going to happen unless they were the source of the plague?"

The major news outlets picked up the story, and within hours, earth's inhabitants were enraged at what they believed was more evidence of the two witnesses' spiteful behavior.

* * *

Romiti had completed nearly three years of his five-year term as the UN secretary-general. The years had been dreadful, and no one could predict when the calamities would end. War, famines, and disease continued to take their toll on humanity. Many more than a billion people had died. The bodies of the dead and dying were everywhere. Large tracts of land were set aside for mass graves, each containing thousands of unclaimed bodies. Most of the dead were unceremoniously dumped into large pits carved into the earth, later marked by small monuments that identified the locations as mass graves.

Starving animals, wild and domesticated, roamed many small towns and villages, crazed by their lack of food and no longer afraid of humans. The fearless animals attacked one another and then humans to quell their hunger. Whenever people found it necessary to leave the security of their dwellings, they were forced to carry guns, clubs, rocks—anything that could be used to ward off the starving creatures.

Romiti was relentless in his pursuit of solutions that would diminish the carnage wrought by the continuous string of man-made and natural disasters. The performance of the Satan-energized dictator was extraordinary, but he knew his efforts would fail until his programs to rid the earth of the God-fearers—Jews and Christians who stubbornly refused to forsake their God—were fully implemented.

CHAPTER TWENTY-SEVEN

Babylon, Iraq

The secretary-general was pleased to hear from his powerful ally James Gladden, the US president. "I understand that Aswad al-Nawawy is looking to increase food imports into the African Regional Zone. Did he convince you to help?" Romiti asked.

There was little congeniality in the president's voice. "Our meetings prompted my call, Mr. Secretary. You delivered 'Abd al-Mumit to me, ensuring my two-term presidency. I'm returning the favor. Al-Nawawy's visit was a pretense for war. He's the spokesman for a trio of regional zone presidents who want to overthrow you. They're convinced you oppose Islam. He asked me to join their conspiracy and even mentioned the possibility of an assassination attempt."

Romiti immediately recalled his confrontation with the three regional zone presidents in his Babylonian office. Suppressing his rising anger, Romiti interrupted the president by asking a pointed question. "Are the other conspirators the regional zone presidents of Mesopotamia and the Middle East?"

"Well, yes, they are. It seems you're already aware of the plot. You must know they intend to coordinate simultaneous strikes on key GSF bases in each of the three regions."

"I was only guessing; this is the first I've heard of their plans. Have you any proof of what you're saying?"

"Conversations—I secretly recorded them as evidence of their plans. I'll e-mail them to you when we get off the phone. The North American Regional Zone will not participate in this rebellion, Mr. Secretary. You have my word."

Appreciative of the warning but angered by the news, the secretary-general ended his conversation with the president and called Commander

Dixon. "I've learned that a small group of treasonous regional zone leaders are plotting to attack GSF targets within weeks. I want you here. Now!"

"Who's your source?" the commander asked.

"Doesn't matter," the secretary-general snapped. "Meet me at the airport in Babylon tomorrow morning. Bring your top lieutenants. Absolute secrecy is a must! You know where I'll be!"

But the co-conspirators had not revealed the full extent of their plans to the president. They had already found an assassin who was willing, actually anxious, to kill the secretary-general. The price was steep but well worth the cost of a successful hit. If the hired gun was captured, a very likely scenario, GSF officers sympathetic to the three rebels would quickly kill the assassin, eliminating any possibility of a link to the co-conspirators' role in the murder.

*　*　*

The Catholic priest in the long black cassock strode briskly through the Babylonian International Airport, ignored by most of the citizens of this once predominantly Muslim city. Since it became home to the United Nations, it was not uncommon for the locals in Babylon to see visiting pilgrims in a variety of religious garb, no longer the object of long stares and careful scrutiny.

After checking into a four-star hotel on the banks of the Euphrates River, the priest relaxed by watching reruns of a couple of John Wayne westerns. Life was simpler back then. There were good guys and bad guys, and the good guys always won.

He was the good guy. And soon he would win.

After watching *Rio Bravo* and *Hondo,* he flicked off the television and began to focus on the purpose of his visit to the Middle East. He wanted to see the secretary-general. Their meeting would be personal. Very personal. He smiled in anticipation of their next encounter.

*　*　*

Jacob often recalled his conversation with Uri about the coming Messiah.

Uri had said the two witnesses would someday be killed and raised to life, their resurrection to be a sign for the nation of Israel. What did Uri mean? Ehud's death had shaken Jacob—how could he know he would see his son again? Could the two witnesses provide answers to these questions and others that were tormenting his soul?

Despite his loathing, Jacob purposefully approached the two witnesses, fearful but determined to learn their purpose for being in Israel. He wanted to know if they were aware of the talk concerning their deaths and resurrection. But before he could open his mouth, the one called Eli'ahu began to speak to him.

"In his great mercy, Yeshua has given us new birth into a living hope through his resurrection from the dead. Concerning this salvation, the prophets, who spoke of the grace that was to come to you, searched intently and with the greatest care, trying to find out the time and circumstances to which the Spirit of Yeshua in them was pointing when he predicted the sufferings of Messiah and the glories that would follow . . ."

Jacob marveled at the timing of the men's words. And their message touched the very depths of his soul. *What prompted them to speak of resurrection? Do they know I'm grieving for my son?*

"I confess I'm a man without hope," Jacob quietly admitted. "What do you mean by a 'new birth into a living hope'?"

Moshe explained, revealing the meaning of "new birth" by telling the story of Nicodemus. "Nicodemus was a first-century Pharisee, a member of the Sanhedrin. He came to Yeshua secretly, at night. Nicodemus admitted that Yeshua was a teacher who came from God, saying, 'No one could perform the miraculous signs you are doing if God were not with him.' Yeshua didn't directly respond to the confession, but said, 'Unless a man is born again, he cannot see the kingdom of God.'"

"Why did Yeshua speak in riddles?" Jacob asked.

Moshe smiled. "Nicodemus, like you, was perplexed by Yeshua's statement. Maybe he accused Yeshua of speaking in riddles too. 'How can a man be born when he is old?' Yeshua explained that he was speaking of a spiritual—not a physical—birth. Yeshua said that unless a person experiences a spiritual rebirth, he or she will be unable to enter the kingdom of God."

Jacob did not offer any comment on Moshe's explanation of spiritual rebirth. "It's strange that you should speak of a 'living hope.' How does the supposed resurrection of Yeshua give us a living hope?" Jacob continued, "My wife and I just lost our son. We believe he will be resurrected in the Olam Ha-Ba, the world to come. But how can we be sure we'll embrace him again? We're beginning to have doubts about some things we've always taken for granted. The Talmud says all Israel has a share in the Olam Ha-Ba. But how can we be sure?"

It was Eli'ahu's turn to answer Jacob's questions as he humbly and carefully responded not only to Jacob's inquiry, but to the unspoken issues that were troubling the heart of this devoted God-seeker. They debated the exclusiveness of Yeshua's claim that "No one comes to the Father except through me." Eli'ahu explained what Yeshua meant when he said, "Whoever believes in him shall not perish but have eternal life." And they thrashed out Yeshua's declaration that "If you believed Moses, you would believe me, for he wrote about me."

By this time, a group of hecklers had surrounded the three men, doing their best to break up the serious discussion. But Jacob would not be deterred.

"I would like to ask one more question. What evidence can you offer that proves the ancient Hebrew prophets were 'trying to find out the time and circumstances to which the Spirit was pointing, when he predicted the sufferings of the Messiah?'"

Despite the harassing taunts of the mob, the witnesses carefully took Jacob through the Torah, marveling at his knowledge of the sacred Scriptures.

Inside, Jacob was trembling as the witnesses opened the Scriptures to him. *Why haven't I seen this before?* he kept repeating silently to himself.

Soon, the throng was shouting so many threats and making such a loud clamor that the men agreed it was best to part company. Jacob thanked the witnesses for spending time with him and began to thread his way through the crowd of scoffers.

"Jacob, God has a unique plan for your brother," Moshe called out. "Soon, Ezra will be known throughout Israel as a mighty man of God."

Jacob was startled by the familiar phrase, and his heart leaped for joy. "Do you know my brother?" he asked.

"We have only spoken to him once, Jacob, and he never mentioned your name," Moshe answered.

"Then how do you know Ezra is my brother?"

"The same Spirit of Christ that was in the prophets is also in us, Jacob. It's by this Spirit that we know you, Rivka, and your brother." Jacob's skin tingled at the mention of his wife's name. How could they know of her too?

Then, turning toward their tormentors, Moshe spoke a few words.

"Pharaoh's heart was hardened, and he would not listen to Moses, the prophet you revere. In response to Pharaoh, Moses stretched out his hand, and total darkness covered Egypt for three days. Like the Egyptians before you, you have also hardened your hearts toward God! How will you escape the judgment to come?"

Moshe raised his hand toward the sky and cried, "For three days, let darkness cover the earth—a darkness that can be felt!"

In a matter of seconds, the sun no longer cast its light. Someone nearby cried out in terror. The darkness was suffocating, almost palpable. Jacob began to tremble as he was enveloped by the thick cloud. A passage from Job came to mind. "There are those who rebel against the light, who do not know its ways or stay in its path." Right now, it would be foolish to reject a flashlight should one be offered to him. How much more foolish would it be to reject the Light that was so clearly presented in the ancient Scriptures?

* * *

The darkness was extraordinary, overpowering the light.

The traffic jams were horrendous as people anxiously headed for their dwellings. Streetlamps barely illuminated the sidewalks over which they stood watch. Headlights could scarcely penetrate the darkness, preventing vehicles from traveling more than ten to fifteen miles per hour. In most homes, even with every lamp turned on, the effect was comparable to the pale light cast by a full moon.

"What's happening to the world, Jacob? I'm so afraid," Rivka was sobbing. She sat with her husband and Ezra in the dark shadows of their living room. After a minute or two, Jacob broke the silence.

"I met with the two witnesses today. I heard them call for darkness to cover the earth."

"Are you serious?" Rivka asked incredulously. "They're the main source of the world's problems, aren't they? How about the darkness? They've been given supernatural powers, by whom no one knows, and they're using their power, voodoo if you ask me, to harm mankind and the environment. Maybe they're in league with Romiti—a conspiracy of some kind, who knows? What were you thinking!"

"What do you mean, 'maybe they're in league with Romiti'? Why are you suddenly down on Romiti?"

"I've just heard some small talk about him, that's all. He's made some pretty wicked remarks about Jews, Jacob. I just don't like the man!"

"Anyway, you asked me what I was thinking when I visited the two witnesses. I really don't know, Rivka. I've never been so confused. Their words are contrary to so many things I've been taught, and yet some of it matches the Tanach so well. And what other man has caused fire to consume his enemies? Remember the plague of flies? The boils? And now this perverse darkness. They're like the prophets of old. They say the purpose of these awful plagues is to catch our attention, to cause us to consider more carefully the one we've rejected, the one they claim to be Messiah. What do you think, Ezra?"

Ezra's shoulders slumped, and a wearied look crossed his face. He appeared to have aged a decade in the last several months. "I'm confused as well, Jacob. And I must confess. I too have spoken to the two witnesses."

"What! Why haven't you and Jacob told me this before now?" Rivka demanded. "What else are you two hiding from me?"

Jacob shook his weary head. "I didn't know Ezra had spoken to them, Rivka. And I didn't tell you because I'm struggling with my conscience. My entire life I've tried to please God, blessed be His Name, and I don't want to disappoint him now."

"I feel the same way you do, Jacob. I've sought counsel with other rabbis and teachers. They tell me these men are empowered by Satan, insisting I stay away from them."

"And yet they speak highly of you, Ezra. They told me you will someday be a mighty man of God. They spoke the very words I've used to describe you."

Ezra seemed troubled, so much so that he hardly noticed the compliment. "The witnesses have revealed things about me that only I would know, and yet I cannot believe them. I cannot forsake the traditions of our fathers or violate the memory of our parents. I will not be called an apostate; I cannot blaspheme the God, blessed be His Name, of Abraham, Isaac, and Jacob."

"But what if they're speaking the truth?" Jacob interjected. "These men teach that most of Yeshua's disciples willingly laid down their lives for their rabbi. The disciples were eyewitnesses to the events chronicled in the Br'it Chadashah. Surely they would not have been willing to die for a lie when they were told their lives would be spared if they recanted their testimony!"

"Perhaps, but we know of suicide bombers who die for their beliefs too, Jacob. Many people willingly die for their cause."

"Yes, Ezra, but it's one thing to forfeit your life for something you *believe* to be true. It's an entirely different matter to willingly forfeit your life for something you *know* to be false," Rivka countered.

Jacob smiled at his wife's insight. "You always amaze me, Rivka. You're blessed with great wisdom."

Jacob looked up, letting his eyes focus on the shadows. "I heard the one called Moshe say the darkness will last for three days. Perhaps they're right. Perhaps we'll enjoy another sunrise. I noted the time darkness fell, and I intend to see what time it lifts. Let's again test the words of these 'prophets.' I cannot reject their teaching, nor am I ready to accept it. I need more time to consider their message."

Each retreated to the solitude of his or her mind, reflecting on the powers of darkness and light.

* * *

The heavy darkness did not diminish the size of the crowds that flocked to hear Sticks's teaching. In fact, this particular judgment was staggering the imaginations of most believers for one reason—it wasn't dark to them.

A young blonde woman was part of a small group that was making its way to an outdoor amphitheater in the park. They had paused to share their stories. "I took my young daughter to school and noticed there were only a few cars in the parking lot. I was puzzled, thinking I might have forgotten a school holiday. As we stood in front of the campus, a woman and her little boy approached us. She asked if I knew what was going on. 'Why is it so dark?' she asked. I had no idea what she was talking about. Her son kept giggling, telling me his mother was playing a game. 'Mommy keeps saying it's night,' he said. 'She thinks she can fool me.'"

The group entered the amphitheater and sat down, waiting expectantly for Sticks to begin. Minutes later, he began without any introduction. "Yes, we're living in difficult times, but what exciting times too! Our God is a powerful, sovereign God, one who speaks his will into existence! His power staggers the imagination, doesn't it?" He flipped his notes but hardly seemed to look at them. "Tonight's topics are the sixth seal, the sealing of the 144,000, and the rapture of the church."

Once again, Sticks had spent the last hour interacting with his congregation, connecting the most needy and hurting with those who could help. While it was sad to see so many in need, it was gratifying and encouraging to witness the unity of the church. It fueled his desire to preach as nothing had ever done before.

"The sixth seal can best be described as cosmic disturbance. The world is experiencing a supernatural darkness right now, but this is a momentary, fleeting darkness that appeared at the command of the two witnesses in Jerusalem. It's not connected with the sixth seal that we'll discuss in a moment."

He grew solemn. "First we must face the fifth seal, and brothers and sisters, this will not be easy for us. The fifth seal represents a soon-to-come time of intense persecution in which most that oppose the Antichrist will be murdered. Remember, the Antichrist's murderous spree begins shortly after he desecrates the temple. We've labeled this period the Great Tribulation. With the sixth seal, God will 'cut short' the Great Tribulation by an incredible display in the cosmos."

Sticks paused a moment, looking out over his congregation as a caring shepherd. "This is not unprecedented in history. God often uses objects in his creation to demonstrate his sovereignty and majesty. For example, at Jesus's birth, magi from the east followed a star that led them to Bethlehem. At the moment of Jesus's death, the earth shook, the rocks split, and many dead were raised to life. When the Hebrews left Egypt, they followed a pillar of cloud by day and a pillar of fire by night. When the sixth seal is opened, the earth will convulse and men and women will cry out in terror, begging to die rather than face the wrath of the Lamb. I believe it's at this moment that the church will be snatched away to be forever with the Lord!"

A smartly dressed middle-aged woman did not approve of what she was hearing. "Hasn't the world seen enough wrath? I came to hear about a God who loves everyone—I'm not interested in hearing about more wrath and terror! God knows we have enough of that already!" She stomped out of the meeting, muttering to herself and anyone who was listening.

Sticks kept silent rather than confronting the angry woman. A few moments later, he commented on the interruption. "I'll see if I can arrange a chat with our visitor, but let me make a quick observation before I go on.

God has been incredibly patient with his rebellious creation. Now it's time for justice—justice brings great joy to some and terror to others. Rather than becoming angry that justice is about to served, wouldn't it be better to make sure you're among those for whom justice will bring great joy?

"Revelation 7 serves as an interlude between the events of chapters 6 and 8. John is taking a big breath, as it were, before rushing on to the trumpet judgments.

"Following the sixth seal, John writes that an angel delays God's wrath from being poured out on the earth while 144,000 Hebrew men are sealed for the purpose of protection. Simply called the 144,000, they'll become God's witnesses on earth as the believers are caught up to heaven. Just imagine that a baton is being passed from the believers we know now to a group called the 144,000. And then, and we're still in chapter 7, John describes a great multitude he sees in heaven that has come out of the Great Tribulation.

"Imagine the scene! John describes this great multitude, so many he's unable to give a figure, from every nation, tribe, people, and language, all wearing white robes and holding palm branches in their hands. Why palm branches? Palm branches were waved to welcome Jesus in his triumphal entry into Jerusalem. It was the method used by townspeople to welcome their king. Palm branches were also used to build the booths used to celebrate the Feast of Tabernacles.

"Do you remember what event this feast anticipates? The coming millennial kingdom. And John hears the songs of the multitude. I believe the great multitude in heaven is singing and waving palm branches in anticipation of the Lord's thousand-year kingly reign on earth! We're gone, folks!"

The smile never left Sticks's face as he described the rapture and the millennial kingdom to follow. But his expression changed as he wrapped up his message. The smile was gone. His somber countenance revealed his sadness at the thought of those who would be left behind.

"And then comes chapter 8! The trumpet judgments begin. We've moved from the seven seals, denoting the worst of what humanity can do against humanity, to the seven trumpet and bowl judgments, which depict the outpouring of God's wrath on an unrepentant world."

Chapter Twenty-Eight

Babylonian International Airport, Iraq

In the initial military planning meeting conducted in a secret bunker of the Babylonian International Airport, Richard Dixon's biggest concern was the size of the rebellion. He was concerned that it might involve all ten regional zones and was relieved to learn this was not the case—at least not yet.

"No, it does not involve all ten zones," Romiti disclosed. "The president of the North American Regional Zone informed me of the plot and said only three zones are involved. Other than the three of them, he's the only other regional president to be informed of the plot. How strong and how prepared is the GSF to conduct war on multiple fronts?"

"The GSF is very strong. Our weapons and multinational forces are far superior to those of any potential adversary, particularly if we're talking about a single nation. The obvious exception is China; our technology is as good or better than theirs, but they have an overwhelming advantage in terms of sheer population size. Is there a chance the Chinese might get sucked into this? They are more powerful than all the armed forces of the North American Regional Zone nations combined."

"I agree, Dixon. I've spent several of the last twenty-four hours in conversations with the Chinese president. While I don't trust him, I don't believe he's even aware of the conspiracy. My guess is that he'll remain on the sidelines unless he senses there's an opportunity for China. For example, if he believes the GSF will be defeated and China could fill the resulting power vacuum, he might turn on us. But he's a true politician, not willing to take a position until he knows the outcome. Obviously, this works in our favor right now. Max, what's coming out of the Center of Intelligence and Security? Where are our blind spots?" Romiti queried.

Max gave a quick summary of the nations in which the most virulent resistance had been documented. "As we already know, there's strong opposition to our policies by Iraq, Syria, and Egypt, mostly caused by the perceived threat to Islam, and perhaps surprisingly, by Israel. The Israeli prime minister was happy to sign the armistice, of course, but is chafing under the leadership of the Syrian who is president of the Middle Eastern Regional Zone."

"We'll leave Israel alone for now, Dixon, but Zagmi, increase your intelligence-gathering efforts in Syria," Romiti ordered. "Let's use this situation to make examples out of the nations that are rebelling against our authority. We cannot allow dissent, or everything we've achieved will be lost."

Dixon briefly outlined a possible strategy, proposing to launch preemptive strikes against the nations in the regional zones that were led by the three ringleaders of the rebellion. His strategy was to cripple their offensive capabilities as quickly as possible.

"What about this cursed darkness—it's worldwide. Are we prepared to launch combat operations under these conditions?" asked one of the commanders.

"We have some recent intel on this," Dixon admitted. "It's supposed to last three days."

"And who disclosed this information?" another commander asked with a smirk. "One of the two crazies in Jerusalem?"

Laughter shook the room as the men and women expressed their amusement at the commander's questions.

Dixon wasn't smiling. "Yes, one of my men overheard one of them make this prediction."

Before the GSF commanders sat down to argue and refine Dixon's strategy, Romiti distributed ops guides labeled *Operation Erichthonius.*

"My ideas are somewhat similar to Dixon's, but take a look."

The commanders, led by Dixon, quickly scanned the document, more out of courtesy to the secretary-general than any belief that his military plans could be of real value. However, the men were startled by the stunning simplicity of the proposed operation. They looked at Dixon, who simply shrugged his shoulders, directing them to move on to the tactics section of Operation Erichthonius.

"You realize, Mr. Secretary, that this technology has never been used in battle?" Dixon asked.

"Until 1945, the atomic bomb had never been used either, Commander. Let's see what happens!"

No one thought to ask the secretary-general why he had named the operation in honor of Erichthonius, the mythical king of Athens who was part-man and part-serpent, raised by Athena, the goddess of war.

* * *

For the first time in three days, light appeared in Jerusalem, exactly seventy-two hours after it had vanished. The peoples of the Middle East were the first to feel the warmth of the sun. They ran outdoors to celebrate, momentarily abandoning their responsibilities.

* * *

I can't believe it! The witnesses called for three days of darkness, and darkness covered the earth for precisely seventy-two hours! Ezra marveled as he considered Moshe's words.

* * *

At the moment light dawned on the Middle East, the Global Security Force launched its surprise attack on the military bases in Iraq and Syria, overwhelming them with a barrage of short-range ballistic missiles followed by a number of ASM missiles fired from GSF aircraft based in Iraq. Given the close proximity of Romiti's enemies to his Babylonian headquarters, the nuclear weapons option was never considered. Columns of rebel ground forces, already moving quickly into position from which to launch their attack on Babylon, were easy targets for the GSF fighter pilots. Within hours, the rebel armies were crushed, no longer a credible threat to the secretary-general.

Syria's infrastructure was moderately damaged by the opening salvo, and then its soldiers were defeated by a vicious UN ground force invasion. The Syrian military, still recovering from the civil war of 2012, was clearly surprised by the strength of the GSF and their ferocity in battle. Like their government leaders, the military had mistakenly come to believe the GSF was primarily a peacekeeping force that would run when it encountered professional, seasoned soldiers. Much to its dismay, the Syrian forces were overwhelmed by the stronger GSF, losing tens of thousands of men and women in the first two days of fighting.

The rebellious Syrian president, who also served as the president of the Middle Eastern RZ, along with his surviving military leaders, surrendered to UN forces outside the smoldering ruins of Damascus, the nation's capital. The general in command of the GSF forces in Syria accepted their surrender and then turned to his second-in-command.

"Execute them immediately. Record the executions and post the clip on the Internet. The world must see what happens to those who defy Romiti."

Egypt fell even more quickly than Syria had. The secretary-general had realized a conventional attack on Egypt would result in a prolonged ground war that would exhaust and discourage the GSF. Instead, Operation Erichthonius called for an electromagnetic pulse attack on Egypt. A small nuclear weapon was detonated high over the target nation, creating an electromagnetic field that radiated down toward the population centers. It caused widespread damage to Egypt's electrical infrastructure but was otherwise relatively harmless. The damage cascaded throughout electrical networks, affecting banking, health care, and transportation systems; food and water delivery systems; and most critically, cyberspace. In seconds, Egypt returned to the dark ages.

GSF assassination teams were embedded in the Egyptian and Iraqi capitals, quietly spirited into the cities during the seventy-two-hour blackout. When the regional zone presidents fled the protection of their offices for fear of their lives, their movements were carefully monitored by loyal GSF operatives. It did not take long for the teams to carry out their mission, and soon the assassinations of the two insurgent presidents were making headlines. Very quickly, Romiti had uprooted his enemies—the three treasonous RZ presidents would no longer pose a threat to his global empire.

GSF battalions continued their southern march through Egypt, easily defeating small pockets of resistance, and then advanced south into northern Africa.

In a communiqué to Romiti, Dixon reported that after several months of fighting, the countries of the Middle Eastern and African Regional Zones, except for Jordan and Israel, had surrendered to the GSF. Romiti was baffled by the inability of Dixon's forces to make significant progress in Jordan, but he decided to address this trouble spot at another time. He wanted the Holy Land, and he summoned Dixon to Babylon to review the ultimate objective.

After its defeat of Syria, the GSF moved south, invading Israel. Ariel Shalev was furious, but his attempts to reach the secretary-general at his UN headquarters were rudely rebuffed. Shalev was told that Romiti was engaged in a private meeting with Commander Dixon and could not be interrupted. In a rage, Shalev finally threatened to unleash his missiles on Babylon if the secretary did not accept his call at once. The threat caught Romiti by surprise, and he tapped the button that represented the prime minister's line.

"Yes, Ariel. What can I do for you?"

"I demand that you remove your forces from Israel. We have not provoked you, Mr. Secretary. Let me remind you that the GSF has been treated well in Israel. Your troops have not gone hungry, despite the famine. We have treated your wounded and have cared for members of the GSF who have contracted HIVE. Yet your forces are behaving like storm troopers!"

Romiti was unmoved. "The president of the Middle Eastern Regional Zone challenged my authority, Mr. Shalev. And now he's dead. Israel is a prominent member of this zone, and while it may not have directly rebelled against me, your nation is suffering the consequences. Let's move on. Since visiting Israel a little more than three years ago, I have thought often of staying in Jerusalem again. I want to tour the temple that was constructed largely because of my efforts. Please arrange my visit with the chief rabbis."

"As you wish," the prime minister sarcastically retorted. "When will you arrive in Jerusalem?"

"Soon enough!" the secretary-general promised.

*   *   *

Despite the strong GSF military presence in Israel, there was no end to the stream of sightseers and religious pilgrims who visited the temple. Various rabbis led the tours through selected areas of the sanctuary, explaining the significance of the religious artifacts and rooms contained within the temple itself.

First-time visitors to Israel were often surprised by the absence of technologically advanced checkpoint security screening systems so prevalent in other public venues around the world. While these readily available systems were designed to detect drugs, firearms, explosives, and other contraband, the Temple Mount system was outdated and unreliable. The security personnel who were screening visitors to the holy sites were far more concerned about appropriate attire, ensuring that the shoulders, arms, and legs of visitors remained modestly covered throughout their visit.

"You've joined this tour every day this week," Rabbi Aaron Judeh commented to the priest, who was uncomfortably attired in a heavy black cassock.

"Yes—today's my third visit. Just enjoyed a brief stay in Babylon, and now I'm wrapping up a month-long vacation in Jerusalem," the priest replied. "I've always been fascinated by the Jews' desire to rebuild their temple. I'm also comparing this temple to the one described in the book of Ezekiel. It's been an interesting study. I've been told it's not possible to sneak a peak at the Holy of Holies, but thought I'd ask again. Any chance to take a quick look, or is it really totally off-limits?"

"I'm sorry, but yes, it's totally off-limits. The chamber is accessed once a year, and only by the high priest. In fact, since its construction, the Holy of Holies has only been entered once—on the day the temple was dedicated."

"I read that the UN secretary-general will be given a VIP tour tomorrow," the priest said to Aaron. "I suppose there's no way to join that group, is there?"

"I'm afraid you know the answer to that question," Judeh laughed. "You'd have to show a personal invitation, signed by Romiti himself."

"Ah," the priest said. "Then this may be my last visit. I'd better review my notes—gotta make sure you've answered all my questions."

The tour continued for another hour and then, as the tourists rounded the corner of a narrow passageway, a short span hidden from cameras and security personnel, an older member of the tour clutched his chest and collapsed to the floor, moaning in pain. A sweaty man with a beet-red face, he looked like he weighed nearly three hundred pounds. A two-hour hike on the Temple Mount was more than his overworked heart could take.

Judeh quickly punched a code on his walkie-talkie. "Possible heart attack in the temple! Victim is a male, late sixties or early seventies. Need aid ASAP!" Gawkers were crowding in, and Judeh stepped in their way and waved his arms. "Move back! Move back!" the rabbi ordered. "Emergency services staff will be here in a few minutes."

While Judeh was attending to his hefty patient, the priest slipped away from the group, creeping unnoticed into a chamber that adjoined the passageway. He ducked into one of the side chambers adjacent to the Holy of Holies, and then, eyes closed, began his patient wait for nightfall.

In less than two minutes, first responders sprinted into the passageway. They quickly put the stricken tourist on high-flow, non-rebreather one-hundred-percent oxygen and made him as comfortable as possible.

"Can you tell me your name?" one of the CPR-trained workers asked.

"Robert Laughlin," came the weak reply from the moaning victim.

"When were you born?"

"December 9, 1960."

"Do you know where you are?"

Groaning and still clutching his chest, he faintly responded, "Yeah—at the Temple Mount."

They continued to render aid until a medical emergency team arrived a minute or two later. The lead medic quickly ran through another series of assessment questions while other team members put the tourist on a twelve-lead EKG and then began to check his vital signs.

"Showing normal sinus on the monitor at eighty. Skin signs are good."

"This pain you're having—can you give me a number from one to ten, ten being the most intense pain of your life?"

"About an eight," the old man whimpered.

"What does the pain feel like? Do you feel pressure? Is it a stabbing pain, or a crushing or burning pain?"

"It . . . it just hit me all at once. Feels—oh, it hurts—like my chest is being crushed. And there's a splintering pain in my left arm."

A medic started an IV while another placed a nitroglycerine tablet under the man's tongue. They gently lifted the man onto a gurney and began to wheel him from the temple. "Code three, rapid transport to a cardiac specialty center," the lead medic barked into his mic as they rapidly made their way to the waiting emergency transport vehicle.

After the brief interruption, the rabbi re-assembled the tourists, and then concluded the tour with a short slide presentation.

Out of concern for the tourist, the rabbi placed a call to the cardiac center. Rabbi Judeh learned that after administering a battery of tests, the attending physicians had pronounced the sightseer in better health than his appearance would indicate but urged him to lose half his weight. The medical team attributed the episode to the excitement brought on by the man's first temple visit.

The rabbi never learned that hours later, the tourist left the hospital in high spirits, duly impressed with his own acting skills and several thousand dollars richer for his Oscar-winning performance.

*   *   *

The next morning, the Temple Mount was buzzing with visitors who wanted to catch a glimpse of the secretary-general as he entered the temple. The anger of the Sephardi rabbi, Isaac Disraeli, roiling at the presence of the unwelcome visitors, was fueled by the carnival atmosphere that enveloped the temple. Vendors, previously prohibited from entering the grounds, were selling T-shirts, buttons, pictures of Romiti, and miniature temples. A temporary food court had been set up too, catering soft drinks, fanola, kebob, falafel, and chocolate babke cake.

To make matters worse, the chief rabbis, Rabbi Isaac Disraeli and Rabbi Jonas Heifetz, had learned that the secretary-general had given orders to forcibly remove the two witnesses from the temple grounds, a move that was certain to cause a commotion. The rabbis preferred that the witnesses leave of their own accord, as they feared that the confrontations would escalate in intensity and eventually lead to violence, defiling the sacred grounds.

A short time later, three GSF units approached the witnesses, apparently unaware of past events or the power that was at the preachers' disposal. "Let's go! Pack up and leave the Mount," one of the GSF soldiers commanded, "and don't return!"

One of the witnesses repeated the response they given so many times before. "We will not leave the Temple Mount until God gives the order. God has given us a message we're to speak to the people. We will remain where we are until he says our mission is finished."

"I see," an officer replied. "God has given you a message for the people. Well, God has given me a message too. Get outta here now, or we'll toss you over the eastern wall!" With that threat, two of the units began to advance.

Once again, the one nicknamed Eli'ahu looked toward heaven, saying, "God, these men have hardened their hearts toward you, choosing to follow the Evil One, the prince of this world. Once more, I ask that you demonstrate your power before these many witnesses. Allow darkness to blind their eyes, just as their evil hearts are blinded to your mercy."

Immediately, the men in the units were groping in darkness, no longer able to see. In a rage at the judgment that had befallen him, one of the sightless soldiers began to fire his weapon wildly, killing a dozen bystanders and several members of his unit. The leader of the third unit shot and killed the berserk soldier while screaming profanities at the two old men. "Shoot them!" he commanded his men. As guns were raised, another ball of fire fell from the sky, incinerating seven GSF soldiers before they could fire their weapons. A half-dozen reporters and at least fifty bystanders were also killed by the fireball.

Instead of falling on their faces in fearful repentance before the awesome display of judgment, the crowd began to gnash their teeth and curse the two witnesses, throwing bottles, scraps of food, and handfuls of dust on God's prophets. The two men stood their ground, silently praying that God would soften their tormentors' hardened hearts.

Standing a short distance away, the secretary-general observed the deaths with an impassive expression on his face. He cared little for the deaths of his men but was enraged by the fearless attitudes of the two witnesses. He ordered the fourth unit to disperse the survivors, and then, alone and contrary to protocol, approached the men who were clothed in sackcloth.

"You will leave this place by nightfall, or by Lucifer himself, I promise to kill you with my own hands," he spat.

The witnesses faced him as though they had expected the confrontation. And in fact, they had.

Moshe was the first to respond to his antagonist. "You have no regard for any god and have exalted yourself above them all. You have said unheard-of things against the God of gods. You will be successful until God's wrath is poured out upon you. And then you, the little horn, will be destroyed. All the kings of the nations lie in state, each in his own tomb. But you will be cast out of your tomb like a rejected branch; you will be covered with the slain. Like a corpse trampled underfoot, you will not join them in burial."

Frighteningly calm, Romiti displayed his anger only in his words and in the intensity of his gaze. "Haman. Antiochus Epiphanes. Herod. Hitler. They will be remembered as choirboys in comparison to me. Do you believe the wrath of your God frightens me? Soon, the Jews and your pitiful followers will experience my wrath, and then the world will worship me and exalt no other!"

In silent fury, Romiti returned to his quarters to prepare for his temple visit, anticipating, relishing the moment when on his orders, the lives of his antagonists would come to a violent end.

Moshe's reference to the little horn had evoked a memory—a curiosity from childhood that Romiti had nearly forgotten. The little horn, a talisman given to him by his mother, was supposed to produce magical effects. For years, it had sat on an entry table in his home in Trento, Italy. *So the meaning of the 'little horn' becomes clear! It must be a religious symbol that represents me—the one chosen to rule the world! The fortune-teller was right—the horn possesses special meaning for me.* He left instructions with his secretary to make arrangements for the talisman to be delivered to his office in Babylon, and then he left for the Temple Mount.

*   *   *

As Romiti and his entourage—including a highly acclaimed, passionately pro-Romiti journalist and his dutiful cameraman—gathered at the base of the Temple Mount in preparation for their tour, Rabbi Disraeli approached the secretary-general. "The deaths of innocent men and woman have marred this special day, Mr. Secretary. Can we schedule the tour for another day?"

Romiti stared at Disraeli with utter disdain. "These deaths mean nothing to me," he said. "Do you understand? Let the world be reminded of my benevolence to the people of Israel. The tour will take place as planned."

Romiti's crass response was more than the old Sephardi rabbi could take. Something exploded inside this mild-mannered teacher, and a bitter retort spewed from his lips. "You're an arrogant fool, Mr. Secretary, but as you wish. We'll proceed with this meaningless charade."

Romiti forged his wicked smile and then fired back, "Let's get on with it!"

Chief Rabbi Disraeli greeted the secretary-general in front of the television crews, welcoming him to Israel and the Temple Mount.

"It is a great honor to welcome you to Jerusalem and to the Temple Mount. You are a great friend to Israel, negotiating the historic Treaty of Babylon that has brought peace to our sacred soil. Through your generosity and tireless efforts, we have accomplished what no generation in two thousand years has been able to accomplish—the rebuilding of the temple."

As Rabbi Disraeli spoke to the secretary-general, he saw only hatred and disdain in the man's cold, serpentine eyes. Even as he spoke, he wondered why the secretary, a man known to have no regard for any religion, had any desire to visit this sacred place.

The welcoming speech over, Disraeli led the secretary-general and his deputy for Religious Affairs, Francois Laroque, into the temple. Although he had made it clear that Romiti and Laroque were not to be accompanied by any GSF troops, his instructions were ignored. Three of Romiti's security detail, all decorated, ex-special-ops-force members, followed the small group into the sanctuary.

The group rapidly toured the temple interior and was soon standing in front of a room known to Jews and Christians alike as the Holy of Holies. "I intend to view what is hidden behind the curtain," the secretary-general stated matter-of-factly.

"I'm sorry," Disraeli replied. "This section of the temple is called the Holy of Holies. Only the high priest is allowed into that area, and then only once a year. It is the most sacred part of the temple. No one can enter, especially one who is not a Jew."

Once again, the secretary-general smiled his awful grin. Turning to his men, he ordered them to draw their weapons. Disraeli cried out, "Please! Not in the temple! Please do not desecrate this holy place!" He jumped between the men and the Holy of Holies, again begging them to leave the temple.

"Don't profane the sanctuary!" he pleaded.

The men laughed at his pleas and then grabbed Disraeli, throwing him roughly to the floor.

Romiti arrogantly marched to the front of the sanctuary, yanking aside the curtain that separated the Holy of Holies from the rest of the temple. If this act of sacrilege was not enough, he turned his back on the area considered most hallowed by Jewish worshipers and then, speaking to the world through the live video feed of the favored cameraman, boasted in poetic cant:

"Who among the gods is like me?
Who is like me, majestic in power, awesome in glory, working wonders?
The nations have heard of me and tremble.
I will reign forever and ever.
I stand alone, and no one can oppose me.
I do whatever I please.
Sing praises to me, for I am the god-man, and I will be highly exalted!"

Suddenly a figure appeared behind Romiti—a priest dressed in a long black cassock.

"You vile dog!" The priest spat out his epithet.

The words startled Romiti, and he whirled around to confront the vaguely familiar voice. He was surprised, and then disgusted, to see only a pathetic priest. As he prepared to push the man aside, he gasped, his eyes opening wide in recognition. Romiti's face quickly turned ashen, revealing his fears to a worldwide audience whose eyes were riveted to their computer monitors and televisions.

"Mahmoud, my friend!" he choked in Ladin.

"Yes, it's me! I've waited for this day!" Mahmoud was also speaking in Ladin, incomprehensible to the ears of the traumatized temple audience. "You call me friend? You betrayed me!"

Mahmoud's features hardened. The happy-go-lucky boy from Italy was gone forever. Romiti looked into the eyes of the terrorist who had destroyed Long Beach, and he saw in them nothing but deep, personal hatred.

And Romiti knew. He was going to die.

A traitorous GSF soldier flipped his compact Glock 27 pistol to Mahmoud, who fired rapidly, striking Romiti twice. The first bullet tore through his upraised arm, severing the brachial artery. The second bullet pierced his right eye, leaving a gaping exit wound in the back of his head. Mahmoud dropped his weapon to the floor, a smirk of satisfaction spreading across his face. He had expected to be cut down in a hail of bullets and was astonished to be alive.

The bloodied secretary-general fell to the floor of the Holy of Holies, grievously wounded. Romiti was lying on his back, unable to move. His mouth moved, pathetically gasping for air. His motionless eyes remained open, transfixed on Mahmoud. Laroque ran to the fallen leader, screaming in anger, crying in disbelief. "Get help! Find a doctor! Oh please, don't die! Don't die!"

The stunned GSF officers quickly recovered from their shock, killing the traitor and subduing the unarmed assassin. They did not remove Mahmoud from the gory scene. He did not bother to fight.

Looking up at Mahmoud, Laroque began shouting, "What have you done? You've killed our lord. This was not to happen! Oh Lucifer, I'm sorry, I'm sorry! I failed to protect my lord!"

Romiti, blood flowing from his horribly disfigured face, stared at Mahmoud and in a barely audible voice, choked out his dying words: "We'll meet again, my friend. We will meet again!"

Seconds later, the secretary-general was dead.

Made in the USA
San Bernardino, CA
06 November 2012